THE HOMEGROWN CAFÉ
BOOK CLUB

MELLANIE SZERETO

amatoria press

PRAISE FOR MELLANIE SZERETO

"A funny, sexy, small-town romp. I fell in love with Big Jim the minute he walked through the door."
 — Bestselling Author Barbara Wallace

"A fun, humorous, and delightful romp with lots of chemistry between the characters. Everything I love in a series."
 — *USA Today* Bestselling Author Jeana E. Mann

"Laugh-out-loud romance with just the right amount of spice and sweetness. You're going to want to read the entire series!"
 — *New York Times* Bestselling Author Donna Alward

BOOKS BY MELLANIE SZERETO

Cowboys of Science series ~
No More Mr. Gneiss Guy
Taken for Granite (coming soon)

Creekside series ~
Sexy Claus (also part of The Naughty List series)
Roll With It
Already Gone (coming soon)

Love on the Menu series ~
Love Served Hot
Red Hot Pepper
Hot Tamale Nights (coming soon)

Love on the Menu...Extra Hot standalones ~
Just Desserts
Iced Latté
A Little Appetizer
The Main Dish
Dressing on the Side
Flavor of the Day

Love on the Menu…Steamed trilogy ~
Egging Her On
Sweetening Her Up
Reeling Her In
Love on the Menu: Steamed Boxed Set

Marry Me series ~
Mom I'd Love to Marry
Dad I'd Love to Marry (in Taking a Second Chance charity anthology)

Nerd Love series ~
Comma Kaze
Comma Sutra (coming soon)

Nerds & Babies series ~
The Nerd Next Door

MAKIN' BACON

CHAPTER 1

TATE MADISON BLEW OUT THE LONE CANDLE, STUCK A BITE OF caramel-apple cheesecake in her mouth, and spit the inedible forkful of grossness right back out on the plate. The gritty texture clung to her tongue, and the flavor of coconut and cashews overpowered the "cheese" filling, apples, and fake caramel drizzle.

"Ew, ew, ew! Tasty alternative to the real stuff, my ass." Why hadn't she taken her mom up on her offer to make brownies and have a party?

Now I have no dessert, and it's the third anniversary of twelve years wasted on a liar and a cheat with the straightest, whitest teeth on the planet.

"Happy damn birthday to me. Again." She pushed away from her desk, grudgingly thankful for the one positive that had come out of her failed marriage to a dentist—the habit of carrying a travel-size tube of toothpaste, a mini spool of floss, and a folding toothbrush in her purse.

After a quick dental-hygiene visit to the tiny bathroom beside her office, she scraped the rest of the wedge and the other seven-eighths of her experiment from the springform pan into the bucket by the service door. Even compostable vegan cheesecake ranked higher than Haydon Spade, D.D.S., in the grand scheme. He didn't deserve a single thought, let alone another critical look at what she could've done differently a decade and a half ago. His deception had spawned lost opportunities she could never recover, and the choices *she* made would now determine the course her life followed.

The delivery buzzer spared her another maudlin hike down the bumpy road of middle age as she washed the base and sides of the pan.

"What other disappointing surprise will I get on this wonderfully sucky day?" She rinsed and stacked the pieces before drying her hands on the way to unlock both deadbolts and open the delivery door.

Flannel-clad broad shoulders and a beefy butt in denim overalls filled most of the doorway, dwarfing her five-ten-in-flats frame. When the giant turned toward her, her appreciation continued to his impressive biceps, buff chest, and calloused hands. He had to be at least five inches taller than she was, even without his enormous work boots. A week's worth or more of scruff covered his jaw, giving him a rough-around-the-edges appeal. A brawny stud was exactly what she wanted.

"Hi, I'm Jim Cochon from Big Jim's Itty Bitty Pig Farm out by the highway. Are you the owner of the new restaurant? I collect food waste from a bunch of the restaurants in the county to feed to my hogs. Less waste going into landfills. Healthier animals. I'll be glad to haul away whatever you have free of charge." He waved toward a massive pickup truck parked near her hybrid hatchback. The bed held a quartet of blue plastic storage drums. "If you're interested, we can schedule days and times for pickup."

Lulled into silence by his deep baritone voice, she nodded.

Tall, built, good-looking. No wedding ring or a hint of tan line. He's perfect.

Although his spiel seemed influenced more by nerves than redneck Ohio farmer, recent studies claimed intellect came from the maternal side. His awareness of environmental impact counted as a plus, in any case. A little bit of nerdiness was never a bad thing.

"Hey, you're Beau Madison's sister, Tate, aren't you? He said you were moving back to Wellington a couple months ago." A slow smile, the kind that usually preceded a proposition, feathered the scant mustache over his upper lip.

Have I got an offer for you, Big Jim. "Yes, Beau's my youngest brother. How do you know him?" She leaned against the doorjamb for a more thorough assessment.

"We've been best friends since kindergarten. Played football together from Pop Warner through high school. 'Course, I wouldn't expect you to recognize me. I was a lot shorter and about a hundred pounds lighter when you went away to college." His gesture suggested he'd been in the neighborhood of four-and-a-half feet tall the last time she had seen him.

About thirty-five years old. Better chance of a high sperm count than someone my age. But then, any man would have a higher sperm count than a jerk who had a vasectomy and neglected to tell his wife about it. For eight damn years. While she underwent fertility testing and treatments.

She sifted through memories of the countless friends who'd hung out with her four younger brothers. On any given day, the Madison household had consisted of enough boys to form its own football team. "Ah, Jimothy Cochon. I remember now."

He sighed and a rosy-pink blush invaded his cheeks. "Mom wanted to name me Timothy and Dad liked James. I'm all for compromising, but I wish they would've picked one or the other and had another kid."

Sorry for embarrassing him, she smiled and reached for the compost bucket. She hardly had grounds to make fun of a name. "It could've been worse. Tames. Jamethy. Or a name they'd already chosen because the doctor was wrong about your gender, like me."

His grin returned, triggering an unexpected flash of heat between her thighs, despite the late-September chill. "Not sure how anybody could confuse you with a boy. Besides, Tate fits you just fine. Are you free Saturday afternoon? About four thirty? You should come to my hog roast." His eyebrows dove into a deep vee above his nose. "Oh. You're a vegetarian, aren't you?"

"Gosh, no. Just the café. With all the pizza and burger places around here, something more unique seemed the way to go. I love pulled pork."

His smile returned, as did the tickle in her tummy. "Well, then, it's an open-house sort of event I started a few years ago. Beau, Everett, Levi, and Archer—and their families, of course—will all be there. And your dad said he and your mom are planning to stop by after the hardware store closes at five."

She handed him her contribution to the healthy diet of his pigs and pushed away from the doorjamb. Gathering her entire family for a meal had proven impossible since her permanent return nearly two months ago, not that starting up a restaurant had allowed much time to socialize. "Sounds like fun."

"Great! This is just food waste, right? No trash?"

"Yes. Vegetable and fruit scraps. Some grains and legumes. Eggshells. Nuts. No meat or dairy. I was going to take it to Mom and Dad's to compost, but you're welcome to it."

"Perfect. Hang on a sec while I empty this into the tub." Four long strides carried him to the passenger side of his truck. He hopped onto the running board, dumped the contents into the closest container, and locked down the lid. "I thought you said no dairy. Isn't that cheesecake mixed in with those vegetable scraps? That's practically sacrilege. You didn't throw it away because you think it'll make you fat, did you? 'Cause you're not. And everybody needs to treat themselves to something special once in a while."

She jerked her gaze from his amazing ass to his adorable face. "No worries. Vegan cheesecake experiment. It was extremely disappointing. Pretty disgusting actually."

"Yeah, I can see why you wouldn't want to eat it. You can't make a decent cheesecake without eggs and cream cheese." He hopped down from his perch and rejoined her, the bucket swinging next to his tree-trunk legs as he walked. "I promise to have real dessert at the cookout. Cakes, pies, cookies. Auggie Hofmeier makes the best chocolate éclair torte. You know the bakery on Main Street? He owns it. I'll make sure the kitchen crew saves you a piece when they plate it. Tuesdays, Thursdays, and Saturdays work okay for you? My route goes right past you. Any less often, and the smell can get a little overpowering for somebody who isn't used to it."

"Hm?" She dragged her attention from his remarkable thighs to the unruly hair peeking out from the edges of his John Deere cap. Genetically speaking, she wouldn't find a better specimen if she spent a year reviewing profiles on the sperm-donor sites she'd found. Although with her luck, he hid a bald patch the size of Antarctica beneath the crown of his hat. "Oh, um, Tuesdays, Thursdays, and Saturdays. Yes, those days will work. I like your hat."

He tugged off the John Deere cap, revealing a thick mat of squished curls covering every square inch of the scalp she could see, and then smacked it on his pant leg. "Keeps the dust out of my hair when I'm working outside and cleaning out the barn. I have a whole stack of brand new ones at home to choose from. They'll be waiting for you on Saturday. We'll see what looks best on you. Gotta protect your face from the sun. Some people call it a curse, but red hair and fair skin suit you."

And polite. "That's very sweet of you." Confident in her decision, she moved the bucket back into its spot inside the doorway. "I should finish my prep work for tomorrow's menu. It was good to meet you as an adult, Jim, and I look forward to seeing you on Saturday."

The cap once again in place, he gave her another wide smile. "Good to meet *you* again, Tate. See you at four thirty on Saturday. Would you rather I pick you up here in the alley or at your house?"

"Um." Had she missed the part where he'd asked her for a date? *"You should come to my hog roast." That's what he said, didn't he?* She licked her suddenly dry lips. Fifteen years was a hell of a long time between dates, and riding a bike wasn't a skill she'd retained well. "Here's fine."

"Great!" He pulled his keys from the front pocket of his overalls as he headed toward his truck. Halfway there, he stopped and looked over his shoulder. "Oh, I almost forgot. Beau shared your secret with me."

Beyond mortified, she wished for the cracked pavement to open up and swallow her. *How did Beau find out I'm planning to have a baby?*

"Happy birthday, Tate! Forty-two looks darn good on you." Jim slid behind the wheel of his pickup and started the engine.

The pitter-patter in her chest struck before the realization that artificial insemination rarely included an affair with the sperm donor. "Well, damn."

&

JIM HEFTED THE LAST TUB OF RESTAURANT SCRAPS FROM THE LOWERED Tommy Gate onto the scooter board and rolled it into the processing room, hoping the exertion burned off the attack of post-meet regrets.

Note to self. If you don't want the woman of your dreams to think you're a redneck, don't wear manure-covered work boots, bib overalls, and ragged plaid flannel to introduce yourself. And leave the cruddy John Deere cap in the pickup.

His mouth had come down with a terrible case of the runs as well, not that he didn't have a tendency to talk a lot to most people. Living alone did that to a person.

In his defense, he'd expected a seventy-something, New-Age, tarot-card-reading hippie to be the owner of the vegetarian café on Depot Street, not the smart, classy, and gorgeous Tate Madison. Building working relationships with the food-service businesses in the surrounding counties kept his feed costs down and community connections strong, but he would've preferred a planned reunion with his redheaded lifetime crush. Even at five years old, he'd dreamed of marrying his best friend's older sister. Thirty years was a damn long time to carry a torch and then blow the first impression.

"Hey, Jim, you in there?"

Glad for a distraction, he turned toward the familiar voice and raised a hand in greeting. "Come on in, Everett. What brings you to Big Jim's? Inspection's scheduled for next month."

The other man's laugh echoed off the concrete floor and cinder block walls as he walked into the room. "You sound like you're looking forward to it."

"I run a clean operation. Why shouldn't I?"

"I wish all our inspections had as few violations as yours." The oldest of Tate's younger brothers tucked his sunglasses into his shirt pocket and hooked his thumbs in the front belt loops of his jeans. "My girls are wanting to show swine again next year for 4-H. I told 'em I'd check with you about getting their order in early. Competition for the best piglets is fierce."

Sifting through the breeding schedule in his head, Jim ticked off the weeks on his fingers. "George and Martha'll have a litter ready to go in early March. I can spare four from their brood. Nice temperament and good musculature. How'd Worf and Jadzia's piglets do for the girls this year? They've produced really healthy litters together. Almost zero mortality rate. Excellent growth and almost no disease. Plus, he's on her before she even starts showing signs of being in heat. I haven't had to inseminate once in the four years they've been mated. I'm adding at least two of their next litter to my breeding stock."

"High scores and the best prices at auction. The buyers look for your hogs and I trust your recommendation. Let's say four from the Washingtons and four from DS9 if you can spare them. I'll have Laura call you about billing and delivery." Everett donned his sunglasses and turned toward the exit. "Better let you get back to work. Good to see you, Jim."

"Later, Rett. Tell the family I said hey. Oh, and see you Saturday."

"Looking forward to it."

The heavy clunk of the outer door announced his visitor's departure and served as a reminder that he had no one waiting for him up at the house, and the handful of workers who helped him run the farm had gone home for the day. He would eat supper alone, unless he brought a thermos of soup and a sandwich to the barn—something he'd done fairly often since his last girlfriend had dumped him three years ago. At least the sows still liked his company when he accidentally called them by the wrong name, not that he'd ever mistake his pigs for Tate Madison.

Cooking, cooling, and storing over a hundred gallons of food waste gave him plenty of time to rehash the slip of the tongue he'd made too many times to shrug off. No matter how hard he tried to fall in love, his subconscious never let him forget the first girl he'd lost his heart to. Now that she was available and home, dating someone else hadn't entered his mind, let alone crossed it. Hopefully, he wouldn't screw up his chance with her on Saturday.

Gotta wash my truck and buy her flowers before I pick her up. Maybe a pair of potted mums from the garden center. Yeah. Some orangey-red ones to match her hair. What else can I do to make her see she's special?

Definitely too soon to give her an engagement ring.

CHAPTER 2

"No, I don't prepare my split pea soup with a ham hock or ham." Tate squeezed until the tines of the olive fork she'd taken to carrying in her apron pocket stabbed into her palm. How did people navigate through life without knowing the meaning of vegetarian? *Patience is a virtue and kindness is free.* "I use a *bouquet garni* and homemade vegetable stock for flavoring."

"Really?" The old woman frowned. "I've never heard of pea soup with flowers. What kind do you put in the bouquet? Because some are poisonous, you know. And I don't want any of that Mary Ju Ana in my food, either."

The blonde behind her in line grinned and patted the old woman on the arm. "*Bouquet garni*, Mrs. Crenshaw. It's a bundle of herbs. Parsley, thyme, bay leaves, or whatever will complement the dish. No marijuana. You put the bundle in soups and broths for flavoring, like you do with a sachet to freshen your unmentionables drawer. I supply Ms. Madison with all her fresh herbs and her vegetables when they're in season."

Riley Fenniman, you're a lifesaver.

The older woman's grip on her pocketbook loosened, along with her grimace. "Well, in that case, I'll try the split pea soup. That comes with cornbread muffins, doesn't it? The sweet kind, not those bland ones they serve when I visit my grandson's family in the South. They're like eating buttermilk pancakes without any syrup."

Releasing the fork, Tate nodded. "Yes, ma'am. They're sweetened with local honey. Would you like something to drink?"

"Hm. I usually drink coffee with my lunch, but I don't know what fair trade means." Mrs. Crenshaw's eyes narrowed. "Do I have to wash my own dishes to pay for it?"

Riley snorted, making the old woman jump, and then lowered the hand she'd raised to cover her mouth. "Goodness! I have no idea where that sneeze came from. Darn ragweed allergy."

Nearly choking on a laugh, Tate pressed her lips together until the giggle trying to get out finally gave up. "Bless you. Fair trade means the people who grow the coffee beans are paid fairly for their crop, their workers are treated properly, and the business follows sustainable practices. It costs a little more, but I want my restaurant to be socially and environmentally conscious."

"Oh, okay." Mrs. Crenshaw opened her pocketbook and removed her wallet. "Coffee then too please. Black."

Tate entered the order on her iPad, grateful for another sale. Business had been steady since the grand opening of The Homegrown Café two days ago, meaning she might not have to dip into the money from the divorce settlement. She had no intention of relying on her ex-husband's reparation fund for this particular endeavor. Only the child he'd passive-aggressively denied her would benefit. As paybacks went, it seemed infinitely appropriate, even though the plan to open her own business had taken longer to fund.

She counted the change into her customer's palm and added a coupon for a dollar off her next breakfast or lunch purchase. "Thank you. You can have a seat. Anabelle will be right out with your order."

"Anabelle Danforth? Wallis's daughter? She works for you?" Mrs. Crenshaw leaned forward, like she expected a juicy bit of gossip.

"Yes." *Don't you dare say anything that'll make me have to insist you apologize to that sweet girl.*

"I hadn't heard. That's wonderful!" A flowery cloud of what

smelled like Chanel No. 5 masked the aromas of the three simmering soups when the woman reached across the narrow glass counter to cover Tate's hand with hers. "Do you think the Garden Club could meet here the first and third Wednesdays of the month after lunch? Just for two hours. From closing time 'til four? We'll be happy to order dessert and coffee if you'll let us use the space for our meetings."

Riley smirked and snuck a thumbs-up behind the older woman's back. She evidently had no qualms about exercising her right to an I-told-you-so. A verbal reiteration was sure to follow as soon as she wouldn't be overheard.

"Yes, I think we can arrange that." Tate offered Mrs. Crenshaw a business card. "Would you send me the details? I want to be sure I have the correct dates and times when I complete the agreement and add your meetings to the calendar. Email or regular mail is fine. Both addresses are on the card."

"Thank you, dear." Looking past Tate, Mrs. Crenshaw waved. "Anabelle! It's so good to see you."

The young woman halted in the doorway between the kitchen and the order counter, the tray she carried wobbling slightly. She steadied it, the effort causing a scrunched forehead and a frown. "Hello, Mrs. Crenshaw. How are you today?"

"I'm well. Thank you, Anabelle. Miss Madison said you're working for her. Are you enjoying your new job?"

After two more steps forward, Anabelle rested the edge of the tray on the edge of the counter and let out a noisy exhale. "I'm still learning, but like it a lot. Miss Madison is a good boss. She used to be a teacher like you."

"Really? I didn't know that." The older woman cast a thoughtful glance in Tate's direction. "I think that might be my order, so I should go find a table."

"Okay." Anabelle trailed Mrs. Crenshaw, her usual care showing in her slow pace.

"Didn't I tell you?" Riley's throaty chuckle drew the beady eyes of a trio of thirtyish businessmen who stood next in line. "Book Club on Thursday evenings. Garden Club twice a month on Wednesday afternoons. Pretty soon you'll have all kinds of private meetings to supplement your income. You should put a sign in the window to advertise birthday parties and bridal and baby showers."

"Fine, you were right about having breakfast and lunch hours, but I'm going to have to hire at least one more part-timer if I add any more events to the schedule. Wally and Anabelle agreed to her working ten hours a week until we see how she adjusts." Tate added the task of contacting the local Down syndrome support organization again to her to-do list and then tapped the New Order button on the tablet. "Cup of butternut squash soup and a side salad with mango ranch dressing?"

"Make it a bowl, skip the salad, and add a peanut butter cookie. Vanilla rooibos. Hot. To go. I have a Chamber of Commerce meeting in twelve minutes." Blonde curls tumbled past the wide collar of her form-fitting jacket as Riley cocked her head to the side and let out a huffy sigh. Then she moved backward, the slender heel of her lipstick-red pump landing on the instep of the man directly behind her.

He jerked away, bumping into the men waiting in line with him. "What the hell!"

"Oh my! Did I step on your foot?" Pivoting toward him, she raised her fingertips to her matching lips, but her congeniality stopped there. "Totally an accident, as I'm sure your hand on my butt was. You know, your mother would be appalled at your behavior. And, yes, I'm old enough to *be* your mother, young man. Is that icky enough to be a deterrent, you pervert?"

The man's cheeks paled, evidently grossed out by the suggestion that he'd felt up someone his mom's age. His snickering companions looked away when he aimed a glare in their direction.

"Sorry." As apologies went, it sounded far from sincere.

Tate cleared her throat and employed her annoyed-teacher voice, the childish antics of adult males too much to bear after twelve years of marriage to their ringleader. "If you're going to behave inappropriately, you can take your business elsewhere. I don't tolerate that kind of conduct here."

Grabbing his buddies by their sleeves, the groper marched through the center aisle between the tables. "Damn, feminazis."

A wall of denim and plaid blocked their path at the exit. Jimothy removed his cap, causing his sleeve to tighten on his bicep and revealing his cute mop of curly hair. "Twerps like you make the rest of us look bad. Now apologize for pawing Ms. Fenniman and for disrupting Ms. Madison's place of business."

Riley perched her hands on her hips and shook her head. "Jim, they wouldn't know an apology if it grabbed them by the nu— Nose. If they know what's good for them, they'll behave like polite little gentlemen next time. Right? Oh, and smile pretty for the security cameras, boys."

Leaning across the counter, Tate smacked her new friend on the elbow. "Antagonizing them won't help. Just let them leave, Jim."

He frowned and stepped aside. "Okay, but I'll be watching to make sure they don't cause any more trouble."

The tickle in her tummy morphed into a backflip, but Tate focused on entering Riley's order. An attraction to the possible DNA contributor of her future child was a distraction she couldn't afford. "I'll be with you in a minute, Jim. I need to get this order ready."

"No hurry." His husky just-rolled-out-of-bed voice stirred up another round of acrobatics in her belly.

Escaping to the kitchen, she willed her hormones to save themselves for insemination. As much as she missed sex, her bucket list didn't include a sexual or romantic relationship.

Been there. Done that. Have the divorce to prove it. And no child custody agreement.

By the time her employee returned with the empty tray, Tate had ladled a bowl-sized helping of soup, bagged the cookie, and filled a to-go cup from the hot-water dispenser. "Anabelle, do you remember how to take orders?"

The young woman nodded. "Yes. I practiced at home last night."

"Terrific." Tate pulled a single teabag from the box on the supply shelf. "Will you please take Mr. Cochon's order while I finish here?"

"Yes, Miss Madison. I like Big Jim. He let me watch the piglets being born once." Anabelle's apron fluttered as she whirled toward the front of the shop.

Their conversation carried to the kitchen—from his cheerful

greeting to the young woman's alternating questions about his lunch choices and his pigs—while Tate spooned vanilla rooibos into the teabag, tugged the drawstring tight, and packed all but the cup of hot water in a reusable tote. Jim's laidback, friendly interaction could easily convince her heart to become infatuated with the perfect man to father her baby. Too bad she wasn't in the market for a boyfriend, not that dating Beau's best friend was a good idea. The age gap posed another sound reason for steering clear of him.

But you agreed to a date with him.

The invisible Jiminy Cricket on her shoulder had a valid point.

She carried the to-go order to the counter and handed it to Riley. "See you at book club this evening. Seven o'clock sharp."

"I can't wait!" The amusement in Riley's eyes warned Tate the discussion was sure to be interesting. "I'll be here at ten 'til. I have a secret to share with you."

"A secret, huh?"

"Mm-hm. And it's a really good one." With a wink, Riley strutted toward the exit, her stilettos clicking on the tile floor.

Every male eye in the room followed her across the room and out the door—except Jim's. He held out his credit card and pursed his kiss-able lips as he locked a disconcerting stare on Tate. "Are you okay? Do you want me to talk to the police chief about sending a patrol around every so often and checking in on you?"

"That's sweet of you, but it isn't necessary. I've taken several self-defense courses and, besides video surveillance, I had an alarm system installed during the renovation. Besides, I really doubt they'll be back. They seem more like the burger-and-fries type anyway."

The worry lines around his mouth softened. "If you're sure."

"I'm sure." She reached out, wanting to reassure him, but withdrew her hand before she made contact with his arm. "Um, Anabelle, why don't you go check on the customers at their tables while I fill Jim's order since the lunch rush has slowed down."

"Okay, Miss Madison. See you at the picnic on Saturday, Big Jim."

"See you Saturday, Anabelle." He shifted his weight from one foot to the other and licked his lips. "Is it okay if I come in the kitchen with you? Easiest to empty your bucket too since I'm parked out back. I hope it's okay that I moved you up in my pickup route. With you closing earlier in the day than most everybody else, it makes sense to do you first."

First, last, and everywhere in between.

A vision of Jim doing her against the kitchen counter triggered a uterine tremor that probably registered at least four-point-seven on the Richter scale.

Holy cow.

His cheeks flushed almost as red as the retro tables she'd chosen for the dining room and probably matched her own. "Pick up, I mean."

"Of course. Yes, you can come with me." As she pivoted away from the order counter, a strangled masculine choke stalled her midturn. *Oh God. What's wrong with my brain?* "In the kitchen. You can come in the kitchen with me. Go. To the kitchen. Yes, let's go to the kitchen."

Biting her tongue to keep any more innuendo vomit from escaping, she hurried to the adjoining space. Steady boot steps announced the presence of her partner in embarrassment as she stopped in front of the order screen above the work counter.

He continued past her to the service door without slowing. "I'll grab your waste while you… Food waste. The bucket."

"Okay. Careful. I dropped a handful of nuts earlier. I'm not sure I found them all."

"Nuts."

"Mm-hm. Pecans. Might be slippery." *Stop. Talking.*

He cleared his throat, his mind evidently going the same direction as hers. "Back in a minute."

Cool air rushed in as he walked out, chilling her heated face and chest. *When did I turn back into a bumbling teenager? It's not like I've never had sex. Most of it mediocre, but still sex. Sex meant to conceive, at least by one of us.*

She plunked a stack of six containers on the counter, determined not to let Haydon's deception turn her into a bitter divorcée, at least in the typical sense. Having a man in her life—or not—didn't define her.

All of the friends she'd made since her return to Wellington were single women, every one over forty and doing perfectly fine on their own.

So what if she was attracted to a younger man?

She didn't have to do anything about it—except ask him to give her some of his sperm.

CHAPTER 3

"Sorry I'm late." Riley plunked into the empty chair beside Tate and pulled the closest serving platter toward her. "My cousin is such a fucking asshat."

Wallis snitched a Brie puff as she slid the last hors d'oeuvres plate in front of Riley. "She's dropping the f-bomb already. What did he do now?"

"He wants me to sell him the north end of the property." Riley's scowl confirmed Tate's guess that her friend was more ticked off at her cousin than usual. Riley stuffed a spanakopita bite into her mouth and added a generous assortment of appetizers to her plate while she chewed. "That's where my water supply comes from. Does that fuckwad really believe I'm stupid enough to sell to him, when he wants to use so many toxic chemicals he'd kill every goddamn plant and insect in the entire county? And probably some humans too."

Tate poured a cup of rooibos chai from the nearly empty teapot and placed it out of reach of her friend's gesturing hands. "That kind of compromises the organic part of your farm. Did you sic your lawyer on him?"

"Kind of? Georgie's busy with a big case this week, but she said she'd send a letter to him and his crackpot lawyer." Riley raised an eyebrow at the fourth attendee of their first book club meeting. "Hey, Petra, will you teach me how to use a meat cleaver? I promise to disinfect it when I'm done."

The tall brunette's slow blink preceded a wide grin. "I've been thinking about taking up axe throwing as a hobby. Want to join me? That way you can make his demise look like an accident instead of having to prevent cross-contamination on my meat-prep equipment. I'd get shut down if the health department thought I was making Soylent Green in the back room."

Nearly inhaling the grape she'd put in her mouth, Tate coughed until she could spit it into her napkin. "That thought is enough to make me give up meat completely. Axe throwing is a thing?"

"Oh yeah." Petra practically purred the words. "There's a place in Medina that has indoor throwing lanes and private party rooms. No worries about the weather. Only about a half an hour from here. Want me to set up a reservation for next week?"

Riley licked her lips and then picked up a baked mac-and-cheese ball. "Count me in. We can go axe shopping this weekend."

"They supply the axes. We'll wait until after we get the feel for throwing to buy our own." With real caramel-cream-cheese dip smothering half an apple slice, the butcher leaned over her plate and took a bite. Her eyes drifted closed as she chewed. "Oh ma gawd. Dis is so good."

Wallis added another of each appetizer to her plate and snickered. "I think Petra just had an orgasm."

Wiping her fingers on a napkin, Riley leaned back in her chair. "If that's the case, pass that dip and a spoon my way. I ran out of batteries last week and haven't had time to stop at the hardware store for more."

"You could ask your accountant to help you with your spread...sheets."

Raucous laughter rang through the dining room at Wally's quip, especially given this week's reading selection—a story about the dating escapades of a middle-aged woman after her husband of thirty years left her for a perky young intern at his accounting firm.

Tate thanked her lucky stars she'd found a group of friends as genuine as the main character's. "From what I hear, he's very good at handling assets."

Wallis winked. "And he's good-looking."

"I've heard he's a master with a grill. You're going to need some fortification for the fornication." Seemingly over her food orgasm, Petra shoved the apple dip toward their silent companion. "Get laid so we can live vicariously through you."

Riley dunked her index finger in the bowl and sucked off the gooey glob. "Mm. That's damn good stuff, Tate. Deacon Jeffries is an excellent CPA and I don't want to have to find a new one, not when a decent toy can perform as well as any man."

"Didn't I tell you Tate's a genius with cheese?" Petra reached across the table to dunk another piece of apple. "You know Deke has the hots for you, don't you? I watched him watching you leave the butcher shop last month. The poor man's tongue almost hit the floor when you bent over to pick up Mrs. Crenshaw's keys for her."

"If I want someone drooling over me, I'll get a dog. Oh, that's not a bad idea. Then I can train it to chase my cousin the dickhead off my property." Riley popped another treat in her mouth and tapped the screen on her cell phone. After several more taps and scrolls, she looked up. "I get to choose next week's book. Another I-must-have-a-man-to-be-happy story, and I may puke. What the hell is wrong with being single and independent over forty?"

"She has a point." Getting up to refill the teapot again, Tate stifled a yawn. "I'm happier now than I've been in a long time. No lies, no manipulation, no trying to make somebody love me when he doesn't. I wasted a lot of years pursuing an impossible ideal."

Wally joined her at the service counter and gave her a sideways hug. "My marriage wasn't perfect, but at least I knew I could always count on Bobby. He was a good man. Speaking of stories, we need a name for the book club. Any ideas?"

Riley frowned into her teacup. "This needs a little kick. Or we could skip the tea and go straight to wine. Then we could call it the Cork-and-Screw Book Club."

"That's depressing. The only screw I want is the good kind."

Petra's snort included a tiny spray of tea out her nose. "Ouch! That stings. Not the good screw. I'm pretty sure that would mean I got a UTI or an STD."

"Which is TMI." Wally added several more snacks to her plate. "Hmm. What do you think of The Homegrown Café Book Club? We can call it THC for short."

Hysterical giggling filled the dining room, but a sinking feeling threatened to swallow Tate whole. "Oh my God. *That's* why Mrs. Crenshaw thought I put pot in my split pea soup! Why didn't somebody tell me?"

With tears running down her cheeks, Petra drew a cannabis leaf— or buckeye, depending on the observer—in the apple dip. "Actually, it's probably good for marketing with all the legalization of recreational marijuana. And everybody's touting CBD as a miracle cure for whatever ails you."

"Yeah, well, I'm not sure I want to be known as the weed supplier in town, especially with the baby plans."

Riley leaned back in her chair and picked up another spanakopita bite. "Hey, how goes the search for a sperm donor?"

A smile snuck up on Tate as she filled the tea ball. "I may have found one."

"Woo-hoo! Can we see his profile? How old is he? Does he have all his hair?"

"Well…" She set the timer on her phone for three minutes and dropped the ball into the pot. "He isn't in the database." *And I have a date with him.*

Petra frowned. "You mean he's some random guy off the street?"

"Not exactly. I've met him." Tate willed her brain to filter what came out of her mouth. "He's in his thirties. Um, tall. Athletic. Has a full head of hair and seems kind and thoughtful. I can get character references before I make a decision."

"Sounds like he might be worth dating." The waggle of Petra's eyebrows implied a date wasn't exactly what she had in mind.

Only once. "Uh-uh. Too young."

"How young? Thirty? Thirty-one? You know that's legal, right?

Who cares if he's younger? More stamina. Less chance of erectile dysfunction. And if he doesn't care how old you are, why should you care how young he is?"

Heat crept up Tate's neck. "Mid-thirties. I have no plans to sleep with him."

"Who said anything about sleeping?" Riley stretched her arms above her head and arched her back, with a *pop* punctuating the motion. "Ah. You know what they say about best laid plans."

Leaning her hip against the counter, Wally giggled. "Yep. The best plans usually include getting laid."

Another round of boisterous laughter filled the room, and Tate's thoughts wandered off into the land of sex—and possibly more—with Big Jim Cochon again. At least her friends hadn't played Guess the Sperm Donor.

Riley's penetrating gaze threatened to burn a hole in Tate's filter, but Petra spoke before Tate could incriminate herself. "A lot of guys come into the butcher shop. What's his name?"

No, no, no. Do. Not. Tell. Them. "You do know the process is usually confidential, don't you? That's the whole point of going through an IVF clinic with a donation center. The donor doesn't know who the mother is, the mother doesn't have actual identifying information about the father—let alone meeting him—and he has no legal claim to the child. No strings to get hung up on. No complications. I've had enough of those to last a lifetime."

Riley drew a tadpole in the dip with a slice of pear. "Then how are you going to get this guy to give you his swimmers? Ask the center to call him? Sneak into his house and clean up with a turkey baster after he jacks off?"

Wally sucked in her cheeks, barely able to pucker up past her grin. "I can recommend a baster with really good suction and ejection."

Wild laughter almost drowned at the chime of the timer, but Tate turned toward the teapot instead of letting her friends see another hot blush bloom across her face and neck. Steam rising from the tea ball as she removed it probably added to her redhead's curse. "I don't know yet. I'll think of something. Or find someone else."

Petra stabbed half a mac-n-cheese ball and paired it with half a spanakopita bite. "But you said he's perfect. Why would you—?"

"I didn't say he was perfect. I said I might have found someone. That means I have options."

"Yes, the option to tell him the truth and see what first-choice donor says. I'm sure you can have Georgie draw up a contract if he agrees. If not, there are plenty of other fishies in the sea."

Tea splashed out of the spout at Tate's attempt to pour. "Tell him? How in the world do you ask someone you barely know to give you some of his sperm?"

Riley reached around her to aim the pot. "With words. How about...I'll pay you a thousand dollars, or whatever the going rate is, for one hand job's worth of your sperm?"

"Hmm..." Petra held out her cup for a refill. "That sounds an awful lot like solicitation to me. Buying and selling semen on the street is most likely illegal."

"Then have Georgie approach him." Riley's eyes widened a millisecond later. "Oh, yeah. That would definitely work. You remain anonymous because your lawyer is your representative. What do you think? Brilliant idea, isn't it?"

With a shaky hand, Tate set the teapot on the table and made a hasty retreat. "Wally, would you mind taking care of refilling every-body's cups? I need a trip to the restroom."

The steady *click-click-click* of high heels behind her sent Tate's heart to her stomach. Only Riley in her trademark stilettos made that sound. "Me too."

Should I try to distract her?

Riley's tight-jawed frown as Tate held the door open for her nixed the idea. Dealing with her cousin's scheming was likely distraction enough. Besides, Riley would see through any attempt at deflection.

Tate willed her bladder to keep her from being a liar, but silence— other than the crinkle of paper from the stall next door—suggested her friend might have had an ulterior motive for tagging along.

"Fucking perimenopause. If there's a God, he's definitely a man, thinking every woman wants a damn uterus. I'm sick to death of bleeding for no reason."

"Do you need a tampon? I have some in the bathroom by my office." *Oh, come on, bladder. Cooperate.*

"Thanks, but I have one. Gotta be prepared when your body is revolting against you. At least the cooler weather is canceling out the hot flashes. Mostly."

A telltale sound came from the stall next to Tate's and then the *whoosh* of the toilet flushing offered cover for her little white lie. She seized the opportunity, waiting until the last gurgle to pull up her leggings and press the handle.

At the double-sink vanity, Riley applied a fresh coat of stiletto-red lipstick and fluffed her blonde curls while Tate washed and dried her hands.

Almost there.

As Tate turned toward the door, her friend hurried around her and blocked her way. "It's Big Jim, isn't it? If it isn't, it should be."

The curse struck again, probably far worse than any hot flash Riley had experienced. "What makes you think that?"

"Red, I can't be the only one who saw the way he looked at you earlier. All smitten-eyed and besotted. He wanted to carry you off to his itty-bitty pig farm in the sky and protect you from the world. Oh, and make cute little Jimmys and Taters with you."

"Do *not* call me Tater." A frown and a glare yielded a snicker from Riley. "And no man has ever looked at me 'all smitten-eyed and besotted.'"

"Uh-huh. The bigger they are, the harder they fall. He wouldn't refuse you anything, especially not the chance to make your wish—and his—come true."

"But…"

"Yes, he has a very nice butt. All you have to do is tell him what you want. Ask and you shall receive. I can practically guarantee it." Riley finally opened the door, leaving Tate to overthink her options as she returned to their book club gathering, especially when she had a date with him in less than forty-eight hours.

CHAPTER 4

"Hey, Jimbo, you in there?"

Jim grunted through the last repetition on the bench press and then swiped at the sweat running into his eyes as he sat up. "Yeah."

The patter of tiny booted feet announced the presence of Beau's three-year-old before she sprinted across the makeshift gym that occupied the south side of the pole barn closest to the house, leaving Beau in her wake. "Unca Jimbo!"

"Hey there, Curlicue. Give me a sec to de-slime." Jim grabbed the hand towel on the end of the bench and rubbed it along the neckline of his muscle shirt and down his arms. "What brings you out to the farm so early? The picnic doesn't start until five o'clock."

"I wike swime. Mommy says it means baf-time. I wike bafs too." As soon as Jim set aside the towel, the girl climbed onto his lap, her full head of rosy-blonde ringlets still bouncing. "She wanted-ed pieces and quiet, so me and Daddy had to go eat wunch at Aunt Tater's res-ront."

Beau grinned. "Molly kicked us out of the house until three because she has a client report to finish before the party. Corey, remember what I said about calling Aunt Tate the right name?"

"But, Daddy, you caw her Tater, and so does Unca Rett, Unca Arsh, and Unca Wevi. 'Sides, taters are my fave-rit, just wike Aunt Tater." The stubborn jut of the girl's jaw signaled her willingness to argue the point until the end of time, given the opportunity.

She's my favorite too, kiddo. Lifting his curly-haired armful as he stood, Jim shared an amused smirk with his best friend. "Want to go visit the piglets while I check on them?"

Corey wiggled against him, her head bobbing and her legs trying to carry her to the pig barn. "I *wuv* the piggies!"

"I know you do. Do you remember the rules? You have to hold your dad's hand. The mommy and daddy piggies are a lot bigger than you, and they might hurt you by accident if you get too close."

"I 'member."

"Promise you'll listen and follow my directions?"

She flung her miniature arms around his neck and kissed his cheek. "I *promise*, Unca Jimbo."

"Okay." He handed her off to Beau, not even bothering to fight the fantasy of having a little girl of his own with her gorgeous mama's red hair. At least that dream had a shot at reality now. "I need to put on my work clothes first. Back in a minute."

"Hurry!" Her clapping echoed off the partially finished walls.

"Yes, ma'am." Hiding a laugh behind a cough, Jim crossed to the changing room for his shirt, overalls, and boots.

Even with a quick-change, his visitors had disappeared from the gym by the time he returned. Following a joyous squeal outside, he found them at the playground he'd built the summer before his first cookout. Back then, he'd had high hopes his own kids would appreciate the clubhouse, swing set, climbing wall, and sandbox by now. His last best chance of marriage and family awaited him at this year's event.

"Unca Jimbo, can I see the piggies now?" Corey zipped into the tunnel slide and landed on her bottom in the grass a few seconds later. Then she jumped up and raced toward him, with Beau jogging along behind her. "Is it piggy time?"

"You bet." Jim set off at a measured pace, although the girl had no trouble keeping up with him. "What did you have for lunch?"

"Tater soup and crackers and cheese. And a banana cupcake wif peanut-budder frossing. Daddy cawed it a muffin, but Aunt Tater says itsa cupcake 'cause of the frossing."

"Sounds like a cupcake to me." He shot a grin at her daddy. "You should know better than to call it a muffin if it has frosting, dude. I remember you having that argument with Tate when we were kids. Carrot cupcake with cream cheese frosting, I think it was."

"Yeah, yeah, yeah. Muffin. Cupcake. Doesn't matter what you call it as long as it tastes good." Beau grasped his daughter's extended hand as they neared the entrance to the farrowing barn. "Hey, speaking of Tate, she told Corey she's coming to the hog roast."

"I invited her when I stopped by the restaurant the other day to see if I could have her food scraps." Dropping to one knee in front of his honorary niece, Jim put on his serious face and crossed his fingers Beau let the subject drop into a bottomless pit. "Are you ready?"

"Yes, Unca Jimbo!" She bounced in place as she spoke, but then she stilled and raised her finger to her lips. "We haf to be quiet, in case the piggies are taking a nap. And I haf to hold Daddy's hand the *hoe* time we're in the barn."

"Good girl. When we're done visiting, I'll give you a piggyback ride to the car."

She flung her free arm around his neck before he could stand. "I wuv you as much as the piggies."

"I love you more than my truck."

Her infectious giggle triggered a chain reaction, spreading from her to him to Beau. "You're siwwy, Unca Jimbo."

"So are you, Curlicue. Let's go." He led them through the outer office and into the prep area. "What do we do before we visit the farrowing stalls?"

She scooted the step stool from beside the sink and held the rails as she climbed to the top. "Haf to wash our hands so the piggies don't get sick."

"You're going to be an excellent pig farmer when you get a little bigger."

Beau's eyebrows rose as he turned on the water. "You plan on putting her on the payroll?"

Grabbing a towel from the shelf, Jim grinned. "Maybe."

"What's pay-row, Daddy?"

"A paying job. Nothing you need to be worried about for quite a while." Beau snagged the towel and helped his daughter dry her hands while he dried his own. "Come on. We need to be home by naptime."

"I don't wike naps." She hopped down the stepstool, barely sticking the landing, and then pushed it back to its spot beside the sink. "I haf too much to do."

"You mean like being grumpy all afternoon while I grade papers? Besides, we need to recharge for the picnic later. You want to be able to play with your cousins, don't you?"

Her lips scrunched into a thoughtful pout, but she reached for his hand instead of arguing. "A widdle nap."

Jim smothered a laugh and shoulder-bumped his friend. "Precocious little bargainer, isn't she?"

"You have no idea." Beau fell into step behind him, Corey at his side.

The animated girl gave way to a reserved child who stayed with her dad outside the pens to *ooh* and *ahh* over this week's new piglets, even as Jim checked on the sows and their young. The toddler's wide eyes and bright smile revealed a subtle resemblance to her favorite aunt, setting off a case of wild butterflies in his stomach.

When he and his guests finally circled back to the hand-washing room, yawns and sleepy eyelids thankfully distracted his best friend from the usual ability to notice something was bothering Jim. "Think you can hold on while Uncle Jimbo gives you a piggyback ride to the car?"

Corey nodded, but Jim had his doubts.

He scooped her off the stepstool, leaving her facing frontward with a forearm supporting her legs and the other across her belly. "How about a kangaroo ride instead?"

"I wike roos." She rested her head against his chest, but it almost immediately lolled to the side.

"Good idea." Beau led the way out of the building and across the barnyard. As he opened the rear car door, he grinned over his shoulder. "Zonked out. Let me buckle her in and then we need to have a talk."

The butterflies morphed into a flock of buzzards. "A talk?"

"Yep."

"About what?"

"Hold on a sec." He eased the seatbelt over his daughter's head and clicked the metal latch into place. After an adjustment to the sliding clip at her chest, he climbed out of the car and closed the door. The relaxed way he leaned his hip against the rear fender suggested a lengthy—and possibly unpleasant—conversation. Beau crossed his arms in front of him. "You and Tate, huh?"

"Tate and I what?" Cold sweat crept along Jim's neck, but a swipe of the bandana from his pocket didn't relieve the sensation.

"You asked her to Big Jim's Annual Hog Roast."

"Well, sure. I told her your whole family would be here. I didn't know if anybody mentioned it to her since nobody bothered to tell me she was the owner of the new café."

"And let you miss out on an opportunity to find out for yourself? She said you're picking her up." Beau's unwavering stare drilled an extra hole in Jim's head. "Like for a date?"

Shit. "Is that a problem? Because our friendship is more—"

"Of course it isn't a problem. You're one of the few guys I know who's actually good enough for her." A smirk replaced the unreadable mask on his friend's face. "Besides, you've been in love with her since we were five."

"Have not."

"Have too, Jimbo. Cut the bullshit. I've watched you watch her from a distance forever."

"So I had a crush on her when I was a kid. That's not the same as being in love with her."

"Don't give me that denial crap. You haven't had a date in…what? Three years?" Beau tossed his keys in the air and caught them without breaking his penetrating stare. "Since about the time I told you she was divorcing the weasel. I'm guessing it's more than just a coincidence."

"I've been busy."

A hoot of laughter sent a flock of starlings into flight from the nearby maple. "Buddy, you're making excuses. Just tell her how you feel about her."

The buzzards in Jim's gut circled over his dying bravery. "I can't tell her I love her! It's our first date."

"See? I know you better than you know yourself. This is why we decided not to tell you about the restaurant. You would've overthought talking to her and chickened out the first time you saw her." Stepping closer, Beau landed a halfhearted punch on Jim's bicep. "At least hold her hand and kiss her good night."

The buzzards completed another circle, adding to the nervousness Jim already had to contend with. "Next thing, you'll be telling me to sleep with her. Aren't brothers supposed to be protective of their sisters?"

"Protect her from what? You'd marry her in a heartbeat if you thought she'd agree to it. Give her a reason to say yes." Beau chuckled as he turned toward the sedan. "And if she wants to sleep with you, make her glad she did, if you know what I mean."

"I'm not talking to you about having sex with your sister. That's weird."

"Weird or not, you both deserve to be happy, and I think you'd be good for each other." Beau climbed into the driver's seat. "My brothers may not be as hands-off as I'm trying to be, so you better make your move pretty soon if you don't want them butting in. Because they *will* tell her after they see you together at the picnic."

JIM CUPPED HIS HAND IN FRONT OF HIS MOUTH, EXHALED, AND THEN quickly inhaled. The minty scent of toothpaste still lingered from the quick brushing before he'd left the house.

Fingers crossed I get to kiss her.

As he climbed out of the pickup, he stowed his keys in his pocket and willed his racing pulse to slow. He hadn't been this nervous since waiting to hear back about the acceptance or rejection of his environmental engineering program application seventeen years ago. At least his attire—ironed khakis, mostly clean hiking boots, and a freshly washed Big Jim's Itty Bitty Pig Farm long-sleeved t-shirt—might make up for the redneck impression he'd surely conveyed earlier in the week.

Clean truck, flowers delivered, and on time.

The service door swung open as he approached the rear entrance of The Homegrown Café, revealing the only woman who'd ever sent his heart into a tailspin.

Tate's smile lit up her whole face and sent his pulse hop-skip-jumping again. "Hi, Jim. Thank you for the lovely planters. Did you see them out front? I've gotten compliments all day."

"You're welcome. Glad you like them. I figured they'd last a lot longer than a bunch of cut flowers in a vase." He stopped an arm's length from her, wishing he could greet her with a kiss. *Maybe next time? God, I hope there's a next time.*

Her ponytail swayed above her jeans-clad butt when she turned to lock the door. "They will, won't they? Anyway, they're beautiful and it was very thoughtful of you."

Will she think I'm crazy if I ask her to marry me right this minute?
Probably.
Definitely.

He offered his hand as she put her keys in the tote hanging from her fingers. "Want me to carry that for you?"

"Thanks, but it's not heavy. Just my purse and a fleece jacket, in case I get cold later. The temperature drops pretty fast this time of year once the sun sets."

"Sure does. There's plenty of room on the seat or the floor for your bag." He led her to the passenger side of the truck and held the door open, grateful for a chance to make a good second impression.

"Thanks." Leaning in to scoot her tote to the base of the center console, she gave him another look at her astounding backside.

His dick stirred behind his zipper, but lust wasn't its only motive.

She lifted her foot to the running board, pulling the denim tighter across her hips. "That's a big step."

"Here, let me help." As he reached to give her leverage at the elbow, she grabbed for the panic handle and his hand closed over her breast.

And there's her nipple.

He jerked away, hoping she didn't think he'd groped her on purpose. Her gasp became a squeak a second before she tumbled backward off the running board straight at him.

"I gotcha!" He braced for the impact, but momentum carried them both to the ground. Pain stabbed through his partial erection and his head clunked against the pavement. "Ouch."

Rolling sideways, she pressed her breasts into his bicep and tugged her trapped arm free. "Oh my gosh! Are you hurt?"

No headache or blurred vision. Dick hurts like hell. Gotta check for bleeding, if I can sit up without being sick. "Maybe?"

However, no amount of blood, sloshed brain, or broken penis would ever erase the spectacular imprint of her body on his.

CHAPTER 5

T<small>ATE EASED SIDEWAYS, TRYING HER DAMNEDEST NOT TO DIG HER HIP</small> into the sizable lump directly beneath her. She'd probably already done enough damage to permanently knock Jim out of the running as the father of her child. *Sperm donor, not lover, boyfriend, or husband.* "Crap. I'm so sorry. I should've been more careful."

"Not your fault." He whimpered as she managed to extricate her legs from his and roll off of him.

Grateful she hadn't rendered him unconscious, she pushed to her knees to survey the damage, gasping at the shooting pain in her kneecap from the pressure. "Are you okay?"

Although his breathing was a bit erratic and he'd curled into a ball, his color seemed almost normal and he was alert. "I just need… Fudge on a stick. Maybe a minute. Or two."

Please let him be okay. "Is anything broken? Can I get you some ice? Or a towel? Are you bleeding?"

He lifted a hand to his hair, wincing when he touched the back of his head. "I don't think so. Little bit of a goose egg, but I've gotten worse playing flag football."

"What about…" She gestured toward his waist. "I'm no lightweight, and I landed on you pretty hard. I, um… You're not…broken, are you?"

"I don't know. It got bent funny and a little squished. Not that you weigh a lot. Bad angle. And landing between you and the ground." After another shaky exhale, he grimaced. "You're not hurt, are you? Did I break your fall?"

"I'm fine, thanks to you." The bruise on her knee would heal, as would the minor twisted ankle, and telling him wouldn't make it happen any sooner. Thankfully, the weave mostly hid the scuffmark on her jeans. She eased her fingers through his thick curls, finding the lump but no broken skin or oozing blood. "You're right. There's no bleeding, but you could still have a concussion. How's your vision? Do you feel dizzy or nauseous?"

"Just the normal hit-in-the-groin kind of sick feeling. No spots or stars." His eyes drifted closed and his respiration steadied. A low hum accompanied his sigh. "That feels nice."

Yeah, it does. "Can you sit up?" She eased her arm under his shoulders, hoping to gain some leverage for him.

He rose several inches from the pavement before shaking his head and letting gravity pull him back down. "Still too much pressure. I'll be okay in a few minutes."

"Are you sure you don't want some ice? Or I have ibuprofen in my purse, if you think that'll help." Guilt guided her fingers away from the lump hiding in his thick hair, but she didn't dare go exploring below his belt to see how badly she'd injured him. *Why couldn't I have fallen on Haydon like that? It's not like he needed his dick for anything but cheating.*

"Yeah, ibuprofen. I'm not good at swallowing pills. Need a drink."

"Okay. Don't move. I'll run inside for some water." She brushed her lips against Jim's head injury before she stood, not noticing the carryover from her teaching days until she reached into the truck for her tote. His mashed penis deserved a make-it-all-better kiss too—and more.

A mini earthquake rippled through her lower belly with that thought, and she grabbed the seat to steady herself. How could she think about giving the poor man a blow job when he couldn't even move without intense pain?

Gotta ask Riley for vibrator recommendations. Seriously.

Or ask Jim to accidentally feel me up again.

She clutched the pill bottle and hurried to the service door, trying her damnedest not to limp. The last thing she needed was to make him feel worse about something that was entirely her fault. Three years without sex had turned her into a jumpy prude with no sense of balance. Her first date in forever and a considerable attraction to him didn't help.

When she returned with a mug of water no more than two minutes later, his position hadn't changed. She gritted her teeth as she knelt beside him, careful not to put any weight on her sore knee. *Eyes on his face.* "I have your water and ibuprofen. Do you want me to help you sit up?"

He shifted onto his back and a euphoric smile spread across his face. "The sun's giving you a halo around all that pretty red hair. You must be an angel."

"I hate to tell you, Jim, but you're delirious. My hair's probably a mess from our scuffle, and I would've thought you'd know more about concussions after playing football for so long." She set the mug and bottle aside and grasped both of his hands. "Come on. We need to get you upright to swallow the pills."

Without so much as a tug on her fingers, he sat up. "No concussion. Just a bump."

"And your...other injury? Will you be able to walk? Drive? Go to the cookout without feeling miserable?"

"I think I'll be okay, although things need some adjusting down there. That is, if you don't mind me running inside to the restroom before we go."

"Of course not." She dumped two tablets into her open palm. "Here you go."

"I usually have to take three. Sometimes four. I'm kind of a big guy." Matching patches of pink bloomed on his cheeks. "I didn't mean... Well, I am, but that's not..."

Big Jim all over, huh? Her nipples tightened against her bra and she barely stifled a groan. Maybe Riley had the right idea after all. Having sex with him might kill two birds with one stone, and spending more time with him had somehow claimed the top spot on her priority list since their collision.

"Tate?"

She shook her head to clear the wayward thoughts. Acquiring a boyfriend wasn't on her to-do list, no matter how much she liked him. "Hm?"

"Were you going to get more ibuprofen? Or do you want me to?" The first two pills had vanished, along with half of the water.

"Oh, um, I can get them." She popped the lid from the bottle and shook out two more. "Here you go."

"Thanks." A grimace and a shudder followed his gulp of water. "I'd rather have a shot than take pills. They always try to stick in my throat, even when they're coated."

"I bet a piece of chocolate éclair cake will help."

"Dessert fixes almost everything."

"That it does." She offered him a hand as she stood and then tucked it behind her back. "On second thought, you should get up by yourself. I'll probably fall on top of you again."

"Better than a two-hundred-thirty-pound lineman. I'd still be laying in a fetal position." He pushed to his feet and brushed the dirt from his pants like she hadn't caused him the ultimate man-pain less than ten minutes ago. "Auggie's bringing an extra cake for me, but I'll share it with you if you promise not to tell your brothers what happened."

"Deal." She led him through the service entrance, unable to keep from imagining Beau's or her other siblings' comments about their mishap. They would have a field day teasing Jim and her if they knew she'd fallen out of his truck and onto him. Much to her consternation, they'd never had any qualms about picking on her where boys or men were concerned. So what if they'd been right about her asshole of an ex-husband? "Employee restroom is to the left, next to my office. I'll put the mug in the sink while you take care of that...adjustment."

"Back in a minute."

"I'll be right here." As hard as she tried, she couldn't prevent a backward glance to watch him lumber into the employee restroom. Curiosity wasn't usually one of her weaknesses, but the feel of his body against hers had reignited an interest that had all but gone into hibernation when she'd discovered her ex-husband's betrayal.

A splash of cool water on her cheeks after she placed the mug in the sink returned her to the here and now. Maybe Riley was right.

"Ask and you shall receive." Am I brave enough? What if I want more?

Heavy footsteps approached her from behind. "Whew! Much better."

Although he didn't sound like a man with a sperm-threatening injury, she'd learned the hard way not to make assumptions. "Nothing, um, broken? Or damaged?"

"Nope." He leaned against the counter next to her, not crowding her by any means, but his presence warmed her from the inside out once again. "Ready?"

"If you are." She tossed the damp towel over the edge of the hamper and pulled her keys from her pocket. "I'll be more careful climbing in the truck this time. I swear I'm not usually such a klutz."

"It was my fault. You were doing fine, and I messed up by trying to help." With color creeping across his face, he looked toward the ground as she locked the service door. "You're not mad at me for grabbing your you-know-what, are you? It really was an accident."

A giggle escaped before she could stop it. Another tumbled out after it, and then another. She gulped in a lungful of air and swiped at her teary eyes, but his sad-puppy expression only made it worse. Aiming the best she could, she wrapped her arms around his waist and rested her head against his chest. "I'm...sorry. I'm not...laughing at... you. The whole thing is just so...funny. I'm not mad or upset or offended. You're the sweetest man I've ever met."

His heart thumped in her ear, beating a little faster than hers, but not by much. Then his palm closed over her lower back, pushing it up another notch.

Hoo, boy! Is he feeling the chemistry too? And those muscles...

He cleared his throat and the low rumble vibrated through her. "That's me, the nice guy. Um, we should get going. The cooking and serving crews are there and everybody knows to grab something to drink and get comfortable, but I probably shouldn't be late to my own party."

"Okay." She raised her head to look up at him, unprepared for the frown that greeted her. "Hey, why the sad face? Being the nice guy is a good thing. I wish there were more men like you in the world."

A sudden smile reached his eyes, possibly because the noticeable bulge pressing into her lower belly meant she hadn't rendered him impotent.

Impotent? Ha! Sweet smile, sweeter man, and amazing muscles. That's one potent combination. It sparked an achy feeling she hadn't experienced in a long time.

She rose on her tiptoes to kiss his cheek and, unable to resist, took a detour toward his mouth at the last second. Maybe it wasn't the smartest decision, but she wanted to prolong the desire building inside her, to enjoy the freedom of expressing herself without caring what anyone else thought.

The first brush of her lips on his sent her back for more. They were warm and soft and sensual. He stiffened for a fraction of a second and then sighed as he tightened his hold on her. His mouth softened against hers, but his uninjured parts didn't.

Holy moly, this is nice.

She parted her lips, eager to take the kiss a step further. A taste of him would make the best belated-birthday gift—better than brownies or the cake he'd promised to share.

Better late than never.

A tentative lick along the seam of his lips sparked a moan and then his tongue glided across hers, triggering a rush of heat through her body. His hand slid from her lower back to her bottom, adding to the sensations pulsing through her long-neglected female parts. Her heart hammered in her chest as he slow-danced his way into her mouth. Each gentle stroke swept her farther from the fact that he was her little brother's best friend and had finished fifth grade when she graduated from high school.

Who cares? The man is a grownup and he knows how to kiss.

He groaned and took a giant backward step, breaking their connection far too soon. Had she misread his interest? "Sorry. I don't usually do stuff like that on the first date. Touching there, I mean. It's just... I guess I've known you so long, it doesn't feel like a first date."

A shaky breath did little to restore her equilibrium. "You already copped a feel of my breast anyway, so no worries."

Regret struck the instant his cheeks reddened again. "I swear it was an acc—"

"Aw, I was joking, Jim. It's okay. Really." She grasped his hand and headed for the truck, suddenly aware of how his big calloused palm and fingers engulfed hers—a testament to what she'd felt against her hip and belly. *Really okay.* "Come on. I don't want you to be late."

"No worries. The crew has everything under control. I'm just the host of Big Jim's Annual Hog Roast."

You're not "just" anything, and I'm in big trouble.

CHAPTER 6

I touched her butt.

And her breast.

Jim willed his dick to calm down, not that his heart was cooperating any better. He wasn't a second-base-on-the-first-date kind of guy, but that kiss had knocked him for a loop—still, after the painfully quiet fifteen-minute drive. It hadn't fallen short of his expectations in the least, even though he'd spent most of his life dreaming of that exact moment.

Thirty years. Definitely worth the wait.

Tate reached for the tote at her feet as he flipped on his signal for the turn into the lane leading to the house. "How's your head?"

Fairly certain she meant what she'd said about everything being okay, he shrugged. "It's hard."

Her choked snort broke a long moment of silence at the same time a cold sweat broke out on his neck and chest.

Hard? Smooth move, dude. Would he ever stop putting his foot in his mouth?

Relying on muscle memory, he made the turn. "I mean... It's fine. I'll just shut up now."

"It was *my* mischievous mind at work." She pulled her phone from the bag and tapped on the screen several times. "I like talking to you, and I'm glad you invited me to the hog roast. I haven't socialized much since I moved back, other than seeing my family sometimes and people at the café and the book club Riley and I started, so this is nice. Better than nice, actually."

"I like books. They're better company than people sometimes." Although he and Tate arrived five minutes before five, more than a dozen vehicles already lined the first row of parking in the field. He followed the unobstructed drive to the garage and parked inside. As the door closed behind them, he shut off the engine and pulled the keys from the ignition, all while reciting the first twenty elements from the periodic table to occupy his brain. "Ready?"

Her frown suggested she wasn't. "Maybe. I just got a text from Levi. He saw us driving in and wants to know if I'm your date."

Jim's stomach rumbled, whether from nerves or hunger he wasn't sure. "What did you tell him?"

"I'm thinking of pretending I didn't see the message. My brothers can be so annoying. I bet they're all here and ready to stick their noses into our business."

"I can't disagree with that. Beau came by with Corey earlier and wanted to know if I was picking you up because it was a date." Telling her the rest of what her brother had said didn't seem like a good idea.

"I hope you told him it is, because…it is."

Elation coursed through him, but he bit his lip to keep from letting out a whoop. "Wait here. I'll come around and help you down."

She dropped her phone into the tote and unbuckled her seat belt, wearing the same happy-go-lucky expression her niece shared with her. "I promise not to fall on you this time."

"That's too bad. I'm prepared for it now."

Her easy laugh cured the heartache he'd tried to ignore when Beau had announced the news of her engagement and marriage a decade and a half ago, even more than finding out she'd divorced the idiot and planned to return home. His chance had finally arrived, and he would do everything in his power not to screw it up.

He exhaled to calm his nerves as he rounded the back end of the truck, but spotting Beau, Archer, Levi, and Everett through the garage-door window wound them back up again. "Your brothers are all here and headed to the house."

When he reached the open passenger door, she placed her hands on his shoulders, reminding him of cowboys helping women down from wagons and stagecoaches in the old Westerns he'd watched growing up.

Mischief laced her smile. "If they want to butt into our business, we'll give them something really good to gossip about."

Grasping her waist, he lifted her out of the pickup and held on far longer than necessary after she stood facing him. The ability to touch her sent his pulse hop-skip-and-jumping again, but he preferred that to nervousness. "Like what?"

"Just follow my lead." She tunneled her fingers into his hair, distracting his dick from its impending nap. "Pull my shirt from my waistband a little in the back and loosen my ponytail some more."

"You want them to think we've been fooling around in here?" As much as he wouldn't have minded the real thing, he didn't like the idea of her brothers teasing her for the next three hours.

"We *are* fooling around. Now untuck my shirt and make this look real. They're going to be here any second." She stepped closer and pressed her lower belly to his waking erection.

A groan escaped as he tugged her blouse free from her jeans and then rocked his hips forward. "You want real? I can do real."

"Mm, then kiss me. I like kissing you."

She met him halfway, her tongue diving into his mouth the moment he melded his lips to hers. The world stood still while he let himself drown in the sensation of having her in his arms and savored the way she tasted him, like she wanted him as much as he wanted her. He'd waited his whole damn life to express his feelings, with the hope that she might feel the same.

His dream had come true.

A herd of footsteps carried from beyond the door leading into the kitchen.

Your timing sucks, guys.

Tate broke the kiss, but she nibbled a path to his ear instead of pulling away. Each deliberate caress added fuel to the bonfire already raging in his veins. Her whisper tickled his neck. "Ignore them. Put your hand up my shirt."

Feel her up in front of her brothers?

"Touch me like you mean it. Focus on me, Jim."

His name spoken so softly, so desperately by the woman of his heart against his ear sparked a shiver that raced through his entire body. Who in their right mind could refuse her?

He slipped his hand past the thin fabric, praying his palm wasn't sweaty. The silken plane of her skin drew his fingers upward until he reached a wide strip of lace traversing her back.

Flat. No overlapping ends. Hooks in front, thank God.

Temptation might've proven too much if he'd had access to the fasteners. Even so, her tongue on his earlobe tested his willpower.

"Ahem."

She sighed and tilted her head away from his, but she maintained the nonexistent space between them. "What are you guys doing in here? Can't you see we'd like some privacy?"

"Auggie wants to know what to do with the extra order for Jimbo." While the voice sounded most like Archer, any of her brothers could've spoken. "We offered to find him."

"He's busy at the moment." She twirled her fingers through his hair again and rubbed her cheek against his beard stubble. "Aren't you, Jim?"

With every cell and nerve ending humming, he barely managed a grunt.

"Hey, Tater, you know this is a family event, don't you? Lots of kids."

She pressed her kissable lips to his and then rested her forehead against his chest. "God, can't you boys take a hint? And don't call me Tater."

Archer stepped into Jim's peripheral vision. "Get a room if you're going to do PG-13 stuff. Or worse. Not that you should be doing that already. Isn't this your first date?"

"Out. What Jim and I do, and when and where we do it, are none of your business, especially when we're trying to do it without an audience." She wiggled against his erection and peered up at him with a wicked smile that added to the snugness of his khakis. "Right, big guy?"

Unable to speak through the flood of lust short-circuiting his brain, he nodded. Never before in his life had a woman made him consider picking her up and carrying her off to his bedroom like a caveman instead of taking care of his responsibilities.

"Did you find him?" The gruff tone meant Auggie had joined their audience. "Dude. You didn't tell me you had a new girlfriend. When did that happen?"

Jim fought a growl, but it got loose anyway. Reluctantly, he withdrew his hand from Tate's blouse, skimming it along the curve of her bottom as he put several inches between them. "Not now since we can't seem to get a few minutes alone. Put the extra package in the pantry and make sure you close the door. Everybody else needs to go outside while I show Tate where to put her overnight bag."

Everett crossed his arms in front of his chest and planted his feet shoulder width apart. "Overnight?"

From the way his voice rose an octave at the end, the oldest of the brothers clearly hadn't expected their big sister to have a sleepover on a first date.

"Yep." She grabbed her tote from the truck and closed the door. Then she linked her fingers with his. "Lead the way, Big Jim."

Hoping his confidence looked stronger to her brothers than it felt, he led her through the gawking men gathered at the doorway. Not slowing, he continued through the kitchen, across the living room, and up the stairs to his bedroom. His pulse drummed in his head by the time he stopped next to the bed. Not in his wildest dreams had he imagined Tate Madison in his bedroom.

Maybe in my wildest dreams. But not today.

She tossed her bag on the covers and grinned. "You were brilliant. That'll teach them to mind their own business."

Juggling the ball of fear in his gut, he sucked in a fortifying breath and slowly exhaled. "So…will you? Stay the night, I mean."

　　　　　　　　　　　*

TATE ADJUSTED HER GREEN CAP SO THE BILL BLOCKED THE EARLY evening sun and concentrated on not tripping over her own feet instead of the comfortable way Jim's hand molded around hers as they mingled with his guests. The last thing she needed was to fall on top of him in front of his friends, neighbors, and business associates plus her entire family, many of her customers, and all but one of the members of her new book club. She was already in danger of falling for him.

He gestured toward the coolers and giant thermos jugs lined up along one side of the shaded picnic tables with his free hand. "Want to get something to drink?"

"Sure, but I need to go find the bathroom first." After all the curious looks and knowing grins from her parents and brothers, a few minutes of alone time would hit the spot. Luckily, her bladder kept her from fibbing, unlike her attempt to escape speculation during Thursday's THC Book Club meeting.

"You can use the one upstairs instead of a porta potty if you want. Iced tea? I'll get it for you while you're in the house."

"Yes, thanks." She held her breath as she slipped her fingers from his and turned toward the deck. The absence of his touch brought a momentary pang each time he let go, adding serious concern to her nervousness. "Back in a few minutes."

"I'll be right here waiting for you."

The pang morphed into a near swoon. Her ex-husband had never treated her with such reverence and thoughtfulness, not even while they were dating. Why was a sweet guy like Jim still single?

She jogged up the steps, hoping to outrun the silly desire to experience romance and falling in love with a man who treated her like a treasure. That kind of head-over-heels and swept-off-her-feet fantasy didn't happen to a forty-something woman with a jaded view of marriage and happily-ever-after. Did it?

Telling him she'd think about staying the night seemed foolish now, even though she genuinely liked him—far more than she'd expected. The what-ifs had hounded her from the minute they'd greeted the first round of guests and developed into a fantasy of co-hosting the event as his wife and the mother of their child with every rapt look he aimed her direction. Equal parts of exhilaration and fear accompanied her across the deck.

"Hey, wait up, Tate."

A groan rumbled in her throat at Riley's demand from behind, but she swallowed it and paused at the sliding door. The harder she tried to avoid a private discussion, the more insistent and persistent her friend would become. "We've barely had a chance to talk. Are you having a good time? The food is amazing. Don't you think?"

"Yes and yes." Riley waltzed past Tate, her wedge sandals every bit as high as the spike-heeled shoes she normally wore. "Have you asked him yet?"

Straight to the point. Tate hurried past the crew loading dessert trays at the kitchen table, hoping to keep the gossip to a minimum. The remainder of the path to the stairs seemed uninhabited, but Tate waited until they reached Jim's bedroom to speak. "Not yet. How do you approach someone about fathering your baby?"

"It shouldn't be too difficult since he already invited you into his boudoir." Riley checked her reflection in the dresser mirror, turning this way and that. "Seriously, you should just sleep with him and let nature take its course. No doctor's office. No turkey basters. And the bonus? You might actually enjoy the sex."

Heat flared on Tate's neck and cheeks on her way to the bathroom. "But..."

A giggle-snort carried through the gap as Tate closed the door. "Yeah, getting to feel his butt is another bonus. Aren't you even a little curious to know if he's big all over? I'm sure it's nothing to be worried about."

Not as scary as falling in love with the wrong man again.

CHAPTER 7

THE MOUTHWATERING AROMA OF SLOW-ROASTED PORK STILL HUNG IN the air, but if Tate ate another bite, Jim would have to roll her home—if she went home. She leaned back in the glider, letting the wispy clouds inching across the color-washed sky lull her toward sleep. The day's warmth faded with the setting sun, and she zipped the jacket she'd layered over her blouse when her date had headed to the barn for a last check on his pigs before bedtime.

A date.

No one at the picnic could've come to any other conclusion since he'd stayed by her side with his hand wrapped around hers almost the entire time. He possessed every quality she wanted in a man worthy of helping her create a child—kind, generous, handsome, athletic, down-to-earth. A few years older and a lot less her brother's best friend, and she might be able to consider exploring a relationship with him, but she couldn't risk creating a rift between him and Beau, no matter how strong the attraction. Could she?

The security light on the end of the farrowing barn buzzed and flickered on, illuminating the only man she'd wanted to get to know better since her not-so-perfect life had taken a one-hundred-eighty-degree turn. Saying no to his invitation to stay the night after the last of his guests departed had taken far more resolve than she'd expected, and the disappointment still smarted. He'd been far more understanding than she deserved, especially after their make-out session in the garage.

His easy gait carried him closer, giving her adequate time to appreciate his physique and wallow in her regret. If circumstances had been different, she might've agreed. Their chemistry had surprised her, allowing her to fantasize about a happily-ever-after, but too many obstacles stood in the way—her wariness among them.

"Everybody's tucked in for the night." He sat beside her and set the glider in motion. If her answer had disappointed him, he hid it well. "Do you want to watch the stars come out? I can turn off the deck lights so they're easier to see."

She smothered the urge to cuddle up next to him and rest her head on his shoulder. Her willpower didn't stand a chance if she touched him again. "I should get going. Bedtime is nine thirty with these early mornings at the café."

The glider abruptly stopped and he nodded. "I'm an early riser too."

Just ask him. The worst he can do is say no.

She grasped his forearm when he started to rise. "I, um, want to talk to you about something first."

"Okay." He sat and sent them rocking back and forth again.

"You don't have to answer right away. And it's fine if you don't want to." *Just be honest.* "So…a little background for context. When I was married, I wanted to have a baby. For reasons I'd rather not go into, I didn't get pregnant. But I still want a baby, even though I'm not married anymore."

He stretched his arm along the back of the wooden seat, looking far more relaxed than most men would if a woman mentioned marriage and pregnancy on a first date. "You'll make a great mom. Anabelle loves working for you, says you're patient when she's learning new things. And your nieces and nephews always talk about their favorite aunt, especially Corey."

"Thanks." Lifting her feet from the ground, she tucked them under her as she faced him. "I was wondering if you might help me. Not financially or anything like that. With conception."

His eyes widened and his jaw dropped. "Like contribute half my DNA?"

"Yes, exactly. Will you think about it?"

"I don't need to think about it. The answer's yes. When do we start?"

Relief and gratitude spread through her insides like the heat his kisses and caresses had inspired earlier. "I'll call my doctor on Monday to see if we can set up an appointment for sperm collection and insemination when I'm ovulating. It should be soon."

His eyebrows dipped into a deep vee, creating shadows across his cheekbones. "Sperm collection and insemination."

"Yes. It sometimes takes several attempts before fertilization, so I'd like to start trying as soon as possible."

His frown and an abrupt end to the gentle gliding, sure signs he'd changed his mind, triggered a twinge of deep disappointment.

"Two things. I suppose three, actually." He huffed out a noisy sigh. "Okay. One. Speaking from experience, intrauterine insemination isn't a particularly enjoyable experience for any of the parties involved. Even my pigs get to try on their own first. And they're successful more times than not. Two." He cleared his throat. "I like getting off as much as the next guy, but I don't really want to do it in a doctor's office while a bunch of people are sitting there waiting for me to, uh, finish. And three. If we're going to make a baby, we ought to at least have fun while we're doing it."

TATE WANTS TO MAKE A BABY WITH ME.

Although her silence was better than an immediate refusal, it also meant she hadn't accepted his offer.

Jim leaned forward, resting his elbows on his knees and his chin on his fists, as he waited for the bout of lightheadedness to pass. Maybe Tate hadn't agreed to stay the night or have sex with him, but asking him to father her child had handed him the opportunity of a lifetime. Had he sounded as desperate as he'd felt when he had spewed out his counteroffer?

What else would convince her?

"Oh, and I have a doctor's report saying I don't have any sexually transmitted diseases. My last girlfriend asked me to get tested and then we didn't even..." *Too much information?* "Anyway, that was a while ago and I haven't been with anybody since."

The faint *hoo-hoo-hoo* of a screech owl echoed the question he didn't dare ask. Who, if anyone, had she slept with after her divorce?

She unfolded her legs, setting off a moment of panic that she'd decided to walk home. "I haven't been with anyone since my marriage ended, and I went to the doctor right after I found out my ex-husband was having an affair. We hadn't used protection in years, so he could've passed all kinds of stuff on to me. Luckily, I only had the beginning of a urinary tract infection. It could've been a lot worse."

"Do you still love him?" The question slipped out too quickly to stop it.

"God, no. Truthfully, I can't remember what I ever saw in him. I saw what I wanted to see, I guess."

"Sorry, I didn't mean to—"

"It's okay. Water under the bridge and lessons learned. I haven't forgiven him for all the lies, but I've moved on and I'm happier than I've been in a long time." She stood and walked to the porch railing, her red hair gleaming in the moonlight. When she faced him, indecision etched barely visible lines around her eyes and mouth. "It was selfish of me to ask you—"

"You don't have a selfish bone in your body. And my offer stands if you change your mind." He pushed to his feet, fairly certain her silence and stern expression meant that wasn't likely to happen.

"I'm not saying no, but I do need to think about it."

"Fair enough. Come on. I'll drive you home. We both have to be up early tomorrow."

Her nod was all the confirmation he needed to prepare himself for a sleepless and lonely night. It wouldn't be the first and probably not the last. Fortunately, thirty years of pining for her had taught him the true meaning of patience.

Light footfalls mingled with his across the deck and into the kitchen, the only indication she followed him. Heading for the garage, he dug his keys from the front pocket of his khakis.

When he gestured for her to go first through the doorway, she glanced toward the ceiling. "I almost forgot. I left my tote upstairs. It has my keys and my phone in it."

"You can go ahead out to the truck while I run up and get it. Doors are unlocked." Grateful for an excuse to wallow in self-pity for a minute, he hurried to the living room and up the stairs.

Although moonlight through the window shone across the bed, he flipped on the switch for his bedside lamp as he entered the bedroom. She wouldn't appreciate him missing any of her belongings, especially if she didn't want to see him again after tonight's awkwardness. She probably thought the only reason he'd suggested trying the real thing first was to get in her pants.

Okay, she's half right, just not for the reasons she thinks.

Man, I thought tonight was finally going to be the night, not that telling her I love her so soon is a good idea.

He dropped his keys next to her bag and put her purse inside with her sunglasses and the John Deere cap he'd given her. Much to his surprise, she'd worn the cap until the sun had set and she'd come inside for her jacket.

"Jim?"

He jumped at her voice and the straps slipped from his fingers, letting the tote fall onto the bed. His keys bounced onto the floor and under the edge of the bed, out of sight. "Yeah, Tate? Did you forget something else?"

She unzipped her jacket as she stepped into the room. "Yes, I did. I forgot that it's okay to be a woman with normal needs and desires. And I… It's like this. I want you."

"Me?" A swell of hope surged through every part of his body before he could consider her meaning. He groaned. "Baby?"

She stopped less than an arm's length from him, letting the outer layer slide off her shoulders. Then it landed at her feet. "Both, but I want you more right now. I started to go into the garage, but all I could think about was the way you kissed me and how wonderful it felt to have your hand on my bare skin. For the first time in a long time, I feel wanted and appreciated by a man."

"I, uh... You... We..." With all his blood rushing south, the likelihood that he'd regain the ability to form a coherent thought or speak anytime soon was slim.

"Yes. We." She placed her open palm on his chest and kicked off her shoes. Her feet looked tiny next to his size-sixteen hiking boots. "I'd like to stay the night, if you haven't changed your mind. You haven't, have you?"

Certain she could feel his heart pounding through his ribs, he shook his head. "Nope."

Her relieved smile said she didn't care that he sounded like an illiterate Neanderthal, replying in one-syllable words and grunts. "Thanks for understanding. This is easier than I thought it would be. It must be because of you. You're kind and sweet, and I truly like you."

A kiss seemed far more effective than another nod or grunt at communicating his pleasure, even if his case of nerves was worse now than when he'd picked her up that afternoon. He leaned in, closing the space between them, and touched his lips to hers. The first light caress led to another and another.

Heaven.

Then her hands slid into his hair as she pulled him closer still and welcomed him into her mouth. Each slow glide of her tongue drained the worries from his mind, transforming the fantasy he'd cultivated into a reality. She wasn't solely motivated by her brothers' presence or the desire to have a baby. She wanted him.

Just me.

Her breath warmed his neck when she eased away. "You seem distracted. Are you having second thoughts?"

"No!" Panic gripped his brain and flooded his veins. "Are you?"

"No." She gave him a gentle peck on the cheek. "But I think we might both be a little nervous."

"Nervous. Yeah." The rollercoaster of yeses and nos had taken a whooshing uphill climb and teetered on the top of a mountainous peak that would lead to a high-speed bottom-of-the-hill crash if she had another change of heart.

"Maybe we need to start with another kiss and untucking my shirt. You know, like in the garage." She licked her lips, pushing the tightness against his zipper up another notch. "Will you help me undress?"

"I can do that." He gave her shirt a gentle tug and eased his palm along her waist to her spine, finding the same band of lace his fingers had discovered earlier. He froze at her shuddering breath when he circled to her ribs. "Are my hands too rough? I work outside a lot and—"

"They feel nice." She guided them upward to the clasp between her breasts. "I think this is what you're looking for. How about if I take my top off first?"

A nod was all he could manage.

She unbuttoned her shirt far faster than his fumbling fingers could have, revealing a deep valley flanked by matching knolls of flesh and wide swaths of smooth skin above and below. Only a modest amount of lace remained when she shrugged away the outer layer.

Swallowing hard, he flicked open the catch. The cups clung to her curves, daring him to free her breasts. "Beautiful."

A faint blush spread from her chest to her cheeks, suggesting she hadn't been complimented nearly enough.

"You are." He slipped the straps past her shoulders and let gravity do its work. When her bra fell to the floor, an involuntary sigh escaped. His daydreams paled in comparison to the real Tate. "Beautiful. Gorgeous. Breathtaking."

Color still tinting her fair skin, she looked away and pulled his shirt from his khakis. Her fingertips grazed his abs, stealing his breath again. "Your turn. Might as well take off your boots and pants too."

"Okay." He yanked the walking advertisement for his farm over his head, turning the sleeves inside out in his hurry. Then he made quick work of all but his underwear. When he straightened, she stepped out of a pair of lace panties the same shade of green as her bra. "You're naked."

"You're not." A mischievous grin chased away the blush. "Wow. You're built like Dwayne Johnson—but with hair. And no tattoos."

"The Rock was my idol when I was a kid." He willed himself to stay relaxed instead of striking a bodybuilding pose. She didn't seem the type to like showoffs. "That was a compliment, right?"

"Definitely." She flipped back the covers and crawled into bed. "Want to join me?"

At her invitation, his muscles sprang into action, taking him to the other side in record time. "Definitely."

Her gaze dropped from his to someplace below his waist. "I don't think you need the boxers anymore."

CHAPTER 8

LORD, HAVE MERCY.

Tate blinked at the bulge growing in front of her eyes and swallowed to keep from drooling down her chin. If she'd known this would be her reward for all those years of disappointment, she would've found a way to move back to Wellington when her divorce was finalized instead of waiting nearly three years to build up her savings.

With his thumbs hooked under the waistband, Jim shoved his form-hugging boxer briefs toward his hips. A bit of stretching eased the elastic past the massive lump and his erection popped free, evidently none the worse for wear from their earlier mishap. "Are you okay? You're breathing kind of hard."

She smiled up at him, happier than she'd been in ages. Every inch of her body tingled, ready to make up for lost time and opportunities. "Perfect."

He resumed his task and then stopped again with his underwear around his thighs. "Did you want me to use a condom this time? I have some."

The moment of truth had finally arrived. She had to choose between Jim Cochon fathering her baby or some anonymous sperm donor she had only a profile to go by. "If we don't, that means I could get pregnant."

"Yeah, but we talked about that. You said you'll be ovulating soon. So, like in a week? A few days?" His erection bobbed at her, daring her to try forcing it into a latex overcoat.

"I, um, I'm not sure. Things have been hectic the past few months with moving and opening the café. I don't know for sure."

He slid his briefs the rest of the way down his legs and sat on the edge of the bed, giving her an amazing view of his back muscles and buns of steel. The mattress bounced as he slipped under the covers. "Maybe it's better that way. We can just enjoy each other. Like a scrimmage. No pressure."

Enjoy. A practice run.

If he made love as well as he kissed, enjoyment wouldn't be an issue. Attentiveness had been his strongest point throughout their date.

Okay. Here goes.

She eased her leg into his space, searching for a foot, a calf, or a thigh to explore. Any part of him would do.

The bed wiggled again as he rolled toward her, putting their faces inches apart. A furrow creased his forehead directly below one of his wayward curls. "Is it okay if I kiss you?"

"Seems like the logical first step since we're here. In bed. Naked." She released the sheet she'd been holding to her breasts and slipped her fingers into his hair. "Plus, I'll be very disappointed if you don't."

"I don't want to disappoint you." He leaned in, starting with a barely there kiss and then gliding his tongue along her lower lip.

She welcomed him inside, pulling him closer still until his chest touched her nipples. The skin-to-skin contact stole every bit of oxygen from her lungs, but it lit her body on fire. Each slow stroke of his tongue along hers promised a night deserving of getting caught sneaking home bright and early in day-old clothes.

His palm spread over her lower back, aligning his body with hers like he had in the garage. The outline of his erection against her leg promised he wouldn't leave her wanting more, unless it was round two. Then he eased his thigh between hers and his fingertips glided over her bottom to her hip, the gentle exploration making her breath hitch and goose bumps scatter over every inch of her skin.

He froze with his hand at the back of her knee. "Did I do something wrong?"

A whimper snuck out before she could consider how he might interpret it. "Oh gosh, no. Except you stopped. I liked what you were doing."

He exhaled and rested his forehead against hers. "Sorry."

"No apology necessary." Snuggling closer, she moved his hand back to her thigh. "I think we're both still nervous."

"I just want everything to be perfect."

Why couldn't she have met a man like him before she'd wasted nearly half her life on a lying cheater? "It is. I'll let you know if I'm not enjoying what you're doing."

"Okay."

"And you'll tell me if—"

"You can do whatever you want to me. I'm all yours." He rolled onto his back, taking her with him.

"Careful!" She kicked her leg straight out to keep from kneeing him in the same place she'd landed earlier and whacked her ankle on what seemed to be his shin. "Ouch!"

In a smooth motion, he shifted her sideways and threw off the covers. A second later, he knelt at the other end of the bed with her feet cradled against his chest. "Are you okay? Which one hurts? You know what? It doesn't matter. I'll kiss them both until you feel better."

The awareness of her utter nudity vanished with the first touch of his lips on her arch and another glimpse at his truly spectacular body. Each successive kiss brought him closer to her thigh, but then he started all over with the other foot, igniting flames that would surely consume her before he reached his destination—wherever that happened to be.

He hooked her legs over his shoulders and nuzzled her inner thigh, the beard stubble on his jaw sparking tingles in her lower belly. "Is this helping the pain?"

A long, low moan rumbled up through her throat on an exhale. "Pain? What pain?"

"Does that mean I should stop?" His chuckle chased away any reservations she had about her decision.

She flexed her thighs and shook her head. "Don't you dare."

He smiled as he slid his hands down to cup her bottom. "So you won't mind a little foreplay? I'm not into wham-bamming and quickies. What's the point of making love to somebody if it's over before you even get started?"

Her heart stuttered, adding to her breathlessness and the wonderful sensations zinging through her body. Had sex ever transported her this far past clinical? "Foreplay would be very nice."

His slightly bristly whiskers feathered over her skin as he nibbled a meandering path toward the needy ache. He once again switched to her other leg before he reached it, intensifying the need to be touched there until her muscles shook. Looking up at her with more desire in his eyes than any man ever had, he slipped his hands along her waist to her ribs and to her breasts, gently cupping them like he was afraid she might break. Then he kissed the folds she wished he would part with his fingers, his tongue, his erection.

She arched her hips and released the moan tickling her throat.

"Can I taste you?" His husky voice caressed her nerve endings, adding to the sweet overload of sensation.

"Yes. Oh God, please, yes." Finally, something in her life was worth begging for. She guided his hands to her nipples, needing more of him. "Taste me. Touch me. All of it."

The heat in his stare flared and he nodded once before his mouth devoured her—kissing, licking, sucking. His fingers strummed her flesh, sending an electric current from her breasts to her clit.

She forced her eyelids open, trying to wallow in the pure decadence and stay connected with his worshipful gaze. Or was it simply lust?

She could live with that, especially considering the immense sexual satisfaction rushing over her from his amazing tongue and hands. Suspended in the endless moment between unbearable bliss and orgasm, she fought to fill her lungs through rough cries she barely recognized as her own. A growl vibrated through her pelvis, sending her over the edge into ecstasy that seemed to go on forever.

Before she floated down to reality, he brushed her hair from her face and stared into her eyes as he slowly pushed inside her, filling her so completely she couldn't imagine ever experiencing sex like this again.

"Ready to make a baby?" He sounded awed by the possibility, as if he truly wanted to give her that gift.

"Yes." Threading her fingers into his curls, she pulled him down for a kiss. Who cared if she hadn't caught her breath yet? Air was far less important than this, than him.

She wrapped her legs around his waist, somehow pulling him deeper still, and matched the easy in-and-out tempo he set for their bodies with her tongue against his.

Synchronized. In tune.

Twelve years in a farce of a marriage hadn't yielded one instance of lovemaking that compared to what Jim was giving her—selfless attention that could easily let her fantasize she was his whole world, someone he couldn't live without, that she was utterly and truly loved.

Thought faded away with the steady rhythm, the slowly rebuilding pleasure, and the measured weight of his body on hers. This was how it was supposed to be.

He panted against her chin as he broke off the kiss, but his lips caressed her cheek and then her ear a moment later. "Is this okay, Tate? I want you to feel as incredible as I do."

She smoothed her palm down his neck to his shoulder blade, amazed that a man this strong could be so gentle and caring. With his next leisurely thrust, she rocked her hips upward to meet him. The motion changed the location of impact, triggering a tremor and a weightless sensation that promised even greater gratification than the first time. "Amazing, Jim."

His rumbling groan assured her he'd felt something too. "I don't think I can last much longer."

"You don't have to." She met him halfway again, gasping when he hit the same spot. "Now…would be good."

He wedged his knees under her hips and quickened his pace, his face still buried in her hair. The wonderful friction carried her higher, but the earthy, animalistic sounds tumbling out of him as he stiffened sent her flying. A burst of heat warmed her insides and she struggled to guide his lips to hers. She wanted—and needed—that connection, to thank him for and share the joy he'd given her.

Her throat stung, suggesting she'd been more vocal than normal, so she tried for a whisper. "I want to kiss you."

"I want to kiss you too." A light peck on her jaw led to another on her cheek, the tip of her nose, and finally her lips. The soft caress became a slow making-love-to-her-mouth kiss that she wished would never end. He raised his head, giving her a peek at his dreamy smile. "I could stay like this forever."

As melty as her bones were at the moment, it was a distinct possibility. "The chances of conception may increase slightly if I lie on my back for fifteen minutes after intercourse. Your little swimmers don't have to fight gravity."

"Better block them inside then too. Don't want anybody to escape, not that they should want to try to leave the exceptional home we gave them." He closed his eyes and touched his forehead to hers. "We should do it again every few hours until morning, just in case this time didn't work."

"Mm-hm." His reasoning made sense, but she had reasons of her own for agreeing.

We should do it again every few hours until morning because being with you is better than a pan of warm gooey brownies.

❧

TATE STRETCHED, OR AS MUCH AS SHE COULD WITH JIM'S BIG BODY curved around hers. Her muscles protested, but the slight soreness reminded her how she'd spent the night. Between the spectacular episodes of intimate exploration and profound physical connection, they'd slept tangled in each other's arms and legs, lying skin to skin until they recharged enough to do it all over again.

Warm lips against her forehead fanned the still-glowing embers, tempting her to steal a quickie before she had to leave. Her brunch-to-lunch hours would then give her time to contemplate what to do about the strange tickle in her insides that had nothing to do with mind-blowing sex, her reproductive organs, and trying to get pregnant.

"Morning." His husky greeting amplified all of the feelings. "I wish we could stay in bed all day, but I need to head down to the farrowing barn pretty soon for a delivery and you need a ride home first. How about some breakfast before we drive into town? I make a decent fried egg sandwich. Not as good as yours, of course."

She burrowed closer, holding him tighter, and kissed his fuzzy chest. "You don't have to go to any trouble."

"No trouble." He combed his fingers through her hair, gently working them through when the strands knotted. "I like doing stuff for you."

Giddiness made her heart swoon. He was kind, generous, and self-less—all qualities she appreciated in a lover and hoped to pass on to their child.

She smiled up at him. "I think that's the sweetest thing anyone's ever said to me. Now we better get out of bed before I can't resist thanking you."

His husky chuckle voiced the amusement and something else shining in his eyes. Exercising far more self-control than she could muster, he rolled toward the edge of the bed. "You're welcome anytime."

"Good to know."

He looked back at her over his shoulder, an adorable blush coloring his cheeks. "I'll go start breakfast while you get dressed."

He rubbed his beard stubble as he sauntered to the dresser, his tightly muscled butt drawing an appreciative sigh from her. Then he pulled a pair of athletic shorts from the middle drawer, tugged them on, and hurried out of the room.

Swoon.

She grinned and hugged his pillow to her face, savoring his scent, their scent.

No regrets. I never thought I'd say that about sleeping with a guy on the first date.

She hadn't really expected him to agree to father her baby, either. Why had she doubted her body's instincts and waffled over spending the night with him?

Still floating on the high of multiple orgasms, a relationship worth exploring, and the possibility of a child nine months from now, she hummed through washing her face, emptying her bladder, and dressing in yesterday's clothes. After a last check of the floor for her belongings, she hooked her tote over her shoulder and scuttled down the steps. The smell of bacon and eggs lured her into the kitchen, where Jim stood at the stove, looking incredibly sexy in his shorts and a bib-style apron.

Wielding a pancake flipper, he turned toward her. "Egg sandwiches are almost ready. Have a seat while I finish up. I've only ever seen you drink tea, so I made a cup of hot water for you. Tea bags are on the table."

"Thanks." She sat, an eye trained on him while she chose an herbal-blend bag from the basket. The muscles in his back rippled and shifted with each movement, making her fingers itch to be sure she'd touched each and every one.

He transferred the fried eggs to a trio of sliced bagels, put on their tops, and placed them in the panini grill on the counter. His bicep bulged when he pressed down the lid. "Auggie's baby Swiss bagels are really good for breakfast sandwiches. Do you get your bread and rolls from him?"

"You bet I do. Riley recommended his bakery when I was contacting suppliers."

"Good. He's a good guy."

"And his chocolate éclair cake is going on my menu board at least once a week if I can talk him into a standing order. Thank you for introducing me to that piece of heaven."

"You're welcome." As he lifted the hinged lid on the panini grill, he slid two plates in front of it.

"Smells delicious." A buzz came from her tote when he set one dish by her mug. Tempted though she was to ignore it, she dug her phone from the depths to check her messages.

Riley's name and number shone on the screen. *"Hey, answer the door! I brought the bundle of parsley you asked for yesterday."*

Crap! Answer or make her wait?

Jim sat down across from her and released a noisy exhale. "So...I was thinking. I really want to have kids. Well, not just kids. I want a wife too. Anyway, what if we got married?"

CHAPTER 9

REPLAYING THE SCENE WITH TATE AT BREAKFAST, JIM PUSHED through another set of reps. The burn in his pecs and triceps barely distracted him from the pain of her rejection.

She hadn't even considered his proposal. Heck, she hadn't taken a single bite of her bagel sandwich before the color had drained from her already pale complexion and she'd raced out the door. Shock and finding a pair of shoes and his keys had waylaid him at least five minutes. When he'd finally gone after her, she had already disappeared somewhere into the pre-dawn darkness.

Twelve hours later, she still hadn't returned his calls.

Man, this is not *how it was supposed to go.*

"Jimbo, you in there?" A knock on the gym door announced Beau's presence, giving Jim no chance to sneak into the changing room.

He closed his eyes and hoped his friend hadn't heard the clank of the weights. Maybe Beau would go away and let him wallow in his regrets alone.

Regret. Only one—asking her to marry me too soon.

"I was on my way home and decided to stop by. Dude, are you taking a nap?" The voice moved closer, too close to pretend he wasn't there. Beau kicked Jim's foot and snorted. "Not enough sleep last night?"

"I don't want to talk about it."

"That bad, huh? The way you were sucking each other's faces off in the garage and all the handholding during the picnic, I figured you'd be planning the wedding today."

"Not funny. I asked her to marry me and she ran away."

The bench on the other side of the machine creaked. "Ouch. What happened? Performance anxiety? She decided things were moving too fast?"

Jim sighed, wishing the problem was that simple. "I don't know what went wrong. She spent the night and everything was perfect. Everything."

"You're sure? Women need a lot more care and feeding than guys do, if you know what I mean."

Throwing a glare at Beau, Jim stood and stalked to the rack of free weights. "Amazing. That's what she said. And I don't think she'd lie."

Beau leaned forward, bracing his elbows on his knees. "Okay, no need to get defensive. Assuming you're right about the, um, physical part, my guess is she freaked about the marriage proposal. You gotta admit asking a woman to marry you on the first date is a little unconventional. Plus, her ex-husband lied to her, cheated on her, and wasted a good chunk of her life. I wouldn't exactly be thrilled to jump off that bridge again without being really, really sure. The worthless prick deserves to have his dick cut off and shoved down his throat. Have you tried calling her?"

"Twelve times. Other than a text saying Riley took her home, she hasn't answered her phone or called me back."

"Hey, that's a good sign. If she didn't give a damn about your feelings, she wouldn't have told you she got home okay. Give her a day or two to calm down and then try again. It's not like she's going anywhere. Speaking of going, I better head home." Beau grinned as he rose. "Let me know if you decide you want to talk about it."

"Butthead." Jim walked his friend outside, ignoring the laughter echoing through the pole barn. His stomach lurched at the crunch of gravel in the lane, but an unfamiliar car dashed the momentary spark of hope.

By the time they reached Beau's sedan, the vehicle had parked next to it and a woman in a red suit and matching lips emerged. "Mr. Cochon?"

He nodded. "Yeah, I'm Jim Cochon."

She rounded the trunk of her sleek black roadster and held out a large envelope. "Georgina Swofford, Tate Madison's attorney. My business card is inside. Please call or email my office once you've had an opportunity to review the enclosed documents. I expect to hear from you no later than Friday at the close of business, as mentioned in the cover letter. Have a nice evening."

Frozen in place, he gripped the envelope while she returned to the driver's side of the car. "Attorney? What for?"

"To represent her interests in the sperm donor agreement, of course."

PETRA'S MOUTH FELL OPEN AND THE SPOON IN HER HAND CLATTERED onto the table. "He *what*?"

With a scowl true to her reputation, Riley set down her wine glass and stabbed her fork into the pickle jar. "He had the audacity to suggest marriage after she specifically asked him to be her sperm donor. Not only that, he insisted on actual intercourse instead of artificial insemination. As if a one-night stand gives him the right to propose to her. Can you believe the nerve of him?"

Petra stuffed a brat into her mustard-and-onion prepped bun. "Please tell me the sex was at least decent and you got a couple orgasms out of it."

Tate pressed her lips together, determined not to incriminate herself any more than she already had since Riley had picked her up at the end of Jim's gravel lane and Georgie had grilled her for details that morning before the restaurant opened for brunch.

Riley's frown deepened. "She wouldn't tell me, and she has a better poker face than I would've expected."

Wally waved a bowl in front of Tate's face. "Sauerkraut?"

Shaking her head, she pushed away from the table. "I'm not hungry."

Her stomach flipped, flopped, and scrambled for cover as a flash of red caught her eye at Riley's patio door. *The blood of her adversaries.* That's how the woman had described the color of her suit earlier when Riley had complimented her on it.

A knock followed and Georgie let herself into the kitchen, the stern-lawyer expression she'd worn during their interview giving way to a satisfied smirk. "It's done. Hand-delivered. And I have a witness. Tall male. About six-two. Reddish hair. Mid-thirties. Wearing an Ohio State sweatshirt and driving a gunmetal-gray Ford sedan with a toddler car seat in the back. One of your brothers?"

"Beau, the youngest. He and Jim are best friends." *Why did I let Georgie and Riley talk me into this? Jim probably hates me and now my family is involved in this mess too.*

Georgie sat in the chair Tate had abandoned and grabbed the bowl of potato salad. "Does he know you planned to have a baby using a sperm donor?"

"No. I didn't tell anybody other than Riley, Petra, and Wally. And Jim." *Why, oh, why didn't I just pick a random guy from one of the websites?*

"And you haven't returned any of Mr. Cochon's calls?"

"No." She hadn't even listened to the dozen or more voicemails Jim had left on her cell, for fear he'd talk her into a second doomed marriage.

Why couldn't he have taken things slowly, giving her time to consider whether she wanted a romantic relationship again? His afterthought about wanting a wife hardly supported a desire to marry *her*, even though he'd acted like the world revolved around her while they shared his bed. His mixed messages made her warier than ever and sorry she'd been brave enough to let her hormones convince to sleep with him.

"Good. Don't respond. The ball is in his court for now." Georgie added a brat and a generous helping of kraut to the bun on her plate. "You should eat. Assuming you conceived is the best approach until we know otherwise. And for God's sake, no moping. He violated the terms of the oral agreement you made last night. You didn't do anything wrong."

"I liked him." The words slipped out against her will, as did the tears blurring her vision.

Wally wrapped her in a hug before the sound of her chair scraping across the floor registered. "Oh, honey, you're such a trusting soul and I love you for it."

"Trusting is just a nice word for gullible." Tate bit her lip to hold in a sob, but the hurt still squeezed her heart.

"Nonsense. Come sit down."

Petra shoved out the empty chair beside her. "Gullible is going back for a sixth helping after the five dicks you were previously engaged to screwed you over."

"I thought one of them died." Plate in hand, Wally loaded it with mound of fruit salad.

"Because he got squished by a cement mixer while he was running from the cops during a drug bust. Pickles. She needs pickles." Her butcher friend guided Tate into the chair. "And I'll get you a bowl of ice cream."

Intermittent buzzing sent Tate's stomach tumbling again and Georgie slammed her hand over the phone next to her glass. "You're not answering that."

Silence reigned for a full five seconds before a single muffled buzz vibrated beneath the lawyer's palm.

She peeked at the screen and laughed. "You got a text from your brother Beau. 'What the hell, Tate?' That's an exact quote. I'm guessing Mr. Cochon let him read the contents of the envelope. That means my intervention had the intended effect."

But was it my intention?

How can I know when everybody's telling me how to feel?

·❦·

RUTHLESS?

Evil?

Tate racked her memory for the exact wording she'd used to ask Jim for his sperm. Had she given him any reason to think his involvement included anything beyond conception?

No, but I told him I wanted him, that I truly liked him. It wasn't only about making a baby.

True to her word to Georgie, she hadn't answered the endless calls or responded to the dozens of texts from Jim, Beau, or anyone who might question her sanity and motives. She had, however, listened to every voicemail and read every message from her brothers and the father of her potential child over the last two-and-a-half days. Her siblings had attacked her on his behalf, using adjectives a thesaurus would be proud of to describe her intent to abscond with the product of their friend's unsuspecting swimmers and her seductive egg. Jim had only asked what he'd done wrong a hundred times, as if he proposed marriage to all the women he dated and had never been turned down.

Maybe he does. What do I even know about him?

Besides the obvious. Her subconscious hadn't let her forget his good-guy friendliness or his bodybuilder physique for a second. Her dreams, both day and night, were a constant barrage of sexual escapades, albeit a rather tame reminder of their night together. Her heart, on the other hand, hurt.

The alley door buzzer interrupted her mindless refilling of salt and pepper shakers.

Delivery?

What day is it?

"Please not Tuesday. God, it's Tuesday, isn't it?" She trudged to the compost bucket and picked it up by the handle rather than lifting the lid. "Full, damn it."

If only she hadn't spent the last forty-eight hours slicing and dicing, chopping and grinding, and cooking and baking to distract herself from her mixed-up feelings.

The buzzer sounded again.

Just tell him the truth.

"I can do this." She bit her lip to distract her nerves. Then she slid the locks and opened the door, not really prepared to face her inadvertent adversary.

A young man in a well-worn WHS Varsity Football t-shirt greeted her with a smile and a wave. "Hey there, Ms. Madison. I'm here to pick up your kitchen waste for Mr. Cochon."

"Oh, um, thank you." Stomping on the unexpected disappointment, she pointed to the bucket. "Careful, it's full."

"Yes, ma'am." He hefted the container and carried it to a smaller version of Jim's massive pickup. Even the same Big Jim's Itty Bitty Pig Farm logo adorned the extended-cab side doors. The clunk of the bucket on the pavement punctuated the stitch of pain in her heart. "See you Thursday!"

As she nodded a farewell, her cell vibrated against her thigh and Georgie's ringtone sang out. Locking herself in the café, she pulled the phone from her apron pocket. "Hello."

"I have news." The brief statement didn't bode well, considering her lawyer's usual long-windedness.

A sigh snuck out and Tate headed to her office. "Give me a sec to sit down." She switched to speaker, set the phone on her desk, and sank into the chair. "Okay, go ahead."

"Jim refused to sign the donor agreement. He's demanding that he be allowed at all prenatal visits, that the baby have his last name on the birth certificate, and that he retain all rights associated with shared parenting. In other words, this is likely to get very messy. Long, drawn out, and incredibly nasty. His attorney claims Jim didn't explicitly agree to your original terms for artificial insemination, so our assertion that they apply, either partially or wholly, is invalid."

Your assertion, not ours. Regret bloomed in Tate's chest and spread to her stomach, her throat, and her eyes. "I guess the best I can hope for now is that I'm not pregnant. I didn't mean to…"

"Didn't mean to what? You can't be nice about this, Tate. Custody cases are often worse than divorces. People fight over houses, cars, and bank accounts, but kids and pets are my bread and butter for billable hours. If you don't want to spend the next eighteen years arguing over whose house your child is going to for birthdays and Christmas, you have no choice but to be brutal, especially since you and Mr. Cochon didn't part ways in an amicable situation. He isn't likely to negotiate terms that are favorable to you."

Her insides threatened to rebel against the little bit of lunch she'd managed to eat after closing and cleanup. "I don't want him to hate me."

"You have a lot to learn about— Sorry, got to go. I have another call I need to take. We'll talk more at book club on Thursday."

The line went dead, but it didn't give Tate a reprieve from the guilt swirling in her conscience.

CHAPTER 10

"Hi, Jim. This is Tate." She held her breath and closed her eyes, prepared for the worst—which she deserved.

His heavy sigh cautioned her the call probably wouldn't go well, not that she had any hope it would. "Hi. Are you still mad at me? I, um, I'm sorry for blurting out a marriage proposal like that. It should've been romantic and—"

"I was never mad, and you don't have to apologize. It's my fault." Her voice cracked on the last word and she squeezed her eyes closed tighter to fight the stinging tears trying to form. "Please try to understand. I don't think I can ever get married again. Not because there's anything wrong with you. There isn't. You're sweet and kind, and if I could change the past... It's just that my marriage was such a disaster."

"But I'd never lie to you or cheat on you. Let me prove it." His gentle proclamation held no animosity, no demand. The sincerity in his request begged her to reconsider.

"I can't. I'm sorry. I can't risk going through that again. If it turns out I'm pregnant, I promise we'll talk about shared custody. I never meant to hurt you. I made a huge mistake by asking you to help me. And now... Anyway, I hope you can forgive me." Before she could cave to his assurances, Tate tapped the icon to end the call and scrubbed away the wetness on her cheeks. Saving herself wasn't supposed to feel like somebody had stomped on her heart and left it to die—while she had to do the same thing to someone she genuinely liked.

She set her phone on the desk, crossed her arms on the edge for a makeshift pillow, and cursed all the big choices she'd ever made. Nothing in her personal life had gone as planned in her thirties, and her forties had already taken a dive straight into a midlife crisis of teenage-drama proportions.

This is why I'm better off staying away from men.

A buzz made her jump, and another followed a few seconds later.

Her insides twisted in knots as she debated looking at the messages or not. Had Jim decided she was a bitch and cussed her out for being selfish? What if he demanded sole custody? How on Earth was she supposed to heal from this mistake if they had to raise a child together but separately?

Just get it over with.

She blinked away the unshed tears and pressed the Home button. Georgie's name appeared.

"At the front door."

"Let me in. We need to talk."

Too beat down for a battle of wills with her attorney, Tate pushed away from the desk and carried her cell to the restroom. *"Give me a minute. Chopping onions."*

At least the little white lie would explain her telltale watery eyes.

After several splashes of cool water, she grabbed the towel and dried her face and hands on a slow trek to the customer entrance of the café. Georgie stood on the other side of the glass, her long blood-red coat standing out against the grayness of the dreary hump-day late afternoon. The unreadable all-business expression she wore only added to Tate's desire to go home and hide from the world.

Unable to look at her visitor, she led Georgie to the corner table. "I called Jim to apologize and explain that there's no way I can marry him. Or anyone, for that matter."

Georgie sat across from her and sighed, the first sign of frustration

Tate had ever witnessed from her lawyer friend. "I know you're upset about the situation, but I told you not to contact him under any circumstances. All communication is supposed to go through me."

"Then you probably don't want to hear that I promised him shared custody if I'm pregnant."

"I'm trying to protect your interests, Tate. What if he tells his attorney what you said? Or worse, he recorded it or had someone with him, listening to everything you said?" Pulling her tablet from her ever-present messenger bag, Georgie pursed her lips. Then her fingers danced on the screen like a troop of River Dance cloggers. "Unless you're going to accept his marriage proposal, you can't talk to, text, email, or otherwise converse in any manner with him until this is settled. Do you understand? The counteroffer will put you in nearly daily contact with him for at least the next eighteen years and nine months. Is that what you want?"

Tate slumped lower in the chair. "I don't know what I want anymore. This whole plan to have a baby was so much simpler in my head."

"My job is to handle the complications." Georgie closed the cover on her iPad and returned it to her bag. "Get your purse and turn off the lights. You're going home to eat, take a nice long bath, and go to bed by nine o'clock. I ordered delivery. It'll be there in twenty minutes."

"I can take care of myself."

Reaching across the table, Georgie patted Tate's hand. "I know you can, but are you?"

PICKLES AND ICE CREAM TASTED SURPRISINGLY GOOD TOGETHER—THE right combination of salty and sweet with the bonus of calcium for healthy bones, teeth, and prospective babies plus vitamin C for eliminating the chance of developing scurvy.

Because the way things are going, there's a good chance I'm cursed.

Tate downed the last tasty bite and transferred mini quiches from the muffin tins to a serving tray. The gooey puddles of cheese in the centers tempted her to sneak a sample before her friends' arrival for their THC Book Club meeting, but pigging out the last two days hadn't provided any relief from her roiling emotions. Stress eating had only made swapping her jeans for leggings necessary.

With a platter in each hand, she carried the rest of tonight's snacks to the dining room. Riley stood outside the front entrance, her fist poised to tap on the glass, when Tate passed the order counter.

Time to put on a brave face.

Almost thankful for her friend's distracted grimace, she opened the door. "Something wrong?"

Riley aimed straight for the food and grabbed a plate. "Deacon Jeffries is such a tool. You'd think he has a death wish the way he antagonizes me all the time."

"I would appreciate you not killing him since he's my accountant too." *And I'm going to need one to help me figure out how to pay for all the legal fees for a fight I don't want to have.* "What did he do?"

"He called me Malibu Barbie because I drove the Bird with the top down to our meeting this afternoon." The tower of quiches on Riley's dish wobbled, but she added a stack of toasted rye rounds and a generous helping of artichoke dip without slowing. "That man deserves a month of hot flashes and night sweats."

A familiar giggle-snort came from behind them.

"You know he only does it to get a rise out of you, right?" Petra squeezed in beside Tate and began loading a plate. "Nice spread. Any word from Big Daddy Jim?"

Turning to hide the distress that was probably written all over her face, Tate nearly bumped into Georgie.

Her lawyer façade instantly fell into place. "I'll be answering all questions regarding my client's case. Mr. Cochon refused to sign and his attorney sent a counteroffer."

"That sounds bad. What kind of offer?"

"I'm not at liberty to say." Georgie traded her grim expression for a relaxed smile. "I only made it through the first four chapters of this week's book, but I'll contribute what I can to the discussion."

No one challenged Georgie's blunt order not to talk about Tate's problems, focusing instead on the reading selection, the food, and permanently adding a second meet-up each Sunday evening at Riley's house that included cocktail hour. Riley, Wally, and Petra wholeheartedly agreed, promising to make virgin versions of every drink if the eventual stick test showed a pink plus sign.

For the first time in over a decade, Tate almost wished her period would start early or the test would announce she wasn't pregnant. Nothing had gone as planned, and a baby would only complicate matters beyond anything she'd imagined having a child on her own entailed.

She stacked the decimated serving platters and dishes and carried them to the sink while her friends gathered the trash and returned the dining room to its previous state. Their voices and raucous laughter made her long for a do-over, one where her past didn't make her have to blow off sexual attraction and a man who seemed to truly like her. Then she wouldn't have to hide in her kitchen to avoid accidentally saying something her lawyer didn't want her to.

Guilt had a voracious appetite, as did missing him.

Riley popped around the corner, wearing a grin that meant she'd either forgotten Deke's Barbie comment or had thought of a fitting payback. "We're all done out there. Do you need help with the dishes?"

Fitting the last tray into the drainer, Tate held it in place to be sure the whole damn stack didn't fall, which would be just her luck this week. "Finished."

"I'll wait for you while you turn off the lights and grab your stuff then. Everybody else already headed home."

"Okay. Meet you out front in a minute." Hopefully, the short walk to their cars would prevent the inevitable question on everybody's mind. What was she going to do about Jim?

The short answer was she didn't have an answer. A legal battle over their child wouldn't end well for any of them, but she'd screwed up any possibility that he would give her a second chance, even if she could convince herself to take one. At forty-two, she still hadn't learned how to navigate relationships with men.

She slung her purse strap on her shoulder, flipped off all but the minimal overnight lighting, and armed the security system. The thirty-second delay ticked off in her head as she walked to the street entrance. A quick scan of the dimly lit dining room revealed all the tables and chairs in their proper places for tomorrow's breakfast customers. The window blinds had been closed and Riley stood on the sidewalk, frowning at her cell.

Phone. Keys. Purse. Tate stepped outside and locked the door with fifteen seconds to spare.

"God, my cousin is such an annoying dipshit." Riley yanked her key ring from her jacket pocket and hurried toward the parking lot across the street, her heels clicking on the pavement. "Gotta go. See you tomorrow at lunchtime."

"Okay. G'night. Drive carefully." Tate adjusted the hold on her keys with her thumb poised over the panic button. As she turned the other direction, she nearly collided with a brunette with her head down and a grimace that probably matched Tate's. "Sorry!"

"No problem! I lose track of where I'm going all the time." The woman scrunched her mouth and peered up at Tate. "Hey, I saw you with Jim Cochon at his big cookout on Saturday, didn't I? I heard he had a new girlfriend. Really nice guy, but— Never mind."

"I'm not his girlfriend. We're...friends. More like acquaintances." *Acquaintances who should be excited about getting to know each other and maybe having made a baby together, not standing on opposites sides of the courtroom.*

"Lucky you. The poor man's up denial without a paddle. Locked himself in the closet, if you know what I mean." Arched eyebrows rose in tandem, disappearing under the brunette's bangs.

Closet? "Are you trying to say he's gay?"

"Or bisexual. Either way, he's in love with a man. Has been for *years.*"

He can't be. I want him for myself!

A hand closed on Tate's forearm. "Yep. He called at least three of his former girlfriends, including me, by the same wrong name when things got, you know, intimate."

That certainly explained why he refused to sign away his parental rights and the possible reason for his casual marriage proposal. Their child might be his only chance to be a father.

But he called me the right name.

The woman leaned in closer and lowered her voice. "I'd really like to know who the guy is. Do you suppose they played football together in college? Anyway, you should be glad you're just friends. Maybe someday he'll work up the nerve to tell Tate he loves him."

CHAPTER 11

"HAVE YOU HEARD FROM MY SISTER AGAIN?" BEAU RESTED HIS HIP against the rear fender of the pickup and crossed his arms in front of his chest. "I still can't believe she expects you to sign away all your rights."

With his stomach alternately chewing on the steak his best friend had fed him and the gristly lump thinking about Tate created, Jim shook his head. "My lawyer told me since I was foolish enough to talk to her on the phone, I have to hire somebody else. I need to get going. I have to check on the new litters and email Deke this week's payroll hours. Thanks for supper."

"I can talk to her if you want."

"No." The refusal came out harsher than he intended, but all his hopes and dreams had crashed down around him without warning, and recovering from it seemed impossible. "Talk to you tomorrow."

He climbed into the cab before Beau could try to offer some other solution to a problem that couldn't be fixed. With a wave, he headed for home to spend another Friday night alone.

An hour and a half later, he plucked a beer from the fridge and parked himself in his favorite chair on the deck. The rise-and-fall drone of cicadas tapered off as the crickets started their nightly song. Then the hum of the vapor light joined in, only to get lost beneath the crunch of gravel under tires in the driveway. If he didn't answer the door, maybe whoever decided to interrupt his evening solace would go the hell away and let him wrestle with his broken heart in peace.

A minute passed and another, both without the wishful-thinking exit noise. Then movement at the corner of the house caught his attention, but long red hair lit up by the security light instantly identified the intruder.

Tate stopped at the bottom of the steps. "I have a new proposal."

His muscles tensed and his brain screeched to a halt at her statement. *Focus. Think. No more daydreaming about a happy ending.* "The only thing I'll agree to is being a father to my kid."

"Are you sure you don't want to read the terms I drew up this afternoon?" She set a sealed business envelope on the deck railing.

He didn't possess the strength to pick it up, let alone read the contents. "Does it say you're accepting my marriage proposal?"

Her unemotional expression gave nothing away. "No."

"Then I don't need to read it." The knot in his gut tangled into a bigger jumble. How could he still love her when she wanted to cut him completely out of her and their possible baby's life?

"Fine. We'll do this the hard way then." She snagged the envelope, marched up the stairs, and crossed to his chair. Slipping her index finger under the flap, she tore it open. The ripping noise accompanied another fissure splitting his heart farther open. "Last chance to make it easier on both of us."

He wrapped his hands around the armrests to keep from grabbing on to her and never letting go. It would only make him look like a bigger pathetic fool than he already was. "Easy isn't always the right way."

Huffing out a sigh, she plopped onto his lap and yanked a paper from the envelope. The new contract tore in her impatience to unfold it, but she shoved it in his face anyway. "Now look what happened. You ruined my proposal."

He blinked, trying to read the words in the dim light. It almost kept him from noticing the erection forming beneath her backside. *This is not a good time, buddy.* "How am I supposed to read when you're wiggling around?"

"You're ready to cooperate now?" She cast a questioning glance at him.

"What choice do I have?"

"I can't force you to say yes, but saying no will definitely complicate matters." With the tear pressed together between her thumb and forefinger, she held the paper a reasonable distance from his eyes. "Read it. Out loud."

Instead of a computer-generated list of concessions, perfectly executed handwriting filled a quarter of the page. A number preceded each of the three items, as they had in the longer typewritten version.

He braced for another disappointment. "Number one. 'I, Jimothy Cochon, agree to abide by the terms of this contract for as long as I live.' I don't promise anything that—"

"No comments, arguments, or rejections until you've read the whole thing." She looked down her nose at him in an obvious former-teacher display.

"But I'm not agreeing—"

"Jim. Read." She frowned at him.

"Okay." Heaving a sigh, he turned his attention back to the paper. "Number two. 'I accept Tate Madison's proposal.' Number three. 'I promise to be the best husband and father I can be to Tate and our baby.'"

"Now we can have a discussion if you want to. Or you can just say yes."

He reread the second and third terms twice, hoping he hadn't misread the words. "Does this mean you're pregnant? This proposal... Are you asking me..."

"I don't know yet. Anyway, it's irrelevant." Flinging her arms around his neck, she kissed his cheek. "Will you marry me?"

"But...you said you wanted a baby. And the sperm donor contract. What if you change your mind again? What made you change your mind?" Pessimism seemed safer than optimism, and he might have to become a hermit if his dream-come-true turned into a nightmare again.

"I won't because I, Tate Madison, agree to abide by the terms of this contract for as long as I live." She cradled his face in her hands. "Waking up beside you made me wish for things I thought I couldn't have. But you waited for me. For a long time. Why didn't you tell me?"

Heat crept up his neck. Had Beau or another of her brothers spilled his secret? "How do you tell your best friend's big sister you've been in love with her since you were five? That—"

"You've been in love with me since you were five?" Her eyes widened. "I thought... Christy, the woman I talked to last night, said you called her Tate three years ago. I assumed that meant... Since you were *five*?"

An inferno spread to his ears and his cheeks. "Oh God, you talked to my ex-girlfriend about *that*?"

"She said she wasn't the only one. I had no idea. Wait a minute. My brothers would've noticed if you had a crush on me. They kept your secret for thirty years? Holy cow. I never would've guessed they could keep their mouths shut about something like that for so long." A heart-stopping smile curved her beautiful mouth upward. "Since you were in kindergarten. I would've been in...sixth grade? That's so sweet and romantic."

"And embarrassing."

She pressed her lips to his for a far-too-short kiss. "You knew. All this time, you knew I was the one. God, I wish I could've been that lucky. I had to make a big mistake first, and then I almost screwed up my second chance with you. So will you marry me?"

The embarrassment finally faded, but her question couldn't seem to sink in. "Are you sure you want to get married? That it's me you want and not just my sperm?"

She wrapped her arms around him, putting her cheek against his. "I did a lot of thinking and realized the reason I wanted a baby so much was because something was always missing. And this week I couldn't sleep because I was missing you. Yes, I'd love to have a baby, but I don't need to be pregnant to feel important to you."

The knots in his gut unraveled, freeing the joy he experienced whenever she was near. "If I say yes, can we try some more, in case you're not yet? I want to give you everything you need to be happy."

She hugged him tighter and wiggled on his lap. "See? This is why I can't help but adore you. I spent all day going over every word you've said to me, every touch, every kiss since you showed up to ask for food scraps for your pigs. How could I not fall in love with you?"

"Hearing those words is better than I imagined." With his forearm under her legs, he scooped her up and stood. "Let's go upstairs and practice our baby-making skills."

"I promise to stay for breakfast in the morning." She nibbled a distracting path along his jaw. "In fact, I was thinking we need to share breakfast every day, starting tomorrow. But you haven't answered my question yet."

Tightening his hold, he carried her toward the sliding door, stopping when their reflection came into view. His inner five-year-old grinned. "You still owe me an answer. After all, I asked first."

THE FARMER TAKES A HUSBAND

CHAPTER 1

"Go take a flying leap into a manure pile, Rudy, and quit wasting my time, Mr. Kresge. I'm not selling or leasing—not any part of the property at any time—while I'm still breathing." Riley Fenniman rose from the painfully uncomfortable Queen Anne chair, taking extra care to scrape its wooden feet across the polished oak floor.

Her cousin and his lawyer cringed through the satisfying screech, but Riley draped her blazer over her forearm and strolled toward the reception area and the exit rather than hanging around for more of their bullshit. Halfway across the room, the heat of a thousand suns set fire to her back, neck, and chest. The sudden hot flash propelled her out of the office, nixing her plan to flip them the finger before slamming the pocket doors.

Late October air kissed her bare face, arms, and calves as she exited the building, cooling her body temperature if not her irritation. "Fucking menopause."

"Who pissed you off this time, Malibu Barbie?" Amusement colored the question, the only not-some-shade of-beige part of the man's entire presence, right down to his tan sport coat and brown hair.

Why did he try to blend in when his sense of humor and realness made him stand out? His cute butt didn't hurt, either.

Of course, if the mouthy inquiry had come from any male besides her accountant, she would've decked the smartass. "Same dickhead as usual. And don't call me that, Clark Can't."

"Good one." Deacon Jeffries stopped next to her at the crosswalk and held out his insulated travel mug, even though he knew damn well she'd given up full-strength coffee in March at her body's insistence and doctor's advisement. "What's your cousin up to this time?"

Her phone buzzed against her lower belly, the closest thing to an orgasm she'd experienced in over a week. Digging her cell from the purse crisscrossing her body, she raised a just-a-minute finger at Deke —although he deserved the middle one for the Barbie wisecrack. "Hello. Fenniman Organics."

"May I speak to Riley Fenniman please?"

"This is Riley." The light changed and she stepped into the pedestrian crossing, her accountant still taking up space at her side.

"Ms. Fenniman, I'm calling from the mammography center. The radiologist saw something that didn't look quite right and wants to schedule a follow-up diagnostic mammogram as soon as possible. It looks like we had a cancellation this week. I have tomorrow, Thursday, at four thirty open. Will that work for you?"

She tried and failed to lock her rubbery knees as a bout of lightheadedness stole her ability to navigate. Then a horn blared and someone grasped her around the waist, leading her away from a blurry red blob.

"Riley? Riley, are you okay?"

"Okay?" Images of her dying mother invaded her mind, the memories as vivid as when they'd been created twenty-six years ago.

"Callbacks are fairly common, so try not to worry. Remember, no deodorant and no lotion from the waist up. And please let us know right away if you need to reschedule for some reason. We'll see you tomorrow at four thirty."

"Tomorrow. Thursday. Four thirty."

Deke guided her down onto a bench and crouched in front of her, his fingers warming her suddenly ice-cold hands. "What's wrong? Can I help?"

She shook her head, still fighting wooziness. *This can't be happening.* "Damn hot flash is making me dizzy. I need something cold to drink."

"The Homegrown Café is half a block away. Do you want to go there?"

"Yes." Her stomach knotted and heaved. *I need to talk to Tate.*

"Are you feeling well enough to walk?" His deeply furrowed eyebrows came into focus, revealing a few stray grays above his serious brown eyes. "You can lean on me if you need to. Or I can carry you."

"Good God, no. I'm fine." She tugged her hands free of his and stood, her heels much less stable than before the call but not so bad she couldn't balance. Leaning was for the weak.

"Are you sure?"

Determined to make the short trek on her own two feet, she aimed a glare at her companion. "I said I'm fine. Don't you have numbers to crunch or something?"

He frowned back at her and extended his hand again. "I have an appointment with Big Jim at Tate's place in ten minutes. I'll go with you."

Finally regaining her equilibrium enough to walk, she sidestepped him and started toward the café. "Why are you being so stubborn?"

"Why are you?" His loafers squeaked in an offbeat rhythm with the click of her heels on the sidewalk as he kept pace with her.

The diversion bombed as a distraction, but she seized the opportunity to redirect the conversation. "You need new shoes. It sounds like the shank is broken."

"I know. I haven't had time. Are you going to yell at me if I hold the door open for you?"

"Probably." She dodged a yippy puppy taking its owner for a walk, giving Deke a slight edge in reaching their destination first, but he slowed as they approached the potted mums that flanked the entrance.

"Then you can hold the door for me." A cheeky grin accompanied his wink.

"I'll open it, but you're perfectly capable of holding it while you go in. Or did you pull a muscle while you were using your calculator?" She reached for the handle, glad for another chance to steady herself.

"Rudy really put you in a mood today, didn't he?" He shadowed her through the door. "Or was it the phone call?"

"You know it was you, right?" Casting another not-quite-serious glare in his direction, she headed for the order counter, where Tate Madison and her soon-to-be husband, Big Jim Cochon, mooned over each other during a post-breakfast, pre-lunch lull.

"Not a chance." Deke's carefree grin said he didn't believe for a second he could possibly be the cause of her rotten disposition. "Hey, Jim. How's business, Tate?"

Riley's best friend shooed her fiancé to the customer side of the counter and smoothed the apron over her still-flat belly, not that it would be for long. "Good. Thanks, Deacon. Word of mouth has kept me under budget for advertising so far. Need a coffee refill? I just made a fresh pot."

"Sounds great. Do you have any scones left? No time for breakfast this morning." Deke set the travel mug on the counter and extracted his wallet from the back pocket of his tan chinos.

"Blueberry and apple cinnamon."

"One of each for me. Riley, do you want a scone? My treat." He raised an eyebrow at her, as if he hadn't enjoyed trying to annoy the hell out of her en route to the cozy restaurant.

"No thanks. Tate, I need to talk to you as soon as you have a minute. In private." Without a wave or a glance at half-the-town's accountant, Riley stepped past him to hide out in the office off the kitchen.

Muffled voices faded beneath the *whoosh, whoosh, whoosh* of the dishwasher and disappeared altogether when she sat in her friend's desk chair. Instead of stripping off her bra to conduct a self-exam that refuted the radiologist's claim, she added tomorrow's appointment to the calendar on her phone and deleted a voicemail from Rudy's jackass lawyer without listening to it.

Tate popped through the doorway and closed out the noises from the kitchen. "What's up? Deacon seems worried about you. He said you had a dizzy spell while you were walking with him. Something about hot flashes and menopause, but I don't think he believed it."

"He should be worried about himself. That man gets too much enjoyment out of antagonizing me and it's going to backfire one of these days." Too antsy to sit, Riley rose, slipped her cell into the outside pocket of her purse, and fought for a calming breath. "I got a call from the mammography center. They saw something. I have to go back tomorrow afternoon for a diagnostic."

"Damn. Are you okay?" Tate wrapped her arms around Riley and gave her a gentle squeeze. "I know it's scary, but most of the time there's nothing there. That happened to me last year. And even if they find a lump, the chances of it being malignant are pretty low."

"Unless you have a family history of breast cancer. It killed my mom when I was in college. She was my age. Aunt Stacy was fifty-one and Great-Aunt Trudy was sixty-eight." The verbal confession stole the air from her lungs, making the room swim.

"God, Riley, I'm so sorry. You must be terrified." Tate guided her into the chair and handed her a tall glass. "Here, drink this. And take some deep breaths. You're paler than I am, and that's saying a lot."

A swallow of cold mint-flavored liquid chased away the hot flash, but the wooziness remained. "Do you have any vodka I can add to the tea? And I don't give a damn if it's only nine thirty in the morning."

"Sorry, I can't help you there. No Ohio liquor license, and I'd rather not get shut down for violating the faulty BYO interpretation." Tate rubbed her palm up and down Riley's spine, calming the wavy floor and walls but not the dread. "Do you want me to call an emergency meeting of THC Book Club this evening? And I can go with you to your appointment tomorrow if you want me to, as long as it's after I close at two."

Shaking her head, Riley forced another swallow of tea past the massive knot in her throat. "I don't want anybody else knowing about it. Not yet. Can I call you about going with me in the morning? I can't decide anything right now."

"That's fine. I'll do extra prep during the Garden Club meeting this afternoon just in case. My lips are sealed. I'm here for whatever you need. Day or night."

Riley blinked away the stinging sensation in her eyes and drew in a slow, deep breath. "Do you mind if I sneak out the rear entrance and borrow your car? I'll give you the keys to the T-bird and we can switch back later."

"Of course I don't mind." Tate removed her purse from the desk and held out the keys to her car. "It has a full tank of gas."

"You're the best friend a girl could have. I owe you." After a final gulp of tea, Riley dug for her keys and stood. "The Bird's parked across the street in the usual spot."

A hand on her shoulder stopped her before she could reach for the doorknob. "Are you sure you're okay to drive? I can ask Jim to take you home."

"I'll be fine. I promise."

The light touch became a sideways hug. "I want you to be better than fine. I was *fine* in a toxic marriage for twelve years. Fine sucks."

"It does, doesn't it? Great big hairy donkey balls." On the verge of her first crying jag in twenty-six years, Riley wiggled free and hurried to the service entrance outside the office. As she opened the door, male laughter stopped her in her tracks.

Tate's fiancé and Deke stood at Jim's pickup with their backs toward her, the beige accountant and her ride home dwarfed by the massive truck and its linebacker-sized owner.

Fuck. Fuck. And double fuck. She backed away, slowly closing the door to avoid drawing their attention.

"Did you forget something?"

Riley nearly jumped out of her skin at her friend's voice behind her. "Jesus, woman, don't sneak up on me like that. And I can't duck out the back way if the nosy Nelly I'm trying to get away from is out there. He's worse than an infestation of tomato hornworms."

"Aw, give the poor guy a break. He's a nurturer. He sees right through your snark to the smart and generous person you are." Tate grabbed Riley by the hand and pulled her toward the prep area. "Plus he likes you. A lot."

Shooting a frown at her friend, Riley lengthened her stride to keep up. "Yeah, well, I don't want or need a man in my life unless he keeps his feelings to himself."

"I didn't think I did, either, and we both know how that worked out." Tate peeked around the entrance to the order counter before continuing toward the dining room. "Come on. You can go out the front and wait at the southwest corner while I lure them into the kitchen."

"This better work."

"It will." After another peek at the main entrance, Tate shooed Riley out the door. "Now go. And call me later."

"Yes, Mother dearest." Riley walked to the corner and counted to thirty—plenty of time for her bestie to distract her almost-husband and everybody's damn accountant. "It'd serve him right if I found him a girlfriend to worry about instead of me."

Silence greeted her as she edged her way into the alley, a sure sign Jim and Deke had taken their conversation inside. Tate's hatchback awaited her on the other side, with barely enough room to squeeze past the pickup. Finally, something had gone right today.

She pressed the Unlock button on the key fob and dashed across the alley, dodging cracks and crumbling spots in the pavement. As she reached for the handle, maniacal laughter echoed off the buildings.

Fuck.

"Going somewhere without saying goodbye, Riley?"

CHAPTER 2

DEACON JEFFRIES STEPPED OUT OF HIS HIDING PLACE NEXT TO THE dumpster, pleased with his foresight into the reason Tate had asked for help reaching something in the kitchen. "If I didn't know better, I'd say you really dislike me."

Leveling one of her last-nerve stares at him, Riley opened the door of Tate's car. "Only when my accountant sticks his nose where it doesn't belong."

He closed most of the distance between them and planted himself at the rear bumper, fairly certain she wouldn't actually back over him. "So you don't consider me a friend? Somebody who worries about you when you try to pass out in the middle of the road?"

"It was a hot flash and I got dizzy. I didn't come close to passing out."

"You didn't answer the question, Riley." Her silence as good as answered it, but he wasn't about to let her off the hook that easily. Even if she wasn't interested in him romantically, she would've fired his ass months ago if she didn't like him as a human being. "Why are you taking Tate's car? Are you having trouble with yours?"

"None of your business. God, you're worse than an overbearing husband." Her smile was as fake as her tenacity was real.

"What do you know about husbands? Or marriage? In fact, as much as you hate men, I'm surprised you haven't traded me in for a female accountant." He softened the teasing accusation with a wink.

She favored him with an eye-roll in return. "Not wanting to get married doesn't mean I hate men. It means I like being single. You know, taking care of myself. Paying my own bills. Nobody else's life interfering with what I want to do. And don't even get me started on children."

"Sometimes it's nice to do stuff for and with other people. Didn't you learn about sharing when you were little?"

"Being selfish is keeping other people from having what I have. I've never done that and I've never forced my choices on anyone else. I can't help it if you gave up your freedom. You should've considered the consequences of marriage before you took those vows. It ends one of two ways. Death or divorce." She slid behind the wheel and slammed the door, but her final jab skewered him where it hurt.

How the hell was I supposed to know I'd end up divorced with sole custody of my girls? I didn't exactly throw my wife out of the house and tell her to chase her dream around the world.

He kicked a chunk of loose blacktop as he moved away from the bumper. The engine revved before he reached the other side of the truck, but at least she couldn't hit him without going through the bed. Although Riley seemed a bit more unhinged than usual, she probably wouldn't damage Tate's and Jim's vehicles for the satisfaction of shutting him up permanently. Her death glare as she backed out of the space proved it.

He met her stare with one of his own. "Drive carefully."

Her frown deepened, assuring him she'd read his lips if she hadn't heard his words through the closed windows. Then she flipped him the middle finger.

Name the day and time, Ms. Fenniman. I'm all yours. He puckered his lips and blew her a kiss as he pivoted toward the service entrance of The Homegrown Café. If she had any idea that he'd jump at her unintended offer in a second, she would definitely risk losing her driver's license for good.

Jim opened the door as Deacon approached. "Do you have a death wish, dude?"

"She wouldn't hurt me. She hates doing her own payroll." If that was the only reason she hadn't kicked his ass to the curb, he'd take it. Deke's stomach growled on the way through the kitchen, reminding him once again that his daughter's meltdown this morning had meant skipping breakfast. He nodded at Tate at the counter. "I'm ready for those scones and a refill now."

Jim sat across from him at their table in the far corner, his eyes still focused in his fiancée's direction. "So when are you going to ask Riley for a date?"

A fleeting denial of interest came and went without voice. "Why should I bother? She'll say no, and then I won't get to flirt with her anymore. Besides, I'm not sure I have the time or energy to date, not with Amanda and Fiona's schedules. And the mood swings. Can you imagine the hormonal disaster waiting to happen if I introduced my puberty-infected girls to a menopausal woman? Not that Riley would ever agree to go out with me. She likes being independent. Taking care of herself—which I admire, but don't tell her that. She doesn't take shit from anybody, including me."

"Or me." Tate set his order in front of him. "She needs you to be her friend right now. I can't tell you why, but don't let her push you away and, more importantly, don't walk away. She might act like that's what she wants, but it isn't."

"I'm not going anywhere. Is something wrong? Besides her cousin being an ass?" Buzzing against his thigh interrupted his first bite of blueberry scone. He pulled his cell from his pants pocket and sighed at the phone number on the screen. "Should've kept my mouth shut. It's the school."

Jim pushed up from his seat and slipped his hand around Tate's. "We'll give you some privacy."

"Thanks." Deke tapped the Answer button and lifted the phone to his ear as his friends walked toward the counter. His stomach growled louder this time. "Hello. This is Deacon Jeffries."

"Hello, Mr. Jeffries. This is Mrs. Merrill, the school nurse."

He closed his eyes and dropped his chin to his chest, hoping his younger daughter didn't need stitches again. "What happened?"

"Fiona may have broken her finger. Or two. I'm not sure." The nurse's sigh carried through the phone. "And the principal would like to meet with you before you take her to the med center."

Well past the oh-shit nerves that usually accompanied that kind of announcement, he waved at Tate and gestured to his scones and then to the door. "I can be there in ten minutes."

"I'll let her and Fiona know."

"Thanks." He ended the call as Jim approached the table with a bag. "Gotta go. I have to go to the principal's office again and my prizefighter needs x-rays. How can we only be two months into the school year?"

Jim grinned. "Hey, at least you don't have to worry about her being able to defend herself. She reminds me of Riley."

Coffee, scones, phone. Halfway to the door, Deke withdrew his keys from his pocket. "Me too, and that isn't necessarily a good thing."

"Do I have to set the table?" Fiona adjusted the makeshift sling she'd created from a pair of baseball pants as she peeked in Deke's office.

"Yes." He saved the spreadsheet on his computer and leveled his best mad-dad stare at her. "You have two busted fingers, not a broken arm, and you can use your left hand. It'll be good practice for when you have to write at school."

"You're so mean."

A snort escaped before he could stop it. "Really? *I'm* mean? You're the one who punched somebody and hurt yourself."

"He deserved it."

"He deserves an apology so you don't get suspended from school, especially since you still haven't told me what he said or did."

Her eyes narrowed. "Not happening. Next time he tells somebody my mom left because of me, I'm going to punch him harder."

Okay, the little shithead deserved it. A glance at the clock in the navigation bar told him quitting time had arrived, but he would have to put in another hour after the girls went to bed to get through his to-do list. He closed the laptop and rolled his chair away from the desk. "There are better ways of getting even than trying to break your hand."

"Like what?" She leaned against the doorjamb and slid downward until her bottom bumped the floor. "Squirting glue in his locker? Or stealing his math homework?"

Deke shook his head as he pushed out of the chair. "No. We've had this discussion often enough for you to know what's acceptable and what isn't."

"Yeah, well, you have a mom and I don't." With far more grace than a girl who wore a sling and loved traipsing through the mud needed, she rolled to her feet. Her noisy stomps down the hallway took his heart with her.

Riley's comments replayed themselves in his head, but he couldn't bring himself to regret a failed marriage that had given him his daughters. No matter how difficult single parenting had become over the last year or two, his girls made him remember how much family meant to him. Of course, he hadn't imagined a life like this when he'd proposed to Trisha sixteen years ago. It sure wasn't what he'd planned for his future.

Fiona had become the tough sister at a young age, the only means of coping with a loss she might never understand. Hell, he still wrestled with the complexity of the situation and the fact that her mother's passing would've been easier to handle than her abandonment. Escaping a possible terminal illness had changed Trisha's priorities to *not* him or their daughters.

A slam and a metallic clatter came from the direction of the kitchen as he trailed after his younger daughter. She evidently possessed enough left-handed strength to take out her frustration and anger on anything she came in contact with.

"Don't set the table with those, Fee! You dropped them on the floor."

Deke braced for another of Fiona's outbursts at her sister's admonishment.

"I don't care. I'm not eating anyway. You're—" The clank of silverware in the stainless-steel sink drowned out whatever else Fiona might have said.

Amanda turned her back on her sister. "More beanies and weinees for me."

He blew out a breath to the count of five and entered the battle zone. "Fiona Louise Jeffries, sit down."

With her trademark death-glare aimed at him, she plopped on the floor.

"At the table. We need to talk." Gesturing to the chair next to him, he sat in his usual spot.

Uncertainty replaced the defiance in her eyes, but the frown remained as she plodded to the opposite side of the table.

Pick your battles. "Amanda, you too."

His older daughter set her knife on the cutting board and grabbed the dishtowel on her way to the dinette. After pulling her seat out of kicking range of her sister, she finally perched on the edge, obviously ready to make a run for it if necessary.

Crossing her arms in front of her, Fiona lifted her chin. "You're leaving too, aren't you?"

The accusation sucker-punched him in the gut, derailing his train of thought for several seconds.

"It's true, isn't it?" More attitude oozed from her follow-up allegation.

"Why would you think that?" As soon as the words were out, he wished them back. *Damn it, I know why. All I wanted was one weekend to decompress, recharge, and remember that I'm doing the best I can.* "Never mind. That happened a year and a half ago and I came home a day late because I had car trouble. No, I'm not leaving, and I want you to stop expecting me to. You're not even close to being right."

"What about all the appointments you have in the evenings and on the weekend? You're always too busy to help me practice my hitting and catching, and we never go bike riding anymore. You care more about your stupid clients than you do me."

Her accusations brought a moment of utter clarity. "Okay, you're right. I've been spending a lot of time working, more than I should lately. I promise we'll do fun stuff this weekend. Just us. But I'm not leaving you. Ever."

"Then, what?" Her matter-of-fact tone all but promised she would hold onto her grudge for now.

He leaned forward to rest his elbows on the table, hoping his next statement didn't ignite another explosion. "How do you feel about dating?"

"Don't you think I'm kind of young? Even Manda's—"

"Me, not you." *God, why did she have to inherit my smartass back-talk?* Barely refraining from rolling his eyes, he scrubbed his hands down his face. "Would you be okay with me dating?"

She scrunched up her mouth. "Eww. You're old. People your age don't date."

"What about Big Jim and Miss Madison? They're *old* like me. Actually, she's a few years older than me. And even older than Jim, for that matter."

"But they don't have kids and they don't act old." A smirk accompanied the cocky tilt of her head. "Besides, women live longer than men."

"Thanks for that reminder. So you wouldn't mind if I dated an older woman?" Anticipation gurgled in his stomach, along with hunger. Why did Fee always pick mealtime to blow a gasket?

"Like who? Mrs. Crenshaw, who taught fourth grade before Big Jim was born?" Dark humor glowed in her eyes, almost exactly like Riley's.

Why the hell do I have to be attracted to a woman who could give my daughter lessons in sarcasm and attitude? He slicked his hand through his hair and grinned. "Yep. Maybe she can educate you on how to behave like a proper young lady."

"Ha. Ha. Very funny."

"About as funny as your snark." Giving up on a straight answer from Fiona, he turned to his older daughter. "What do you think, Manda?"

Amanda's expression revealed nothing but impatience with her sister and boredom, which usually meant she was analyzing everything he said. "I think you're too chicken to ask her out."

"Who? Mrs. Crenshaw?" As deflections went, it wasn't his best attempt.

Manda looked down her nose at him and rolled her eyes. "Puh-lease. The blonde lady who owns the farm where Miss Madison gets her produce. *Miss Fenniman*. You were staring at her when we went to the café for lunch last week. Boys are always so obvious."

Her sister giggled. "Dad and his crush sitting in a tree. K-I-S-S-I-N-G. First comes love. Next comes marriage. Then comes Dad with a baby carriage."

Finally cracking a smile, Amanda pinned him with a stare. "I dare you to ask her out."

CHAPTER 3

OH GOD. BREATHE.

The room blurred and pitched, and the radiologist's voice faded under the growing roar in Riley's ears.

Fuck. Fuck. Fuck.

Biopsy.

She gripped the arms of the chair, hoping like hell she'd misheard the B-word. That word had meant cancer to her mom, her aunt, and her great-aunt.

Death sentence.

She closed her eyes to slow the motion sickness creeping its way from her stomach to her chest. A warm hand closed over her ice-cold fingers and another circled her other wrist, but neither calmed the nausea or the chills suddenly triggering goose bumps up and down her bare arms.

Where's a damn hot flash when I need one?

"Riley, listen to me." Dr. Porter's nasally timbre cut through the noise and some of the fog. "I need you to take some slow, deep breaths. There's no need to panic. I know you have a family history of breast cancer, but the spot is small, which means we caught it early. It might not even be cancerous and the odds are low. We'll know more after the biopsy."

She forced out the question that would determine her future, if she had one. "When?"

"I'd like to fit you in next week if I have an opening. We'll check with my nurse as soon as you get your color back and your pulse stops break dancing. I don't want to add x-rays to today's procedures." The younger woman snorted a laugh.

The room steadied when Riley opened her eyes, but her insides continued their Tilt-A-Whirl spinning. "The sooner, the better. And I'd gladly exchange this for a broken arm. At least I could use the cast to beat this anxiety into submission."

"I wish I could manage that trade." Dr. Porter released Riley's wrist as she straightened. "Are you feeling okay to walk out to the waiting area? No rush if you're not."

With a curt nod, Riley scooted forward in the seat and planted her stiletto-clad feet. "Ready."

The room wobbled slightly when she stood, but another deep breath steadied it enough for her to follow the radiologist into the hall. Two gray-haired women with the requisite cotton wrap-and-tie tops stood outside a changing room, their conversational tones assuring her they had no worries about lumps or biopsies or cancer. Did they know how lucky they were?

Probably not.

They would live to ninety-eight and die peacefully in their sleep of old age.

Walk. Right. Left. Right. Left.

The door to the waiting area opened in front of her as she continued the simple mantra in her head, and she amplified the chant to block the hum of low conversation trying to distract her from her task.

"Riley? Riley?" Dr. Porter guided her into a chair. "Are you okay?"

"No." Leaning back, Riley closed her eyes to ease the rocking sensation.

"Wait here while I see what times I have available next week. Is someone with you? Or would you like me to call a friend for you? I'm not sure you're in any condition to drive yourself home."

"Tate. My best friend. She offered to come with me, but I told her I'd be fine. I just need to sit here for a little bit."

"Take as long as you need. I'll have someone bring you a cup of water."

Ten minutes later, Riley stepped outside with an appointment card and a pre-op instruction sheet crumpled in her fist. The car key dug into the palm of her other hand, the tiny stab of pain reminding her she hadn't died—yet. It was only a matter of time.

Each step required too much energy, too much focus. She paused on the sidewalk to scan the parking lot for her car. A lone yellow car stood out in the sea of black, white, gray, and red vehicles, but the shade resembled a dandelion instead of butter. Where the hell had she parked? Had she driven her T-bird? Or did she still have Tate's car?

"Riley, get in!" The familiar voice yanked her from the tunnel vision of searching the lot.

Biting the inside of her lip, she opened the passenger door of the silver hatchback idling at the curb. *I will not fucking cry.*

"Buckle your seatbelt and we'll go for a drive." When the belt tried to slip from Riley's grasp, Tate reached across the center console to push the latch into the hole. "Before you ask, I've been having these creepy, uneasy feelings all day, so I had Jim bring me here after we dropped off the Bird at your house. You should've let me come with you."

Unable to speak past the pain in her throat, Riley shrugged.

"They confirmed the lump, didn't they?" As she pulled away from the curb, Tate glanced in Riley's direction. "Biopsy?"

Riley nodded.

"God, I can't imagine how scary that must be. Do you know when? And I'm driving you, by the way. No excuses, not even if it's during restaurant hours. I'll find somebody to cover for me or I'll close for the day."

A hard swallow barely budged the knot, not that she could

remember the day or time of her next appointment, and her cramped hand refused to unfold. "Next week?"

"Never mind. We'll figure everything out later." Tate flipped on her turn signal at the street. "First, you need a distraction. We're going for ice cream."

The hum of the engine lulled Riley into numbness as a steady line of cars prevented a quick exit. Patience hadn't been a virtue she possessed since college and her mother's illness, and the looming presence of death pressed closer now, like it waited for her. She hated waiting, never wasted time, always conscious that her life would likely be cut short at some point.

Finally, a break in traffic allowed Tate to make the turn.

Riley closed her eyes to keep from having to look at the approaching cemetery, even though it didn't make the reality of the situation disappear from her thoughts. Death might come to everyone eventually, but knowing what awaited her—a hopeless attempt to prolong her life—hit the only vulnerable spot in her heart.

Too soon, the car slowed and made a turn that shouldn't have happened.

"The usual?"

Tate's question cut short the pity party. "Usual?"

"Yeah, we're at the ice cream place. Forget it. I know what to order for you."

"Something with alcohol?"

The car inched forward at a snail's pace.

"A scoop of brownie batter and another of coconut cream pie in a cup with whipped cream on top for my bestie. And a single scoop of lemon meringue in a waffle cone for me. Extra napkins please." Tate eased forward to the payment-and-pickup stop in the drive-thru.

Tears prickled and Riley blinked to clear her vision, grateful for a friend who knew her so well. "I love you, girlfriend."

"I love you too, Riley. Whatever you need, I'm here for you, even if it's just ice cream and a hand to hold." After a quick swap of cash for the order, Tate handed Riley their treats and drove to the exit. "We'll go to Findley and you can cry on my shoulder. No judgment, and I promise not to tell anybody."

"I hate crying."

"I know. You can scream instead if you want to. Now start eating before it melts." As soon as Tate merged back into traffic, she tapped the volume control on the steering wheel and then grabbed her cone.

Metallica filled the car, the angry guitars and angrier lyrics embodying the rage and fear creeping through Riley's soul. Every pulse of bass vibrated through her body to join the sensation of ice cream melting in her mouth and the heavenly flavors of chocolate, coconut, and whipped cream coating her tongue. They cooled and comforted her from the inside out with each bite and beat. If ever the perfect therapy session existed, this was it.

Tate crunched the last bite of her waffle cone, more heavy metal thumping in time with her chewing, and steered into the nearly empty picnic area parking lot at the state park down the road from Wellington. She swiped a napkin across her mouth and chin, and then shut off the engine.

The song continued while Riley scraped every last drip from the cup, more grateful for their friendship than she would've expected. That first phone call about buying produce for a new café in town six months ago had been the best day of her life. Six months of having a best friend like Tate was better than not at all, wasn't it?

The stereo suddenly went silent, bringing an end to the distraction.

"Trash." Tate held out an empty plastic bag. "Ready to cry, scream, talk? I'm yours for the rest of the evening if you want to skip book club. I can text the girls and say something came up. Jim's helping my brothers build a tree house at Beau's house. Pizza and beer as payment."

So many fucking loose ends to tie up. "You tell him when he gets home that he has until Monday to marry you."

Her friend ducked her head and sighed. "He promised no more than two weeks, but I know he's delaying because he's worried I'll be stuck with him if he can't get me pregnant."

"But you are, aren't you? It's been almost three weeks since you guys had first-date sex. And other than the few days after that you spent being stubborn—"

"It was five days, and he asked me to marry him the next morning. It was...unexpected."

"Whatever. You two need to stop playing musical chairs. You're living together. You *love* each other. Get married and take the test already."

"I'm six days late. I was going to take the test this morning, but then you got the call yesterday and I didn't want to celebrate, in case the diagnostic confirmed the lump. If I'm pregnant, a few more days of waiting to find out isn't a big deal. Supporting you is more important."

"Stop being so fucking considerate of my feelings. You should be living the whole happily-ever-after thing." Riley snagged a napkin from the stack and scrubbed away the damn tears leaking from her eyes. Streaks of mascara and eyeliner stained the thin white paper. *Raccoon eyes too. Great.* "Take the test in the morning and go to the courthouse in the afternoon tomorrow. No excuses."

"Okay." Tate reached across the console and grasped Riley's hand. "You know Petra and Wally will want to help any way they can too, right? Oh, wasn't Georgie going to try to make it tonight? We can meet at your house if you want. All the vodka sours you can drink, and you won't have to drive home. We'll take care of you."

"Only if nobody gets weepy. God, I have so much to do before..." *Before what? I die? I get too sick to put my affairs in order? An affair. I deserve to have sex at least one more time.*

"No talking like that, Riley. I know you're scared, but we don't know that the lump is cancerous. If you want to update your will and stuff just in case, fine. But no doom and gloom until we know for sure." Her friend released her hand and picked up her cell phone. "What do you need to do? We can make a list."

"You don't understand. The women in my family *do not* survive breast cancer. The chances I'll die from it are a lot higher than the average person. I have to be realistic, and I can't pretend everything might be okay when it probably won't." Kicking off her shoes, Riley swung open the door. Tiny pieces of gravel stabbed the bottoms of her feet as she stood, affirming the fact that she was alive for now.

The driver's door clunked closed behind her. "I'm calling Georgie and telling her to meet us at your house. She can get everything organized and figure out what needs to be done. I hope you're not leaving your shoe collection to me. My feet are a lot bigger than yours, not that I can walk in four-inch heels anyway."

Riley spun to glare at her friend, wincing when the stones bit deeper into her skin. "You're asking me about shoes?"

"Would you rather I ask if you have a burial plot? That's how f-ing crazy this conversation is." Tate rounded the front end of the car and pulled Riley into a tight hug. "I'm selfish and I don't want to lose you."

Fighting a sob, Riley wiggled free and marched to the closest picnic table, glad for the pain knifing through her feet. "Damn it, I'm telling Georgie to arrange for one of those tree burial things in your front yard. Then I can haunt you every fucking day for the next fifty fucking years."

"Good. I want to see your scowling face and hear you throwing f-bombs all over the place. And you'll finally be paler than I am. You can't scare me." Tate plopped onto the concrete curb and thumped her fingers on her phone. As she lifted her cell to her ear, she aimed a glare at Riley. "Besides, your bullshit will help fertilize the lawn instead of stinking up this conversation. Georgie, hi. It's Tate. Are you free? Riley got some news today and she needs legal advice. No, not on the phone. Oh? That doesn't sound good. Her house in twenty minutes? Book club is meeting there tonight, so plan to stay. It doesn't matter if you didn't have time to read the book. Okay, see you then."

"I hate it when people act like I can't take care of myself." Riley picked a stone from her big toe and heaved it into the woods. "Except you. Sometimes. I hope you plan on ordering pizza, because I'm sure as hell not cooking for anybody."

"I brought everything to make spaghetti and garlic bread."

"Leave it to the motherer to have Italian carbs wherever she goes.

No wonder Big Jim's been in love with you forever. You better text Petra and Wally."

"Already done, Ms. Micromanager." Brushing the butt of her jeans with one hand as she stood, Tate flipped Riley the middle finger with the other. "Get your ass in the car or we'll be late meeting Georgie."

"That bird needs more attitude, Ms. Bossypants. We'll work on it later." Most of the funk now flung far and wide by the venting her best friend had encouraged, Riley returned to the car and sank into the passenger seat. "I'm going to be so pissed if I die."

Tate's grin held a bit of wistfulness. "Me too."

"Is Georgie having problems with a case? What doesn't sound good?"

Silence dragged on for at least a full minute. "She talked to Rudy's lawyer right before I called. There's a problem with Trudy's will."

CHAPTER 4

"Do you have a big pot?"

Riley shot Tate a scowl on her way to answer the knock at the patio door. "Fuck if I know. I haven't looked in any of the cabinets except the pantry and the ones with glasses, mugs, and plates since right after I moved in."

"You really should learn to cook, woman." Tate silently opened and banged closed cupboard after cupboard—from the bottom cabinets closest to the stove to the ones flanking the dishwasher. She produced what looked like Aunt Trudy's favorite canning pan as Riley unlocked the deadbolt and twisted the knob. "Finally. Your kitchen needs some serious reorganization."

"Have at it." Riley waved her lawyer inside and grabbed a bottle of red and another of white from the wine cooler.

Georgina growled and held up a legal pad with bullet-point notes filling half the page. "We need to make a plan ASAP, and your cousin's attorney needs to retake his ethics class from law school." She set the notepad and her computer bag on the table before pulling out a chair. "You might want to pour a drink, Ri. It's bad. Hey, Tate. Did you and Jim set a date yet?"

"Bad? It can't be any worse than the rest of my day." Riley

detoured into the work area to fetch her battery-powered corkscrew and two glasses on her way to the seat next to Georgie's. "They're getting married tomorrow. What's wrong with Trudy's will? It's been thirteen years since she died. Why would Rudy contest it now?"

"Tomorrow, huh? It's about time. We'll need to update your will. Jim's too. I'm penciling you in for Monday at three. Let me know where you want to meet by Sunday night. My secretary will email you a reminder Monday morning." Looking up from her laptop, Georgie adjusted her reading glasses and pinned Riley with her divorce-attorney face. "Rudy isn't contesting the will. However, Mr. Kresge called me about an hour ago, asking if you were ill. He said your cousin's wife saw you at the medical center and that you'd mentioned needing to meet on Tuesday instead of last Thursday because of a doctor's appointment. He sounded a bit too hopeful and my gut was telling me it wasn't just some random attempt to annoy you, so I did a little research. Long story short, unless you have an heir to the farm by blood or marriage, it goes to Trudy's next-in-line blood relative when you pass, which is Rudy."

Her equilibrium taking a nosedive, Riley crossed her arms on the table and rested her forehead on the makeshift pillow. "Fuck a goddamn duck. Tell her, Tate."

"Tell me what?" The wariness in her counselor-friend's question was more fitting than she could know.

Footsteps approached from the work area and then a chair bumped across the tile floor, a clear announcement that Tate had joined them. "Her mammogram showed a suspicious spot last week. She had to go back for a diagnostic today and they need to do a biopsy."

For the first time since Riley had met her lawyer three years ago, Georgie didn't instantly and profusely respond. She didn't offer an eloquent and decisive solution with the confidence of a legal genius, either. "Damn."

The hum of the corkscrew broke a long silence, followed by a welcome *glug, glug, glug* and another.

"Drink up." Tate sighed. "I wish I could join you."

"More for me." Riley sat up and chugged most of the glass. "Give it to me straight. What are my options?"

Georgie slid the notepad toward her. "I made a list, but you're not going to like any of them. Depending on the timeline and prognosis, we may have to eliminate some. When's the biopsy? I'll cancel whatever I have on my calendar to go with you."

"Next Thursday at ten." After another gulp of cabernet, Riley pulled the paper closer. "Have a baby? Are you fucking kidding me? Besides the fact that I don't want one of those things living inside me for nine months, I'm forty-seven years old and working on menopause. Finally."

"Why do you think I didn't add any pros and cons? Technically speaking, it's an option, so I wrote it down. Keep reading."

"Fine. Adoption. Pros: strong legal grounds for inheriting property; can choose an older child or children; no childbirth. Cons: time-consuming process; requires parenting skills and commitment. Jesus, I'm supposed to adopt a kid who's already lost her family so I can die and leave her alone? I may have been a grownup when my mom died, but I remember what it's like to lose a parent. I might put someone I hate through that, but I'm not doing it to a kid."

"Okay, I'll take that as a no." Georgie tapped on the keyboard, obviously crossing that option off her list.

"Wait a minute. What if somebody adopts me? Mr. and Mrs. Madison have five kids. What's one more? Then Tate can have a sister. And they don't even have to try to mold me into a responsible adult."

Georgie's glasses slipped to the tip of her nose as she frowned at Riley. "Nice try, but no judge would ever agree to that. Next."

Riley moved her finger down the lines to find her place. "Get married? Hell no! What would I do with a husband, besides bury him in the compost heap?"

A snort came from Tate as she hurried toward the stove. Steam from the pot rose beyond her. "Wow, it's been a long time since you had a date, hasn't it? You know, you might save money on batteries."

"Husband doesn't equal good in bed any more than boyfriend, fuckbuddy, or one-night stand." *Besides, I only know one hot guy I don't want to string up by his balls.* Riley emptied her glass and reached for the bottle.

Georgie snatched it away before she could wrap her hand around it. "I need you sober for this discussion. Or at least mostly sober. Unless you can prove Rudy isn't a blood relative of Trudy's, you're going to have to choose one of these three options or resign yourself to him being next in line to inherit the farm."

Her heart in her stomach, Riley pushed away from the table and paced to the arched entrance into the living room. "Those aren't choices. They're punishments. Fucked, fucked, and more fucked. Without foreplay, an orgasm, or lube."

"You don't have to decide right this minute, but it needs to be soon, in case..."

"In case I have cancer and die." The words came easy after so many years of practicing them, but they still yanked on the ever-present knot in her stomach. Her blouse suddenly strangling her, Riley forced the button at the back of her neck through its loop. "I'm going to change clothes."

Murmurs chased her up the stairs, her friends probably speculating about which of the three evils she would choose. Marriage and children had never been part of the plan for her life, not even before her mother's death. Aunt Stacy's passing eight years later and Great-Aunt Trudy's five years after that had only bolstered her decision not to add to the divorce rate and the planet's overpopulation problems.

She stepped out of her pumps and stripped off her skirt and top, leaving a trail of clothing on her way to the big brass bed she'd coveted as a teenager. The cheval mirror drew her to her reflection, and she shed her bra to inspect her worst enemy. Not a pucker or dimple hinted that a lump lay hidden in the flesh of her left breast.

"I'm not ready to die. They can have my boobs, but I want to live." Turning her back on the perky traitors, she snagged her favorite pair of silk pajamas from the bedpost. The smooth fabric caressed her skin as she dragged on the lipstick-red lounge pants and camisole. Her nipples tightened from the soft touch, like they didn't have a care in the world. "We'll play later. I earned at least one big O today."

Muffled voices—too many to be only Tate and Georgie—came from downstairs as she padded barefoot out of her bedroom. If everyone in the book club had arrived, she would tell them her news and get it over with. Recognizing Petra's throaty sex-kitten drawl among them, Riley paused midway down the steps for a calming breath.

"So we're all agreed?"

Wally's here too. Her motherly diplomacy was unmistakable.

The chorus of yeses abruptly ended when Riley rounded the corner into the kitchen. "What are you guys up to?"

Petra glanced up from an open bakery box on the counter. A smear of chocolate spanned her chin. "Nuffin'."

"Don't give me that bullshit. Spill." Riley made a beeline for the doughnuts and snatched the lone maple-iced cream stick. "What did you have to do for Auggie to score these so late in the day?"

Despite her dark hair and olive complexion, an angry blush swept up Petra's cheeks to accompany her scowl. "A kiss. One kiss. I offered him sixty bucks for six goddamned doughnuts and he wouldn't take it. Jackass."

Wally waggled her eyebrows and shoulder-bumped their butcher friend. "Oh, a kiss! With tongue? How was it? Or don't you kiss and tell?"

"What's to hide? It was okay."

A giggle followed Wally's snort. "Just okay? And what about tongue?"

Stuffing the rest of her Boston cream pastry in her mouth, Petra stomped to the bar someone had set up on the sideboard. She popped the cap off a Guinness and lifted the bottle to her lips.

"Eww!" Tate made gagging noises near the sink. "You're not really going to mix chocolate and stout to get out of answering, are you?"

As Petra tipped up her beer, Georgie transferred the pumpkin cake doughnut to a napkin. "That's a sure sign the kiss exceeded her expectations, and tongue was most definitely involved. I wonder what he'd give you if you slept with him."

Petra leveled a narrow-eyed glower in the lawyer's direction.

THE FARMER TAKES A HUSBAND

"Probably an STD, considering how much he flirts with every female who sets foot in his bakery."

Wally's hoot of laughter filled the kitchen. "If I didn't know better, I'd say you were little jealous."

"Like hell I am."

The bowl of spaghetti cradled in both hands, Tate wove her way to the table. "Come and get it!"

Still savoring the first taste of maple goodness, Riley snagged the chair beside Petra. "No matter what it cost you, I appreciate the cream stick. Want to go axe throwing this weekend? My treat."

"They're already booked full. I checked after I picked up the doughnuts. You can help me hack up cow carcasses Saturday night instead if you want to." Her butcher friend piled a helping of spaghetti on her plate and passed the bowl to Riley. "It's very therapeutic."

A shudder rippled up Riley's spine. "I think I'll pass."

Petra passed her the basket of garlic bread. "Hypocrite. The only difference between butchering a cow or a pig and chopping vegetables is animals make noises you can hear when you kill them. I tried to explain that to my PETA-propaganda-spouting ex-fiancé, but he claimed it wasn't the same. You know the yeast in this bread used to be alive too."

"Really?" The question came from Georgie. "You were engaged to a member of PETA?"

"He joined *after* I said yes."

Wally handed Petra the cheese grater. "And a guy who cheated, another who died in a traffic accident, one who got a job in Dubai. Hmm. That's only four. There were two more, but I can't remember the details. Oh yeah. One went back to his ex. What was the last one?"

Wielding her fork, Petra stabbed it into the center of her pile of pasta and twirled an enormous wad. "Oh my God. Can we please not talk about my poor relationship choices?"

"That's it!" Her nearly empty glass raised, Wally leaned around Tate and looked toward the opposite end of the table and their newest member. "The gold digger who thought she was rich because her parents own a vacation cabin down in Hocking Hills. It barely has indoor plumbing."

The fork clattered against Petra's plate. "Damn it, I thought we were going to give Riley advice about how to keep Rudy's poisonous hands off the farm."

Midchew, Riley pushed her chair away from the table and stood. As she turned to the sideboard for something stronger than cabernet, the chatter behind her fell silent. After pouring a hefty dose of vodka into her half-empty glass, she took a swig for courage. "Besides the fuckery with the will and keeping the farm in the family, I found out today that I have a lump in my breast. The biopsy is scheduled for next week."

At least one gasp momentarily broke the silence, but no one spoke for at least a minute.

"This changes our timeline and eliminates some options." Georgie's authoritative tone lacked its usual confidence. "She has to make a decision now so I can make immediate changes to her will, just in case the lump is malignant and the cancer is aggressive. Otherwise, the property will go to her cousin. Her aunt set up a trust that allows her to farm, reside on, or basically do whatever she wants with the property, except sell it if there's a living heir. While it prevents Rudy from buying the farm or even a portion of it, the wording also ties her hands in regards to naming a beneficiary other than a family member, unless there are none."

Although Riley suspected she already knew the answer, she asked the question making her insides churn. "What options are left?"

"Find a husband. And after talking to Tate, Petra, and Wally, I have an idea where to start."

CHAPTER 5

"Fee, hurry up! You're going to miss the bus! And, no, I don't have time to drive you to school this morning. I have a meeting. Let's go." Deke chugged the rest of his lukewarm coffee, praying the caffeine kicked in soon.

Her backpack slung on her shoulder, Amanda hefted it higher as she headed out the front door. "Bye, Dad. Love you."

"Love you too. Good luck on your math test."

"Thanks." She waved and pushed open the storm door.

"Are you coming, Fee?"

"I had to tie my shoes." Heavy footsteps trudged down the hall, announcing Fiona's presence before she arrived in the kitchen.

"Why are you wearing hiking boots? Wouldn't sandals have been fast— Never mind." More than likely, he wouldn't like the real reason.

She continued her plodding pace across the tile floor to the entry, her arm no longer in a sling. Instead, multiple Ace bandages covered her from elbow to fingertips, transforming her splinted fingers and forearm into a club. "I have detention today."

"You're lucky you didn't get worse. Grab your backpack and go. I'll see you this afternoon. Love you."

She stared at him for several seconds before she dragged her pack from the table and along the floor. "Don't forget to pick me up."

"I won't." *Not in a million years.* The only thing that kept him from going after her was the emergency meeting his most frustrating client had demanded via text message a few minutes before midnight. *This better be damned important.*

A rumble outside drew his attention to the school bus approaching the end of the driveway. Its blinking lights changed from yellow to red when it jerked to a stop. His daughters climbed the steps, freeing him from the strain of single parenting for a few hours—unless Fiona found trouble again today, which was always a possibility.

What am I supposed to do?

With no forthcoming answers, he locked up and headed into the garage. Yesterday's carryout bag still sat in the center console cup holder, reminding him he'd forgotten to eat breakfast for the fifth time this week. Stale scones were better than an empty stomach, weren't they?

Thankful it hadn't turned into a triangular hockey puck overnight, he bit into the blueberry pastry as he followed the bus through the neighborhood to the main road leading into and away from town. A pile of crumbs accumulated in his lap during the short drive to the two-hundred-plus-acre spread, but he washed down the ones in his throat with the shudder-worthy dregs from the travel mug he'd neglected to carry into the house after taking Fiona for x-rays.

Do other single fathers have these problems?

His pulse ticked up a notch when he spotted Riley under the security light outside the greenhouse closest to her garage, the same way it did every damn time he saw her. He parked in the turnaround and crossed his fingers she hadn't decided to fire him after their run-in yesterday at The Homegrown Café. Teasing and sparring came as close to outright flirting as he dared venture, considering her aversion to marriage and kids.

Luckily, the crumbs on his lap landed on the ground instead of his seat when he climbed out of the car. He waved, hoping to get a feel for her mood. "G'morning, Riley."

Her hand popped up without her middle finger sticking out to greet him—most definitely a good sign. "I'll meet you in the kitchen. Help yourself to coffee. There's a fresh pot."

Maybe she didn't plan to fire him, but her offer meant she had a true emergency, especially since she'd quit drinking the high-octane stuff months ago.

Audit?

He grabbed his computer from the passenger seat and his travel mug from the cup holder before heading to the patio door. The aroma of good French roast lured him inside to the coffeemaker. After a quick rinse of his mug, he filled it with the enticing brew. A thunk behind him interrupted his first slurp of hot coffee.

Riley dropped into a chair at the kitchen table and gestured for him to join her. "Thanks for coming out so early."

"Not a problem." Her polite demeanor put him on edge, but he sat across from her with his mug and computer bag in front of him. "It sounded urgent. What's going on?"

Dark smudges under her eyes and wrinkled clothes warned him the problem was bigger than he'd anticipated. The woman never looked less than ready to kick ass, take names, and model whatever sexy outfit she wore that particular day. "You have to help me, Deacon."

"I'll do what I can. What do you need?"

She rubbed at a spot on her chin and sighed. "Great. A zit. I need a husband."

What? He sipped his coffee, pretty sure the situation called for a large dose of caffeine but afraid he'd choke on it. "What do you mean you *need* a husband?"

Her jaw tightened and the faint lines around her mouth deepened. "Need. You know, must have."

"For what? A practical joke? Nobody in their right mind would ever believe you'd willingly get hitched." The hot brew scalded the tip of his tongue, but it went down smooth—no bitter aftertaste like the cheap crap he bought.

She pushed out of her chair and slogged to the counter in her sneakers, a far cry from the customary fuck-off heels. Then she poured coffee into the mug by the sink. "I know."

"You shouldn't be drinking that. Didn't your doctor—"

"Yes. I'm drinking it anyway." The scowl she aimed at him eased some of his concern, but it lacked the if-looks-could-kill strength it normally had. "I have to get married as soon as possible."

This isn't the woman I know. Alien abduction or did she go off the deep end? "Is somebody blackmailing you, Riley?"

She slammed the mug onto the counter, making coffee slosh over the top. Her hand shook as she crossed her arms under her breasts. "I wish. I'd tell them to go fuck themselves. It's Aunt Trudy's will. If I don't get married, my asshole cousin will get the farm."

Now we're getting somewhere. "But you already inherited the farm."

"And I have no heirs. I found out yesterday that Aunt Trudy's will —trust, whatever—says the farm has to stay in the family unless there's nobody left to inherit. At the moment, that leaves the shithead who loves to poison everything and his equally annoying wife and man-child. Where the hell am I supposed to find a husband I won't strangle within a week?" Something that sounded an awful lot like panic laced her words.

What about me? Was this the opportunity he'd been waiting for? Of course, he'd sort of planned to date her before he risked asking her to marry him.

He wrapped his hands around the cool metal exterior of the insulated cup, formulating a convincing response instead of blurting out a proposal guaranteed to get him tossed out on his ass. "We've known each other for almost a year and a half, and you haven't put your hands around my neck yet. Not even when I told you your last accountant underestimated your quarterly estimated taxes."

"That was *his* fault, and you made him pay the penalty so I wouldn't have to strangle him. See? This is why I'm asking you for help. I trust you."

There's no way in hell she'd admit to trusting me if she didn't like me. At least he stood a fifty-fifty chance of her falling in love with him if he'd gotten that far. "Um, that's not exactly what I meant."

"Then—" Her eyes widened. "Oh. *Ohh.* You mean... You? Why would I ruin a perfectly good working relationship with my accountant?"

Here come the arguments and excuses. Time to fire back. "What makes you think I'd let something like marriage ruin our client-CPA relationship? And you better not expect free or even discounted book-keeping and tax services, especially payroll. I have bills to pay."

She had the decency to look offended. "Of course not."

Here's the tricky one. He braced for the answer that would shoot his chance to kingdom come. "You don't hate me, do you?"

Her gaze fell toward the floor. "Well, no. Not yet anyway, even though you aggravate the hell out of me sometimes."

"Thanks. I love you too." The words slipped out far too easily, the truth colliding with the sarcasm he'd managed to inject. "Let's look at this logically. We get along pretty well and I'm not married. I have two kids, adding another layer of protection to your claim to the farm. Even if my girls decide not to have children, we could potentially lock your cousin and his heirs out for a long time."

Damn, I'm good.

She picked up her mug and swallowed a noisy gulp of coffee, like it might kick-start her sleeping snark. "I suppose. But..."

Going in for the kill. "Do you have a better option? Some secret boy-toy hidden in your attic or basement?"

Her visible exasperation should've sent her pretty hazel eyes rolling across the kitchen floor. "The only boy-toys I have are in my nightstand drawer with a stash of dead batteries."

An impromptu image in his mind of Riley pleasuring herself nearly sidetracked his brain, and his khakis tightened at his groin. "I don't think those qualify as next of kin, blondie, no matter how much you enjoyed their company or how intimately they knew you before you killed them."

A bark of laughter kept him from begging for a chance to prove himself more proficient than a vibrator, even though trepidation stood out beneath her wide smile. "Fuck it all. You're hired, Deke. At least you have a decent sense of humor."

His stomach fought with his heart over which of them had the worse case of nerves. "It's better than just decent and you know it. So... When's the wedding?"

The color drained from her cheeks and her white-knuckled grasp on the edge of the counter spoke volumes about her desire to take the plunge. "Tomorrow, if possible. Preferably not today. Tate and Jim are supposed to be getting married this afternoon. Monday, at the latest. What's your schedule look like?"

"Tomorrow? I'm not saying I won't do it, but what's the rush? I mean, marriage is serious business, especially with kids involved. Don't you think we should go on a date first?"

She glanced toward the ceiling, as if her patience had hit its limit. "I could be run over by a tractor or buried under an avalanche of potatoes today. I can't afford to wait."

The hypothetical instruments of her demise might be a tad melodramatic, but he couldn't argue against the possibility of them happening. People died unexpectedly all the time.

Am I willing to risk her marrying somebody else if I don't say yes right away?

Absolutely not. He had one shot and one shot only. "Okay."

Relief written all over her face, she picked up her mug. "Thank you. I appreciate this more than you know. We need to discuss the terms for the contract so we're both clear on the expectations and responsibilities. Georgina Swofford emailed me a contract to use as a template so everything's in writing."

"Good idea. Once we work out the terms, we can make copies and sign and add them to our will portfolios. Those will need updated after the wedding." He pulled his laptop from his bag and opened a new document for notes.

"If we get that far. First off, if I die, you're not allowed to sell or give away the farm or any portion of it to just anybody if there are no remaining Fenniman heirs. You'll oversee the farm, but it'll run basically the same as it does now, with my managers for the different aspects of the business making day-to-day decisions. They would consult with you on big decisions and you'd handle the financial stuff that I've been doing. Georgie already incorporated all the details into the template."

"Makes sense." A quick check of his calendar yielded nothing but weekend father-daughter time, the first Saturday this month to allow it. "I can spare an hour tomorrow."

She took another long swallow of coffee. "Fine. We can get the license today. Second, I expect one basic benefit for my sacrifice—sex."

Holy shit, I've died and gone to heaven. "Hmm. Now I'm wondering if you're more interested in my body than keeping your cousin from—"

"Ha. Ha." She glared at him from over the rim of her coffee cup. "Since we're going to have a physical relationship, you have to agree to undergo testing to prove you won't give me any sexually transmitted diseases. And you have to have a vasectomy while you're getting tested. Babies are *not* part of the deal under any circumstances. Those two items are non-negotiable."

"That's three items, Riley. No selling or giving away the farm, testing before any hanky panky, and a snip to prevent babies." He typed the second and third conditions, ready to agree to whatever terms she demanded.

"Fine. Those three items are non-negotiable, even though they're technically item one and items two a and two b. Oh, and I'm not changing my last name."

"Of course not. I agree to your terms, even though you're being argumentative. Now it's my turn." Casting a glance at his bride-to-be, he prioritized his top two requests, pretty sure asking her to fall in love with him would obliterate any chance of his other condition coming true. "My girls need a woman to talk to. You know, about girl things."

She perked up, as if the task didn't challenge her skills in the slightest. "You mean like periods and bras and making sure they know women deserve orgasms every bit as much as men? I can do that."

He swiped his hand over his face, hoping it hid his urge to show her he was up for the job. "Jesus, Riley. They're thirteen and eleven. Don't you think that's kind of young to be talking about sexual pleasure?"

A lewd grin replacing her humorous one, she strutted to the table and straddled his lap. "There's the problem with men. They treat sex like it's some sacred rite of passage into manhood, but they expect their daughters to cross their legs and save themselves for marriage. Who the hell are all those boys having sex with when they're out gaining experience? Huh? Girls need to know it's okay for them to have sex too, if they want to. And it damn well better be good for them too."

I'll do my damnedest to make it the best you've ever had. Too bad he couldn't tell her that—yet. "I'd rather you didn't make it sound so..."

"So what? Enjoyable? I'm beginning to think I need to take you for a test drive before we sign on the dotted line. If I have to get married, I'll be damned if I'm settling for mediocre sex for the rest of my life."

"Then I better get my results. Wouldn't want that to stand in the way of your test drive." He wiggled beneath her, enjoying the pressure against his erection. "Oh, and I got snipped before my ex-wife decided she preferred traveling the world with a camera to a husband and kids."

"Ouch. I figured your wife had passed away since you never talk about her. How long were you married?"

Curiosity is a good sign, isn't it? "Five years. The girls were three and one when she left. She doesn't visit or communicate with them and they don't remember her at all. I guess she just wasn't cut out to be a wife and mother."

"Some women don't want to be, but society projects its expectations on them. When they cave to the pressure, they sometimes regret it. Me? I have absolutely no desire to go through pregnancy, childbirth, or parenting of anything that can't feed itself when it's hungry or go to the bathroom when it needs to pee." She nailed him in place with a warning stare. "And no amount of how-can-you-know-if-you-don't-try wheedling is convincing me otherwise."

"I admire that about you, the ability to know exactly what you want and the strength to go after it. Not caring what other people think.

You're a what-you-see-is-what-you-get kind of person. I like that."
Slipping his arm around her waist, he nuzzled her neck below her ear.
"By the way, Amanda and Fiona have a far broader repertoire in the
kitchen than I do and they both passed Advanced Potty Training a long
time ago."

"Okay, so back to the test drive." She rocked her hips forward and
groaned. "How soon do you think you can get tested?"

He slid his hands along her thighs, over her ass, and up her back.
"Already done. I keep the paperwork in my wallet."

CHAPTER 6

RILEY COULD'VE KISSED DEKE FOR BEING SO DAMN EFFICIENT. Actually, she would—after they exchanged documentation and before she ripped the boring beige clothes off the body she'd wondered about on several masturbation occasions. "Mine's upstairs. In my bedroom."

"Invitation or spiteful teasing?" His tongue and then his teeth caressed her earlobe.

Tiny tremors vibrated through her lower belly, and her nipples ached for someone's touch other than her own. She ground her pelvis into his erection, working the crotch seam of her gauzy palazzo pants against her clit. "Request to be accompanied. And be quick about it."

"Hold on tight." He gripped her ass and stood, pushing the seam into the perfect spot.

Caught in a swift upward spiral, she tightened her legs around his waist and clung to his shoulders. His first step into the living room bounced her past the edge, setting off spasm after wonderful spasm like she hadn't experienced in months. She buried her face in his tan sport coat to keep her cry from busting his eardrums as the ripples continued.

He snorted a laugh as he started up the stairs. "Couldn't wait for me, huh? Why am I not surprised?"

Her pulse throbbed through every part of her body, making up for all those dead batteries she had yet to replace. "Fuck you."

"That was the plan, Riley, but you jumped the gun. I guess we'll have to try again, not that I mind. That was an amazing orgasm I just gave you."

"You didn't give me anything, smartass. I took it."

"My sense of humor turned you on and carrying you got you off." His low chuckle tensed his abs enough to create an aftershock. "I felt that. I deserve at least partial credit."

He isn't wrong. "Whatever."

He slowed at the top of the steps and brushed his lips on her cheek. "Which way?"

"Left." A whiff of shaving cream and coffee tempted her to rest her head on his shoulder and simply breathe. How had she never noticed how good he smelled?

"Dresser or nightstand?"

"Hm?" How had she lost track of the conversation?

"Your paperwork, bride-to-be." He stopped at the bed and lowered her bottom to the mattress. "I'll show you mine if you'll show me yours. Gotta finish that test drive."

"Yeah, paperwork." Leaning back, she shook off the brain fuzz and loosened her hold on his hips. "Top drawer of the nightstand on this side."

"In the hole next to the money slot." He worked a brown wallet from his butt pocket and set it on her belly. Without moving from between her legs, he opened the drawer, setting off the usual rattling. "That's quite a collection of boy-toys and dead batteries you have. How about I buy you a jumbo pack of batteries and incorporate your toys into our wedding night?"

"The boring accountant has a kinky side, does he?" His wallet unfolded when she picked it up, opening to pictures of two girls with his dark hair and brown eyes. The younger-looking one wore an annoyed expression that almost matched the troublemaker twinkle Riley had seen many times in photos of herself at that age.

"You'll have to wait and see." He removed her ancient report from its envelope. "This is dated almost eight years ago."

"Is that a problem?" A zippered plastic bag occupied the spot he'd sent her in search of. She opened it and unfolded the wrinkled document.

"Only if you've had sex with somebody since then. There are a lot of batteries in the drawer, but I highly doubt it's seven years' worth."

She flipped him the finger as she noted his date and the mention of a vasectomy. "The last time I had real sex was on my fortieth birthday. The only reason I remember is because it sucked, and not in the good way. FYI, I always empty and restock my drawer after you send me the bill for my quarterly taxes."

"Good to know I've been useful." He tossed the envelope back in the drawer and then hooked his hand under her right knee, bunching her pant leg above it. "Now I'm not so embarrassed at having gone six years without sex. My excuse is kids. What's yours?"

"I'm better at getting myself off than most men are."

"Obviously." His left hand glided from the back of her knee to her ankle, triggering a not-unwelcome tingle as he untied her shoe. The sneaker thudded on the floor. "I'll do my best to be the exception. Top or bottom? Do you have a preference?"

"Both." Another tiny spasm rippling through her abdomen, she raised her other leg for him to continue taking off her shoes. "No preference as long as you're not selfish about orgasms."

He dropped the second sneaker and looked down at her with a wicked grin. "I plan on giving you so many you're limp as a wet noodle and begging me to let you rest. You should take off your pants and shirt so I don't rip them. I can get a little impatient when sex is on the line."

How could a blandly dressed man who exasperated the hell out of her push all the right buttons, too? "You have to let go of my foot."

He swirled his tongue over her anklebone and up her calf, inciting more of those damn tremors. At her knee, he halted and kissed the sensitive underside. "Shall I strip for you, my queen?"

"Yes, and be quick about it." She tugged on the drawstring at her waist. "I want to see something besides beige. Do you even own any clothes that aren't some shade of brown?"

His blazer flew toward the dresser and he loosened his tie. "Jeans. With work clothes, tan is easiest to match. I'm colorblind."

"Really? Here I thought you were just dull." Lifting her hips, she shimmied out of her pants and underwear.

He raised an eyebrow and worked his way down the front of his button-down oxford. Then his gaze skipped toward her lower body. "I guess I have a lot to prove to you."

"Not necessarily." She sat up and pulled the long-sleeved tee over her head. The slight chill caressed her bare skin. "I can tolerate boring clothes if you're good in bed."

His eyes narrowed as he shrugged out of his shirt. Although he didn't exactly sport a weightlifter's muscles, he could claim he hadn't yet fallen victim to a middle-aged dad bod, much like she'd imagined. "Good is subjective. Compatibility is more important and good together works best. You always go wandering around the farm without a bra on?"

"When I want to." Leafing through the remaining slots in his wallet, she didn't find the item she expected. His driver's license, however, gave her new ammunition for teasing. She propped herself up on her elbows to enjoy the rest of the show. "If you'd copped a feel in the kitchen, you might've noticed sooner."

"You would've slugged me if I'd gotten handsy before this conversation." His shoes creaked ever so slightly as he kicked off one and then the other. "No, I haven't had time to replace them."

"How can you be sure? And did I say anything about your squeaky loafers?"

"You didn't have to." He paused with his pants unfastened and his hands poised to shove them down his legs. "Does that mean you've been lusting after me the last year and a half?"

"I'd hardly call admiring a fine ass lusting. Besides, you're practically a baby. Just turned thirty-nine last month. Got a thing for older women, do you?"

"You're the first, although I never would've guessed your age when you hired me. How about you? Got a thing for younger men?" Turning his back to her, he disposed of his khakis and underwear. Despite its paleness, his butt fit into her favorite category—firm and nicely rounded. Then he cast a sly grin over his shoulder. "Speechless, huh? Wait until you see the rest."

A bubble of laughter kept her from foolishly revealing her curiosity. "You know damn well I don't have a thing for any man."

His eyebrows rose almost to his hairline.

"Wait. That didn't come out right." She nearly climbed off the bed to slap the smirk that followed the surprise off his face. "Ah, hell. Turn around and show me the goods."

DEKE SWALLOWED HIS NERVES AND BELTED OUT SEVERAL BARS OF THE most well-known striptease tune on the planet as he swiveled his hips and pivoted toward Riley. *My wife, if I don't screw this up.*

She sat up, staring toward his dick with her lips parted. Her tongue snuck out to wet them, making him harder than he already was. "Do you know how to use that thing?"

"Does a duck know how to swim?" He stripped off his socks, adding them to the assortment of clothing littering the floor.

"You're not a duck and I don't want any swimmers within ten feet of me, especially since you don't have a condom in your wallet."

"I took it out several years ago after my daughters found it and asked if it was a balloon. Besides, we've already established that we're both disease-free and I've been snipped." Fairly certain she was having second thoughts, he climbed onto the bed and stretched out beside her. "If you're not a hundred-percent sure about this, tell me. No hard feelings. Actually, that's a bad choice of adjective."

She rolled to face him and used her hand to prop up her head. Blonde curls fell across her cheek, giving his temptress an unwarranted hint of innocence. "I've never had sex without a condom. It goes against all my rules."

"All joking aside, I would never risk anybody's health for an opportunity to get laid. Not yours or mine. The only woman I've ever not used protection with was my ex-wife when we were trying to have a baby and when she was pregnant. That said, I'll wear a condom if you want me to and you have one." He barely resisted reaching out to wind a curl around his finger.

Her eyes flicked toward the nightstand and back to him, but her neutral expression gave nothing away. "You can go without since the damn things are probably past their expiration date anyway. But if I end up with crabs, warts, or worse, I'll sue your ass and take your accounting business."

"I'd expect nothing less." He hooked his arm under her waist and pulled her on top of him, smashing her breasts against his chest. Her legs ended up flanking his and put his erection in direct contact with her lower belly. He sucked in a breath and slowly blew it out. "Damn, you feel nice. How about a smorgasbord of positions to see what works best? We can start with the cowgirl. Well, after a kiss."

"You talk too much." She covered his mouth with hers and shoved her tongue past his lips when he tried for a rebuttal.

Pretty sure she meant to test his doormat qualities, he met each aggressive thrust with one of his own and placed his palms on her butt cheeks. If she wanted a challenge, he'd give it to her.

Even as their sparring continued, she moaned and shifted to her knees, pressing her nipples into his ribs. He seized the chance to stand his dick up beneath her and guide her body onto him in a single swift motion. A rush of lightheadedness threatened to carry him away, but being surrounded by and connected to her so fundamentally gave him everything he needed to survive.

She dragged her mouth free and grunted as she arched upward, her breasts not quite close enough for a taste. "Holy fuck."

His patience shot to hell, he cupped the two handfuls and pushed until she was upright and seated against his balls. Simultaneous brushes across her taut peaks earned him a groan. "Ride me or we're moving on to the next position."

She rocked forward and jerked her hips back, taking him even deeper. Her fingers dug into his thighs behind her as she did it again and again. Ragged breaths mixed with sexy whimpers and squeaks, and her eyes glazed over like she suffered from feverish delirium. Every advance and retreat produced the perfect amount of friction along his length, confirming what he'd imagined in his self-induced relief for months.

Their chemistry would burn him alive and he'd enjoy every damn minute of the fire.

Her noises took on a frustrated quality, so he rolled sideways, putting him on top, rather than prolonging her suffering from the elusive goal. He hooked her knees over his forearms and locked gazes with her as he thrust deep enough to steal his breath. His heart hammered in his chest, as much from the ability to finally make love to her as the pure lust in her eyes.

"Tell me what you want, Riley." The words came out raspy, but she didn't seem to notice.

She arched upward and licked her lips, evidently—and incorrectly —thinking he needed more seducing. "Mutual orgasms. Now."

His dick twitched, more than willing to comply with her request. "Fast and hard then. Put your arms above your head and hold on."

She squeezed him with her vaginal muscles and flicked his nipple as she stretched like a cat, making him jump when his balls clenched. Then she bunched the comforter in her fists. "This better be worth all the hype."

He bent forward to kiss the snark out of her delicious mouth. The rough sweep of his tongue along hers ratcheted his horniness higher. "Always the skeptic."

Not giving her time to respond, he lunged into her, setting a frantic pace that held no guarantee he wouldn't finish before her. Every deep thrust forced a groan from his throat, but high-pitched cries filled the room. Her thighs trembled against his arms and she shook her head back and forth like she didn't want to drown in the sensations she had to be feeling. Her body pulsed and vibrated around him, dragging him under with her.

Then heat shot through him, the accompanying roar warring with her scream. The room, the bed, everything faded away as he let their releases carry him to the clouds. He had fantasized about this moment since he'd met her, and it hadn't fallen short of spectacular.

Collapsing on top of her, he waited for his pounding heart to slow, savoring their skin-to-skin contact and listening to her breathe. "Ready to sign on the dotted line?"

CHAPTER 7

THE FIRST TIME HADN'T BEEN A FLUKE. NEITHER HAD THE SECOND.

Or the third. Rubbing her damp hair with a towel, Riley walked out of the bathroom on rubbery legs, not sure they would carry her as far as the bed, let alone her dresser. She flopped on the tangled covers, too sated to bother with clothes or flip the bird at the chuckling sex fiend shadowing her.

"Limp as a wet noodle. I won't make you beg for a rest since we still need to sign the agreement and I can't be late to my ten-o'clock appointment." Deke grinned at her before leaning down to kiss her big toe. "God, you have sexy feet."

"I don't beg." That was a lie. She'd begged him to make her come in the shower. "Shut up."

He laughed again and shoved an arm into his shirtsleeve. "I didn't say a word."

"But you were thinking it."

"Maybe." The swagger toward the rest of his clothes confirmed it, but his magnificent butt made up for his exasperating ego. "Mostly I was thinking about how I'm going to explain all the moaning and screaming to my daughters."

"You could tell them the truth." She rolled to her belly to get a better view while he dressed.

"I'm pretty sure they don't want to know their dad is having sex and enjoying the hell out of it. Fee already thinks I'm too old to date."

The blood in her veins froze. "You're dating someone?"

He smirked at her as he stepped into his underwear. "Jealous?"

Much to her dismay, his allegation struck a little too close to home. "Fuck, no. I just don't like cheaters."

"I'm not cheating because I'm not dating anybody." The stretchy cotton clung to his ass and upper thighs, allowing her to continue her admiration. "The topic of dating came up in conversation recently. As a hypothetical situation."

"And your daughters don't want you to date? Why didn't you say so earlier? How are they going to react to you getting married and them acquiring a stepmother?" Frustration rejuvenating her muscles, she climbed off the opposite side of the bed and shuffled toward the dresser.

"Amanda's okay with me dating and Fiona hates that she doesn't have a mother." With his pants hanging open at the waist, he caught her in front of the mirror. His eyes met hers in their reflection. "They'll be fine with it and even if they're not, they'll get over it. You're hunting for trouble, Riley. You have to make up your mind we're doing this, or you have to be willing to risk your cousin inheriting the property."

The concern trying to turn into panic lessened somewhat with his reassurance, but it didn't disappear. "I have no parenting experience at all, so you're going to be on your own for the most part. Same goes for the relationship part. I don't do high maintenance."

"I've been doing the single parenting thing for a long time. If you can be there when they need a woman to talk to, we're good." He twirled her around to face him and rested his palms on her hips, setting off more tingles. "For us, all I ask is that you're honest with me. If something's bugging you, tell me. We can argue for a while and then have make-up sex."

"I never would've guessed you were such a horndog."

His hands glided to the lowest part of her back. "It's your fault for insisting on a test drive and wandering around naked. You can only expect so much self-control from a guy who's been celibate for six years. Besides, I didn't hear you complaining fifteen minutes ago. Or an hour ago."

She shrugged, making his hands slide a few inches lower. "Why would I complain? Last time I checked, eight years is longer than six."

"Quit trying to pick a fight. I have to go soon." His mouth closed over hers and he licked the seam of her lips, seducing her into opening for him. The lazy pace of each gentle caress of his tongue threatened to melt her into a gooey puddle. As her knees weakened, he ended the kiss and sighed. "I have to go."

She grasped his biceps for balance. "You said that already."

"I mean it this time. Put some clothes on before I get distracted again." His gaze dipped toward her breasts and he growled. "Don't you have orders to invoice or something?"

"Yes, but tormenting you is much more fun." Reaching for the dresser, she managed to pull open her underwear drawer. "Red, black, or nude thong for our trip to the courthouse for the license?"

"You're a truly evil woman, Riley Fenniman."

"Yeah, so?"

He shook his head and backed away from her, amusement evident in his glittering eyes. "Red. Bra to match?"

"Of course." She pulled out the matching undergarments, the weight of his stare still feathering across her skin while he tucked his shirt and zipped his pants. "Any chance you'll wear a color other than tan tomorrow?"

"I have a black funeral suit and a white shirt. Amanda bought me a new tie to go with it for Christmas last year. White, gray, and blue." Standing at the mirror, he re-knotted the one he'd tossed on the floor earlier.

"That'll work since I'm planning to wear black too."

His snicker didn't surprise her. "Got a black lace bra and panties for under your mourning clothes?"

"What do *you* think?" She shimmied into her thong and then threaded her arms into the racer-back bra.

"I think you really enjoy riling me up." He sat in the rocker and yanked on a sock as she hooked the front clasp and adjusted her breasts in the cups. "I'm free from twelve to one and three to four to get the license. Shit, three thirty. I have to pick up Fiona and Amanda from school and I'll have to stop by the house to pick up my divorce papers on the way."

"You're easy to irritate. I can meet you there at twelve fifteen." Instead of giving in to the slight nausea the thought of getting married instigated, she padded to the closet for her red pencil skirt and matching flowered blouse. "Georgie said to fill out the application ahead of time and print it to make things go faster. We'll also need picture IDs and cash to pay the fee. I'll take care of it since it's my problem that got us into this situation."

"Sounds fair." He followed her into the closet and stopped at the floor-to-ceiling shelves of footwear. His laughter filled the space. "It's exactly how I imagined it. Which pair goes with today's outfit?"

"These." With her skirt zipped but her top still drooping at her neck, she grabbed her laser-cut D'orsay sling-backs from the middle shelf by the heel straps and dangled them in front of him.

"Nice. You should wear them to bed sometime." He waggled his eyebrows at her, his not-boring side catching her off-guard again.

"Why? So I can stab you when I'm done with you?"

A grin spread across his face and his low chuckle sent a shiver up her spine. "You wouldn't hurt the man who does your payroll and knows how to keep you sexually satisfied, now would you?"

He had a point, but she tapped the spike heel against his chest anyway. "Maybe. Maybe not."

"It looks like the only boring part of being married to you will be my clothes."

She snorted as she trailed him out of the closet. "That remains to be seen. I don't have high hopes."

Stopping at his sport coat and loafers, he clutched at the left side of his chest. "I'm so wounded. Maybe I should cut my losses and run. I mean, getting laid three times in one day is probably a reasonable consolation prize, especially after six years of jacking off."

Every muscle in her body tensed before his intent to annoy her pushed past the possibility that he had no intention of following through on their agreement. "God, you're such a smartass."

"Takes one to know one." The rest of his belongings in hand, he led the way downstairs. His jacket landed next to his computer and his shoes clunked beside his chair as he sat. "I need to leave in twenty-five minutes. Where's the template? I'll start filling in my terms while you find the link to the marriage license form."

She fastened the hook on her blouse and walked to the coffee maker for a refill to calm her nerves. Unfortunately, the rich aroma sparked a twinge in her gut reminiscent of the ones that had sent her to the doctor. "I need to get it from my office."

Without touching the carafe, she retraced her steps to the living room and crossed to the parlor she'd transformed into her workspace. The silence gave her a minute to sort through the contradictory emotions swimming in her mind. His familiar teasing brought a degree of normality to the situation, but it also reeked of easy banter between two people who genuinely enjoyed each other's company and chose to spend time together.

It's nothing personal, Deke. Even though I like you, I don't want to marry anyone.

What other choice did she have?

None. Fucking none.

She snatched the contract from the printer tray and picked up the laptop on her desk, disgusted by her wishy-washy whininess. The lesser of two evils could've been a lot worse than her beige number cruncher with an unexpected skill set. He was tolerable, unlike Rudy inheriting and destroying everything she'd built.

The faint clicking of fingers on a keyboard greeted her halfway across the living room and Deacon didn't look up when she entered the kitchen. "I added another item to the list. Since the farm is your business location, the girls and I should probably move into your house. Then I can make a few repairs I've been putting off before I put my house on the market. If you have the space and you don't mind, I can set up a new home office here. I prefer to meet with clients at their businesses, so you don't have to worry about people coming and going all the time."

Taking the seat beside him, she shoved the contract at him and tried to ignore his effort to be agreeable. "Fine. Your daughters can have the two downstairs bedrooms and you can use the spare room upstairs or the finished attic above the garage for an office."

His attention turned from his computer to the paper in his hand. "Whatever works best for you. And I'd like Manda and Fee to meet you before we do this. Springing a wedding on them at the last second isn't a good idea, even if they're okay with me dating."

"Be here at six with pizza. Any toppings. I'll pick up dessert from Auggie's bakery on my way home from the courthouse. God knows I deserve a huge piece of his lemon pound cake." The link from Georgie's email popped up in a new tab on her screen, whipping her stomach into recurring somersaults with a full twist. Would he still marry her if she puked all over him?

"Good call. Two of the girls' favorites." He glanced her direction and frowned. "Hey, are you feeling okay? You're looking a little green around the edges. I warned you about the coffee."

"It's not the coffee, damn it." She slapped at his hands when he reached for her.

"Bend over and put your head between your knees."

"I don't need to look up my skirt. I'm already acquainted with what's in there." His face blurred, and she sucked in a deep breath to counter a bout of dizziness.

"So am I, but that isn't the point." He pressed on her back, forcing her face into his lap. "Is this better?"

Her cheek brushed the unmistakable contours of what lay behind his zipper. "If you wanted a blow job, why didn't you say so?"

"Because you look like you're about to pass out and I have to leave soon. Stop arguing with me and breathe while I fill out these forms." He rubbed his fingers up and down her spine, distracting her from the sick feeling impending matrimony had brought on.

"I don't need a fucking boss."

"Maybe not, but you need a keeper at the moment and I've appointed myself. Now be quiet for five minutes."

The steady movement of his hand on her back and the rhythmic scuff of pen to paper on the table slowly calmed her whirling insides enough that her vision cleared. Then both stopped and faint clicks took over, but she closed her eyes to fully appreciate the comfortable pillow his lap made instead of sitting up.

"Feeling better yet?" His voice held a hint of concern, sparking a pang of guilt she shouldn't feel, and he brushed her hair off her forehead.

She faked a yawn that morphed into a real one as she rose from her makeshift bed. "Just a little tired. Your clothes put me to sleep."

He chuckled and shook his head. "Liar. Good sex put you to sleep. We just need to fill in a few places on the license application with your personal information and it'll be ready to print. I've also added all the terms we talked about to the contract. Do you think we should have a witness when we sign it? I mean, normally I'd trust you, but..."

"But what? Do you think I'm going to—" A knock at the patio door channeled her annoyance to the person interrupting her interrogation. "For fuck's sake, what now?"

"Here." He slid her laptop in front of her. "Why don't you fill in your information while I answer the door?"

She grunted instead of bothering with a yes or no since he'd already stood.

"And you need to work on using the F-word less. The girls hear enough cursing at school and on TV, and I've been trying to watch my language around them."

"Oh, you mean fuck?" The expletive eased some of the anxiety of typing her social security number into the corresponding box. She clicked on the next empty space and added her deceased father's full name, which brought her another step closer to completing the form. "Fuck. Fuck. Fuck."

"Yeah, that's the one." He waved the visitor inside, but his body and the door blocked the person's identity. "Come on in. I appreciate your coming over on such short notice."

"Yeah, well, I don't like owing anybody a favor."

She tried and failed to place the man's testy voice without looking up from the final blank applicant box.

Deke cleared his throat and a chair scraped across the tile floor. "Riley, do you know Oscar Banyan? He's agreed to notarize our signatures and perform the ceremony this evening, so I thought you might want to meet with him ahead of time."

Done with her part of the horrid application, she sent the document to her printer before she could change her mind and pilfered a gulp of coffee from her CPA's dented travel mug. The flavor barely compensated for the painful burn all the way to her stomach. "What a fitting way to lose my singlehood. Married by The Grouch. Fuck! Did you say *this evening*?"

CHAPTER 8

WITH ALL HIS BODY PARTS SURPRISINGLY STILL IN WORKING ORDER, Deke slid into the driver's seat and buckled his seatbelt. Two more clicks followed, but he waited until he exited the school parking lot to make his announcement. "We need to have a family meeting as soon as we get home."

Fiona met his gaze in the rearview mirror, her chin up and eyes narrowed. "You're sending us to live with Grandma and Grandpa, aren't you?"

"No." He gripped the steering wheel tighter to keep any further comments locked inside his head. Allowing her to bait him would only give her more room to dig her heels in.

"Then what do we need a family meeting for?"

Amanda's audible sigh from the passenger seat harmonized with his internal one. "We'll be home in five minutes, Fee."

"I don't care. I want to know now."

"So do I, but you don't see me having a temper tantrum."

A storm erupted in the mirror as he glanced at the reflection of the road behind him. "I'm not having a temper tantrum, Miss Perfect!"

Not in the mood to referee a shouting match, he tapped the Power button for the stereo and turned up the volume until Nirvana drowned out their voices. When his older daughter reached for the volume control, he slapped his hand over it, plunging the car into deafening silence. "Not another word. You both have two minutes to take your stuff to your rooms and grab a snack when we get home. Then I expect you to sit down on the couch and listen to me. When I'm done talking, we'll have a civilized conversation like civilized people."

Amanda stared at him from the passenger seat. "I didn't—"

Curt Cobain once again shouted over his daughters' attempt to test his patience, and Deke cast a warning frown at his older daughter. Busted eardrums couldn't be any worse than Manda's and Fee's arguments and accusations. In fact, the head-banging music gave him an excuse to sing along at the top of his lungs, releasing some of the tension in his neck and shoulders.

Turning in to their neighborhood, onto their street, and then into their driveway took his stress level down a few more notches, but he left the volume up until he shut off the engine and the garage door closed behind them.

Fiona bailed out of the car first and hurried to the kitchen door, tapping the toe of her boot on the concrete in her usual show of impatience as he juggled his computer bag, the contents of the cup holder, and his keys. "Manda sings lots better than you do."

Her sister snorted. "She's right, Dad. You sound like a sick moose."

Handing off his keys to Amanda, he shrugged. "So what? I enjoyed myself, and that's what matters. Living room. Two minutes."

His younger daughter crowded past Manda as soon as she unlocked the door and twisted the knob. Thunderous footsteps and giggles carried to the kitchen while he threw away his trash and set his laptop and mug on the counter, reinforcing his notion that he would never understand how his daughters could fight with each other one minute and conspire together the next. At least the sniping had stopped.

He slipped his hand into his sport coat to be sure Riley hadn't somehow picked his pocket for the license when he'd kissed her goodbye in the courthouse parking lot. The whole thing still seemed surreal—making love with her, arranging their marriage, not having to hide his attraction anymore. He wouldn't, however, count on being married to her until she said her vows and they were officially husband and wife.

"Dad, we're ready!" The synchronous yell came a minute and a half sooner than it should have, stirring up his nervous stomach.

"Coming." He took a fortifying breath and forced his legs into motion. If he'd learned anything during a decade of single parenting, it was that delaying usually made the situation worse and a strong show of confidence kept the pushback to a minimum. *And never, ever fall for the tears trick.*

The girls sat side by side in the middle of the couch, presenting the most united front he'd seen in years. Fiona opened her mouth like she might have something to say and then glanced toward Amanda before shutting it again.

Not trusting her cooperation to hold, he dragged the armchair closer and sat. "I have some pretty big news and it affects you almost as much as it does me. So, anyway… Okay. Do you remember the conversation we had last night about me dating?"

His older daughter cocked her head to the side and raised her eyebrows. "You said we weren't allowed to say anything until you were done talking."

"You're right. I did. Yeah, so…me and dating…but not." *Just say it.* He rubbed his sweaty palms on his khakis and bit the bullet. "Riley. Miss Fenniman, the blonde woman you mentioned, and I are, um, getting married."

Fee popped up from her seat, her eyes wide and her mouth open far enough for a bug to fly in with lots of room to spare. "When?"

Amanda's eyebrows dove downward, the stern look pinning him in place. "Is she pregnant?"

He choked halfway through a swallow. "What? No, of course not!"

"When, Daddy?" Fee didn't seem to notice her slipup, one she hadn't made since she was seven—when she'd started asking why she didn't have a mother and why Trisha had left. Those conversations had led to the beginning of walls and mistrust and so much anger.

"Tonight." Resting his forearms on his thighs, he focused on the overlapping layers of Fee's makeshift cast. "It's sort of like a business deal, not that we don't like each other too. We do. I've liked her since she became a client. I know it's out of the blue, and I wish you had more time to get used to the idea, but we're having supper at her house. And then the ceremony." *If she actually goes through with it.*

"Can I call her Mom?"

The question pierced his heart, even though he should've expected it. "You'll need to ask Riley about that."

"Okay." With a contented smile, Fiona sat back down.

Amanda frowned and wrapped her hand around Fee's, clearly in protective big-sister mode. "What's the plan? Are we supposed to dress up for the wedding? Is she moving in with us? Does she like you as much as you like her?"

"I'd like for you to dress up—you know, to make a good impression—and it *is* a wedding. Mr. Banyan will be marrying us, but we don't really have time for all the fancy stuff, not that Riley seems to care about that." Hell, she'd probably stomp on the bouquet he'd picked up for her on his way home from the courthouse.

"You should buy her flowers, even if she doesn't want a big wedding."

"Already done."

Her frown softened a little. "Good. Where are we going to live?"

Not surprised by Amanda's practicality, he sifted through the conversation he'd had with Riley during their brief wait for the license. "We're moving to her house over the next week, so you'll need to pack enough clothes to last the weekend. She needs to be close to the farm to take care of her business and she has a bigger house than we do. You each get your own bedroom and you'll share a bathroom."

Fiona's smile drooped, even though she constantly complained about how girlie her sister's half of their room was decorated.

"And does she love you? Or at least like you a lot? As much as you like her?" Amanda scooted forward, as if his answers dictated her acceptance or rejection.

They were also the most complicated of her questions.

He pushed out of the chair and paced to the window to gather his thoughts. Then he crossed to the couch and crouched in front of his girls. "We've been friends for a while and we trust each other. I think that's a good start, considering we agreed to do this to protect her farm."

"Does she know you like her as more than a friend? Like a girl-friend? Did you tell her?"

Looking from Manda to Fee and back again, he covered their clasped hands with his. "Not yet, but I will once we get settled. In the meantime, I'd appreciate if you didn't say anything to her about it. She isn't exactly thrilled about acquiring a husband."

Both girls slouched backward into the cushions, but only Fee spoke. "What about us? Does she hate kids too?"

"She doesn't hate kids. Actually, she said she wouldn't mind talking to you about girl stuff." He tucked an escapee from her ponytail behind her ear and injected as much confidence as he could muster into a grin. "You have no idea how happy she was to hear you're potty trained and can cook."

A snicker from Amanda suggested her biggest concerns had been addressed.

"So you're not having any babies?" His younger daughter's expression gave no hint about her feelings on the subject.

"No babies." He held his breath, waiting for her reaction.

"Good. You're too old." A hint of a smile ruined her delivery.

He pulled her into a one-armed hug and reached for her sister with his other arm. "If I'm old, it's because of you two, but I love you right down to my gray hairs anyway. Now go pack your suitcase, and remember a toothbrush and pajamas."

"Love you too, Dad." After a quick squeeze, Amanda sprang up from her seat and hurried toward the hall. "Gotta pack and do my homework."

Fiona held on longer than he expected and took over the space her sister vacated. "This was the best surprise. I've waited forever for a mom. I promise to be good so she likes me."

"Just be yourself, Fee, and she'll like you fine." He closed his eyes to savor the few moments she'd let him into her wounded little-girl heart. "I'm glad I could make you happy."

"I hope marrying Riley makes you happy too." The typical contentious tone had completely disappeared from her voice.

A lump formed in his throat and he buried his face in her hair, wishing he could've taken a chance on the woman he'd fallen for sooner—as much for his daughter's sake as his. "You bet it does, kiddo."

"Do you love her?"

He nodded. "Yeah, and it's kind of scary."

"Some things are, at least a little bit."

"But loving somebody mostly feels good."

She kissed his cheek and wiggled free. "Is it okay if I bring my ant farm?"

જ

"WE BROUGHT PIZZA!" FIONA ROLLED HER OVERNIGHT BAG THROUGH the open patio door and stopped in front of Riley. "I'm Fiona, but you can call me Fee if you want to. Dad and Manda do, except when they're mad at me for getting into trouble. Then I get the full-name treatment. *Fiona Louise Jeffries!* Can I call you Mom?"

No beating around the bush, huh? Not that he should've expected any less from the girl who clearly needed a mother in her life, Deke shrugged when his bride-to-be glanced sideways at him.

Her expression hinted at horror, amusement, and an urge to strangle him, but knowing what she wore under her red skirt and flowered top jumped to the forefront of his thoughts.

A smirk said she knew exactly where his mind had gone. "I need to think about it, Fee. What happened to your arm?"

His younger daughter raised her mummy club and grinned. "I punched a boy at school for teasing me. I got two broken fingers and detention, but it was worth it. He's a bully."

"The doctor wrapped your whole forearm for broken fingers? Seems like overkill to me, not to mention it lets the bully think he hurt you worse than he did. I would've asked for a finger splint or to have my fingers taped together to show him how tough I am, but that's me."

Damn, she's good.

Riley waved Amanda into the kitchen and gave her a Mary Poppins inspection. "You must be Manda. Short for Amanda?"

His older daughter maneuvered her suitcase inside. "Yes, Ms. Fenniman. You can call me either one. I don't get in trouble."

"Good to know. You can call me Riley for now. I'm not sure how I feel about Mom yet." Her heels clicked on the floor as she walked toward the living room. "Follow me, girls. I'll show you to your bedrooms while your father brings in his luggage. Pizza can go on the table and you can put your stuff in my room, Deacon."

He followed her progress until she disappeared around the corner, fantasizing about her sexy shoes on her sexy feet at the end of her sexy legs while he explored new positions on their wedding night. She would be his wife and he would be her husband. His patience had finally paid off.

Female voices carried from somewhere off the living room as he hauled the garment bag with his suit and the bag with the rest of his weekend necessities upstairs. Most of the noise was laughter—Fee's and Riley's from the sound of it. Hopefully, that meant they'd hit it off like the two peas in a pod they were and his bride planned to go through with the wedding, come hell or high water.

He stowed his belongings and the surprise bouquet in the master bedroom, keeping alert for any sudden outbursts and doing his best not to get distracted by memories of that morning's test drive. Even knowing the location of her underwear drawer tempted him to linger, but he left her boudoir without peeking at the lacy bits that left almost nothing to his imagination.

When he returned to the kitchen, the trio had already placed dishes, silverware, and napkins next to the takeout boxes and stood at the counter with a row of glasses, not a scowl or grimace among them. Manda seemed a little detached, but she'd always been slower to warm up to new people than her quick-to-judge sister.

So far, so good.

"Deke, how about making yourself useful and grabbing the salad from the fridge? Dressing too." Riley handed him a nearly empty milk jug as he walked toward the refrigerator. "And put this away please. You'll need to go to the store tomorrow. Remind me to text you a list in the morning."

"I can bring over—" The vast abyss where she should've stored leftovers, condiments, and jars of every flavor of pickles on the planet held only a bowl of salad, a safety-sealed jar of raspberry vinaigrette, and less than half a bottle of white wine. "You don't have any staples in the house? Like eggs and flour and butter?"

"I'm a farmer and a businesswoman, not a chef. I don't cook. If I want food, I go to the packing barn for damaged produce or I eat out. If *you* want food, cook something or use your phone and order it." The fists she perched on her hips dared him to challenge her suggestions. "And I have staples. There's cereal in the pantry and milk in the fridge. Well, not much anymore, but I have coffee and tea. Wine. During the off-season, I grow fruits and vegetables in the greenhouse. Most are for my customers, but I grow enough for me to make a salad for lunch or supper. Produce is better for you when it's raw. More nutrients. More fiber."

"Fiber helps you poop." Fee picked up two full glasses and shuffled toward the table. Despite her best efforts, milk sloshed over the rim and dripped on the floor. "I learned that today in health class."

So much for first impressions.

"That it does." Riley tore a paper towel from the roll on the counter and wiped the bottom of the glass and then the puddle. "Looks like the cleaning service will be earning their pay this month. Maybe we should pour drinks at the table next time."

"You have a cleaning service? Like somebody who cleans the toilets and mops the floors?"

"Of course. Otherwise, my house would be a disaster area."

"Dad, you should've asked Mom to marry you a long time ago." Fee's quick peek in Riley's direction wasn't nearly as stealthy as she probably thought it was.

A howl of laughter came from his almost-wife. "For your information, I asked him, Fiona Louise Jeffries, and you evidently inherited his affinity for pushing people's buttons, even your stepmother's."

Fee rested her injured hand—minus the Ace bandage—on the back of her chair and donned a triumphant grin. "Ha! You gave me the full-name treatment. That definitely means I get to call you Mom."

CHAPTER 9

Using the cheval mirror for guidance, Riley adjusted her black corset top high enough to cover the edges of her strapless bra and low enough to show a bit of cleavage. If she had to go through with the damn ceremony, she deserved a man who was prepared for his husbandly duties on their wedding night.

"Mom, I need help with this stupid zipper." Fiona's reflection stomped closer until it stood beside Riley's. "I wanted to wear pants, but Manda said I should wear a dress. I hate dresses."

"Turn." Grasping the girl's hand, Riley twirled her a full rotation and a quarter. Then she eased the zipper up her spine. "There you go."

"Thanks." Fee sprinted to the bed and jumped onto the mattress. The flared skirt of her sundress poofed out like a parachute and the bed scooted an inch or more across the floor, probably in the same groove Riley had made as an equally rebellious child. "Aren't you going to tell me why I should like dresses?"

"No, but how about not destroying my bed? Your father and I need to be able to sleep in it tonight." Satisfied with her mourning clothes, Riley slid her feet into the tapestry pumps that complemented Deke's black, silver, and blue ensemble.

"You mean have sex, don't you? That's what people do when they get married." The girl's smirk said she expected an appropriately shocked or embarrassed reaction.

You're dealing with an expert, kid. "Yes, of course we'll have sex, but not the whole night. I need a minimum of six hours of sleep to function the next day, especially since I stopped drinking full-strength coffee." Taking one last glance in the mirror, Riley pivoted toward her audience. "What do you think? Will your dad have trouble keeping his hands off me?"

"Eww. You aren't supposed to say stuff like that." Fee added some realistic gagging sound effects.

"All I did was answer your question. Don't ask what you don't want to know." As ready as she would ever be, Riley shooed her mini self toward the bathroom. "Let's see if your sister's dressed yet."

After three raps on the door, Fiona cupped her hands around her mouth. "Manda, are you done?"

"No." A sniffle suggested the older girl had been crying. "My stomach hurts and I want to go to bed. Tell Dad I'm too sick for the wedding."

Riley almost returned to the dresser for the key she kept in her underwear drawer, but something in Amanda's voice suggested her illness wasn't exactly a fake stomach bug or food poisoning. While the girl hadn't welcomed her into their family the way her younger sister had, Manda hadn't been hostile. "Can I come in? I need to see if you have a fever."

"I don't."

But you have cramps, don't you? "Fee, go on downstairs and find your sandals. I'll be down in a few minutes."

The girl hesitated, like she might argue, and then she headed toward the hall. "Okay, Mom."

Waiting until footsteps sounded on the steps, Riley braced for a serious stepmother-stepdaughter talk with Deke's teenager. "Amanda? I sent Fiona downstairs so we can have a private chat."

The knob turned and the door cracked open several inches. "I'm okay with my dad marrying you. Really, I am. I just feel awful."

"I think I know why." A peek inside revealed a hunched form on the floor. "Period, huh? Oh, and I appreciate you not being a pain in the ass about us getting married. I mean butt."

Manda raised her head from her knees, but her hair hid part of her pink-cheeked face. "How did you know?"

Riley stepped into the bathroom and closed the door behind her. "I'm a woman. I might be nearing the other end of having them, thank God, but I still remember the beginning. First time? Second?"

"First, and I didn't bring any of the stuff Grandma bought for me. It wasn't supposed to happen like this." Another sniffle preceded a swipe at the damp trail to the poor victim's jaw.

God, do I have perfect timing or what? Spotting the empty tissue box on the vanity, Riley retrieved a new one from the cupboard. "Dry your eyes and we'll take care of your annoying venture into womanhood."

The girl straightened, looking a little less worse for wear after wiping her face and blowing her nose.

"Okay." Riley tapped the cabinet drawer closest to the toilet. "I have an assortment of tampons, pads, and panty liners in every bathroom in the house. The last two are peel-and-stick to your underwear. Pads are simplest, but they can be bulky under some clothes. Panty liners are for light flow and backup for tampons on heavier days. Tampons are usually more comfortable once you're used to them, but they require some basic knowledge. You don't want to stick them in the wrong hole and they need changed fairly often. Do you know where your vagina is?"

Amanda's color deepened and she glanced toward her lap. "Mm-hm."

"Before you go getting all embarrassed, there's nothing wrong with knowing your body. Touching it and learning about it is a good thing, especially when you're ready to have sex. That discussion can wait until another day, but you need to be aware that you can get pregnant now that you're having periods. Do you need instructions for using tampons? They're pictures on the paper in the box and I can answer basic questions if you need help."

"Um, I think I can figure it out." Her soon-to-be stepdaughter blew her nose again and tossed the used tissue in the trash.

"Oh, and no flushing feminine hygiene products. They'll clog up my septic system, so wrap them up in toilet paper and throw them in the trash." Happy with her matter-of-fact lesson, Riley patted her student on the shoulder. "I'll be right outside if you need anything. Wash your face and put on your dress when you're finished. Then we'll find a pain reliever for the cramps."

"Riley?" Manda looked up, her frown now gone.

Itching to escape the reminder of her own horrible pubescence, Riley grasped the doorknob. "Yeah?"

"Thanks." The girl pushed to her feet and set the tissue box in its spot on the counter. "I'll try to hurry."

Being a stepmother isn't so hard. "Okay. And you can call me Mom if you want to since Fee didn't exactly give me a choice."

Seven minutes later, Deke's older daughter emerged from the bathroom. She'd pulled her hair back from her slightly flushed face and the cute babydoll dress was the perfect style for hiding even the worst case of menstrual bloating. Her ballet flats matched the tiny lavender flowers on the field of sage green, even though heels would've been Riley's first choice. Of course, the girl stood at least two inches taller in her bare feet.

Amanda brushed her palms down the skirt and glanced downward. "Do I look okay?"

"Gorgeous."

"You're not just saying that to make me feel better?"

"I never say things I don't mean." Riley hooked her arm through Manda's. "Let's go see if your sister found her shoes."

"I know she packed them. I watched to make sure." At the top of the steps, the girl paused. "Thanks for…everything. Mom. It would've been awful without anybody to help me. Dad tries, but he doesn't understand girl stuff."

"Most men don't. Come on. Let's get this wedding over with so we can have cake."

HOW IS SHE GOING TO KILL ME?

As Deke turned toward the patio doors, Big Jim gave him a thumbs-up and Tate offered a wide smile from their place to his right. He cradled the bouquet of black roses in his left arm and quadruple-checked his suit-coat pocket for the rings he'd bought from the window of his ten-o'clock appointment's shop. Then he nodded at the former corporate attorney turned small-town mayor turned wildlife preservationist slash notary public slash wedding officiant to hit the Play button on his phone.

Electric guitars and Billy Idol's voice welcomed his daughters and his bride through the open doorway. Riley's gaze locked on his before her laughter harmonized with the first verse of "White Wedding."

God, she's so damn beautiful.

Her eyes widened, evidently noticing the only two wedding guests at his side. Although she shook her head at him, she greeted Tate with a hug. Her lips moved, but the chorus drowned out their quick exchange. Another hug followed before Riley stood beside him and took the bouquet he offered.

Oscar tapped the screen again, plunging the venue back into relative silence. "We are gathered here this evening to witness the joining of Deacon and Riley in marriage. We're also gathered here to witness the joining of Jim and Tate in marriage. You, Deacon and Riley, and you, Jim and Tate, have chosen to commit yourselves to one another in matrimony. If you've changed your mind, now is the time to speak up."

Deke dared a glance at his bride with his heart in his throat. *Please go through with it.*

She licked her lips and gripped the flowers tight enough to turn her knuckles white, but no renunciation exited her mouth.

After an eternal count to fifteen, Oscar thumbed his phone screen in rapid succession, his scowl screaming he would rather be doing anything besides officiating a wedding. "This is my first double ceremony, so bear with me as I work through each set of vows. Listen for your name, because I don't have time to repeat everything. I have a sick buzzard to take care of. Deacon Jeffries, do you take Riley Fenniman to be your lawfully wedded wife, to honor and cherish her, and be faithful to her as long as you both shall live?"

Deke willed his racing heart to return to normal. "I do."

"Riley Fenniman, do you take Deacon Jeffries to be your lawfully wedded husband, to honor and cherish him, and be faithful to him as long as you both shall live?"

A slow inhale and exhale became two and then three. She smashed the bouquet into her other hand.

Oscar's frown deepened. "Either you do or you don't."

"F—" She cleared her throat. "Fine. I do."

Almost there.

Oscar repeated the rapid-fire question for Big Jim and Tate, with no faltering "I do" from either of them. "Rings symbolize the eternal circle of life and love. Deacon and Riley, will you be exchanging rings?"

With a noisy sigh, Riley shook her head. "No. Can we please get to the end already?"

Deke dug for the rings in his pocket and handed her the larger one. "Yes, we will."

"You didn't think to tell me?" Her low voice carried as much irritation as if she'd shouted at him.

"I wanted it to be a surprise."

"Well, you succeeded there." Her all-too-familiar glare couldn't hide the anxiety lurking in her eyes. "I don't like surprises."

Tate wrapped her arm around Riley's shoulders and hissed something in her ear.

"Oh my God, fine. We'll do the ring thing." Riley grabbed his left hand and licked the plain gold band before sliding it onto his third finger. "With this ring, I have the right to nag you."

"You already do, blondie." Surrendering to a laugh, he lifted her hand, positioned the diamond-and-emerald estate piece at her knuckle, and gently wiggled it until it slipped into place. "With this ring, I have the right to kiss you until you quit nagging."

She glanced toward a giggle and a snort behind them—his daughters, no doubt—and back toward Oscar. "Are we married yet?"

"No. Now shut up so Jim and Tate can *do the ring thing.*" Their grumpier-by-the-second ordained neighbor turned toward the other couple. "Exchange your rings and say whatever vows you wrote. And they better be short. I need to feed my critters."

Jim nodded and slid the band onto his fiancée's finger. "With this ring, I give you my heart and promise to love you my whole life, no matter what the future brings. You are my world, for always."

With a smile that sparked a twinge of envy, Tate brushed a tear from her cheek and then bound herself to her true love with a matching band. "With this ring, I ask you to be my husband, to accept all the love I have for you, and to share my life. Being with you makes me happier than I ever dreamed I could be and I hope I always do the same for you."

Oscar referred to his phone again before stuffing it in his jeans pocket. "By the power vested in me by the Ministry of Ordained Officiants and the State of Ohio, Deacon and Riley, I pronounce you husband and wife. Kiss if you want to. Or not. You're married and it isn't my problem. The same goes for you, Jim and Tate, but I think you stand a better chance of not getting divorced. I'll file the signed licenses when I go to the county seat next week."

Hooking his arm around his contrary wife's waist, Deke planted a kiss on her lips before she could protest the public display of affection. "Back in a minute, honey-sweetheart-darling. Hang on, Oscar. I'll walk you to your truck."

A grunt served for an acknowledgment as his very first accounting client in town lumbered toward the driveway. "The next time I ask you to do me a favor, tell me to go to hell. I'm sick of weddings and I can't wait until my license expires in December so people will stop begging me to officiate."

"Yeah, well, this was sort of an emergency. Otherwise, I wouldn't have asked. I really appreciate the last-minute exception and I'm calling us even. Here's fifty bucks for your trouble."

Oscar cast a steely glower over his shoulder as he climbed behind the wheel. "You know damn well I don't need it. Keep your money for the divorce lawyer."

"That's a really shitty thing to say, especially considering you know how I feel about Riley."

The Grouch slammed the rusty door shut and leaned his elbow on the ragged seal at the bottom of the stuck-open window. "Just calling it like I see it. She married you for the wrong reasons and you married her for the right ones without telling her. You're doomed."

The observation stabbed a dull needle in Deke's high hopes.

CHAPTER 10

Fiona switched off the nightstand lamp and burrowed into her blankets. "Goodnight, Mom. Goodnight, Dad."

Never look a gift horse in the mouth. Deke followed his wife out of the bedroom, closing the door behind him. "She never goes to bed that easily."

Riley's smirk warned him she knew exactly why. "It might have something to do with the conversation we had while we were getting dressed for the I-do-you-do ring swap."

"Oh? What kind of conversation?" He stopped outside his older daughter's room, fairly certain no discussion involving Fee and Riley could be fit for public consumption.

"She jumped on my bed a little harder than necessary, so I asked her not to break it since you and I have to sleep there. She tried to shock me by saying we were probably going to have sex, not sleep." Riley raised her fist to the door.

He grasped her wrist before she could knock. "And?"

"And what? I told her the truth—that, yes, we're going to have sex. She thought it was gross. Next time, she won't ask personal questions just to get a reaction."

Fighting laughter, he shook his head. "Is there anything else I should know?"

Her dipping eyebrows and scrunched nose were a sure sign something else had happened. "Sort of. Probably. Manda got her period for the first time today, but don't you dare say anything about it unless she brings it up. She had cramps and she was worried because she didn't pack any pads or tampons."

"Geesh, they really threw you in the deep end, didn't they?"

She shrugged and knocked on Amanda's door. "We talked. I told her where to find supplies and to ask if she needed help. This parenting thing isn't as hard as you made it sound."

"It can and will get worse. A lot worse." At his daughter's call to come in, he gestured for Riley to enter. "You just wait."

"I'll believe it when I see it." She turned the knob, sashayed into the room, and plopped on the edge of the bed. "All settled in?"

Amanda didn't fling her arms around Riley the way Fee had, but her smile was wider than he'd seen it in a long time. "Yep. I love having my own room. Thanks for everything."

"You bet." Riley initiated a hug, the spontaneous kind she shared with Tate whenever the mood struck her. Then she popped up and walked toward the hall.

Regret that he hadn't recognized how much his girls needed a feminine influence fought with the new surge of love for his wife. Deke kissed his daughter's forehead and focused on not letting his voice crack. "Good night, Manda."

"Good night, Dad. Good night, Mom."

Riley paused at the doorway. "See you in the morning. Hurry up, Deacon. It's time for bed. I need to be out at the packing barn by six to sign off on Saturday's delivery paperwork, and the pumpkin patch opens tomorrow."

"Right behind you." His eyes strayed to her swaying hips as he shadowed her to the living room. "Do we have time for a quick toast? Seems like we could use all the good luck we can find."

She continued into the kitchen without slowing. "I don't know what The Grouch's problem is, but he's wrong. I have every incentive in the world to stay married, even if I'd rather strangle you sometimes."

"Oscar's a little antisocial and a lot cynical about marriage. After the way his ex and her lawyer made a public spectacle of their divorce, who can blame him?"

"Still, he could've just kept his opinion to himself."

"You mean like you do?" He dared a chuckle.

"I keep lots of comments to myself."

"But plenty of them you don't."

"Maybe, but I've never told a couple they were doomed to divorce in the middle of their wedding."

"I have no chance of winning this discussion, do I?"

"Nope. Grab the wine bottle from the fridge while I get the glasses." Her above-the-knee skirt inched up her thighs when she stretched toward the middle shelf of the cupboard.

He traced the curve of her hip with his fingertips on a much-needed detour before retrieving a surprise from the refrigerator. "Jim and Tate brought over a mini bottle of Moët as a thank-you for making the wedding arrangements."

"Nice. Let's take it upstairs since we can finish off a split in about three swallows each and get to the really good stuff sooner." A pair of champagne flutes dangling from her left hand, she crooked a finger at him. "I want to take advantage of the limited benefits of being married."

"You're planning to let me sleep some tonight, aren't you? Gotta stock the kitchen and start moving stuff from my house to yours tomorrow. Oh, and be sure to add batteries to the grocery list." Well-chilled bottle in hand, he trailed after her up the stairs. "Quarterly taxes are due by the end of the month. I emailed you the forms this afternoon."

Her throaty laugh as she flipped on the master bedroom light assured him she remembered every detail of their conversation prior to the spectacular test drive. "You're a lot less boring than I expected."

Although the move skated as close as he dared to a romantic gesture, he scooped her into his arms and carried her over the threshold. A carefully aimed kick sent the door thunking closed as he approached the bed. Then he lowered her to her sexy heels-clad feet, holding her snug enough to enjoy the slow glide of her body down his. "I'm full of surprises."

"I'm beginning to see that." Her free hand closed over his butt cheek and a devious smile curved her lips. "Why don't you open the champagne while I lock the door? I wouldn't want to traumatize the girls if they come looking for you."

"Planning to have your wicked way with me?"

"Damn right I am." She ground her hips into his and nipped his earlobe, an unexpected but not unpleasant combination of sensations. "And it better be mutual."

"It is. Go lock the door." He switched on the bedside lamp and set to work on the foil seal. "And turn off the light. Neither of us is going to be able to move when we're done being wicked."

"You better keep that promise." The ceiling light went out, leaving his sexy wife bathed in lamplight and shadows. "Do you know how to open it without hurting yourself?"

"Yep." With his thumb against the cork, he loosened the wire cage. "I watched a YouTube video on my phone while I was waiting for you and the girls to come downstairs for the ceremony. Turn the bottle, not the cork, and voilà! No injuries or waterfalls and plenty of bubbles. Sort of like a vasectomy—all the fun without any accidents."

Her laughter filled the room, reminding him again why he'd fallen for this truly genuine woman. "Pour the champagne so we can take off our clothes. I'm ready for some safe fun."

He divided the contents between the pair of flutes, adding a little to each one until he emptied the bottle. Holding out a serving of bubbly to Riley, he lifted his own glass in preparation for a toast. "Ladies first."

She closed the space between them and grasped the champagne with her left hand and his tie with her right. "To compatibility, because life's too short to go without great sex."

"Amen to that." After a fizzy swallow of barely tasting the stuff, he touched his glass to hers. *To us.* "To happy endings. May our orgasms be mutual and many."

"Mutual and many." She drained her flute and set it and his on the nightstand. "I want you naked."

Glad to grant her wish, he kicked off his black loafers as he unbuckled his belt. "Leave on your shoes. And your bra and under—"

Urgent knocking froze him midway through unzipping.

"Daddy? My stomach feels yucky." Retching, followed by the distinctive sound of vomit splattering on the floor, deflated his half-hard dick faster than a bucket of ice water.

RILEY REACHED FOR THE INSISTENT ALARM, HER HAND CONNECTING with something smooth and rounded. She pried an eye open and caught the scant outline of an empty bottle in time to steady it in the early morning darkness. The momentary glint in a narrow strip of security light rays through the blinds jerked her attention to the ring on her finger.

Wedding ring.

She stretched her leg toward the other side of the bed and strained to hear breathing, snoring, or any kind of sleep noises beside her. Even after she managed to find the Off button on the clock, utter silence and cold sheets assured her she was alone.

Deacon—her husband—had never come back to bed last night and their wedding night had been a bust. As much as she wanted to rage at him for reneging on the promise of exceptional sex, she couldn't begrudge him needing to care for Fiona. He was a devoted father and one of the more decent human beings she'd ever known. He might tease her until she wanted to lose him in her corn maze, but his unconditional love for his daughters made up for his faults. He'd been mother and father to them for a decade, doing the best he could to be a good parent through it all.

She rolled out of bed and hurried through her Saturday morning routine, anxious to check on him and her stepdaughter, even though the feeling somewhat disconcerted her. Concern didn't necessarily equal the kind of affection often associated with marriage and kids, and what was wrong with liking her husband? Besides taking care of his daughter, he'd removed all evidence of the vomiting mishap in the hall.

Dressed in her weekend farm-work clothes, she detoured to the bedroom Fee had chosen instead of heading straight to the kitchen for a bowl of dry cereal and no coffee. The door stood partly open, allowing light inside from the hallway and giving her a clear view into the room. The man slumped against the headboard cradled his little girl against his chest with a large bowl at the ready near his elbow. His hair needed a comb and the white dress shirt with its sleeves rolled up past his elbows could use an iron. His heart, on the other hand, was perfect.

I wish...

No getting too attached.

The urge to straighten the blanket around his shoulders and kiss her sleeping husband chased her to the kitchen. She wasn't a sentimental fool or a woman with any inborn tendency to nurture. The very real possibility of cancer had turned her into an emotional wreck, nothing more.

She plunked a cereal bowl on the counter and dumped in a helping of cranberry-almond granola. Her charging phone vibrated and lit up an arm's length away, providing a distraction from the depressing thought.

Georgie's name flashed on the screen. *"You didn't tell me what happened yesterday. How did the discussion with D.J. go? Any luck finding a suitable candidate(s)?"*

Riley crunched on a clump of oats, nuts, and dried fruit while she tapped in a response, deleted it, and started over again. Her friend probably wouldn't be amused by her criteria for suitable. *"He offered to sacrifice himself and arranged for the ex-mayor to officiate. It's done."*

"That was fast. Good. He agreed to all our terms? We need to update your wills ASAP. He has kids, doesn't he? Did you talk about you becoming a legal guardian? Is he divorced? Widowed? We need to file paperwork for you to adopt if their mother is out of the picture. Do you have time to meet later this morning? Lots to discuss. 10:15 at your house?"

Did her attorney eat, sleep, and breathe family law every minute of every day?

Referring back to the message, Riley kept her answers to Georgina's rapid-fire interrogation brief and in order. *"Yes. Okay. Yes. No. Yes. No. No mom. I think so. Okay."*

Less than five seconds passed before another text popped up in the thread. *"Tell D he needs to be there too. See you then."*

"Tell him yourself. I'm not his damn secretary." Riley added the ten-fifteen appointment to her calendar and popped another piece of granola in her mouth.

"What's the matter? Besides the fact that you had to get married. Was the wedding night sex that bad?"

"What wedding night sex? His younger daughter threw up outside my bedroom door while we were undressing. He never came to bed. At least not mine. Call or text him."

Fuck it. I deserve coffee. Riley stalked to the coffeemaker and groaned when she found yesterday's grounds in the filter basket. "Ugh."

"Let me make the coffee." Deke's husky offer shimmied along her spine before he padded across the kitchen and nuzzled her neck. "It's the least I can do after last night. I'm so sorry."

She closed her eyes, wallowing in the instantaneous rush of desire his lips triggered. "It's not your fault. Is Fee feeling better?"

"Yeah. She told me she snuck a third piece of pound cake while we were saying goodbye to Jim and Tate. I don't think she'll do that again. She hates puking." His hands closed over her bare shoulders and he kissed the sensitive spot behind her ear. "Do we have time for a quickie while the coffee's brewing?"

A glance at the microwave clock gave her something to smile about. She grabbed his hand and dragged him toward the laundry room. "Forget coffee. I'd rather have ten minutes of sex."

His familiar low chuckle made her nipples pucker instead of scraping across her last nerve like it usually did. "Good to know I rank higher than caffeine."

She stopped next to the dryer and shoved her capris down her legs. "Only if you're ready to go right now."

He grinned and lowered the zipper of his rumpled suit pants. His erection pressed against his underwear, trying to escape. "What do you think?"

"Daddy, where are you? I'm hungry." The words were somewhat muffled, suggesting Riley and Deke had a few seconds to regroup.

Dropping his forehead to hers, he whimpered. "Son of a Fudgesicle. Not again. My dick's going to fall off if I don't get inside you soon."

She snorted and yanked her pants back up. "Probably not, but this better not be the story of our marriage."

"In the laundry room, Fee. I'm checking to see if the towels I washed last night are dry." With a grimace that spoke of pain, he rezipped. "Not if I can help it, wife. We're going on a date tonight, even if it's just parking somewhere so we can have sex in the backseat."

CHAPTER 11

RILEY SAT AT THE CORNER TABLE WITH HER BACK TO THE WALL, IN case the conversation got too private for prying ears. Under normal circumstances, she wouldn't have given a damn if someone overheard she'd gotten laid. A public announcement about her marriage was a whole other ball of wax. Everyone in the book club knew, but she'd used the excuse of helping Deke and the girls settle in at her house to get out of Sunday evening's meeting and the inevitable questions. Truthfully, she'd enjoyed spending time with the family she couldn't risk getting too close to.

"Here you go." Tate set two glasses of iced herbal tea on the table and plopped into the chair across from her. "How's the arrangement going?"

A long sip cooled the simmering heat on Riley's chest and back. "Well, let's see. So far, Fiona threw up on our wedding night and Deacon slept in her bed instead of mine, we had to have sex in the woods to get any privacy on Saturday, and I got poison ivy in places you don't want a rash. That was fun explaining to the doctor yesterday afternoon. It definitely put a damper on the good part of being married. And wouldn't you know? He didn't get so much as one damn itchy spot. Me, I got a shot in the ass and a prescription.

The upside is his daughters aren't as much of a pain in the ass as I was expecting. Manda can cook and Fee always takes my side. He's a good father."

Tate's amusement seemed confined to a snicker. "Sounds like things are working out pretty well."

"Better than I expected." Riley fiddled with the ring on her left hand, spinning it round and round to keep from scratching her crotch and thinking about the unexpected feelings that had developed over the last few days. "But I'm not getting too comfortable. Life always finds a way of fucking you over, just for the hell of it."

Tate failed to hide a frown behind her glass. "We talked about Thursday's plan at book club Sunday night. Georgie's driving you to your appointment and staying with you in the waiting area. Wally's going to be there to pick you up when you're done. She'll stay with you until Petra takes lunch at one and I'll relieve her after I close the restaurant at two. Have you told Deacon?"

"No, and don't even start nagging me that I should. We did this thing to save the farm, whether it's for the short or long term. And with the girls adjusting and quarterly tax forms going out right now, he doesn't need the distraction." *They shouldn't have to worry too.*

"But—"

"What about you and Jim? You never told me what the test said." Riley took a long drink, hoping the redirection tactic worked.

Her friend's dreamy smile instantly gave away the results. "I decided to wait until after the wedding. Baby or not, we love each other and that's what matters. So we got up Saturday morning, I peed on the stick, and we waited the two minutes together. You should've seen him when the plus sign appeared. He kissed me and then he kissed my belly. And he kissed me again and made me breakfast in bed. We already started planning the nursery."

Leaning across the table, Riley wrapped Tate in a hug. "That's so disgustingly sweet. Congratulations!"

"Thanks. Without Georgie's and your devious intervention, I'd probably be crying on your shoulder right now." Tate wiped at her eyes as she eased back into her seat. "Looks like I am anyway. You—"

Riley's phone vibrated on the table and the caller ID demanded she not let the call go to voicemail. "Hang on a sec."

Her friend pushed up from her chair. "Do you want me to wait at the counter?"

Riley shook her head as she lifted her cell to her ear. "Hello. Riley Fenniman."

"Hi, Ms. Fenniman. This is Dr. Porter's nurse. She's had a cancellation at eleven thirty this morning and wanted me to check with you to see if you're available to come in for your biopsy today instead of Thursday."

The chance to know her fate two days sooner brought equal parts dread and relief. She sucked in a slow breath to fend off the woozy feeling making the walls spin and the floor wobble. "I... Um... That's in...like an an hour...and fifteen minutes? Okay. I'll be there."

DEACON DUMPED HIS COMPUTER BAG, TRAVEL MUG, AND THE LAST BOX from his old home office on the kitchen table while his daughters rushed past him with their backpacks and shopping bags. "Manda, remember to preheat the oven and, Fee, it's your turn to set the table."

"Yes, Dad!" The response came in unison a moment before they disappeared into the living room.

Although cooperation had ruled since Friday afternoon, he had no delusions that it would last.

After another trip to the car for their carryout supper and the bag containing a new pair of brown shoes and a surprise for his wife, he went in search of her. The master bedroom was empty and the bathroom door stood wide open, meaning Riley hadn't returned from the daily meeting with her farm managers or she'd barricaded herself in her office to catch up on Fenniman Organics' accounts receivable.

As he arrived at the bottom of the stairs, the crunch of gravel carried through the open window on the other side of the living room. Tate's car flashed in and out between the trees lining the driveway and his pulse kicked up a notch when he spotted her blonde passenger. A week ago, he never would've guessed he'd be sharing her bed, let alone married to the woman he loved. Someday he might even work up the courage to tell her.

The oven sang its done-preheating ditty and the patio door opened when he rounded the corner into the kitchen.

His wife smiled at his daughters, but it didn't quite reach her eyes. "Hi, girls. I have a crapload of paperwork to finish by Thursday. Would you mind bringing supper to me in my office when it's ready?"

Fee frowned, but Riley didn't seem to notice. "I'll put everything on a tray. I promise not to drop it."

"If you do, we'll clean it up. No biggie." Pressing her lips together, Riley walked toward him, looking like the task took far more oomph than she possessed. She hadn't complained much about her poison ivy rash itching, but it clearly had taken a toll on her ability to sleep.

He shoved his fists in his pockets to keep from pulling her into his arms and insisting she take a nap. "Hey, you okay?"

Her tight jaw loosened ever so slightly. "Just a little tired. I'll take a break to say goodnight to Manda and Fee."

Her slower than usual pace said she was more than a little tired, and concern settled in his chest like a bothersome case of heartburn. "Let me know if you need anything."

She didn't look back as she crossed to her office. "This week to be over with. I'm pretty sure you can't do anything about that."

THE STAIRS CREAKED, ALERTING DEKE SOMEBODY HAD COME UPSTAIRS —preferably Riley. He leaned out of the new home office he'd been setting up most of the evening in time to see her shuffle into their bedroom, her sexy shoes dangling from her fingers and her shoulders slumped. For the first time since he'd met her, she looked exhausted.

Instead of hooking up his new monitor and keyboard, he moved the empty boxes onto the pile in the corner and turned off the switch inside the doorway as he left the room. Lamplight cast a wedge of rays onto the wood floor, lighting his way to the woman he loved more every day. A backrub and a foot massage might put her to sleep, but he'd gladly give her a reason to feel half as much toward him.

A trail of clothes led to the bed, where she lay with her pillow half under her head and half under the sheet draped over her body. Her eyes were closed, but her stiff muscles promised she hadn't fallen asleep in the three or so minutes since he'd heard her come to bed.

He exchanged his clothes for the pajama pants he'd worn after the mishap in the woods and crawled under the covers. When he smoothed his palm over the muscles at the base of her neck, she tensed. "What's wrong?"

"Nothing." She tried to scoot away, but he levered up on one elbow and moved with her.

"Liar. There's definitely something wrong. Are you mad at me for something? The Riley I know doesn't hide her feelings to spare anybody else's. Now talk to me."

Her impatient sigh warned him she wasn't in the best of moods. "It's not you. I'm tired and I just want to sleep."

The words and the finality in her tone didn't fit the tension rolling off her body.

"Okay." Unwilling to risk a major argument so early in their marriage, he stretched around her to turn off the lamp.

She gasped and jerked away. "My breast is kind of sensitive today. So don't touch it."

He shoved away the covers, revealing a bruise peeking out from the armhole of her tank top. "What happened? It looks like somebody punched you."

"It's nothing. Just an accident."

Like hell it's nothing. He eased the fabric past her ribs and the lower curve of her breast, baring her nipple and a mottled patch of red and purple skin the size of a golf ball. A tiny incision with specks of dried blood at the edges rested in the center of the bruise. His heart dropped to his stomach and tangled in the knots already forming there. "This looks like you had a biopsy. And don't you dare tell me I don't know what I'm talking about. My ex-wife had a lump the last year we were married."

"Fine, I had a biopsy."

Not again.

She yanked her shirt down, her squeak instantly confirming the motion had caused her a significant amount of pain.

He pushed out of bed and paced to the bathroom and back to keep his roiling stomach under control. The thought of losing Riley scared him a hell of a lot more than becoming a single father had ten years ago. "And you didn't think to tell me?"

"What would you have been able to do about it? It wouldn't have changed anything."

"I'm your husband. I would've been supportive. I would've held your hand and worried with you. Damn it, Riley. How could you think you had to do this by yourself?"

Her jaw flexed, a sure sign her stubbornness had overridden every other emotion. "What makes you think I *can't* do this by myself?"

She was right. She was strong enough to face cancer alone, whether it included a false alarm, months of chemotherapy, or a death sentence.

He clutched at the corner of the dresser, the realization of what a fatal diagnosis would mean hitting him without warning. "That's why you needed to get married. You think you're going to die and you didn't want Rudy to get the farm. Gotta keep those priorities straight. Who the hell cares if you leave behind a husband who loves you and two girls who finally have a caring mother as long as your precious farm is safe from evil?"

"Bullshit. You don't love me. We've only been married four days." She narrowed her eyes at him, like she could see through him to his soul. "Fuck. This was your plan all along, wasn't it? When I told you I needed a husband, you volunteered for the big sacrifice without taking a breath. How long have you been waiting to put your hooks into me, Deke? Six months? A year? Since the day you overheard me firing my accountant for screwing up my taxes?"

"Hooks? Is that what you call being a friend and falling in love with a woman I liked and respected? Every damn day I looked forward to seeing you, talking to you, getting to know you, but superficial friendship seems to be all you want from me. Oh, and sex. Can't forget that, can we? At least I haven't been using you." Not bothering to fight the frustration churning in his insides, he grabbed his robe from the bedpost and headed downstairs to the couch.

The hurried tempo of his footfalls on the steps remained unbroken and unaccompanied. She wouldn't follow or try to stop him, of that he had no doubt, despite the disappointment that singular truth held. He couldn't force her to accept his feelings or to lean on him, even if the thought of her dying ripped him apart. No matter how much time she had, he didn't have the power to save her or make her love him.

The near-full moon shining in the windows lit a path to the living room, where his bed for the night waited, not that he'd be able to sleep. Maybe by morning, his choices would be clearer—and easier to face— because make-up sex couldn't fix their problems.

UNEXPECTED LIGHT AND THE RICH SCENT OF FRENCH ROAST GREETED Riley when she opened the bedroom door, leading her toward the room Deke had claimed for his home office. She owed him an apology for overreacting last night, for not telling him about the biopsy and the underlying reason she'd married him. His declaration of love had caught by surprise, pushing her to acknowledge that he had become more than a friend.

He didn't look up from the box on his desk when she stopped in the doorway. "I called Oscar."

"Oscar?"

"Oscar Banyan."

She crossed her arms under her breasts a second before the massive bruise reminded her of its presence. A slight adjustment eased the pain to a bearable level. "About what?"

"The possibility of an annulment. But he hasn't filed the license at the county courthouse yet, so technically speaking we're not actually married." He added a calculator and a picture frame to the box. "If the paperwork isn't filed, the marriage isn't legal. That's easier than an annulment, if that was even an option."

Her fist tightened of its own accord, pushing against her sore breast, but the pain distracted her from the inability to pull in a breath from his announcement. "Is that what you want? To end our agreement?"

He dropped another frame on top of the last one, still not giving her so much as a glance. "Look, I know you don't want to be married and you sure as hell aren't interested in anything more than playing house with me. Honestly, I don't think I can risk having you decide you don't need me anymore if the biopsy comes back okay."

"What if it doesn't?" *Can't you see that's my greatest fear? And I don't know what I want anymore.* "What about the girls?"

"I'll tell them I changed my mind. This is a lose-lose situation all the way around, but I'll be damned if I'm the one left watching you leave me, whether it's by cancer or a divorce when you realize you're not dying." He finally faced her, his teasing grin hiding behind a grim line. "I went through that once and I won't do it again, no matter how I feel about you. I can't do it."

The agony in his eyes matched the physical ache in her breast, but she couldn't argue against his logic, even if it meant Rudy inherited the farm.

He turned away and returned to his packing. "I'll move our stuff back to my house while the girls are at school and you can go back to what makes you happy."

CHAPTER 12

"You're such a hypocrite." Fiona heaved her backpack at the couch and leveled a glare at him that put every previous one to shame. "You keep promising me you'll never leave, and now I can't have a mother anymore because you're too much of a wuss to stay and fight for her. I want to live with Mom."

"Fee's right." Manda's lower lip trembled and a tear trickled down her cheek as she grabbed her sister's hand and led her toward their shared bedroom. "Me too."

Deacon sank into the armchair. He'd expected anger, disappointment, and a lot of pushback when he informed his daughters of his marriage's demise. He hadn't prepared to have the truth thrown in his face, not that he'd been able to see it through his own heartache.

It doesn't change anything, and it's too late anyway.

His second marriage had failed before it was official. At least Oscar hadn't laughed at him and tossed an I-told-you-so on the disastrous shit heap that was his non-relationship with Riley. Banyan hadn't pointed out the money they'd saved on a divorce, either. His only comment had been that he would shred the worthless piece of paper to use for bedding in his rehab barn.

That's a hell of a metaphor for my love life.

❧

SILENCE GREETED RILEY WHEN SHE BRAVED A RETURN TO THE HOUSE at five o'clock. No one stood at the stove over a crazy concoction in a casserole dish. The table wasn't set for four—or at all. The chatter she'd gotten used to existed only in her memories now. Her home wasn't a home anymore.

The refrigerator contained the half-empty bottle of wine and an opened jug of skim milk—the same as when Deke had arrived, minus the salad and dressing. She forced her legs to carry her to her step-daughters' bedrooms, but each one resembled guestrooms once more. Upstairs, all evidence of his presence had been removed—from the nightstand, the closet, the bathroom, the spare room turned office. All their belongings were gone.

Like always, he'd been true to his word. She couldn't have made him stay, even if she'd tried.

Nothing from her brief not-quite-real marriage remained, except a stab of regret for the accusation she'd heaved at him and an empty hole in her heart. He may have offered himself up to play her husband, but she had asked him for suggestions and accepted his proposition when all was said and done. She'd brought the whole damn mess on herself and lost a reliable friend, an amazing lover, daughters she'd never planned to have, and probably her accountant.

She stripped off the farm clothes she'd worn to take care of business and finish the weekly invoices while she stayed off everyone's radar in the equipment barn. A bath and pajamas called her name, as did the wine in the fridge and the cereal in the pantry.

Her phone buzzed on the counter when she entered the kitchen, sparking a fleeting hope that Deacon had changed his mind.

I don't deserve a second chance. Besides, I'm better off single.

The sentiment didn't possess the same vigor it had a week ago, but only because she'd gotten used to having three other people sharing her space. It had nothing whatsoever to do with any affection for her pretend husband or dreading the report Dr. Porter had promised to call about by Friday.

Liar.

A second message set off her phone while she poured a glass of chardonnay and another when she flipped open the top of the granola.

"Fuck it." She grabbed the cereal box in one hand and the wine in the other. "I'm going to bed."

"WHY HAVEN'T YOU ANSWERED MY TEXTS? I'M WORRIED SICK ABOUT you."

Riley tapped on Tate's contact and switched to speaker so she could add laundry detergent to the washing machine. If she had to spend another minute in bed with Deacon's scent, she would lose her damn mind. Why couldn't sex-filled dreams have awakened her as darkness fell instead of his phantom arm wrapped around her waist, holding her close enough that his heartbeat pulsed against her back while they slept?

Maybe she had liked having him in her bed for more than sex, but missing the man implied romantic feelings. How had that happened?

"Riley? Where have you been? I tried checking on you practically all day to make sure you were doing okay after the biopsy and you dropped off the face of the planet. And then Jim told me Deke asked to borrow his truck this afternoon. What's going on?"

"I'm washing sheets." The washer played its obnoxiously cheery notes as Riley changed the settings and pushed the Start button.

"Smartass. One more chance, or I'm coming over."

Grabbing her phone, Riley retreated to the kitchen. "I still have poison ivy on my butt and the anti-itch cream is a fraud. My boob has a bruise the size of a beefsteak tomato, which Deke found and got pissed off about last night. He and the girls moved out today after he told The Grouch not to file the marriage license. Life is just peachy. Come on over and we'll have a party."

After a long stretch of silence, Tate sighed. "You should've told him. He's your husband—"

"Evidently not."

"—and he cares about you."

"Shit. You knew he was in love with me, didn't you? That's why you and Georgie pushed me to ask him for help."

"Partly, but mostly because I know you care about him. How could you not when you let him tease you and still go back for more? If you opened your eyes, you'd see you're in love with him too."

"Like hell I am."

"Think about it, Riley. You go out of your way to antagonize him and create excuses to challenge him. Why is it so hard to admit you have feelings for him?"

"Even if I do have feelings for him, what's the point now? We're not married, living together, or speaking to each other. It seems to me that ship has sailed and sunk."

"Oh, so what you're saying is Jim and I shouldn't have bothered, either, despite you and your cohort interfering? Spare me the do-as-I-say-not-as-I-do crap. I just texted Georgie to stop Oscar from destroying the license, if he hasn't already. The next move is yours, girlfriend. Are you going to go after what you want or act like a scaredy-cat?"

❧

"Running two minutes late and can't stay long. I have a deposition at two thirty. Would you mind ordering a hot herbal tea of the day in a to-go cup for me?"

"Will do." Riley stepped up to the counter, wishing her stomach would allow a large black coffee into its confines without igniting a bonfire all the way to her throat. "Hi, Anabelle. I'd like two vanilla rooibos teas please. One hot in a to-go cup. One iced. Both large."

"Hi, Ms. Fenniman. How are you today?" The young woman tapped on the tablet screen. "One large hot tea of the day for carryout and one large iced tea of the day in a glass. Would you like a scone or a muffin?"

"No thanks." Pasting on what she hoped was a passable smile, she handed Anabelle her credit card. "I'm okay. How are you? Tate said you're working more hours. You must be doing a good job. Be sure to add a twenty-percent tip."

Dimples formed in the server's cheeks. "Fifteen hours a week. I have seniority."

"Excellent. I bet your mom's really proud of you." Riley took the card and receipt. "I'll be at my regular table."

Anabelle gave her a thumbs-up. "The new boy will bring your order out to you. Thank you and have a good day."

"You too." Cheered somewhat by Wally's perpetually friendly daughter, Riley wove through the tables to the far corner of the café. The rest of the world hadn't stopped, in spite of her problems.

Georgie's signature blood-of-her-enemies red coat flashed past the window and the woman entered the empty dining room with a determined glower leading the way. "Sorry I'm late. Banyan insisted on knowing why you want the marriage certificate filed before he would agree to do it, especially when Jeffries asked him not to. How are you feeling today? Any word from Dr. Porter?"

"No. Tea will be here in a minute." Riley pushed out the chair closest to her as her attorney collapsed the umbrella that matched her trench coat. "What did you tell him?"

Georgie sat, but she waited until Tate's newest part-timer placed their drinks on the table and headed back toward the kitchen to speak in her low everyone's-a-spy voice. "The truth. That you entered into the union in good faith and a divorce provides a more lucrative settlement for you than pretending no vows were taken."

"I'm not asking Deke for alimo— Wait a minute." Riley aimed a glare at her friend. "It may have worked on Tate, but I'm not falling for your reverse psychology bullshit. Remember? I was in on that scheme."

Not even glancing in Riley's direction, Georgie shrugged and eased the lid off her steaming tea. "It was worth an attempt."

"You can't fool me, so don't even try. What do you have up your sleeve?" A long sip of iced tea cooled the hot flash simmering between Riley's shoulder blades.

"Speaking as your friend, I think it's time you tell him how you feel. It's obvious to everyone in the book club, and we know you best. Speaking as a divorce lawyer, some marriages are worth saving. Yours is one of them." Georgie blew across the cup, sending wisps of steam floating upward.

Her friend's missing cutthroat approach caught Riley off-guard as much as the ache in her heart. "I don't want to make him a widower."

"No matter how long it lasts, you deserve to be happy. Deacon thinks he's meeting me here to talk about a divorce settlement in less than two minutes. Please use this opportunity to be honest with him. By the way, Banyan hand-delivered your signed marriage license this morning. I verified it. You should probably share that information with your husband." Georgie put the lid on the cup and rose as a soaked tan-clad man with a computer bag over his head rushed into the café.

"Fuck. Thanks for giving me plenty of warning." Riley swallowed a gulp of tea, but it didn't quell the swarm of locusts in her belly when he frowned at her.

"A kick in the ass, you mean." Her friend walked toward him and extended her hand. "Mr. Jeffries, your wife would like to discuss terms. In this instance, I think a private conversation will be more productive than a negotiation with her attorney."

His frown deepened and he continued to drip in the puddle forming around his feet. "She isn't my wife."

"Lorain County Probate Court begs to differ. Shall I ask Tate for a towel?"

He waved her away. "What's the point? I have to go right back out in the monsoon anyway."

Georgie shook her head. "Why are married couples always so stubborn? Sit down and talk to your wife. Or better yet, listen to what she has to say. Call me later, Ri."

A blob of red marched past the window before Riley could respond, but her drenched husband hadn't budged. She downed the rest of her tea, in hopes of drowning the locusts, and then grasped her umbrella as she stood. *Be honest with him.* "I'd rather we weren't interrupted during this discussion. My car's in the alley."

He hesitated for a moment before slogging beside her to the

counter and through Tate's kitchen. "Have you heard anything about the biopsy?"

"No. The doctor said probably tomorrow. I'm sorry I didn't tell you. You deserved to know what you were getting into."

"Yeah, I did."

The total lack of a teasing insult or comeback in his response stung, but she opened the umbrella and held it between them. "No sense getting any wetter."

"I'm not sure that's possible." The patter of raindrops filled the silence as he walked beside her to the passenger side and climbed in.

She hurried around the front end of the car, glad for the distraction of cool rain on her skin. Sucking in a last breath, she slid into the driver's seat and laid the wet umbrella on the floor at her feet. *This is it.* "Georgie convinced Oscar to file the license. She thinks our marriage is worth saving."

After several slow inhales and exhales, he turned to face her, his body stiff and his expressive eyes shuttered. "What do you think?"

"I..." His emotional distance hurt more than the bruise on her breast. She tried to clear the lump in her throat to no avail. "I really am sorry for not telling you. You've always been a good friend and I... wasn't."

His features softened slightly, giving her enough hope to brave the rest.

"I think... So, here's the thing. I might be in love with you."

"Might." The windshield fogged, a testament to his heavy breathing. "That word isn't part of your vocabulary. Either you are or you aren't. I don't see how we can be worth saving if you're not sure how you feel about me."

She dropped her forehead to the steering wheel, embarrassed by the admission she was about to share. "I've never been in love before. I don't know what it feels like. This isn't the same as Jim and Tate's sickening-sweet hearts-and-flowers kissy-face crap. I miss your obnoxious teasing and waking up in the middle of the night trapped under your hairy thigh. And if I die, I want your boring tan clothes to be the last thing I see to remind me how unboring you've made my life."

"I don't want to watch you die." His voice cracked over the last word.

The ache in her soul convinced her he spoke the truth. Was that how love felt? The deep longing to take away someone's fears and pain? To make them laugh and smile?

"Yeah, well, I don't want to die. And I don't want you to have to watch me die, either." She sat up and gave him a halfhearted punch in the bicep. "Not when I figured out I really am in love with you. But if I have to die, I'd rather spend the time I have left arguing with you than living without you."

He captured her fist and brought it to his lips, sending tingles up her arm from the simple touch. "Are you sure? A hundred-percent positive? No doubts whatsoever?"

"Hey, how about cutting me some slack? I'm forty-seven years old and this is my first serious relationship." She pulled his hand toward the fogged up front window and unfolded his index finger. Guiding the tip through the moisture, she drew a heart and wrote their initials inside it. "Is ninety-nine point nine close enough?"

"Not into hearts and flowers, huh? And some kissy face would be awfully nice right now." His familiar grin finally made an appearance.

Her heart tripped over its own beat at the sight, but buzzing against her hip interrupted the action she wanted to take. "Hold on. I'm expecting a call from a new client. It'll just take a sec."

He threaded his fingers through her hair as she dug her phone from her purse. "I'm sure I can find a way to occupy myself for a few minutes."

The number on the screen killed the mood in an instant. *I don't want to die.* "Hello. Riley Fenniman."

"Hi, Riley. This is Dr. Porter. I have the results from the biopsy."

Fuck, fuck, fuck. Breathe. Breathe.

"I haven't had a chance to read the full report yet, but I wanted to let you know the tissue samples came back benign. Good news. No cancer."

Disbelief kept a surge of relief on a short leash. "You're sure?"

"Yes. I do, however, want to go over the full report with you at your convenience."

Good news. No cancer. Her eyes blurred and she blinked to clear her vision. "I, um, can I call back later to make an appointment?"

"Of course. I'll see you soon."

The line went dead, but Riley couldn't move.

Deke brushed his fingertips over her cheeks. "You're crying. What's wrong? Was that your doctor? Is it cancer?"

The panic in his questions unfroze her, but liberation from the years of fear came slowly. "No cancer. Benign."

He dragged her across the gearshift onto his lap and held her tighter than anyone had hugged her before. "You're not allowed to change your mind. You said you love me and we're married. That means forever, whether one of us gets cold feet or not."

A bubble of laughter cut through the thickness in her throat. "Hot flashes. I don't get cold feet."

"Mostly I was talking about me. I left instead of fighting for you and I promise not to do that again. Things won't be perfect, Barbie, but that's okay."

"Shut up and help me steam up the rest of the windows, Clark." She covered his mouth with hers to celebrate life, love, and making out with her husband.

THE BUTCHER AND THE BAKER

CHAPTER 1

"ONE KISS FOR A BOSTON CREAM DOUGHNUT. RIGHT." PETRA Lochsley slapped a twenty—twice what she'd offered three and a half weeks ago—on the counter and gave the baker her best stink-eye. "Keep the change, because I'm not falling for that bullshit again. My tonsils still haven't recovered from the last time."

"I seem to recall my tonsils getting a workout too." Shoving the cash back at her, Auggie Hofmeier grinned, the net over his shaggy brown hair doing absolutely nothing to detract from his masculinity. "What's the matter, Pet? Afraid you won't be able to stop at just a kiss this time?"

"You wish, Casanova." She grabbed her money and spun on her wet wellies toward the exit, punctuating her parting jab with a squeak louder than any pair of sneakers could achieve. Her long braid whipped around too, smacking her in the chin. "Fine, I'll take my business elsewhere from now on. I hear Betty Crocker doesn't proposition her customers for kicks. And don't call me Pet, Auger, you boring boor." *No more steaks for you.*

His maniacal laughter followed her outside, past his arriving part-timer, and chased her along the sidewalk through the cold early-November rain to The Butcher. Although the drizzle chilled her temper somewhat, most of the exasperation finally faded when she stood at her worktable two doors down, with a meat cleaver in her right hand and a mountain of hacked-in-half racks of baby back ribs to her left.

"Keep it up, Hofmeier, and that pile of bones is gonna be you one of these days." She added the ready-to-sell cuts to the display case before she clomped to the front entrance to turn around the OPEN sign.

A pair of Wellington Garden Club ladies stood under the awning, waiting for nine o'clock like they did every Monday morning. Their cheerful chatter as they entered the butcher shop brought Petra's mood back to its usual even keel for the most part, although a giant chocolate-frosted cream-filled pastry would've helped considerably more. "Good morning, ladies. Any good gossip from the beauty shop this morning?"

Her former third-grade teacher stepped up to the service counter and removed the plastic rain bonnet from her freshly styled white hair. "Good morning, Petra. Just the usual. Things have been pretty quiet since last month's unexpected weddings. Did you have a good weekend?

"I did, thank you, Mrs. Crenshaw. Riley and I went axe-throwing on Saturday, and we had THC Book Club and cocktails Sunday night at Tate's house."

"Axe-throwing?" Wide eyes accompanied the woman's horrified tone. "That sounds dangerous."

"Less dangerous than not having an outlet for my frustrations. What can I get for you?" Petra snapped on a fresh pair of gloves, slid open the glass door to the ground beef, and dug a scoop into the closest pan. The woman's order was almost as predictable as the baker's obnoxious come-ons. "Two pounds of ground sirloin? It's a dollar off per pound this week."

"Oh, wonderful! Better make it four. Two packages of two pounds each. I'm making sloppy joes for my great grandson's birthday party tonight. I can't believe he's a year old already. Where does the time go? Do you have any ham shanks? This cold spell calls for a pot of navy bean soup."

"Sure do. I smoked a big batch over the weekend." With the first two-pound tray of hamburger wrapped in freezer paper and labeled, Petra weighed the mound for the second package. "How many would you like?"

"Three please, dear. I like to keep some extras on hand." Mrs. Crenshaw pointed to the bin of ribs through the glass. "And two of those. Do you have any of your special dry-rub seasoning?"

"No, but if you don't mind waiting, I can mix up a bag for you in a jiffy."

"Perfect. And while you're finishing up my order and helping Doris, I'll pick up the birthday cake I ordered from the bakery." Donning her rain bonnet again, the older woman hurried toward the door. "I'll only be a few minutes. Oh, and I'd like to order two twenty-five-pound turkeys for Thanksgiving."

After stripping off her gloves, Petra added the order to the spreadsheet tacked on the wall. "Got it. I'll have everything ready when you get back. Be right with you, Mrs. Wills." *I bet Hofmeier doesn't have the balls to tell Mrs. Crenshaw she has to pay with tongue hockey.*

The retired pharmacist looked up from the notepad she held and grimaced. "No hurry. I'm still finishing this week's menu. You don't happen to have any suggestions, do you?"

Moving one spice jar after another from the upper shelf to the wide counter opposite the meat case, Petra smiled at the same question her customer posed every Monday. Predictability was underrated. "How about a pork tenderloin with veggies in the slow cooker? A batch of your homemade biscuits would go great with that. Let's see. White chili and cornbread muffins. Um, roast chicken. Whole roasters are on sale this week. And you can't go wrong with breakfast for supper. Omelets or French toast with bacon or sausage. Fried apples and hash browns on the side. I'm getting hungry just thinking about it."

"You always have such good ideas. All set." Doris Wills put away her pen and laid her shopping list next to the scale as Petra rang up the sealed bag of dry rub and finished bagging Mrs. Crenshaw's order.

"Glad to contribute." Thankfully, she'd learned early on in her butcher-shop-owner days to keep a running list of serving suggestions right outside her tiny office. It had been a lifesaver on more than one occasion.

Mrs. Wills sorted through the packages of premade sausage patties in the smaller freestanding case and set two near the register as Petra wrapped the loin. After another search, the eighty-eight-year-old added a roll of braunschweiger to her growing pile.

"Good stuff, isn't it?" Movement near the entrance caught Petra's attention when she placed the last item in the former druggist's bag, spurring Petra around the end of the case. "Uh-oh. Looks like Mrs. C needs a hand."

The baker appeared behind the white-haired former teacher a moment later, steadying the cake box in her arms a moment before it would've flopped onto the sidewalk. In a single smooth motion, he opened the door and set a bakery bag on top of the cake as he relieved her of the load. "After you, Mrs. Crenshaw. Good morning, Mrs. Wills. Miss Lochsley."

Miss Lochsley? You two-faced, good-for-nothing-but-pastries jerk. Pasting on a smile, Petra pulled a double-tier shopping cart free from the nested line near the window and gestured at the top basket. "You can put those in here, Mr. Hofmeier."

Mrs. Crenshaw grasped the white sack and handed it to Petra. "This is for you, dear. I've heard it's your favorite."

A peek inside revealed a Boston cream doughnut, its chocolaty-creamy aroma creating an immediate sugar high. She set it out of harm's way next to the scale and bit her tongue to keep from sticking it out at her nemesis since he'd probably view it as an invitation. "Thank you, Mrs. C, from the bottom of my stomach."

"You're welcome, dear." Pulling her checkbook from her purse, the older woman offered the same smile that had welcomed a slightly disruptive eight-year-old girl into her classroom thirty-five years ago. "Did you put the receipt by the bags? I just need to fill in the amount on the check."

"Yes, ma'am." Petra rolled a second cart toward Auger the Boor, barely resisting the urge to ram it into his ankles. "You don't mind loading Mrs. Wills' purchases while I take care of Mrs. Crenshaw's, do you?"

"'Course not. I'll push the cart to her car and you can get Mrs. C's." His flirtatious wink fanned her flaming temper.

She rested a hand on each side of the empty top basket and leaned toward him. A slight press of her biceps against her outer boobs drew his gaze lower, obviously to the cleavage peeking out of the V-neck tee under her apron. After a slow bat of her eyelashes, she employed what her friend Riley called her sex-kitten drawl. "My assistant asked for the morning off, so I can't leave the shop. It wouldn't be too much trouble for you to help both ladies with their groceries, would it?"

He didn't even have the decency to look guilty when he raised his eyes to hers again. "No trouble at all."

So predictable.

Moving out of touching range, she turned her attention to Mrs. Crenshaw's bags at the register. "Would you look at that? The rain's coming down harder. Ladies, would you like to borrow my umbrella? No reason to risk messing up your trip to the beauty parlor. Mr. Hofmeier can return it with the carts when he's done helping you to your cars."

The retired teacher gave her a one-armed hug. "Thank you, Petra. That's very thoughtful."

"You're welcome. Anytime." Without a backward glance, she finished loading the basket under the cake box and then hurried to her office, grabbing her orgasmic treat on the way. The temptation to sneak a bite proved too strong, and she tore the pastry in half, careful not to let any filling drip onto her desk. "I'm not playing patty-cake with you, baker-man."

"Patty-cake is definitely not what I have in mind, Pet." Auggie's husky voice interrupted her with breakfast almost to her lips. "Covering you in cream filling and chocolate buttercream and licking it off is more like it."

A tremor raced through her lower belly, stealing her ability to breathe for several seconds. She stuffed two-thirds of the piece of doughnut in her mouth, not trusting herself to keep from accepting his proposition. *I don't want him. Damn it, I don't! The only way I'm ever having sex again is if I get married, and hell's freezing over before I agree to another engagement.*

"What's the matter? Did I finally suggest something you're interested in?" His slow grin made a perfect target for her annoyance.

She smashed the remaining bite of the pastry half into his face, taking extra care to stuff plenty of icing up his nostrils. Talking past her mouthful, she cupped his ass and wiped her gooey hand up the rear seam of his snowy-white baker's pants. "Uck oo."

His tongue snaked out and licked his lips, triggering another spasm, this one between her thighs. Then he grinned, creating a pair of dimples above the dark stubble covering his jaw. "Name the time, Pet. I'm all yours whenever you want."

So you can throw me away too?

"Geh out." Bits of cream filling mixed with frosting and doughnut crumbs sprayed toward him. She grabbed the umbrella from beside her laptop and jammed the blunt end into his gut.

Why does he have to keep teasing me?

"Oof." He winced and doubled over, sparking a split second of remorse, but it quickly passed. "Some day, love."

The pain he'd experienced couldn't begin to compare to the stab in her heart his word caused. How many men had said they loved her and lied?

All of them.

She dropped the umbrella and spun away, choking on the wad of doughnut and emotion lodged in her throat. "Geh da fuck ou now."

Several seconds passed before retreating footsteps announced his departure, but she stood frozen and shaking. That direct hit to the one weakness she'd never been able to move past hurt like a son of a bitch, more so than it should after four years since her last broken engagement—last being the key adjective. Broken didn't bother her. It had hardly been the first time.

Six. Six. Six. The number of the beast. Who would've thought a person could amass half a dozen broken engagements and no weddings in eighteen years?

And the one man I thought was my friend wants to use me like all the rest.

The doorbell rigged to announce customers when she was in her office buzzed, signaling either Auggie's departure with one of the ladies or the arrival of another of her Monday morning regulars. She wrapped the remainder of her doughnut in its waxy paper and stowed it in the bag. As much as she would've preferred smashing the rest in his face, the bite she'd already sacrificed would have to do.

She eased around the corner, careful to stay out of view in case her nemesis hadn't left. The curved glass in the meat case distorted the new arrival, but the blood-red trench coat gave away her identity.

Mrs. Crenshaw greeted Petra's lawyer friend with a bright smile. "Georgina, how lovely to see you."

"Good to see you too, Mrs. Crenshaw." Georgie extended her hand, but the older woman enveloped her in a hug. Unsurprisingly, the attorney stiffened, barely tolerating the touchy-feely action.

"I can't thank you enough for helping my granddaughter and her husband save their marriage. They're happier now than when they were newlyweds."

Backing away, Georgie met Petra's gaze over the case. None of her unmistakable discomfort showed in her bland expression. "Sometimes divorce isn't the answer. Petra, do you have a few minutes to discuss a business matter?"

Petra nodded from her ineffective hiding spot. "Sure. Come on back. We can talk while I grind some more sirloin."

The least squeamish of her friends rounded the end of the counter, her no-doubt-designer heels clicking on the linoleum. Her voice was low as she joined Petra by the grinder. "The owner of the empty space next door finally returned my call. He's willing to sell for the right terms."

"What're the right terms?" Petra fed a hunk of beef to the machine.

Georgie recited a price that matched the most recent tax assessment she'd quoted last month. "And he wants a guarantee you won't turn the storefront into one of those discount stores or a flea-market junk store. He wants a family-owned business that fits the small-town atmosphere.

Non-chain and non-franchise restaurant, hair salon, or other service-based company. He really likes the idea of expanding the butcher shop into the space."

"How soon can we sign a purchase contract?" A faint buzz carried from her office, announcing someone at the entrance. Unfortunately, the prickling along Petra's spine told her Auggie the Boor had returned to assist Mrs. C to her car. "See you next Monday, Mrs. Crenshaw. Have a good week."

"Thanks, Petra dear. You too." Although the woman's exit wasn't audible with the grinder hum, she never lingered over goodbyes.

Ten, nine, eight, seven, six, five, four, three, two, one. "How soon?" Petra cast a glance at Georgie, who stared in the direction of the door.

"As soon as your nosy neighbor quits trying to eavesdrop on our conversation. Yes, you, Mr. Hofmeier." Georgina's narrowed eyes flashed like they could set fire to the object of her irritation. "I believe Mrs. Crenshaw is waiting for you to follow her to her car."

CHAPTER 2

AUGGIE TOSSED ANOTHER BROWN-GOO-COVERED TISSUE IN THE restroom trashcan and hoped his employees didn't think he had a bad case of the stomach flu. At the rate he was going, he might blow through an entire box of Kleenex before he managed to remove all the chocolate frosting from his nose. He hadn't bothered to change his pants yet, not that the whole town hadn't already seen the shit-smear lookalike all over his ass on the two round trips helping the Garden Club ladies with their groceries. For a cold and rainy Monday morning in northern Ohio, a lot of people had been out and about. However, he refused to complain since the woman of his dreams had touched his butt.

He'd seriously pissed off Petra, and the reason was worthy of cele-bration. She might've thought she'd hidden her reaction from him, but the glazed look in her eyes had shouted orgasmic anticipation when he'd suggested eating her for dessert. He had finally cracked her impenetrable shell. Of course, he still sported a respectable hard-on from thinking about licking every inch of her.

"Hey, Auggie!" A trio of loud knocks followed his full-timer's summons. "You about done in there? Phone call for you."

"Yeah, just a sec." After a last look in the mirror and a swipe at a smear he'd missed on his chin, he washed his hands and exited the employee restroom. On his way to the office, he grabbed a clean pair of drawstring pants from the stack of laundry inside the supply closet. "Any idea who's on the phone?"

Nate shrugged without glancing up from the half-sheet cake on the turntable and piped a yellow daisy into the overlapping leaves at the corner. "Don't know. He didn't say. Just asked for Augustus."

Since Auggie had talked to his grandpa yesterday, that left one other old codger who would use his full name. "This may take a few minutes, but bang on the door if you need a hand."

The tattooed biker grunted as he switched bags and added a pink flower to the birthday cake.

Auggie closed the door behind him when he entered his office and then toed off his shoes. A quick change allowed him to sit without making a mess of his new ergonomic desk chair. He leaned back, appreciating the first time off his feet since four in the morning. "This is Augustus. What can I do for you?"

"How've you been, young man? I have a proposition for you." The older man's voice hinted at the usual rascally twinkle in his eye.

"Great to hear from you, Mr. Collier. I'm above ground and in love. How about you? Pop said you had knee-replacement surgery a few weeks ago."

His grandfather's friend chuckled. "In love, huh? How's the lucky lady feel about that? The knee's almost good as new."

Settling deeper into the chair, Auggie sighed. "I'm not so sure she considers herself lucky. She smashed a doughnut in my face this morning and threw me out of the butcher shop. Let me know when you're up for a game of horseshoes."

Raucous laughter rang through the phone, causing him to temporarily hold the receiver a few inches from his ear. "Petra? Eddie's granddaughter? You sure you can handle her? She's something else when she gets a thorn in her britches. I'm selling the building and thought you might be interested in it."

Auggie sat up, ready to talk business but all too aware the old man couldn't have a single-track conversation to save his life. "Petra doesn't need handled. She deserves a guy who's willing to accept her as she is and treat her like a queen. I'm listening. What kind of deal are we talking about?"

"You know what you're up against, right? Five engagements—"

"Six." *But who's counting?*

"—that ended badly can leave a woman bitter. Eddie, Otto, and I agreed that if one of us decided to sell, the others would get dibs on buying it. Since you and Petra took over your grandparents' businesses, that means I'm asking both of you if you're interested. You can expand, open a new small business, connect the butcher shop and the bakery. That's up to the two of you."

"Have you talked to her about buying the shop?" Tapping the space bar, Auggie woke his laptop. "She may be bitter, but she's also still single. I'm looking at it as an opportunity to show her not all men are idiots and creeps. Plus, I have a few tricks up my sleeve to sweeten her up. Did you know my Boston cream doughnuts are her favorite treat?"

"Talked to her lawyer this morning. She's been after me to sell for a couple months, but the knee was giving me hell so I just got back to her. You think you can sweet-talk a gal who has the stomach to electrocute a cow and turn it into T-bones and hamburgers? Eddie said she's taken up axe-throwing for fun."

Interesting. Auggie double-clicked the expansion plans he'd had drawn up in July. "I want in on the storefront, no matter what Petra decides. Sweet-talking is for liars and cheaters. I want to feed her and take care of her. Besides, who am I to judge her for making sure I have steaks to grill? Somebody's got to do it. Oh, and I know about the axe-throwing. Tried it myself last week. If it makes her happy, I'm all for it. Last I knew, she still holds every county pitching record for fast-pitch softball. Not bad for somebody who graduated from high school twenty-five years ago."

"Sounds like you're wandering into stalking territory there, Augustus. I'll set up a meeting for this afternoon and we can work out the particulars. Just the three of us. No lawyers. Four o'clock okay? Hold on a sec." The old man mumbled something, suggesting a side conversation on the other end of the phone. "Joanie said I have a doctor's appointment at four. Are you free at two?"

"Two is good. Why don't we meet at the shop? Knowing Petra's interests doesn't make me a stalker. It means I want to plan things she likes to do for when I ask her out." Bringing up his calendar, Auggie added the meeting to his schedule, along with a reminder alert.

"I'm thinking maybe it's time for you to shit or get off the pot. See you then."

Auggie returned the receiver to its cradle, unsurprised by Hugh's challenge and the old guy's penchant for getting the last word. "Hm. Since my pants looked the part, I guess that's a sign I better up my game."

"YOU." PETRA SCOWLED AND CROSSED HER ARMS UNDER HER BREASTS, pushing more cleavage past the low-cut vee at the front of her shirt. "What are you doing here?"

Despite the frigid greeting, Auggie grinned and raised his gaze from her deliciously curvy body to her if-looks-could-kill brown eyes as he joined her on the sidewalk outside the defunct metal works shop between the bakery and the butcher shop. "Right now, I'm imagining what it would be like to—"

"You're both here. Good. I hate when people are late." With the assistance of a polished cane, Hugh Collier hustled toward them, moving faster than he had in years. He unhooked a ring of keys from his belt loop and wasted no time unlocking the decorative security gate of the storefront. "How are you doing, Petra? You still driving the pickup I sold you right out of high school?"

"You know I sold that rust bucket fifteen years ago, you old coot." The glare she drilled into the retired artist-welder's back said Hugh hadn't told her their meeting included a third wheel. "I'm willing to beat whatever offer Hofmeier makes. Business is booming and I need the additional space for the butcher shop."

"We'll talk about money later." After another jangle of keys at the glass door, Hugh gestured for her to go inside. "I made a deal with Eddie and Otto, and I'm following through on that promise. Look around all you want. Then we'll negotiate."

"What kind of deal?" Afternoon sun lighting her face through the windows, she glanced in Auggie's direction, eyes narrowed and accusing. "You know all about this underhanded bullshit, don't you? Jesus. You know what, Hugh? Let's cut to the chase. Have you already signed a sales contract with Otto's grandson?"

Mr. Collier tapped his cane on the floor, creating a hollow thump that echoed off the walls. "Why would you think that? Didn't I say we'd negotiate after you look around?"

"I don't trust either of you not to try to pull a fast one on me, especially when you didn't tell me he'd be here and he obviously knows all about your deal." Planting her rain-boot-clad feet, she held up the index and middle fingers of her right hand. A Band-Aid circled the first knuckle of her pointer finger. "Two strikes against you. If this is a done deal or a bidding war, just say so up front and quit jacking me around. Otherwise, I'm having a chat with Gramps and Otto about your shifty scheme."

"Now, honey—"

"Don't 'honey' me like some helpless bimbo who can't string a sentence together with a needle and thread. I want the truth, and I want it now." Her clipped tone suggested her normally negligible patience had surpassed its limit hours ago, probably when her body had betrayed her during their morning clash.

The old man opened his mouth as if to speak, but Auggie raised his hand. "It's me she's mad at, Mr. Collier, not you. Here's the truth, Petra. Hugh called me this morning about the space, shortly after he talked to your lawyer, as I understand it. Our grandfathers had an agreement with him that if one of them closed up shop while the others were still in business, the remaining two could buy out the third if they wanted to. He's honoring that agreement since the butcher shop and the bakery are owned and run by family. You and I can decide if we want The Candlestick Maker space before he puts it on the market, but we have to settle on mutually acceptable terms."

Although her gaze remained hard as the proverbial rock, the tension in her jaw softened a hair. "And what exactly constitutes 'mutually acceptable terms,' pray tell?"

A warning look to Hugh yielded a nod, so Auggie related the rest of what their host had told him about the deal. "Since you've made it clear you're interested and I'd like to add seating to the bakery, I propose we become equal investors."

The shadow that appeared and disappeared from her face in not much more than a second made him cringe at his word choice. "Equal investors. Like partners? I don't want a partner. If I have no other choice than to share, I'll buy half and you buy half."

Hugh shook his head. "Why would you want to tear down two walls to build another one in between? Seems to me it'd be cheaper and better for business if you connect your shops instead of making folks go outside to get from one to the other. Maybe a place for people to sit and enjoy a doughnut while they wait to buy a roast for supper. Update the restroom for customers and—"

"And who's going to clean it? It sure as hell isn't going to be me." She perched her fists on her hips, drawing Auggie's attention to her long legs—legs he wanted to explore inch by inch with his tongue. "What're you looking at? Eyes up here when I'm talking, buster."

Auggie took a leisurely visual stroll up her gorgeous thighs, along her flared hips, past her tapered waist, over her full breasts to a pair of lips made for kissing. "I'll hire a part-time janitor. Somebody to wipe down tables, clean the restroom, empty the trash, sweep and mop the floors. You can pay the monthly security fee, and we'll call it even."

"That sounds like a partnership. What if I want to own my half outright? You can buy the half with the restroom since you want to hire a new employee." She scanned the empty storefront and took four steps to the left. Dragging one rain boot on the dusty floor, she drew a line down the middle. "There. That looks pretty even, doesn't it? How much do you want for half, Hugh?"

"Well..." Frowning in the direction of the smudge marks, the old man scratched his head. Then he pulled a folded paper from his shirt pocket and handed it to her. "The top number is if you and Augustus buy it together. The bottom one is if you each buy half."

"This isn't fair. Why should I have to pay twenty-five percent more just because I don't want to share the building with the bane of my existence? Did you know he won't even sell me a doughnut? Not for money anyway. As if I should prostitute myself for chocolate frosting and cream filling."

Mr. Collier leaned heavier on his cane. "Having my lawyer handle two purchase contracts costs more than having him handle one. Besides, the whole point of selling to you and Augustus was to keep the shop among friends. What's this business about prostitution? Just what is he expecting you to pay with?"

The sunlight caught a flush on her cheeks even near the back of the showroom. "A kiss."

A noisy snort filled the space. "Not very original, is he? A little forward if you ask me."

Whose side are you on?

Her hint of a smirk came as no surprise. "Presumptuous too."

Mr. Collier nodded. "Did you tell him you might consider kissing him after a date or two?"

"Well, no. He hasn't asked me out." She stuffed the paper in the back pocket of her jeans and lifted her chin, sending her dark choco-late-colored braid swinging back and forth above her beautiful back-side. "Not that I'd say yes. He flirts with every female who sets foot in the bakery. God only knows how many women the playboy's juggling at any given time."

"Sounds to me like trying to make you jealous has backfired on him."

"Hey!" Auggie forced his gaze from her butt to Pop's longtime friend. Pouring lighter fluid on Pet's flaming temper wasn't helping his cause. "I've never done anything but be friendly to my customers. Plus, I'm standing right here, so stop talking about me like I'm not. Can we get back to discussing the shop?"

Pointing his cane directly at Auggie, the old man leveled a hard stare at him. "As soon as you show Petra you're not playing with her affections and ask her on a real date. A nice dinner, polite conversation, an activity she enjoys. Then we'll finish talking about business."

Way to put me on the spot. Battling the worst case of nerves in his entire life, Auggie turned to face the woman he'd known most of it and fell for out of the blue six months ago like somebody had flipped on a short-circuited switch. *Damn near electrocuted.* "Petra, will you go axe-throwing and have supper with me at the Brown Derby tonight?"

CHAPTER 3

PETRA DOUBLE-CHECKED HER TOTE FOR THE FILE CONTAINING notarized copies of the purchase agreement and every other possible document she might need as she strolled along the sidewalk toward the Lorain County Justice Center. The fact that she'd had to overpay still stuck in her craw, but at least she'd had the pleasure of refusing Auggie's invitation since she always spent Monday evenings playing euchre with her grandparents. His obvious disappointment that she'd already made plans had surprised her, deflating the satisfaction telling him no had brought.

He just wants in my pants. I bet he doesn't even have a clue how to use frosting and his tongue to please a woman.

Grateful for two days of successfully avoiding him, she paused at the intersection to check for traffic and then stepped into the crosswalk.

"Petra? Is that you?"

Shit. I know that voice.

Ah hell, not Number Six.

Don't turn around.

"It *is* you. Wait up."

Can this day get any worse?

Without slowing, she continued toward the sidewalk. "What do you want, gold digger?"

"Ah, come on. Don't be like that."

"Like what? Rude to the asshole who proposed to me because he thought I was rich?" She tossed an eye roll over her shoulder as the ground slanted upward beneath her feet. *Please make him go a different direction.* "I definitely earned that prerogative."

The jerk didn't even have the decency to look embarrassed, let alone repentant. "So...are you still single? I'm getting married in a couple weeks."

None of your goddamn business. "Give your wife-to-be my condolences." She tried to turn toward the next crosswalk, but an arm hooked her around the waist and a pair of soft, welcoming lips met hers. She almost melted into a puddle, despite the need for long sleeves and a hoodie today. *Holy moly.*

"Mm, I missed having lunch with you, love." Auggie winked at her and then nuzzled her neck.

Not you.

"Play along." His whisper tickled her ear, shooting sparks all the way to her lower belly.

Faced with the minimally lesser of two evils, she nipped at his chin, making sure she caught his skin between her teeth. "Me too."

He grinned and shoved a hand toward the jackass behind her. "Auggie Hofmeier, Pet's fiancé."

The gold digger snickered. "Gonna try again, huh, Petra? You know she's been engaged six times, right?"

Auggie rubbed his palm over her hip and tucked his fingers into her back pocket. "Good thing none of them worked out too. I'm lucky seven and I don't believe in long engagements. I asked her this morning in bed and the wedding is happening right after we fill out the application."

What the hell? She surreptitiously elbowed him in the ribs when he draped his arm around her shoulder.

Number Six's eyebrows almost reached the spot where his hairline used to be. "Hm. Well, congratulations, I guess. Looks like we're headed to the same place. We can walk to the Probate Court office together."

Great. Just fucking great.

Falling into step with her ex-fiancé, Auggie chuckled. "I hope you don't mind if we get a little, you know, affectionate on the way. We can't keep our hands off each other, not that I mind."

I'll put my hands around your throat, mister. She aimed a fake smile at her fake fiancé and pinched his butt hard enough to make him wince and possibly leave a bruise.

With his mouth next to her ear again, he lowered his voice. "You're going to kiss it and make it all better later, aren't you? After I lick dessert off you, of course. I'm really looking forward to the honeymoon."

A whimper snuck out, but she covered it with a cough. "Damn ragweed allergy."

His smirk assured her he hadn't fallen for her ruse. "I promise to put you to bed and take really good care of you as soon as we get home."

Laying it on a bit thick, aren't you, lover boy?

He held the door for her at the building across the street from the one she'd planned to visit. Then he pressed kisses to her forehead, cheeks, and nose while they waited for the elevator. The public show of affection continued when he trapped her in the back corner with his thigh between hers. His feigned excitement at the entrance to the sixth-floor office drew sideways looks from Number Six and the standoffish bleached and spray-tanned blonde he'd greeted a few feet from the elevator doors.

"I can't wait to marry you." Auggie lifted Petra off her feet and spun her in a circle. "I'm the luckiest guy in the world."

She clung to him, keeping her chin against his jaw as she hissed in his ear. "Lucky there're too many witnesses for me to get away with strangling you."

A slow glide along his body revealed how lucky he thought he was going to get—and the lump cuddling against her thigh was nothing to sneeze at. He smiled at her, amusement and something unthinkable in his eyes. "I love you more, Pet."

Her stomach flip-flopped and her heart squeezed. *Oh no. I'm not falling for that line of bullshit again.* Six times was her limit, no matter how sincere the words sounded. She waved the other couple past them. "You were here first. Go ahead."

The blonde statue moved forward, following the gold digger into the room while she removed a key ring with the Tesla logo on it and a leather wallet from her designer purse. He'd evidently hit the jackpot with the woman who didn't speak to anyone but her financial equals. Too bad she didn't know the jerk beside her wasn't.

Fifteen minutes later, Petra tapped the toe of her welly on the floor and barely suppressed an impatient growl. *What's taking so long? Aren't they ever going to leave? And what the hell am I going to do with another marriage license?*

The man behind the counter finally called Number Six's and Miss Rich's names, quelling Petra's anxiety. Only a moment passed before he spoke again, announcing to the room she and Augustus could pick up their approved license and reenergizing the nerves that had prematurely begun to settle.

Stay calm. If I excuse myself to go to the restroom, they'll be long gone by the time I get back and I can shred the stupid paper into the trashcan.

Her legs turned rubbery as she walked to the counter, but Auggie's hand at her lower back steadied her. He grasped the paper and led her toward the hallway, where her former fiancé and his bride-to-be waited.

Six smiled at her, like he could see through the whole ridiculous scenario. "I was thinking we could be witnesses at your wedding. You know, to show there are no hard feelings."

Good God, no.

Auggie cast a glance at her and then at something over her shoulder. A lengthy debate seemed to go on behind his eyes in a matter of two seconds. "Oscar, you're right on time. We just got the license. I need to talk to you for a minute before we can start. Pet, I'll be back before you can miss me."

Oscar? The Grouch? Not Oscar Banyan. Panic struck faster than she could polish off a Boston cream doughnut during her period. What was Wellington's former mayor and only internet-ordained wedding officiant doing here?

He'd recently performed a double ceremony for two of her friends, but that didn't mean she wanted the same favor. Trapped between the gold digger and her fake fiancé, she had nowhere to run.

The Grouch muttered something unintelligible and walked several yards away with Auggie. His perpetual frown deepened, but he nodded. After a long moment, he glanced toward her and nodded again. After another brief exchange, they walked back to her and their witnesses.

Auggie linked his fingers with hers and brought her hand to his lips. "Oscar's on a tight schedule and the weather looks a little iffy, so he wants to marry us here instead of at the gazebo. Is that okay? All that matters to me is the commitment we want to make to each other. We can always go to the park and take pictures when we're done here."

His question offered her an out, but creating a scene would only give her ex a reason to doubt she could actually move beyond broken engagements to an actual marriage. Thankfully, based on her friends' experiences, Oscar wouldn't immediately file the signed license, giving her the option to tell him not to.

Complications.

Why hadn't Auggie left well enough alone and let her ignore the shallow jerk?

She stabbed her cut-short fingernail into his palm and pasted on a serene smile that made her cheeks hurt. "That's so sweet. Me too, honey."

Pulling his cell phone from his pocket, Oscar faced Auggie and her. The glare he aimed in their direction shouted his disgust loud and clear. "If you two lovebirds are ready, we'll get started."

Auggie grinned like he was enjoying every second of the farce. "Ready."

Grudgingly, she forced the word from her mouth without choking on it. "Ready."

Their makeshift minister tapped the screen several times. "We are gathered today to join Petra Lochsley and Augustus Hofmeier in marriage. They've asked me to keep this simple since their love binds them much deeper and stronger than spoken vows. Do you, Augustus, take Petra to be your partner, your lover, and your wife? To be true to her and cherish her as long as you both shall live?"

Suddenly more serious than she'd ever seen him, Auggie met her gaze. "I do."

"And, Petra, do you take Augustus to be your partner, your lover, and your husband? To be true to him and cherish him as long as you both shall live?"

The moment that had eluded her for eighteen years had come, daring her to take the leap, despite the circumstances, the setting, and the groom. She might spend the next month hating herself for needing to prove her worthiness, but her curse would finally be broken. "I do."

Oscar placed his hand over theirs. "As you've chosen to get matching tattoo wedding bands, due to the nature of your occupations, we'll forego the exchanging of rings. By the power vested in me by the Ministry of Ordained Officiants and the State of Ohio, Auggie and Petra, I pronounce you husband and wife. Congratulations."

Auggie leaned closer, putting his mouth within a hairsbreadth of hers. "Can I kiss the bride now?"

"If you want to."

Halfway through Oscar's less-than-enthusiastic go-ahead, soft lips closed over hers, the gentle but firm caress spreading warmth through every inch of her humming body.

Anger? Maybe a little lust?

Who the hell cares?

She thrust her tongue past his teeth, savoring the tingles in all the right places and grabbing the chance to seize control. Each stroke he matched distanced her from the reality that their sham nuptials would likely end in her first and only termination of marriage. The least she deserved was a wedding night to remember before she confessed her worst mistake to Georgina, her divorce-lawyer friend.

The bulge pressing into her thigh expanded, but the groan that rumbled into her from her temporary husband made the need all the more urgent. Moving her hand to his ass, she pulled him closer.

"Ahem. How about taking that somewhere private?"

Auggie eased back at the admonition from The Grouch, blinking at her like she'd kissed him against his will.

I guess you didn't mean it when you said you're all mine whenever I want. Too bad, because I'm holding you to it now, hubby.

His breath raspy, he took a backward step, putting him almost out of her reach. "Uh…yeah. Thanks, Oscar. Come on, Pet. Let's go home and celebrate."

Number Six and his fiancé blocked their path to the elevator. Slipping their folded license into the inner pocket of his suit coat, he looked Petra in the eye and then glanced toward Auggie. "Congratulations. Looks like seven really is your lucky number."

Auggie guided her around the asshole wearing the same self-absorbed sneer he'd worn when she called him out for being a greedy jerk. "Nah. Lucky is finding true love and making it stick, even after a bunch of idiots manhandled her heart."

He might be a boor, but Auggie Hofmeier could give Cyrano De Bergerac lessons on romantic prose. Chin up and heart hardened against the impossible fantasy, Petra let him lead her into the elevator and then out of the building. No way in hell would she allow herself to believe he actually meant the words he spouted so easily, whether Six swallowed the poetic notion or not.

Auggie stopped at the crosswalk and pulled his phone from his jeans pocket. "Almost five. Are you hungry? We can stop somewhere before we head back to Wellington."

"What's the matter? Afraid of what's going to happen next?" She tugged him forward, more determined than before to claim the silver lining from her surprise wedding. "Order a pizza from someplace that has a drive-thru. We'll pick it up on the way to the honeymoon."

He fell into step beside her. "You're taking this a lot better than I expected."

"And you didn't answer the question."

"I'm just kind of confused—and maybe a little concerned—that you're not plotting my untimely demise. You aren't, are you? I only did what I did because your ex was being a spiteful shithead. And, in case you're wondering, I had no idea Oscar was going to be there. That part... I guess I got carried away, especially when the dickwad offered to be a witness, like he didn't believe I'd actually marry you."

"You're rambling." She kicked a pebble several feet down the sidewalk, not sure why he hadn't jumped on the opportunity to annoy her. "I get why you did it, but I don't give a damn what anybody thinks about how many times I've been engaged. You should've let me handle it."

"You're right. I should've, but..." He glanced sideways at her and shook his head.

"But what?"

"You could've said I don't instead of I do. Besides, I couldn't pass up the chance to kiss you again, not after you wouldn't play along Monday morning." A wide grin replaced his contemplative expression.

Tugging on his hand, she picked up the pace toward her truck. "Then we're even. Because if I have to be married, even temporarily, I'm not passing up a chance to get laid."

CHAPTER 4

Do not screw this up.

Auggie followed Petra—his wife—into her kitchen, carrying a large deluxe pizza, an order of Jo Jos, a box of breadsticks, a dozen spicy-garlic wings, and a side salad. Either she thought he ate a lot or she planned to burn thousands of calories on their wedding night. The latter aroused him beyond belief, which scared him a little. Did thirty-seven-year-old men usually get so hard they could barely walk?

Pet dropped her keys on the butcher-block table and yanked off her boots. "You can put those in the fridge for now. We'll heat stuff up in the oven later."

He kicked off his shoes by the door, hoping a few seconds of standing still relieved some of the pressure behind his zipper. "Okay. So…I only have one condom in my wallet."

"I have most of a box." Her sweatshirt landed on the back of the closest chair. "Any STDs I need to know about? No matter what Mr. Collier says, you're a big flirt."

The salad almost slid off the top of his pile as he turned to frown at her. "Glad to know you think so highly of me. No. I got tested after my last girlfriend decided she wanted an open relationship and told me after the fact. You?"

She looked away, but not before a telltale rush of color flooded her cheeks. "I got tested when Number Five admitted he'd been talking to his ex about a reconciliation. Six insisted on waiting until we were married to have sex, so no STDs."

He shoved his load onto the middle shelf and closed the refrigerator door, giving him time to consider his words. "You have nothing to be embarrassed about. Actually, all those broken engagements saved us from having to show divorce papers when we applied for the license. Like I told the loser, I'm a lucky guy."

"Lucky because—"

"Because I was in the right place at the right time. Now I'm all yours whenever you want." He shed his jacket as he took two steps toward her. "Let's go start the honeymoon, Mrs.— Hm. Do you prefer Mrs. Hofmeier? Mrs. Lochsley-Hofmeier? Or do you want to stay Ms. Lochsley? Personally, I don't have a preference. I'll be Mr. Lochsley if that's what you want."

Her eyes narrowed on him and she shifted her weight from one socked foot to the other, hinting that she might be having second thoughts about inviting him home. "You understand this is temporary, right? It wasn't supposed to happen, and I'll be contacting Oscar about not filing the license. If he already has, Georgie Swofford will be my first call in the morning about an annulment. Or divorce. Whichever it needs to be."

The missed opportunity to deck one of the men who'd mistreated her flitted through his mind, but getting charged with assault wouldn't convince her to trust him. "I'll go along with whatever you truly want, even if you change your mind about tonight. However, you need to understand I'm a strong believer in fate, Pet."

She gnawed on her lower lip and pinned him in place with a stare that dared him to break his promise. "Follow me. And you better be undressed by the time we get to my bedroom."

Pretty sure he'd finally discovered a crack in her tough shell, he trailed her out of the kitchen and through the living room, leaving his shirt, t-shirt, and socks in their wake. In the hall, she widened her lead while he hopped one-legged out of his jeans, but he wore only his boxer briefs when he reached the master bedroom doorway.

With his thumbs hooked in the waistband, he shoved his underwear to his knees and let them slide to his ankles. Stepping out of the leg holes, he crossed the finish line with only a condom to his name. *Ready or not, here I come.*

"Get in and suit up." Without looking back at him, she grabbed the edge of the covers from her mostly made bed and flipped them toward the footboard.

"What if I want to undress you?" He placed the foil packet on the nightstand as he approached her from behind. The chilly air did nothing to cool the heat that had been simmering inside him since they'd exchanged wedding vows. "Wham-bamming isn't much better than jacking off in the shower. Besides, I've been looking forward to tasting every inch of you and finding out what makes you feel like you've died and gone to heaven. You know, like when you eat one of my cream-filled doughnuts."

A barely audible whimper was all the warning she gave him before she whirled around and plastered her mouth to his. Her fingers tunneled through his hair, tangling and pulling him closer, and her palm seared his skin as she smoothed a hand over his ribs and down to his bare ass.

He groaned, drowning in the sensations coursing through his body but afraid to touch her for fear of breaking the spell. Each aggressive stroke of her tongue threatened to steal what little control he had. Then her lips were gone.

"Undress me already." Her husky order barely allowed him time for a breath before she kissed him again.

"Mmm." Still lip-locked to her mouth, he tugged her shirt from her jeans and took half a step back to pull it upward. Stuck at her under-arms, he followed the hem to the middle of her back and the hooks holding her bra in place. A twist of the strap popped the fasteners free, allowing him to peel the cups from her breasts and press his chest to her soft flesh. "Mm-mm-mm."

Again, she broke the kiss, this time yanking her shirt over her head with the bra straps tangled in the sleeves. "Too slow."

Her arms stretched toward the ceiling, providing the perfect opportunity to taste one of the nipples that had puckered against his skin. It tightened even more when he circled it with his tongue and then sucked it between his lips. Anxious to explore more of her gorgeous curves, he unfastened her jeans and worked them and her underwear over her hips while he showered her other breast with equal attention.

Every sexy noise she made urged him to drop to his knees and lick a path down her belly to the triangle of neatly trimmed curls he'd uncovered. He bared her thighs and then her calves as he neared the sweet scent calling to him. When she freed one foot from her jeans, he hooked her knee over his shoulder, putting his target in line with his mouth. With his first slow lick through her slick folds, her muscles trembled under his fingertips, and a throaty moan seemed to give him the go-ahead to continue his foreplay—as if he needed any encouragement.

His next leisurely venture from her vagina to her clit earned him a stinging tug on his hair and a rock of her hips toward his face. He flicked back and forth over the swollen bud and cupped her breasts, strumming her nipples with the same steady rhythm.

Her lips parted, and sharp cries accompanied her shallow gasps for air. She jerked against his mouth, an orgasm apparently pulling her over the edge into bliss. The pulsing and shaking went on while he switched from flicks to sucking and another louder cry suggested the second wave bested the previous one. She melted into him, her legs no longer tense, and he caught her as she collapsed onto him. He lowered her to the rug and kissed a path to her euphoric half smile, savoring every inch of skin along the way.

His imagination hadn't done justice to the simple act of going down on her.

Still panting, she blinked up at him. "Condom. Hurry."

He levered up on his elbow and patted the top of the nightstand, in hopes of finding the packet without moving any farther. *Aha!*

After a flip to position the protection correctly, he rolled it on and then cradled her flushed cheeks in his hands as he rested against her slick opening. The moment he'd waited for had arrived at last. Pressing his lips to her forehead, he sank inside her, losing himself in her body and finally expressing the love he'd kept silent about for months.

She wrapped her legs around his hips and arched into him. With every measured motion, her pulsing muscles pulled him deeper and her breathless cries grew louder and higher pitched, stealing his control.

He nuzzled her ear with the next thrust. "Tell me how you feel, Pet."

Her near sob accompanied a rapid squeeze of his dick, dragging him toward the point of no return. "So good. So damn good."

Slow and steady had been the plan, but her words banished every thought of it from his mind.

"I want to make you feel even better." Needing to see her face, he rose over her, clasping her hands in his and holding them above her head. Finesse had no place in the rush to bring her the ultimate pleasure, so he rocked into her with every ounce of his strength. The erratic in-and-out strokes burned his knees on the rug, but only the friction of their joined bodies mattered.

Her eyes widened a second before she contracted around and beneath him. Then they closed as she trembled and let loose a half cry, half scream—an invitation to surrender to his release.

His balls tightened and heat shot from his dick, sending him chasing after her with a chance to catch her. He collapsed on top of her and rolled away from the bed to keep from crushing her. She clutched at him, holding him tight while their breath mingled and his heart drummed against her chest, trying to reach hers through the aftershocks moving from her belly to his. Only the sound of their shallow panting filled his ears for several minutes.

Maybe, just maybe, the sex will convince her we should stay married for the next fifty or sixty years.

She loosened her hold and shifted to her back, breaking their physical connection. "I need food so we can do that again."

"It *was* pretty good, wasn't it?" Staggering to his feet, he grinned down at her. "I'll go put supper in the oven while you recover from your multiple orgasms. We passed a bathroom in the hall, didn't we?"

She flipped him the bird as she laid her forearm across her forehead. "Second door on the left."

"You know, I'm all yours all the time now. Just tell me when you're ready, and I'm more than willing to accommodate your desires." At the doorway, he paused to pick up his underwear and drink in the view of the beautifully naked woman stretched out on the floor.

Without uncovering her eyes, she waved a dismissive hand at him. "We'll see about that."

He blew a kiss at her and set off for the bathroom with weak knees and a smitten heart. Nothing in his wildest dreams compared to making love to Petra—his wife, the female who would just as soon strangle him as talk to him.

His plan for a quick stop to dispose of the used condom turned into a shell-shocked stare in the mirror to weigh his options. A tear in the latex could mean complications he hadn't foreseen, not that he had anything against babies. He did, however, have a problem with a surprise pregnancy influencing Pet's feelings for him. Should he even tell her about the mishap?

Keeping secrets isn't a good way to start an accidental marriage.

Washed and dressed in his boxer briefs, he shuffled to the kitchen, gathering the rest of his clothes along the way. He dropped the pile next to the laundry room and went in search of a suitable implement for warming up their supper. With the oven preheating and half their carryout order transferred to a baking sheet, he made the much-longer-than-before walk back to the master bedroom.

Better to know it's a possibility and obsess for a couple weeks than to not have a clue and freak out over a plus sign.

Clad in a t-shirt that barely covered her gorgeous butt, Petra stood with her hands braced on the dresser as he entered the room.

Her sigh didn't bode well. "So…in case you didn't notice, I think the condom leaked. Actually, based on the amount of goo running down my leg when I stood up, I'd say *leaked* is a vast understatement. Exploded is more like it."

While she didn't seem upset by the observation, she didn't exactly convey happiness, either.

He crossed to her, but he stopped an arm's length away to be on the safe side. "I was just coming to tell you it had a hole in it when I took it off. What are the chances of…you know? Is the timing right?"

Her frown answered both questions before she opened her mouth. "I'm in the middle of my cycle, so the odds are probably about as high as they can get. How cliché is conception on the wedding night?"

Maybe she isn't going to hack off my dick and grind it into sausage. "Pretty damn cliché. At least we're married and not teenagers."

"True, not that I care what other people think." She blew out a long, slow breath. "God, I'm forty-three years old. I haven't thought about having a kid since I was engaged to Number Four."

He risked a step closer and rubbed his palms along her scrunched up shoulders. "It's totally your decision as far as I'm concerned, but have you thought about taking the morning-after pill? I'll pay for it if you want me to. My condom. My fault."

"I can't take synthetic hormones. Otherwise, I'd be on the pill and a broken condom wouldn't be an issue, at least not as far as getting pregnant." She dropped her head forward and groaned.

A tiny stab of guilt pricked at his conscience for the involuntary surge of relief her predicament potentially created. Nine months would give him more opportunities to convince her they shouldn't get divorced. A sing-songy string of notes from down the hall saved him from suggesting fate had chosen them as its recipients for a bonus pack of surprises.

Straightening, she looked over her shoulder at him. "The oven's done preheating or the timer went off. We'll continue the backrub after supper."

"Preheat." Not giving her time to argue, he grasped her hand and led her toward the kitchen. "We have about ten minutes after I put the food in the oven to work some more on this part of the massage. I'm planning on saving the best for later."

She planted her feet when they reached the dining table. "You're not seriously suggesting we have sex again, are you?"

"Of course I am." He trailed his fingertips along the back of her thigh at the lower hem of her t-shirt. "Think about it. What's the likelihood of a second condom busting its seams?"

CHAPTER 5

Petra reached for the passenger door handle, but Auggie leaned across the center console and lured her into a breath-stealing kiss, igniting memories of his mouth on various parts of her body through the most decadent night of her life. If he stuck to those skillfully executed tasks and left talking to people who didn't enjoy antagonizing her, she might tolerate being married to him long enough to take a pregnancy test. At least none of the four condoms they'd used from her supply had ruptured on impact.

With a groan and a last soft brush of his lips on hers, he shifted his upper body back to his side of the car. "See you at nine. Have fun."

His husky voice and silly grin triggered a tremor in her lower belly, as if her traitorous body couldn't get enough of him. "Don't be late."

She pushed out of the car, careful not to juggle the bakery box on her lap as she stood, and hurried down the sidewalk to the entrance of The Homegrown Café before he could try to talk her into a quickie. A familiar laugh from behind sent heat rushing up her neck to her cheeks.

Riley caught up with her when Petra adjusted her hold on the box to open the door. "I'll get it. Looks like Auggie gave up the goods for a kiss again."

Unable to look Riley in the eye and lie, Petra trudged past her with the knowledge that no secret was safe in their tight group of friends—not Tate's sperm-donor fiasco with Big Jim Cochon and not Riley's breast-cancer-scare-induced marriage contract with Deacon Jeffries. "Save it. It gets better."

"Better?" Riley followed her to the snack table. "This, I gotta hear."

"As soon as everybody's here." In need of something sweet to soothe her nerves, Petra plopped the only Boston cream doughnut—her second freebie of the day—on a plate. "I'm only telling this story once, and it damn well better not leave this room."

Carrying a tray of assorted goodies, Tate rounded the order counter of her cozy restaurant. "Hey, Petra. Riley. What happened?"

"More than a kiss evidently. That man is a genius with frosting and cream filling." Riley snapped up the maple cream stick and bit off the end. "Mm."

You have no fucking idea.

"Ah, doughnuts." Tate set the snacks beside a platter of fruit and dip. "You didn't threaten to bury the hatchet in him, did you?"

Instead of acknowledging the question, Petra grunted and loaded her plate with mac-n-cheese bites, bruschetta, mini quiches, and an assortment of apples, pears, and grapes.

"Hi, everybody!" Wally waltzed in with Georgie on her heels. "Oh, doughnuts! What did they cost you this time, Petra?"

Riley's grin made Petra's stomach sink. "We're about to find out. Grab some snacks and come sit down."

Her friends wasted no time filling their plates and the seats around their book-club table. Then all eyes turned toward Petra.

She leaned back in her chair and swallowed to wet her suddenly dry-as-a-desert mouth. "Okay, so I guess I should give you a little background. You know how I've been wanting to expand? I signed a purchase agreement for half of The Candlestick Maker shop on Monday."

With the cream stick halfway to her mouth, Riley frowned. "Half? I thought you were going to try to buy the whole thing."

"I wanted to, but Hugh refused. Supposedly, he and Gramps and

Otto had an agreement that whoever closed first had to give the others first dibs on the shop. Auggie wanted it too and I didn't want to share the space, so we each got half."

Georgie nodded. "Makes good legal sense since verbal agreements have a precedent for being binding in many cases. I'm happy to look over the contract before you close, if you want me to. Actually, if Auggie will agree to it, I'd like to look at his as well to be sure there aren't overlapping claims to any areas of the building. Better safe than ending up in litigation."

"Shit, I hadn't even thought of that." Wishing her mug contained Guinness instead of tea, Petra took a drink to wash down a quiche. "Anyway, I went up to Elyria yesterday to request a reassessment for property taxes, and guess who shows up while I'm walking to the county building. The gold digger."

Wally snorted. "What did he want? Still holding out hope you'll be his sugar mama?"

"He was headed to the probate office to apply for a wedding license. And, of course, he had to ask if I'd ever gotten married." Petra lifted her hand when Riley opened her mouth. "I planned to ignore his question, but then Auggie shows up out of nowhere, saying he missed me and getting all kissy face. And he introduced himself to Six as my fiancé."

Three chins dropped. Only Georgie seemed unfazed by the story. "I see where this is going. You and Auggie have a marriage license, don't you? You don't have to use it. Just destroy it or let it expire. Technically speaking, you're not even engaged since you didn't agree to marry him."

Too humiliated to look at her friends, Petra buried her face in her hands. "Auggie said we were getting married right after we got the license, and Six and his plastic girlfriend asked to be witnesses. Then Oscar Banyan showed up in the hallway."

"Oh. My. God." For once, Georgie seemed at a loss for words.

Daring a peek between her fingers, Petra sighed. "Needless to say, things got out of hand before I could stop them. So…Auggie and I are legally married. And he'd dropped off his car for service, so taking him home seemed like the nice thing to do."

Wally popped out of her chair and wrapped an arm around Petra's shoulders. "You look like you're still in shock. What are you going to do?"

"It gets worse."

Tate's eyes widened. "Worse?"

"I figured since we were married, I deserved some conjugal benefits for my trouble." Petra straightened and clasped her hands in her lap. "He spent the night at my house. And one of the condoms—"

"No way!" Riley held out the last inch of her pastry. "You mean he creamed you too?"

Hysterical chortling spilled out of Wally and quickly turned into a bad case of the giggles. "*One* of? How many did you use?"

Georgie, on the other hand, donned her attorney glower. "You don't have to answer that. Have you done the calculations? What's the likelihood of conception? Pregnancy will make a divorce significantly more complicated."

"It's very possible." *Divorce. Pregnancy.* The sick feeling in the pit of her stomach forced Petra to her feet, and she paced to the order counter. "He apologized and took total responsibility, but I'm the one who invited him on a honeymoon. It's as much my fault as his. When I told him the morning-after pill isn't an option because of the synthetic hormones, he gave me a backrub and fed me."

Pulling a legal pad from her messenger bag, Georgie morphed into full-blown lawyer mode. "That doesn't sound like a man who's concerned about an unintended wedding or a condom failure. Are you sure he didn't prearrange the chance meeting with Banyan and try to impregnate you intentionally?"

"The Grouch seemed kind of put out, like he didn't want to perform the ceremony, and it was over in less than two minutes. Not the sex. That was…" Although she wasn't a religious person, "spiritual" fit better than any other description. "Never mind. It would've taken a lot of planning to set up something that elaborate, especially when it was my idea to go to my house."

"Okay. I trust your judgment until or unless we acquire evidence to the contrary." After a few more scribbles on her notepad, Georgie set down the pen. "How soon do you want to proceed with the divorce? I can meet tomorrow late afternoon to discuss options with you and Auggie."

Troubled by her friend's obvious anticipation of ending a marriage, even though it was accidental, Petra shrugged to hide her discomfort. "I don't know. I just needed to tell somebody for now. Can we talk about the book and eat instead?"

"You bet." Tate waved her back to the table. "We're here if you need us—and if you don't. Did anybody make it past the part where the brother hears knocking noises in the basement and his flashlight dies when he gets to the bottom of the steps? I made Jim double-check the locks on the doors and windows before we went to bed."

Riley refilled her mug and passed the teapot to Wally. "I stopped when the neighbor girl saw the strange light in the woods and went by herself to see what it was. Her dog never should've saved her. I made Amanda and Fiona read that scene. No stepdaughters of mine are going to be dumb as a cow patty. Too stupid to live means you should be the first to die. A cookbook would've been more entertaining."

Sliding her legal pad and pen into her bag, Georgie frowned. "I thought you hated to cook."

"I do. That's my point. I hate stupid people more."

Wally snickered. "Riley's just grumpy because she has to be careful about not using the f-word in front of Deacon's kids."

"Damn right I am. Swearing is like exercise. I need to do it regularly to stay healthy." Riley's prescription drew laughter from around the table.

The predictable banter continued through the book discussion, decimation of the snacks, and cleanup, lulling Petra into a mostly normal mood. Her accidental husband's appearance on the sidewalk as she exited the building with Georgie set off another round of stomach acrobatics.

Auggie leaned against the front fender of his car, looking too much like an irresistible bad boy from her high school days. "Hi, Pet. Georgina. How was book club?"

"Auggie." After a polite nod in his direction, Georgie glanced toward Petra. "It was interesting. Yes, very interesting. Call me, Petra."

Impressed by her friend's ability to turn her facial expressions on and off at will, Petra directed her gaze at Georgie. "I will. See you Sunday at Wally's. Drive safely."

"You too. Good night." Without another acknowledgment of Auggie, her lawyer friend set off at a good clip toward the parking lot across the street.

"I'm glad you told your friends what happened." He opened the passenger door and gestured her inside.

His gentlemanly behavior instigated warring feelings, but she sat and folded her legs into the space in front of the seat. "What makes you think I did?"

Instead of responding, he closed her door and rounded the car to the driver's side. He settled behind the steering wheel and started the engine before looking at her. "Georgina implied a lot more than what she said. She's ready to file divorce papers on your behalf and probably sue my ass for child support as soon as we know if you're pregnant."

"You got all that from her telling me to call her?"

"Yeah. Are you saying you didn't tell them? And a straight answer would be nice."

She crossed her arms under her breasts and returned his disconcerting stare. "Fine, I told them. Everything."

He shifted into gear and pulled away from the sidewalk. "I don't get why you think it's a big deal. I talked to Jim and Deacon about what happened at the courthouse. Considering what they went through with Tate and Riley, I thought they might have some advice for me."

Hoping the alternating dark and light between streetlights hid her wavering emotions, she turned to look out the window. "I can't wait to hear how that conversation went."

"When we get to your house. I brought a change of clothes and my shaving kit, but I'll only stay if you want me to. If not, we'll talk and then I'll leave. No pressure." He didn't say another word during the ten-minute drive, but his silence and the absence of his usual teasing spoke volumes.

After months of blatant innuendo and flirting, his sudden transformation into Mr. Kind-and-Considerate sparked as much annoyance as concern. Did he truly believe she would sic Georgie after him and leave him destitute? Or did he hope for an expedient divorce now that he'd finally succeeded in getting her into bed?

The headlights flashed a pair of expanding circles on the garage door as he pulled into her driveway. Then they vanished, leaving only the porch light's faint glow in the darkness. "Do you mind if I come around and open your door?"

Damn it, men need to come with an instruction manual. "How about if you get your overnight bag and I open my own door?" Not waiting for confirmation, she climbed out of the car and dug her house keys from her purse.

He trailed her up the porch steps, still uncharacteristically quiet. "I'll go if you change your mind."

"Damn right you will." She waved him into the house and locked up behind him. "Put your stuff in the bedroom and come back out to the couch."

A baker's dozen of reasons for his behavior formed in her mind as he traipsed down the hall and disappeared. None of them improved her mood or relieved the confusing jumble of concerns wrestling in her belly, not the least of which was the possibility that she might actually like him. How middle-school hormone-ish would that be?

She dropped into the recliner, determined to banish any romantic notion her subconscious mind conjured up. Good sex had nothing to do with the heart.

Footsteps added a twist to the activity giving her insides a workout, and Auggie sat on the end of the couch closest to her. "Jim and Deke gave me some advice tonight, based on mistakes they think they've made. My gut says they're right, so I'm just going to lay things out now so there's no misunderstanding."

Steeling herself against everything from elation to disappointment, she gripped the arms of the chair. "Okay. Good. I prefer total honesty."

"Good." He rested his elbows on his knees and glanced down toward his clasped hands. Then he pinned her in her seat with an unreadable stare. "We've known each other a long time, ever since we were kids, and I've always thought of you as a friend, even though you're older than me by six years."

Son of a jacking-off prick, I'm getting the friend talk. Well, that's a new excuse for being dumped.

Not needing to hear more, she stood. "Friends with benefits works for me, as long as neither of us is dating or screwing anybody else. Not that you'd purposely expose me to an STD, but my health is more important than getting la—"

"That's not what I meant at all!" He bounded to his feet and placed his hands on her shoulders. His jaw twitched and he huffed out a breath. "Remember that day last spring when I caught you playing in mud puddles in the parking lot? It was pouring down rain and you were stomping around in those boots you always wear with this giant grin, like it was your birthday and Christmas all rolled into one. Something clicked on."

"Clicked on?" Her stomach fell to her knees and panic flooded her veins. *No. Not another guy claiming he loves me and changing his mind when he finds out I'm not rich, making me choose him or my career, finding out he's a cheater, etcetera, after I decide I can trust him.*

His expression softened. "Yeah. I fell in love with you that day. And I don't want a divorce."

CHAPTER 6

WHETHER SHE PREFERRED HONESTY OR NOT, PETRA OBVIOUSLY HADN'T seen his admission coming. The color had drained from her face and she seemed a bit wobbly on her feet.

Auggie guided her onto the couch and sat down beside her, torn between relief at admitting his feelings and trepidation that he'd blown his chance with her. "All the flirting and teasing... I was kind of hoping you'd figure out why on your own. After all the idiots who treated you like crap, I thought I should take things slow. Give you time to notice and get used to the idea. I guess I should've just told you the truth and taken your rejection like a man."

She gave his foot a half-hearted kick. "Why do men always assume women can't handle directness and that they have to think for us?"

"It was me I was trying to protect, and our friendship. I know you can take care of yourself. It's part of what I respect about you. And in case you're wondering, everything that happened yesterday was... I don't know. I don't think it was an accident, but it wasn't premeditated. I had no idea that ass and his mannequin girlfriend would be at the courthouse, and Oscar never would've agreed to marry us without your consent. In fact, he tried to talk me out of it—and not because he hates performing weddings. He told me the same thing you did—

that the creep's opinion doesn't matter." Fairly certain his rambling was only digging the hole deeper, Auggie sighed. "Anyway, I'm sorry for not just telling you back then. I probably don't deserve it, but I'd like the chance to show you I'm serious about staying married to you."

"Is this about—"

"No. It has nothing to do with the broken condom." Turning toward her, he lifted her legs across his lap and tipped his head to look her in the eye. "One way or the other, I love you. It's that simple."

"How am I supposed to know if you're telling the truth? I suck at choosing trustworthy men." Her lower lip vanished behind her upper one.

"You didn't choose me. I chose you." He nudged her chin higher. "Not on purpose, but that's okay. My heart seems to know what it's doing. It's been keeping me alive for a long time."

A hint of a grin warmed him from the inside out. "That could change in a hurry if you're messing around with me."

"But I really enjoy messing around with you. How about if we go do that right now? Four in the morning will be here before we know it." Unable to resist, he kissed her cheek, her nose, and then her lips. "Unless, of course, you want me to leave."

Indecision appeared and disappeared in the blink of her eye, but the enduring desire there didn't mean she would fall victim to it. She clambered off his lap and extended a hand toward him. "Let's go to bed before I change my mind. We can discuss this some more tomorrow."

"How'd it go last night?" Deacon Jeffries closed the empty folder that had held The Baker's October financial report printouts and raised an eyebrow at Auggie. "Petra's almost as stubborn as Riley."

While he wasn't too sure "almost" was accurate, Auggie chuckled. "Better than I expected. I'm pretty sure Georgina Swofford's ready to swoop in with divorce papers at any moment, but I told Petra how I feel about her and she didn't kick me out of her house. I think she might even believe me when I said I didn't set up the whole fiasco with her ex-fiancé and Banyan."

"I'm glad it's working out. She seems pretty level-headed, even if she and Riley like to throw axes for fun." His accountant returned the folder to his computer bag and stood. "Fiona asked if she could go last time. Thankfully, Riley's flat-out no probably saved us from another trip to the emergency room, besides the fact that Fee's fingers are still healing from the latest incident at school. The I-have-a-mom honeymoon period seems to have worn off with that round of head-butting."

A ripple of dread made its way along his spine and into his chest. Auggie leaned against the desk to steady himself.

"Hey, are you feeling okay? You look a little queasy." Deke stared right at him for several seconds and then burst out laughing. "Sorry, buddy. You should see your face. Birth control failure or are you and Petra trying to have a baby?"

Auggie sank into his chair, wondering what fate had in store for him today. "That obvious, huh? Condom broke."

"Before or after you told her how you feel?"

"Before, not that the timing matters. I have no idea if she wants kids." The sudden realization triggered a new bout of lightheadedness that didn't fade with a slow inhale and exhale. "She didn't threaten to castrate me, but she's not exactly open about her feelings unless she's pissed off."

"Maybe you should follow the same advice Jim and I gave you last time. If you want to know what she thinks about it, ask her. She might not even be pregnant anyway." Deke slung the strap of his bag over his shoulder and patted his pants pockets. "Keys. Phone. I have to head to my four-thirty appointment, but call me if you need moral support."

"Thanks, buddy. I appreciate it." Auggie accompanied his accountant to the front of the bakery. "Talk to you later."

With a wave, Deacon headed for the door and then held it open for a woman and her teary-faced, wobbly on his feet toddler. After a glance in Auggie's direction, he hurried outside.

Yeah, I'm already aware that could be Pet and our kid in a couple years. And, no, I don't know how I feel about it yet. Auggie greeted his customer with a smile as he washed his hands. "Can the little fellow have a sugar cookie? With or without icing."

"You're a lifesaver. He just dropped his last fishy cracker in the parking lot and had a meltdown because I wouldn't let him eat it. No icing please." The woman hefted the boy into her arms and helped him grab hold of the treat. "Thanks. I have an online order to pick up. Markley."

At the cubby with prepared orders, he checked the receipt and then the contents of the only remaining shopping bag. As he set the sale on the counter, his wife coming in the door snagged most of his attention, setting off a familiar flutter in his stomach. "A dozen dinner rolls, half a dozen croissants, and a loaf of brown bread. Can I get you anything else? There's not much left this time of day, but everything except special orders are half off during the last half hour we're open."

"Do you have—"

"Mo!" The kid clapped, sending the crumbs on his fingers and jacket flying every which way.

"Cookies are all gone." The woman grabbed for his hands and sighed. "Sorry. He made a mess all over the floor. He's a total barbarian with food."

Auggie chuckled and offered her a napkin. "Don't worry about it. I need to sweep and mop pretty soon anyway. What else can I get for you and Conan?"

"Nan-nan-nan-nan-nan." The kid clapped again and aimed a wide semi-toothless grin in Auggie's direction.

Shaking her head, his mother cracked a tired smile. "That's what his daddy calls him. Some hoagie rolls or subs? I'm hoping the butcher shop can slice a couple pounds of rib eye steaks for me."

"I'll see what I have left, and you can ask the owner about the steaks without going anywhere. She's right behind you." He rounded the counter and gave Petra a too-short kiss on the lips on his way to check the rack. "My wife. She's the butcher. I think I see a package of hoagies on the top shelf."

Instead of filleting him with a scowl for publicly outing their relationship, Petra wore a thoughtful expression when she glanced toward his customer, at him, and then back again. "Thin, like for Philly cheesesteaks?"

The woman nodded as she adjusted her hold on the miniature barbarian. "Yes, exactly."

"Not a problem. Stop by when you're done here and we'll take good care of you." Walking with Auggie to the counter, Petra pinched his ass and smirked at him. "You gotta watch out for this guy, though. He could sell milk to a cow."

"Moo-moo!" The kid flung his arms around his mother's neck and giggled.

Petra's belly laugh matched the one that had made Auggie fall madly in love with her out of the blue six months ago—and it dragged him deeper still. "I have just the thing for you at my shop, kiddo. Do you have a cow in a can?"

The woman grinned as she set her purse next to the shopping bag and withdrew her wallet. "No, he doesn't, but a few days ago my husband was talking about the cow in a can he had when he was a kid and wondered if anybody made them anymore. He'll be so surprised. Do you have children?"

Auggie rung up the hoagie rolls and added them to her purchases instead of risking a peek at his wife's reaction to the question. "Nope. We've talked about it a little, but we just got married two days ago."

"Really? Congratulations!" Somehow juggling her son and her money, his customer handed him exact change for the half-price afterthought. "How did you meet?"

Petra grabbed the grocery sack by the handles. "I've known him his whole life. I even babysat him a few times when I was a teenager. He was quite the little hel— Uh, troublemaker. If you're ready, I can carry your bag for you."

"Thanks! Ooh, a younger man. Good for you." With a wink and a wave at him, the woman followed Petra toward the exit. "And good for you, marrying an older woman. It's nice to know I'm not the only one who thinks age doesn't matter for women and their men."

Hoping for another kiss to hold him over until closing time, Auggie caught up with them at the door and pulled his wife into his arms. Her lips softened against his. "Mm. Sometimes, love just happens. Wrap up some T-bones and I'll throw them on the grill for supper when we get home."

Petra hummed her approval. "Garlic bread?"

"Yep. See you in about half an hour." He kissed her again before stepping aside to let his customer out of the door. "Thanks for coming in."

The woman hefted her wiggling son higher and rubbed his back when he rested his head on her shoulder. "Thank you. Conan says thank you for the cookie too. Have a nice rest of your day."

"Nan-nan-nan-nan-nan." Without lifting his head, the kid giggled and waved.

Leaning toward Petra, his mother stepped out onto the sidewalk. "You two are such a cute couple."

Yeah, but will we still be a couple at Thanksgiving? Christmas? New Year's?

Auggie made a mental note to snap a selfie with his wife after supper, in case she decided to take Georgie's advice.

Will a baby make any difference?

Yeah. I could end up divorced and paying child support if—

He shook off the doubts on his way to the broom closet. Despite the wariness her past relationships had wrought, she wouldn't punish him unless he earned it—like the smashed doughnut in the face. The lack of immediate retribution for their impromptu wedding proved she at least partially appreciated his attempt to protect her.

Leaving his part-timer to handle the few last-minute shoppers, Auggie busied himself with sweeping, mopping, and prepping the front for closing. By the time he locked the door and closed the blinds, the kitchen had been transformed into its nightly spotless space as well.

Now he could spend time with his wife—his first Friday night date since well before Cupid's arrow had buried itself in his heart.

Nate met him at the service entrance with the key to his Harley dangling from his fingers. "How the hell did you get Petra to marry you?"

A glance toward the back of The Butcher shop and the sassy, sexy love of his life as Auggie locked up sent his pulse thumping. "Long story."

His expert cake decorator smirked and slipped his helmet onto his bald head. "I bet it's an interesting one."

"It is, but I don't think she'd appreciate the whole town gossiping about it. I'll see you tomorrow."

"Don't do anything I wouldn't do." Nate slapped Auggie on the back and then chuckled as he headed toward the sleek machine parked in its usual spot.

That's not saying much. Pocketing his keys, Auggie walked to Petra's truck, arriving in time to relieve her of the bag she carried and greet her with a mostly chaste kiss. "This is much better than teasing you so you'll pay attention to me."

Her lips twitched before curving into a wide grin. "Still six years old, are you?"

"Maybe, but you're the one who likes playing in puddles. Besides, if I'm six, that makes you twelve, and that's definitely robbing the cradle." Determined to get the much-needed conversation out of the way, he rounded the front end of the pickup while she climbed in the driver's side. As he buckled his seat belt, he pulled in a calming breath and waited for her to start the engine. "Speaking of cradles, I think we should talk about what happens if you're pregnant."

CHAPTER 7

A POST-WORK SHOWER AND AN AMAZING STEAK DINNER GAVE PETRA lots of time to mull over how to respond during Auggie's what-if conversation. Unfortunately, her thoughts on the matter were no less muddled than they had been since their honeymoon mishap. She added the last plate to the dishwasher and set it to start, half hoping he'd forgotten about the must-have discussion.

He patted the cushion next to him as she joined him in the living room. "Come sit with me. We've procrastinated long enough."

Using his lap for a pillow, she stretched out on the couch with her bare feet hanging over the far end. "It's not procrastinating if you don't know what you want to do."

He combed his fingers through her damp hair, looking far more serious than normal. "I'll go first then. Like I told you yesterday, I love you and I don't want a divorce, whether you're pregnant or not. If you're not, I'm okay with it. I never met a woman I wanted to marry before, so having kids wasn't really on my radar. If you are, I'm mostly okay with it too, even if I'll worry about you the whole damn time. Not that you're old, but having a baby over forty seems like it would be high-risk. Plus, you work harder than a lot of people I know and I don't want anything bad to happen to you. And last but not least, I'm selfish. I kind of like having you all to myself."

Moved by his concern, she hooked her hand around the back of his neck and tugged him forward for a kiss. "I appreciate your being honest. I'm a little worried about trying to balance work and motherhood. Actually, more like a lot. I don't know if I can do my job with a belly the size of a watermelon, and I can't close the shop for three or four months. It's not that I hate kids or anything, but I like my life the way it is."

"With or without me in it?" His directness shouldn't have surprised her.

She frowned and narrowed her eyes at him. "Is. That's the word I said. Not was or will be."

He frowned back at her, his face still inches from hers. "With or without me? You're hemming and hawing."

"You sound like my grandmother."

His sigh tickled her cheek and his breath smelled like a perfectly grilled T-bone and garlic. "You're still doing it. I'm not asking you to tell me you love me, not unless you really do. I just want to hear you say you want me in your life. That you like me. Not just for sex. Romantically."

She licked her suddenly dry lips and swallowed to wet her parched throat. "Every time I've ever told a guy—"

"We're already married. No more broken engagements. I promise." He brushed her hair away from her forehead. "Pet, I get why this is hard for you, but humor me. Please?"

His light touch and soft plea allowed him past the wall she couldn't seem to tear down, and the tightness in her chest eased. "Okay. I *like* you. As more than a friend."

"Thank you. That makes me very happy." He smiled and then kissed her nose. "Does it make you happy?"

Surprisingly, it did. For the first time in ages, being in a relationship didn't mean waiting for one shoe or the other to drop. "Yeah. Ready to go to bed?"

᪥

"SORRY I'M LATE!" PETRA DROPPED HER PURSE AT HER FEET AND HUNG her jacket on the coat tree in Wally's foyer.

A chorus of greetings came from the direction of the kitchen and this week's Sunday night books-and-cocktails host popped her head around the corner. "Hurry up! You're missing my online dating stories."

Cell phone in hand and a genuine smile on her lips, Petra hurried down the hall. "This ought to be good."

"You have no idea." Wally pointed to the empty chair squeezed between Riley and Georgie. "Have a seat and help yourself to whatever you can reach on the table. Since you and Tate aren't drinking, I decided to go with virgin options to remind us of our youth."

Snickers came from Riley, Tate, and Wally, and Georgie cracked a smile in her usually buttoned-up sense of humor.

Riley bumped Petra's shoulder and grinned. "How's married life treating you?"

Petra poured a hefty portion of what looked like mango daiquiri into a tall glass. "A hell of a lot better than engaged life. He likes to cook, he isn't a slob, and the man knows how to—"

"Fuck?" The favorite word from Riley's vocabulary drew laughter from around the table.

"Well, yeah, but that's not what I was going to say."

Tate let out a blissful sigh. "He's not the only one with that skill. Bake? Jim ordered one of Auggie's chocolate éclair cakes for our one-month anniversary tomorrow."

"Also true, but not what I was thinking." Petra added a straw to her drink and slurped up a sinus-numbing mouthful of the frozen concoction.

Georgie picked up a cracker topped with Easy Cheese. "Follow directions, I hope, for your sake. There's nothing worse than a man who ignores your instructions."

Shaking her head, Petra grabbed the can of cheese and sprayed a glob on her finger. "He's better at it than most men I've known, but, no."

Their host set a bowl of assorted candy in front of her. "The way you're glowing, I'd say he knows how to make you feel like you're the only woman in the world he'll ever love."

"Exactly. How did you get to be so smart, Wally?"

"Once upon a time, I had a husband just like that. Not a day went by that Bobby didn't tell me I was important to him in some way or another. Mostly with actions. Sometimes with flowers or books or a box of my favorite chocolates. Or he'd make supper if I had a rough day with Anabelle or throw in a load a laundry before he left for work. Not too many men like him exist, at least not from what I can tell. Besides, Auggie's been mooning over you for months. A man who's truly in love doesn't give up when the woman of his heart needs time to figure out she might feel the same."

Tate nodded and took a turn with the Easy Cheese. "Jim waited thirty years for the right time to tell me how he feels. That's dedication."

"And so romantic." Wally stretched past Georgie and snatched a Kit Kat from the bowl. "The creeps on those dating sites want a mother or a booty call, not a partner or a companion. Geesh, all I want is a man to go to the movies with and talk to once in a while now that Anabelle is becoming more independent. She doesn't need me as much as she used to. And she went out on a date last night. Eat some of this leftover Halloween candy so I don't pig out on all of it."

After another squirt, Tate passed the can to Riley. "You're an awesome mom, Wally, and you should be proud of yourself for teaching Anabelle she doesn't have to rely on you for everything. Did she tell you I'm training her to manage the café while I'm checking in deliveries?"

"Yeah, right after she told me Darren asked her to a movie and dinner. She was so excited when I picked her up from work on Friday." Wally gave Tate a one-armed hug. "I can't tell you how much I appreciate the opportunities you've given her and the other Downs kids."

"Aw, you're welcome." Tate sniffled and wiped her sleeve across her cheek. "They're some of the sweetest people I know."

Digging for a Reese's Cup, Petra scrambled to change the subject to something less worrisome, considering the possibility that she might be pregnant. "I didn't know you signed up for an online matchmaking service. Call me if you need me to kick somebody's ass."

"I don't think that's going to be a problem. I'm on day sixteen of the thirty-day trial, and I haven't gotten past a first message exchange yet. You'd think men in their forties and fifties would've aged to at least the maturity of a twenty-two-year-old by now." With a glass of raspberry-colored liquid in one hand and a Kit Kat stick in the other, Wally raised her drink toward Georgie. "To the two remaining single women of our club. May we continue to find happiness in ourselves and our dear friends, because I have no confidence in men contributing to it."

A rare grin curved across Georgie's face as she clinked her daiquiri glass against Wally's pint canning jar. "To being single, happy marriages, and good friends."

More clinking made its way around the table, but the mood and conversation were far less raucous than their usual biweekly gatherings. So much had changed in their club since their first meeting almost eight weeks ago. Three weddings—one of which almost hadn't been official until after some arm-twisting and another that was accidental. Two possible pregnancies—one of which had been intentional and confirmed, plus another that had been neither.

What had happened to their over-forty, single-and-loving-it group?
We're dropping like flies. And I don't even hate it.

"HAPPY ONE-WEEK ANNIVERSARY. I WANT TO GIVE YOU A WEDDING ring."

Still floating on a cloud from spectacular early morning sex, Petra lifted her head from Auggie's chest, where his heartbeat had erratically and then steadily thumped in her ear. "I appreciate the sentiment, but I can't wear a ring to work. Too dangerous with the meat grinders and saws."

He rolled sideways, taking her with him. The faint glow from the clock lit up half of his face and the sexy shadow of stubble on his jaw. "What if we got matching ring tattoos? Remember from our wedding ceremony?"

"You know tattoos are permanent, right?"

"That's the point, isn't it?" He slid his palm against hers and linked their fingers together. "Or I wouldn't mind wearing a real one on a chain around my neck. Just as a reminder that we're committed to each other, even though we started out a little unconventional. You want to stay married, don't you?"

A lot had changed in the week that had passed since the incident at the courthouse.

Not that much. She'd been attracted to him before their inadvertent vows, despite her efforts to the contrary. "Possibly. You're growing on me."

His mischievous chuckle sparked a tremor in her lower belly. "Any time you want."

"Sex fiend. You know what I meant."

"Nope. You should tell me exactly what you mean so I don't misunderstand." He kissed her forehead, setting off an equally shaky feeling in her heart.

"The thing is..." She licked her lips to buy some time to sort out her thoughts. "Okay, so... I think maybe I might be... Damn it, I love you. And don't you dare tease me about it."

His soft exhale warmed her face, but his barely visible smile warmed her soul. "Never. Not in a million years. Those are the words I've been waiting to hear for months. They're beautiful, like you. I love you too, Pet."

"I guess we better stay married then." She tugged him closer for the kind of kiss he'd awakened her with. Annoying chimes interrupted as soon as she touched her lips to his. "That alarm has sucky timing."

"Sucky timing would've been going off before we got off or before you could tell me you love me." He reached over her and killed the noise coming from the clock. "Grab another ten minutes of sleep while I take a shower."

"You just earned yourself barbecued ribs for supper."

"Sounds almost as delicious as you." After a brief kiss, he crawled out of bed and sauntered toward the bathroom.

Captivated by his naked form, she burrowed into the covers to watch him until he was nothing but a dark blob. *It's about damn time I got lucky in love.*

As she drifted off, the phone on her nightstand buzzed, pulling her from sleep. Then it buzzed again a few seconds later.

"This better be important." She snatched her cell and squinted against the brightness while she opened her text messages. Didn't Georgie ever sleep?

"Closing on the storefront is today, isn't it? We need to meet before then. Are you free this morning?"

What could be so important that it couldn't wait until at least sunrise?

"8:15 at your shop?" Dots bounced in the text bar, indicating her lawyer friend had more to say, which was often the case. *"This is too serious for a phone call or text."*

Autocorrect kept Petra from having to put forth too much brain-power to answer. *"8:15 is fine. Go to bed."*

"Can't. Working on co-parenting negotiations. See you at the shop."

She yawned as she located the thumbs-up emoji. "I need coffee."

When Auggie joined her at the counter eight minutes later, she poured two mugs of French roast, savoring the robust scent permeating the kitchen.

He wrapped an arm around her waist and nuzzled her ear. "You're up. Couldn't go back to sleep?"

"I tried to, but Georgie texted me. I swear that woman works at least thirty-eight hours a day." Petra slid a mug toward his free hand. "We're meeting at the shop this morning."

"She isn't trying to talk you into divorcing me, is she? Or a pre-nup, after the fact?"

"Nah. Something to do with Hugh and today's closing, I think. She was being vague, probably on purpose. Anyway, it's too damn early for…" His lips on her neck short-circuited her train of thought. "Stop that, or we're going to be late. Eggs for breakfast?"

"I'm just happy that I'm capable of distracting you." He released her and picked up his mug. "Since you made the coffee, I'll cook the eggs. Scrambled and rye toast or breakfast burrito?"

"Burrito with pepper jack and salsa verde." Cursing the steam still wafting from the cup on the counter, she shuffled to the fridge for the ingredients. The rattle of pots and pans and utensils brought an involuntary smile to her face. Their morning routine ran like a well-oiled machine—or an old married couple's ability to finish each other's sentences. "Cheddar and ketchup?"

"I'll have what you're having."

"I thought you liked cheddar and ketchup on your eggs."

"God, no. I only ate it to make you laugh. Now that I know you love me, I don't have to try so hard to be a goofball."

"But what if I like the goofball?" She removed an egg from the carton and grinned at him. "Catch."

Spying her husband outside The Butcher's street entrance, Petra set aside the pan of freshly ground sirloin and stripped off her gloves. Her heart pitter-pattered when his gaze met hers through the glass as she approached the door. Had love ever felt this good before?

Auggie held up a pair of bakery bags and the words on his lips were unmistakable.

Boston cream. God, the man knew her weakness and exploited it every chance he got—making up for his devious deals of spit-swapping for doughnuts.

She flipped the locks and greeted him with a smirk. "No time to trade sex for a pastry. Georgie'll be here any minute."

Raising a hand to his chest, he sighed. "You wound me, dear wife. I brought you—and your friend—a gift. No payment expected in return, except that you love me until the end of time."

The giddiness morphed into a giggle. "Well, in that case, I suppose I can accept your offer of sweets, Romeo."

"I'm not some melodramatic teenager suffering from infatuation. Cupid used a full-sized arrow on me, Pet, and I'm not stupid enough to think you'd kill yourself over any man." He handed her the bags and kissed her cheek. "I need to meet with one of my contractors at lunchtime, so I'll see you at the closing appointment."

"Sounds good." Tugging on the front of his baker's jacket, she pulled him back for a more satisfying kiss. "Thanks for the doughnuts, Mr. Lochsley."

"You're very welcome, Mrs. Hofmeier." His wink and wide grin as he headed back outside sent her pulse skipping again. A moment before the door swung closed, he grabbed the handle and held it open. "Good morning, Georgina."

"Auggie." Georgie nodded once and stepped inside. "Thank you. Petra, can we talk in your office?"

"Sure." Dragging her attention from the most amazing guy she'd never dated, Petra locked the door and led her friend past the counter. "He brought doughnuts for us."

"Resorting to bribery already, is he?" Georgie gestured toward the chair behind the desk. "You'll want to sit down for this."

"This?" A disconcerting shiver slithered up Petra's spine as she sat.

"I finally had a chance to go over the purchase agreements." After slipping on her reading glasses, her friend set out two sets of papers, both with several places highlighted in yellow. "According to the documents you emailed to me, you're paying significantly more per square foot than Augustus Hofmeier, except the parts don't add up. Did he and Mr. Collier discuss the selling price in your presence?"

"No. Hugh wrote his asking price on a piece of paper and gave it to me. Actually, two prices. One if Auggie and I agreed to buy the storefront as partners and one if I decided to buy half of it by myself. They talked like they'd discussed terms before..." The shiver froze into a solid knot at Petra's neck. Pounding her fist on the desk, she silently cursed herself for not seeing the conspiracy between her grandfather's buddy and her husband. "He knew, damn it. I should've thrown that egg at him. Hell, the whole flipping dozen."

Georgie's normally unreadable poker face sported a grimace. "It gets worse."

CHAPTER 8

LIFE IS GOOD.

Auggie slid the blueprints for The Candlestick Maker into their tube and stood it in the corner next to his chair. His plan had come together perfectly. Construction would begin in the new space on Monday and end in time for a Black Friday grand opening.

A glance at his computer screen warned him he needed to leave for the title company now to be on time for the closing. As he rose, his office door banged open.

Mr. Collier hobbled inside, his cane swinging toward the desk. "What did you do, Augustus? Petra left a message that she changed her mind about the shop and she canceled the appointment to sign the paperwork. She even threatened to sic Eddie, Otto, and her lawyer on me."

"*What?*" Auggie jerked backward when the cane swooped toward his head. "What did *I* do? I signed the purchase agreement you had drawn up."

The old man dropped into the only other chair in the room and thumped his weapon against the floor. "And from what I gathered from her yelling, you married her sometime since our meeting at the shop last week."

"Yeah, so?"

"So you were supposed to wait until after the closing. Didn't you read the fine print in that darn purchase agreement? My lawyer and I had it all laid out. Then you had to go and throw a wrench in everything by running off to the courthouse like your pants were on fire. Haven't you heard of premarital sex? If it was good enough for Joanie and me sixty years ago, it's good enough for you now."

"Geez, sex had nothing to do with it!" Shoving his fingers through his hair, Auggie tried to wrap his brain around the mess. "Start at the beginning, because I don't have the foggiest idea what you're talking about. And, for the record, Pet and I didn't run off to the courthouse. She was outside when one of her ex-fiancés showed up and started harassing her. Long story short, we ended up at the probate office, applied for a license to get the loser off her back, and got trapped into a ceremony in the hallway, as luck would have it. But, until today, everything was working out just fine."

"Oh, this is not good." Mr. Collier balanced the cane across his knees and tapped his fingers on the polished wood. "Any chance of talking you into a divorce while we get things straightened out?"

"No. Actually, hell no. I love my wife and she loves me. Rewrite the contracts. And no funny business this time." Spying his notes on the desk, he sighed. "You know this completely screws up the renovation schedule, right?"

The cane thunked on the floor as the old man rose and again when he walked to the door. "Hey, I'm not the one who didn't read the whole agreement."

"I'm not done talking to you! Get back in here!"

The rhythmic *thump, thump, thump* grew fainter and the *click, click, click* of high heels took its place. Georgina Swofford stood in the doorway a second later, the manila envelope in her hand standing out against her red coat. "May I come in?"

"Why the hell not?" Auggie gestured toward the chair Hugh had vacated.

"Thank you, but I don't have time to chat." She stepped into his

office and set the envelope in front of him. "I'm Petra's legal representative in the divorce proceedings."

His stomach turned inside out and his heart followed suit.
"Divorce?"

"You can pick up your belongings at her house between five thirty
and six today. She's having the locks changed, so there's no need to
return the keys she gave you."

"Locks changed? What does she think I'm going to do? Sneak into
the house in the middle of the night?"

"It's a precaution I recommend to all my clients. My contact information is included—"

"What if I don't want a divorce?"

"Then we'll do this the hard way." She pivoted toward the kitchen,
her lawyer mask in place and her spine rigid. "By the way, thanks for
the apple cider doughnut this morning. It was delicious."

*She's thanking me for a doughnut when my life is going up in
flames?*

Stunned into silence, he could only wish spontaneous combustion
on the damn envelope, saving him from having to face some unbearable facts. First, he'd screwed up by not reading every single word of
the stupid agreement. Second, he should've let Petra handle Six. Third,
telling her the truth about his feelings six months, three months, or
even one month ago would've saved him from the consequences of this
situation. Fourth, he'd destroyed her love for him in less than twelve
hours. Fifth, not having a sex life was a lousy excuse for not replacing
the condom in his wallet a year ago.

The list could go on, but he closed his eyes and leaned against the
headrest to contemplate his options. Having been the recipient of her
wrath last week, he couldn't exactly expect her to take this kind of
manipulation sitting down. Of course, serving him with divorce papers
hit a much higher level of fury than a smashed doughnut in his face.

How can she think I'd jeopardize our relationship for a building?

*Because every loser who proposed to her made sure she knew she
wasn't the top priority in his life. Why would she think I could be any
different?*

A week of showering her with attention couldn't erase twenty years of bad boyfriends and broken trust.

Okay, so think.

He retrieved his copy of the paperwork and read every word on the two-page document. The triple asterisk in the middle paragraph of the second section sent him in search of the footnote. Buried between the second and fourth notations, small print detailed a diabolical plan guaranteed to pour gasoline on Petra's sometimes-short temper.

"Each purchaser agrees to legally wed the other party within two months after closing, or property in its entirety reverts to the original owner and all payments are forfeited by both purchasing parties."

Jesus, no wonder she filed for divorce. Hugh, you're a sneaky, lowdown, conniving busybody who doesn't know when to leave well enough alone.

Now what?

I have to talk to her.

The solution wouldn't be as simple as walking into her shop and asking her to listen to his side of the story. If divorce had been her first thought, she was far beyond the kind of pissed off she'd been when he'd bartered for kisses. She wouldn't hesitate to bloody his nose or blacken his eye. Castration might also be among her top choices for retribution. Maybe he hadn't meant to deceive her, but he had most definitely screwed up.

A text wouldn't cut the mustard, either.

He dug his phone out of his pocket and tapped in her number, his insides churning more with every digit. The call went to voicemail before the first ring.

Disappointed but not surprised, he took a calming breath. "Pet, I'm sorry. It doesn't excuse anything, but I trusted Hugh and didn't read the entire purchase agreement. I know. It was incredibly stupid of me. You're absolutely right to be upset. If I'd known about the fine print, I would've made him take it out. You deserve better than to be manipulated by a nosy old man, well-intentioned or not, especially after what happened at the courthouse. Anyway, I love you and I hope you'll forgive me for being an idiot. I swear I had no part in his crazy scheme.

Call me? Please? Just to talk. We have something really special, and I want to fix this. Our relationship and the contracts."

Stuck for the moment, he ended the call and rolled the chair away from the desk. Light knocking drew his attention to the open door.

Chewing her lower lip, his afternoon part-timer shifted her weight from one foot to the other. "So, I just got here and I noticed a dent in your rear fender and a broken taillight. Looks like somebody clipped you when they were parking. Nate said it wasn't there this morning."

"Seriously? You have got to be kidding me. I don't have time for this." Auggie resisted the urge to bang his head on the desk. With the way things were going, he'd probably give himself a concussion at the very least. "Thanks for letting me know."

"You're welcome." She turned partway and then stopped. "I thought you had a meeting or something."

"It got canceled." Blowing out a hefty sigh, he pushed to his feet and followed her into the kitchen. "I'll be out looking at my car if anybody needs me."

She grabbed an apron and a hairnet from the supply shelf on her way toward the sink. "Okay. I'll tell Nate."

Without slowing, Auggie headed out the service entrance to survey the damage. A crease several inches long but not very deep marred the passenger side near the back bumper, and pieces of red and yellow plastic littered the pavement. The streak of light paint across the charcoal gray confirmed his part-timer's guess, assuring him Petra hadn't taken a baseball bat to his car as payback for Hugh's underhanded dealings. Her truck also rode too high off the ground to have created the indentation, even though it was nowhere in the parking lot.

The police report and insurance call killed the rest of his workday, but his mind never strayed from the unopened envelope on his desk.

Divorce papers. Does she really believe I married her to get my hands on Collier's shop?

After a cursory check of the front of the bakery and another of the kitchen, he pulled on his sweatshirt and grabbed the dreaded packet.

Nate aimed a frown at him as they exited the building. "Hey, boss, you okay? I overheard some of what Georgie Swofford said, not that I was listening or anything."

"Nope." His mood darkening even more, Auggie veered toward his damaged car. A few feet from the driver's door, a vaguely familiar stench permeated the air. A glance at the ground revealed a mound of dog crap the size of a giant cinnamon roll—with his foot dead center. "Shit on a goddamn stick."

"That's your shoe, not a stick." Deke's voice came from behind him, suggesting the CPA had witnessed him stepping in it. "I'm glad I caught you. Got a minute?"

"Only if it's good news. Otherwise, I don't want to hear it." Auggie lifted his foot from the pile, nearly gagging from the pervasive odor when it slurped free. "Jesus, why can't people pick up after their critters?"

Maintaining a hefty distance, Deke pinched his nose. "Saw-wy, buddy, yaw gettin' audited."

"Of course I am, but that's the least of my worries." Auggie yanked off his shoe and heaved it at the dumpster several yards from his car. The metallic *thunk* and shit splatter at the point of impact did little to relieve his frustration. The only consolation was he hadn't worn his newer pair to work today. "You ever have a day where everything starts out perfect and goes straight to hell like a fucking snowball from there?"

"It must be pretty bad. You're mixing some peculiar metaphors." His friend pulled a plastic fast-food sack from his computer bag. "Want to talk about it? Riley and the girls are having a ladies' night out. Or do you need to head home to Petra?"

"There's no 'home to Petra' anymore." After a wave of the envelope, Auggie set it on the trunk above the broken light. "Georgie dropped off divorce papers this afternoon—after I found out Petra canceled the closing because Hugh tried to con her and put some idiotic fine print in my purchase agreement."

Deke frowned as he stepped close enough to pass off the bag. "She thinks you were in on it? That doesn't make sense. You've been in love with her for months. Why would you jeopardize your relationship when everything's finally working out?"

"Exactly." Holding his breath, Auggie scooped the mushy pile into the bag covering his hand and tied it shut. On the one-shoed walk to the dumpster, he kicked off the lone cross-trainer that wouldn't do a bit of good without its mate. "And Georgie just so happened to be circling like a damn buzzard, waiting to swoop in to handle the divorce she probably instigated."

"Have you tried talking to her? Petra, I mean."

The shoes clattered when they landed in the bottom of the mostly empty trash container, and Auggie tossed the bag of dog crap on top of them. "I called her right away, but it went straight to voicemail. Evidently, she isn't speaking to me. How the hell did that happen?"

"Marriage has a learning curve. In some cases, a painfully big one." Deke pointed toward the fender as Auggie returned to his car in his stocking feet. "Where'd the dent come from?"

"Somebody must've hit my car when they were backing out of the space next to me. Another one of the snowballs on the road to hell today." A heavy sigh escaped. "She told me she loved me this morning, and now I'm supposed to come get my stuff from her house by six o'clock."

"Ouch. I don't know if you're going to make it. It was almost quarter 'til when I got here."

"Damn, I gotta go. I'll call you tomorrow." Grabbing the envelope, Auggie pressed the unlock button and then climbed behind the wheel.

Friday evening traffic crawled through town, every block turning into a marathon.

Come on, people! Drive!

The clock on the dashboard read one minute after six when he finally turned in Petra's driveway.

Late.

Only the fixture above the kitchen sink lit up the interior, and the garage light flickered on against the deepening dusk when he shifted into Park. No gym bag waited for him on the back step. No clothes decorated the front lawn. The silver key on his ring tempted him to try it in the door, but his wife's lawyer would probably have him arrested for trespassing and attempted breaking and entering.

"I guess I have to buy new shoes or go to work barefoot tomorrow."

CHAPTER 9

THE *THWACK*, *THWACK*, *THWACK* ON HER BUTCHER-BLOCK WORKTABLE brought minimal satisfaction, but Petra positioned another cutlet and pounded it flat with the tenderizer mallet. The stack of flattened chicken breasts, incarnations of Hugh Collier's and Auggie Hofmeier's heads and other body parts, for her Stuffed Chicken Breast Saturday promotion had grown steadily in the last hour, exhausting her arm if not her anger—and hurt.

God, her heart hurt like hell. After all the failed relationships she'd endured, it shouldn't have been possible for any man to cause her this much pain. Somehow, her soon-to-be ex-husband had wormed his way into the only undamaged part of her heart and hacked it to pieces.

After I told him I love him.

I'm never doing that again. Ever.

She slammed the mallet onto the paper-thin cutlet until it resembled ground chicken. *Never, never, never.*

Then she tossed the mess into the pile of cordon bleu wraps she'd destroyed—a pan full that had grown faster than the stack of usable ones. After stowing the salvageable chicken breasts in the walk-in fridge to finish later and running the rest through the grinder, she added seasonings and binding agents for meatballs. The repetitive scoop and squeeze-the-handle-to-release motion allowed her mind to wander again while she filled tray after tray.

Two envelopes sat side by side on her desk, one with the marked-up contracts and the other still sealed. She didn't have to—or want to —open the second. It only confirmed what she'd suspected after Georgie's revelation. Auggie may not have set up what happened at the courthouse, but he'd taken advantage of what he thought was a golden opportunity to bypass Hugh's footnote to the contract. One word had nullified the benefit, putting her in the middle of a game she refused to play.

Within two months after *closing.*

She would divorce her husband, like the paperwork in envelope number two requested, according to Georgie. She wouldn't, however, remarry him after the new closing on the building. One marriage and one divorce was her limit after six disastrous engagements. Thankfully, her attorney had promised to handle all the details.

With the last tray filled, Petra loaded them all in the flash freezer, wishing she could do the same to the balls of the two men who'd manipulated her. Instead, she would do what she should've done when she hadn't been able to buy all of the shop next door. The real estate agent she'd called late yesterday afternoon had promised to line up viewings as soon as possible at several commercial properties that met her requirements. Wouldn't the conspirators be surprised when a For Sale sign went up in her window?

Agreement between the original three musketeers or not, no Hofmeier or Collier descendant would be allowed to buy her storefront as long as she was selling.

She patted her back pocket as she headed to the walk-in for the cordon bleu supplies, but the missing phone reminded her that Georgie had insisted on confiscating it until Sunday night's book club meeting. Fury-driven calls and texts didn't fit into the quickie divorce plan. Neither did listening to fake apologies and bullshit explanations if Auger the Boor called her.

A glance at the clock on the wall assured her she had more than enough time to roll and bread four dozen ham-and-cheese stuffed chicken breasts. Maybe she should start work at two in the morning every day. Besides increasing her productivity, the new schedule would allow her to avoid running into her worst mistake in the parking lot. Other than euchre night at Grams' and Granddad's on Mondays and book club on Thursday and Sunday evenings, she had nothing better to do.

And sleeping alone is for the birds.

She set up the assembly line for the Saturday special and nudged her thoughts toward the list of features that would create the ideal butcher shop. New inventive ways to get even with all the men who had made her love life hell couldn't compare with the satisfaction of stringing Auggie's underwear, other clothing, and personal care items on a clothesline crisscrossing his front yard.

"WHICH PAIR DO YOU THINK HE'S WEARING? THE HEARTS OR THE devils?"

Snickers, giggles, and whispers from a gathering of Mrs. Crenshaw's Garden Club younger cohorts met Auggie as he wheeled the restocked bread rack into the front of the bakery. Word had evidently spread through Wellington about the lawn decorations he'd found in his yard last night after a trip to the store for new shoes. Every streetlight in the neighborhood had made sure all passersby saw the exhibit well after nightfall. The light drizzle had guaranteed none of his belongings were fit to wear, including his spare shoes.

He raised his chin and smiled to keep from telling them to take their goddamn gossip somewhere else. "Bananas."

Half the women burst out laughing, a few turned red-faced, and several aimed lewd grins at him. Did they honestly believe he would jump into bed with one of them because Petra had kicked him out of hers?

Glad his baker's jacket hung to his hips so they couldn't speculate about other things, he locked the cart's wheels and returned to the kitchen.

Nate glanced up from the cake on the turntable. "You okay, man?"

"No, I'm not okay. I've been married for a week and about to get divorced. My new shoes are rubbing a blister on my heel. Oh, and most of the customers are here to catch a glimpse of the loser whose wife put his boxers on display for the whole damn town yesterday." Bypassing the empty cooling carts, Auggie headed to the sink to catch up on dishes. "The only upside is most of them are buying and we'll be sold out within the hour."

"Your life sounds like a country song. The only things missing are your dog died and your ex slashed the tires on your truck."

"I stepped in dog shit and somebody hit my car. Close enough." Water ricocheted off a mixer paddle, spraying Auggie in the face. He adjusted the faucet and grabbed a towel from the shelf. The whole stack tumbled into the dishwater. "Damn it."

Nate's chuckle added to his annoyance. "Maybe you should go hang out in your office until closing time. I just finished the lettering on the last two o'clock pickup, so I can help out at the counter."

"Hiding won't help." If anything, the downtime would allow his brain to formulate more worst-case scenarios, like a positive pregnancy test and eighteen years of co-parenting and child support to go with the very real possibility that he wouldn't be able to convince Petra to stay married. "I'll clean up the kitchen while the rest of you handle the unruly hordes."

"Sounds like a plan." With the boxed cake balanced on his left forearm, Nate saluted and headed toward the front of the bakery.

A plan.

Why hadn't he formulated a plan?

Winging it hadn't gone well at all. Sitting on his ass to give the woman he loved time to notice his feelings hadn't worked any better than jumping at the chance to tie the knot and see what happened. Any effort he made to talk to her now would likely end with a restraining order and a jail sentence. Then she'd probably have a party with her friends to celebrate his demise.

In any case, spending the night in the county lockup couldn't begin to compare to a future without her.

He balanced the last paddle in the drainer and wiped all the counters with his abundance of wet towels, ready for the next pile of dog crap or dent in his car. Giving up wasn't his style, and Georgina Swofford's divorce papers wouldn't stop him from fighting for his wife.

Step one. Feed her.

Every pastry had vanished by eleven o'clock, the pies were gone by twelve, and a lone carrot cake had remained when the Garden Club arrived to harass him at one. By now, somebody had almost certainly chosen it as payment for gawking at the object of today's gossip.

New step one. Make a plan.

Step two. Make a cake.

If he expected any chance of winning her back, a well-laid plan was his only option. He gathered the filling ingredients for Petra's second favorite item from his bakery—Boston cream pie—and racked his brain for the most sincere and romantic gesture he could offer Petra.

Rings on top? Nah, too cliché.

He needed an original idea, one that only she would appreciate. Then he would send one of his part-timers to deliver his masterpiece to The Homegrown Café Book Club's Sunday evening meeting. A bit of peer pressure from her happily married friends couldn't hurt.

Would a mini bonfire from the unopened envelope be over the top?

FEEDING ANOTHER FIVE POUNDS OF COW TO THE GRINDER, PETRA WILLED her irrational subconscious to stop detouring to the dream she'd had during her most recent catnap. Even if she wanted to have sex with Auggie, which she absolutely didn't, her period had started this morning. What should've been relief was tempered by the realization that nothing but a marriage license and a divorce-in-progress tied her to him now. Updating her website and sending out the newsletter with the week's specials at four in the morning had taken her mind off him only for a little while, sort of.

The switch blurred and she bit the inside of her cheek to stem the tears stinging her eyes. Crying wouldn't change a damn thing, especially the fact that his entire motivation for pursuing her revolved around getting his grubby paws on The Candlestick Maker shop. She—her heart, her emotions, her feelings—had been expendable, like they'd been with every other man she'd ever known.

Swiping her sleeve across her eyes, she pivoted toward the sink to wash her hands before moving on to the next part of prepping for tomorrow's new sales gimmick, Meatloaf Monday. Her leaky eyes started again when she cut the first onion in half, but at least she had an excuse this time.

Thirty-six regular and eighteen mini loaves later, she stood at the peephole of the service door. A view of the parking lot yielded her truck and no other vehicles, meaning she wouldn't run into the baker or any of the nosy customers they shared. By now, everybody in town likely knew the details of her final failed relationship.

Keys at the ready, she ducked out the door, locked up, and jogged to her truck. As she climbed into the driver's seat, gravel crunched behind her.

Go, go, go! Do. Not. Look. Back.

Keeping her eyes on the empty part of the lot in front of her, she pulled forward and turned toward the closest exit. Her heart pounded long after she reached the street, but she refused to look in the rearview mirror for a possible glimpse of the man who had fooled her so completely.

Three familiar cars lined her driveway, two on the left and one on the right, leaving a pickup-wide path between them leading to the garage. Riley and Tate climbed out of Riley's T-bird as Petra squeezed through the narrow space. A package of baguettes stuck out of the grocery bag in Tate's arms. Evidently, her friends had decided to change the time and location of their books-and-cocktails meeting and have supper instead of snacks.

God, I hope Tate brought pasta and garlic bread.

The garage door hummed closed while Petra trudged into her house, ready for an ice-cold Guinness straight from the bottle. After a quick stop at the fridge, she snagged the opener and popped off the cap on her way to the front door.

The whole crew stood on the porch, looking like they were ready for an intervention, with Riley leading the way. "Why didn't you tell us what happened? Tate had to hear about it through the gossip mill at the café and fill the rest of us in."

"I didn't want to talk about it. I still don't." Leaving her friends to follow or not, Petra returned to the kitchen. Footsteps and whispers said they trailed after her, but she took a long swig and then moved her supply of vodka, Jameson, and rum from the cabinet to the counter. The two envelopes, along with a handful of commercial property listing printouts she'd placed on the table yesterday, almost made her glance in their direction. "Help yourself. Anybody want coffee or tea before I hop in the shower?"

"I can take care of it." Wally set a white bakery box next to the liquor supply, triggering a pang in Petra's gut. A printed label with her address obscured the lower corner of The Baker's logo. "You got a delivery while we were waiting for you to come home."

"Who's it from?" *If it's a dozen Boston cream doughnuts, I'm smashing every last one of them in his face.*

"The young lady seemed to think you ordered it online and paid extra for delivery after the bakery closed." Wally picked up the teakettle from the stovetop, sloshed the water inside, and set it back down on the burner. "I tried to give her a tip, but whoever did it included that in the payment. Go clean up while we make supper."

"Back in fifteen minutes." Not about to argue with a free meal and the opportunity to delay sharing her relationship woes, Petra retreated to her bedroom.

Auggie's belongings no longer cluttered the vanity among hers, but his presence remained. Memories of one short week with him seemed to appear out of the steam from the shower, clinging to her body and mind as she tried to wash them away with the blood, sweat, and tears of another day's work. Only the aroma of tomatoes, Italian seasonings, and garlic when she emerged from the bathroom chased the ghosts into hiding again.

Clad in her rattiest sweats and the careless attitude she'd learned to wear after her second broken engagement, she sauntered back to the kitchen.

Riley met her at the doorway and waved the printed listings in Petra's face. "Hey, what's this? You're moving the butcher shop?"

Smacking the listings away, Petra aimed a glare at no one in particular. "Damn right I am. I'm done being manipulated. And if nobody besides Hugh or the boor wants to buy my shop, it can sit empty for the next fifty years for all I care. Spite can be incredibly satisfying."

Georgie carried a napkin-covered platter to the table and set it beside a stack of plates and forks. "I told that old codger to mind his own business."

"You knew about this before—"

The doorbell drowned out the rest of her accusation, announcing someone at the front door, immediately followed by insistent knocking at the patio and more ringing.

On the verge of telling everybody to get the hell out of her house, Petra growled and pointed to Georgie. "You. Go see who's abusing my doorbell and then bring your ass back in here. I want to know exactly what you've been keeping secret. And, Riley, make that stupid door pounder stop."

The two women headed in opposite directions while Tate and Wally added a giant bowl of spaghetti and drinks to the spread between wary glances at Petra.

"If she doesn't want to see me, she can say so herself." Auggie stomped into the kitchen with Riley tugging at his hooded sweatshirt. The manila envelope in his hand matched the one someone had moved to the head of the table, reigniting the burning ache from his betrayal. "We need to talk, Petra."

Crossing her arms at her chest, Petra straightened her spine, determined not to show an ounce of weakness. "Here's the deal. You pay for the divorce since you started the process, and I'll sign the papers."

His jaw flexed and his eyebrows dipped toward his nose. "I didn't start the process. You did. Your attorney hand-delivered the paperwork to me. And, for the record, I refuse to cooperate."

Had he lost his mind?

Tightening the grip on her elbows, she frowned. "I didn't—"

"About the divorce..." Georgie stood at the table with Hugh leaning on his cane next to her. She picked up the still-sealed packet and flipped over the one in Auggie's hand. The color drained from her face. "You haven't opened the envelopes yet? They're filled with blank paper. The divorce, the wording in the contracts... It was all Mr. Collier's idea."

CHAPTER 10

H UGH SMACKED THE TIP OF HIS CANE AGAINST THE HARDWOOD FLOOR. "Dagnabbit, Georgina! You weren't supposed to tell them!"

Holding his breath, Auggie slid his index finger along the seal of the envelope he'd dreaded opening and pulled the papers free. As he flipped through empty page after empty page, a mix of relief and fury swirled inside him. He tossed the handful at Pop's lifelong friend, sending paper fluttering everywhere. "You let Petra think I wanted a divorce? Just so you could force us to become partners under your terms? You hurt her, even knowing all she's been through."

The old man looked toward Georgie like he expected her to defend his actions. "I did it for the two of you. There you were, crazy in love with her but too chicken to tell her, and she needed a man who'd treat her like a queen. You needed a nudge. How was I supposed to know you'd go and marry her at the drop of a hat?"

A rumbling growl from Petra brought absolute silence to the kitchen. Her fists clenched and unclenched as she glared in Hugh's direction. "Let me get this straight. You were trying to sell me to Auggie so I'd have a husband."

Bushy eyebrows rose and a frown sat perched on Hugh's wrinkled chin. "Aw, now. I wouldn't exactly put it like that."

"How exactly would you put it, you conniving scoundrel?"

"I, um… I just wanted you to be happy."

"Right." She took two steps toward him, pausing near the bakery package. "What's in the box and who sent it?"

Struggling to tame the butterflies in his stomach, Auggie chanced joining her at the counter and tore off the tape holding the flaps shut. The sides of the box fell open to reveal the contents. The position of the cake topper on the chocolate glaze and the smudge-free message below it confirmed delivery had gone off without a hitch. "I did. It's a Boston cream pie. I wanted to show you I wasn't giving you up without a fight."

She touched a fingertip to the groom kneeling at his bride's feet, but her expression didn't soften. "'I promise to love, honor, and cherish you every day of my life.' We didn't have a wedding cake."

"I know. We barely had a wedding." He grasped her hand and dropped to one knee. "I'll marry you as many times as you want, with all the hoopla, to make up for it."

"Get up. Once was enough. I just want a piece of cake." Wielding the knife Wally handed her, Petra cut a narrow wedge from the cream-filled layer cake. Then she transferred it to the plate her friend set on the counter and shook her head at the fork Tate tried to give her. "I don't need it. Not yet anyway."

The determined gleam in his wife's eyes warned him to take a step back, but he stood his ground, ready for any punishment she dished out for his inadvertent part in the scheme.

Her gaze flicked toward her attorney and the instigator of the whole mess. She stalked across the room, detouring to the table halfway there and dipping her free hand into the bowl of pasta. Gooey strands swung, dripped, and plopped onto the floor as she completed a backswing.

Wally's gasp came a second before Riley snorted and ducked behind a chair.

Georgie closed her eyes, but Hugh's widened and he tried to use his partner in crime as a shield against the handful of spaghetti winging its way toward them. The glob landed on her cheek, ricocheting into her hair and onto his shoulder. A second ball followed the first in quick succession, landing square on the old man's nose before it rolled down his chest and plopped on his shoe. Not a single drop of sauce stained the wall beside them, proof that Petra deserved those longstanding pitching records.

The plate still in her left hand, she padded closer to her victims and then mashed a chunk of cake against each of their foreheads. "Fix those purchase agreement terms, and we'll call it even."

Despite her grimace, Georgie seemed resigned to accept any further sentencing by the judge and jury. "I'm sorry for my part in this, Petra. When I found out what happened, I thought I could fix it. Auggie didn't—"

"He didn't read the dad-burned contract." Hugh tugged his jacket from her white-knuckled grasp and swiped his palm over his face, spreading the cream filling and spaghetti sauce to his chin. "If he'd—"

Petra shoved the remainder of the cake in his mouth. "Shut it, you nosy buzzard. And go home before I decide to dump that whole bowl on you."

You tell him, Pet. Auggie swallowed a chuckle and bit his tongue to keep from grinning.

"Do it!" Riley came out of hiding and reached for the spaghetti.

Prepared for the worst, he quickly moved the wedding cake to the farthest corner of the counter and took up a defensive position between his wife and the food on the table. A wobbly wad of pasta flew at him a second later, but he deflected it with a baseball swing, sending it into the back of Wally's head.

A hoot of Riley's laughter rang through the kitchen moments before Wally bounced a slice of garlic bread off the blonde's cheek. It bowled over a glass of wine, splattering red droplets onto Tate and painting orangey polka dots on her yellow blouse. The rest formed an expanding puddle and a multilevel waterfall off the table, onto the edge of the chair, and to the floor.

Righting the glass with one hand, Tate grabbed a handful of salad with the other and then stuffed it down the back of Wally's sweater. Since a trio of bottled dressings stood next to the basket of bread, she'd probably gotten away with the least goopy attack.

One by one, the three women succumbed to hysterical giggles and collapsed onto the floor, leaving Petra, Georgina, and him standing. Hugh had evidently taken advantage of the distraction to make his escape.

Georgie scooped the remainder of the chocolate, crumbs, and cream off her forehead and eyed the mess like she might stuff it in her mouth. "I deserved that. In spite of the fact that we all knew you secretly liked Auggie, I should have told you everything when I found out what Uncle Hugh had done. I prepared the fake packets to pacify him. I never imagined you wouldn't open them right away. It went against my better judgment and I should've listened to my conscience. I'm so sorry. Can you forgive me, Petra?"

Uncle Hugh?

"Uncle Hugh?" His wife spoke in unison with his thought.

"He's my grandmother's younger brother. He and Aunt Joan helped me pay for law school. They didn't have any children and..." The attorney shook her head, sending a dangling strand of pasta tumbling off her shoulder. "Suffice to say, I'm grateful for their generosity. That, however, doesn't justify causing you to question Auggie's loyalty... and love. He does love you, you know. I amended the original contracts this morning and told Uncle Hugh if he didn't admit what he'd done, I would tell you."

His wife's sigh suggested she wouldn't stay mad at her friend forever. "Fine, I forgive you. But I'm still mad at you."

"As you should be." Still cradling the glob in her hand, Georgie stepped over the strings of red-, yellow-, and brown-coated spaghetti and walked to the sink. "Tate. Riley. Wally. Let's clean up and get out of here so Petra and Auggie can talk."

The women's slipping and sliding as they tried to stand led to more giggling, but they finally managed to work their way to their feet. In short order, the kitchen was no longer decorated in food fight décor and the remains of the meal had been stowed in the fridge.

The first three book clubbers, with evidence of the wild party only partially noticeable on their clothing now, hugged their host and trooped out the front door in a single-file line. Georgie brought up the rear, hesitating for several seconds before following the others without a hug. Her tentative expression was a drastic change from the usual confidence and aloofness. A heavy *clunk* left the house free from chaos for the first time since his arrival.

Auggie gestured toward the bakery box on the counter. "Do you want dessert?"

"God, yes." Exhaustion colored Petra's voice, but she followed him to the safe corner he'd found for their wedding cake. "A big piece, and with a fork this time."

"You're not going to smash it in my face?" He lined up the knife and shot a grin over his shoulder. "Is this big enough?"

"I'm not wasting any more of it, not that I think you did anything wrong. At least not anymore." Placing her hand on his, she added another inch to the wedge. "I shouldn't have jumped to conclusions. It's just that—"

"You don't have to explain." He cut where she indicated, somewhat resigned to the fact that her past wasn't something either of them could easily overcome. "I get it."

The cupboard door swung open near his head and she set a dinner plate on the counter. "I wish you didn't have to."

"Me too, but I wouldn't change who you are for anything." Plate in hand, he turned toward her. "Grab a fork."

She held up two as she led him to the dinette via a quick detour to the fridge for a Guinness. "One for you and one for me. We have some things to celebrate."

"I'll take that to mean you've forgiven me for not reading the fine print in the contract. It was a stupid mistake, one I won't make again."

"You didn't read the fine print?" Her right eyebrow rose, like she hadn't listened to his voicemail. Then she reached toward the center of the table. "You're a lot more trusting of the old coot than I am. Looks like Georgie decided to give my phone back to me."

"She had your phone?" A sinking feeling renewed his irritation with the co-conspirators, even if Hugh had basically blackmailed his niece into sticking her nose where it didn't belong. "For how long? I left a message for you on Friday after she delivered the fake divorce papers."

"When do you think? I can't believe she let that old goat manipulate her. Of course, another day or two of stewing in her guilt won't hurt her." Tapping on the screen, she frowned. Then she tapped some more and held the phone to her ear. A full minute passed before she lowered the cell and turned it facedown on the table. "Damn busybodies. Don't they have anything better to do than screw with my love life when it's actually going well?"

She loves me. Utter happiness warmed him as he lifted a forkful of Boston cream pie to her lips. "How about a bite of cake, Pet?"

She opened wide and then shut her mouth around the heaping helping. Chasing it with a swig of stout, she closed her eyes. "Mmm. Heaven. Thank you, Mr. Lochsley."

"Guinness and Boston cream? Hm, interesting combination. Wait a minute? Guinness? Does this mean—"

"Yep. No worries about baby Auggies. My period started this morning."

Relief joined contentedness. "That's good news, because I don't feel like sharing you, Mrs. Hofmeier. I'm thinking maybe I should get snipped to be on the safe side from now on."

She blinked at him for several seconds and then offered him a bite every big as the one he'd given her. "You'd do that for me?"

Chocolate and cream filling melted on his tongue, confirming her assessment that it tasted like heaven—almost as good as his wife. "You bet. I love you and I want to make you happy."

Her smile widened with every word, but it faltered a moment later. "Boo. No sex tonight, and I want you to show me how much you missed me."

He pulled her onto his lap and kissed his way along her jaw to her ear. "I'm not opposed to broadening our repertoire of lovemaking techniques, especially if I get to hold you all night long and wake up with you in the morning."

Looping her arms around his neck, she wiggled closer. "Tell me what you have in mind, sweet talker."

WHEN HARRY MET WALLY

CHAPTER 1

POSITIONED WITH A CLEAR VIEW OF THE HOMEGROWN CAFÉ'S entrance, Wallis Danforth crossed her ankles for good luck and tapped her fingertips on the table to calm the butterflies in her stomach. She'd been on first dates before. So what if her last first date had been almost thirty years ago?

Well, maybe it wasn't really a date. Meeting for a chat over break-fast qualified as more of a let's-get-acquainted meet-up, didn't it?

Wally pressed the Home button on her phone and sighed. *Fifteen minutes late. Why can't people be on time?*

As the screen darkened, movement through the window over-looking the street sent the swarm in her belly fluttering again. A dark-haired man pulled open the door and stepped inside. While his face resembled the picture from the dating app, only platform shoes and a year of daily workouts would make him six feet tall and a hundred-eighty pounds.

Liar, liar, pants on fire.

Did he really think I wouldn't notice? It's not like I care about a perfect body. I just want somebody nice to talk to.

She pasted on a smile when he met her gaze. "Daniel?"

A frown accompanied his slow nod. "Wallis?"

"Yes." She stood and offered her hand, keeping the table between them. "Did you have a hard time finding the place?"

"Yes. I was looking for someplace nicer than a greasy-spoon hole-in-the-wall diner. I hope the coffee's drinkable." He seemed to take in the cozy café as he sat—without shaking her hand. The frown deepened. "How old is your picture? You said you were a young-looking fifty."

"Excuse me?" Sitting back in her chair to glare at him, she crossed her arms under her breasts. *Jackass.* "There's nothing greasy or tacky about my friend's café. And are you kidding me? Have you looked in a mirror? Athletic build? Really? Were you referring to your ego? If anybody could insist on having the lights off, it's definitely me, you shallow hypocritical jerk."

He raised his hands as if to fend off her rebuttal. "Easy there, Wallis. I'm just used to dating younger women and eating at restaurants with real waitstaff, not ordering at the counter and having meals delivered by kids who should probably be in an institution for the mentally retarded."

"How dare you?" Wallis shoved the table against the creep, pinning him in his chair as she rose. As hard as she tried, she couldn't force her voice into the low not-draw-attention volume she would've preferred. "For your information, one of those *kids* you think is *mentally retarded* is my adult daughter and she's a heck of a lot smarter than you are where it counts. You could learn a lot about being polite from her, not to mention being on time. Oh, and you have hair dye on your neck, you hateful butthead. Get out before I do something we'll both regret."

With wide eyes, he scrambled backward, knocking over his chair as he escaped from her trap. Two seconds later, he rushed out the door and past the window.

Applause filled the busy café, bringing heat to Wally's cheeks and tears to her eyes. Her daughter's face blurred in the crowd, but not before Wally caught an eye-roll. She plopped into the chair with her face in her hands, ready to give up on trying to find a decent guy to go out with and share a little companionship once in a while.

"Breakfast is on the house, mama bear." After the distinctive *clack* of a tray on the Formica table, a chair scraped across the floor. "Are you okay?"

Wallis peeked through her fingers at her friend Tate Cochon. "Yeah. I'm sorry for causing a ruckus and for the loser insulting THC."

"No apology necessary. None of it was your fault, and my other customers are telling Anabelle and Darren what a good job they do and not to listen to bullies like dye-job Dan." Tate's hint of a smile grew into a huge grin. "I expect mom lessons over the next seven months and eighteen-plus years. You were awesome. I can't wait for you to tell this story at book club tomorrow night."

Falling victim to her friend's infectious mood, Wallis dropped her hands to her lap and snickered. "I need to write that name down! It's going in the one-act play I'm working on about dating at fifty."

"Ooh, that sounds fun."

The heavenly scent of cinnamon, ginger, nutmeg, and cloves carried to Wally's nose. "Is that a pumpkin-spice scone?"

"Pumpkin-spice scone plus a helping of potato, spinach, and mushroom breakfast bake and a cup of vanilla chai with almond milk." Tate unloaded each item in front of Wallis and then set aside the tray. "Eat while it's hot. You know, I bet tips are going to be amazing today. What do you think of me donating them to The Up Side of Downs in Dan's name?"

"As long as he doesn't get the tax benefit for a charitable contribution. I can't believe I thought he was worthy of a first date. The self-absorbed misogynistic weenie."

"Speaking from experience, I'd say this mistake was a pretty minor one." Grabbing the empty tray, her friend rose. "I need to get back to the kitchen, but I'll see you tomorrow evening at my house."

"You bet. Thanks for breakfast." Wally scooped a bite of casserole, more grateful than ever for her book club friends. Her cell buzzed and lit up with a vaguely familiar number next to the plate. Exchanging the fork for the phone, she tapped the Answer button and lifted the device to her ear. "Hello."

"Hello, Wallis? This is Norma Jenkins. Do you have a minute?"

Wally's pulse kicked up like she'd hoped it would for her date.

Technically, it had, but for the wrong reasons. "Norma, hi. A minute. An hour. Do you have news about the inspections?"

"Other than a minor leak in the employee restroom and one outlet that needs replaced, all the reports came back with no issues. Closing is still set for ten o'clock Monday morning. I'm emailing a copy of the reports and the amount for the check right now."

"That's really good news."

"It is! Wallis, I can't tell you how pleased I am that you're making sure the bookstore stays open. It's one of Wellington's oldest businesses. My newsletter goes out on the first Tuesday of each month, so let me know if you need help promoting the changes you have planned."

Warmed by her real estate agent's enthusiasm, Wally made a mental note to add the information to her calendar. "That would be awesome. I appreciate all you've done to make this happen. I'll send you the new logo and schedule this afternoon. You should probably remind me in the email you're sending now, though. Menopause is harder on my brain cells than parenting."

Norma's hoot of laughter chased away the last of Dan's negativity. "I remember those days and sympathize. Reminder added. Oops! Gotta go. I have another call. Talk to you soon, Wallis!"

The line went dead, and the moral support of her female friends tempted Wally to relegate dating to the same cemetery. Bobby might chastise her from the grave for giving up on men, but he wasn't the one trying to navigate the dating world.

Ten years. Has it really been that long?

"Excuse me. Do you mind if I set my coffee on your table while I look for my keys? I hope I didn't lock them in my car again."

Looking up from her phone, she barely smothered a giggle at the man's outfit of high-water red pants hiked up to his chest paired with a white-collared yellow shirt and a droopy blue bowtie beneath his corduroy blazer. "Sounds like me lately. Take your time."

"Thanks." He patted the front and back pockets of his trousers and moved on to the large one on his shirt. After checking beneath his whirligig cap, he stuffed his hands into his jacket pockets. "I feel like I should apologize for all the decent guys of— Aha! Found them. Anyway, your date was a cad. You're beautiful, no matter your age, and way too good for the likes of him. And Anabelle—your daughter, right? She's better than most at waiting tables and taking orders. Always polite and helpful. She's quite fortunate to have you for a mother."

Despite the thicker-than-necessary compliments, Wally offered him a genuine smile. "Thank you. You're very kind to say so."

"Just calling it like I see it." He scratched at his reddish-brown beard stubble with his keys and then picked up his to-go cup. "I'd better get going to play rehearsal or I'll be late. It was a pleasure to meet you, Anabelle's mother. I hope to see you again."

Hmm. Me too. "Wallis. Wallis Danforth. I enjoyed meeting you too."

"Wallis. Like Wallis Simpson, Edward VIII's wife? Lovely. Absolutely stunning." Laugh lines formed at the corners of his bright blue eyes to accompany his charming demeanor. "You, I mean. A name makes a person neither beautiful nor ugly. Harry Kreiger at your service, my lady. I'm thoroughly enchanted, but I really must go or the director will have my head."

A bubble of laughter escaped. "Of course."

He bowed and turned toward the exit. Then, digging in his back pocket, he spun back around, sending the propeller on his cap twirling. Less than a minute later, he handed her a pair of what appeared to be tickets. "For tonight's performance. I hope you and Anabelle can attend."

Bold text on the cardstock proclaimed to admit one to the high school's production of *The Misadventures of Alice* this evening at seven o'clock.

Intrigued by his unassuming and unaffected nature, she slipped the tickets into the outer pocket of her purse. "We'd love to, Harry. Thank you. Break a leg."

"Thank you, dear Wallis. I shall endeavor to do my best." After another bow, he dodged a family of four entering the café and dashed out the door.

An involuntary grin tickled her lips as he disappeared past the window, his black-and-white Converse high-tops leading the way. Harry Kreiger seemed to be the Dread Pirate Roberts, Ichabod Crane, and a British royalty expert all rolled into one funny and adorable nerd.

Curiosity got the better of her as she savored the rest of her breakfast, and a quick Google search produced a photo—minus facial hair—and a brief bio of a Wellington High School history teacher, performer, and playwright. Not only did he write plays and act, he played the saxophone and sang. The man was evidently as talented as he was kind, witty, and intelligent. He also didn't seem to care about her age, since the creep had announced it to the whole café. Was he older, younger, the same age as she was?

Now why couldn't I find a guy like him on the dating app? Probably a married flirt with my luck. Sigh.

"Mom, you were awesome." Anabelle wrapped her arms around Wally from the side and kissed her cheek. "I'm so proud of you."

Resting her head against her daughter's, Wally gave her a one-armed hug. "Thanks, sweetie. I'm proud of you too. You and Darren have every right to be upset about the things he said, but you didn't let it bother you."

"He's a dumb old meanie. What he thinks of us doesn't matter." Anabelle loosened her comforting hold and began gathering the empty dishes. "Can I get you anything else before you go?"

How did you get to be so grown up already? "No, thank you. I'm fine."

"Okay. Thanks for coming in for breakfast. See you again soon." Clearly pleased with her ability to remember all Tate had taught her about waiting tables, Anabelle grinned and carried the loaded tray toward the kitchen.

That's my girl.

Wally slipped her phone into her purse and reached for her jacket on the back of the chair. Life consisted of one adjustment after another, leaving her no choice but to go with the flow. She'd discovered happily-ever-after and survived losing her husband. Their only child might have been born with an extra chromosome, but she'd taught

Wally the meanings of true love, happiness, and blessing. Anabelle's developing independence was simply the next step.

"Are you okay, Wallis?" The white-haired president of the Wellington Garden Club stood where Harry had a minute ago with her lips pursed, looking every bit like the long-retired teacher she was. "You're not crying over that horribly rude man with the bad dye job, are you?"

"Goodness, no, Mrs. Crenshaw." Wally swiped at the wetness on her cheek and sucked in a slow calming breath. "I'm just feeling emotional because my baby is so much more exceptional than I ever imagined she could be."

The old woman grasped Wally's hand and gave it a firm squeeze. "That's because she's had a wonderful role model to emulate. Keep up the good work, young lady."

Although a chuckle got free, Wally managed to stop an unladylike snort. "Young? I don't think so. Some days I feel a hundred years old."

Mrs. Crenshaw clucked her tongue. "Pish. Age is just a number. Being young comes from the heart. Take it from someone who's *a lot* closer to a hundred than you."

"Wiser too."

"Maybe about people, but all this new technology makes my head hurt. Oh, here comes my granddaughter. You have a wonderful day, dear." With a wave, the oldest resident in town weaved through the order line that now extended out the exit.

Gathering her belongings, Wallis could only hope the changes she planned for the bookstore generated half as much success as The Homegrown Café since its grand opening two months ago. At least Black Friday and the holiday season would boost sales in the failing business she wanted to save.

Certain Tate didn't have a spare moment to say goodbye, Wally followed the path Mrs. Crenshaw had taken to the sidewalk. The November chill forced her to turn up her collar for the short walk to the parking lot across the street, but it reminded her that Thanksgiving was only days away and she had a lot to be thankful for.

The car finally blew warm air from the vents as she approached the bookstore. Police lights flashed on in front of her, bringing her to a full stop next to the two-story building wedged on the corner between an insurance office and a florist.

My new adventure.

Maybe it wasn't official yet, but she'd already worked out a transition plan with the seller and his employees. The assistant manager and the three part-timers had agreed to stay, and The Homegrown Café Book Club would add The Corner Bookshop to its biweekly meeting rotation. Besides book signings and poetry readings in the semi-private room at the back of the store, the possibility of other performances popped into her head—with Harry Kreiger topping her list of people to ask.

She crept forward as the police car and another car pulled into the next available parking spaces. When she eased past the poor soul who'd been foolish enough to violate a traffic law in town, a familiar frown caught her eye through his window.

Poor soul? Ha! That's what you get for being an ass, dye-job Dan.

CHAPTER 2

HARRY GRABBED THE BILL OF HIS CAP AND PULLED IT FROM HIS SWEATY head as he took a final bow with the rest of the cast. The house lights came up and the stage lights dimmed as he straightened, finally letting him see into the sold-out audience.

Six rows back near the center of the auditorium sat Wallis Danforth and her daughter, Anabelle. The woman who'd barely left his thoughts all day nodded when she met his gaze. Her bright smile widened, sending his pulse hammering and his stomach cartwheeling.

After raising his index finger at her in a just-a-minute gesture, he jogged to the front of the stage and hopped into the exit aisle ahead of the first-row audience. The crowd surged as he made his way up the aisle, but his guests had only reached the end of their row when he arrived at his destination. Luckily, the other patrons seemed to be headed to the opposite aisle.

He handed them both a lollipop from the stash in his shirt pocket. "I'm so glad you could make it! Did you enjoy the show?"

Anabelle grinned. "Yes. It was funny. Thank you for the tickets."

"You're very welcome." More than willing to risk a heart palpitation, he turned his attention to her mother. "And you, Lady Wallis?"

Amusement sparkled in her pretty brown eyes. "Most entertaining, Mr. Kreiger."

"Please. Call me Harry. I feel old enough when my students call me Mr. Kreiger."

"Harry." The smile that accompanied his name on her lips stole his breath and at least half of his brain function.

Wow. Just wow. Ask her. "So...I hope you won't think I'm being too bold, but... Do you like to dance? I need to learn the basics of salsa, the ballroom-dancing kind, to try out for a part in the spring perfor-mance. If I set up a few lessons, will you be my partner? I promise not to step on your toes."

"I'd love to. Dance lessons, not toe squishing." She tucked a wayward hank of wheat-colored hair behind her ear, revealing a dimple in her right cheek and three small hoops and a gold stud in her ear. "Learning to salsa has been on my bucket list for years."

A bottleneck in the exit aisle pushed him close enough to see light freckles on the bridge of her nose. "Perfect. Do you have anything to write your email or phone number on?"

She glanced down toward her tiny purse and frowned. "I hope you won't be offended if I err on the side of caution, but could we meet at The Corner Bookshop on Monday afternoon? About four thirty?"

Disappointment annihilated the butterflies in his stomach. Why had she feigned interest in his invitation if she didn't intend to go? "Doesn't it close at four on Mondays?"

She leaned in, tickling his ear with her warm breath. "It isn't offi-cial yet, but I'm going to be the new owner, so we can meet there anytime I say. Closing for the sale is Monday morning and inventory starts at the close of business."

"You're buying the bookstore? How cool is that? Monday at four thirty it is." A loud whistle from the direction of the stage burst his happy bubble. "I need to head backstage for a cast meeting."

"We have to be going too, but it was good to see you again." Her bright smile sent his pulse racing once more. "Tell everyone they put on a great show."

"I will, Wallis. Thanks for coming, and I'll see you Monday. Good-night, ladies."

She stepped into an opening in the waning crowd with her daughter's hand tucked into hers. "Goodnight, Harry."

Anabelle grinned and waved with her free hand. "Goodnight."

After a polite nod, he zigzagged his way toward the stage, feeling lighter than he could ever remember. If love at first sight existed, his heart most certainly had found it—and fallen hard.

"Hey, Mr. K!" Duncan, one of his fifth-period kids, stood several feet above him at the end of the covered orchestra pit and offered him a hand up. The stagehand smirked as they walked toward the crowd of students and staff. "Is Mrs. Danforth your girlfriend?"

"Not yet, but I have high hopes."

"Cool. Did you know she used to be the librarian here back when Anabelle was in school? That was before you started teaching here. Maybe like five years ago. Anabelle was in my sister's class."

Librarian, huh? I can picture that. "No, I didn't know. Too new, I guess."

Duncan lowered his voice when the director climbed several rungs up the ladder and cleared her throat. "My sister gave her Kit Kats to look the other way when she went over the limit for checked-out books. King size, not the regular or snack size."

Harry filed the information away for later. "Good to know. I'm a Krackel guy myself."

"Really? I would've guessed M&Ms or Reese's pieces. Maybe Skittles."

Even though the director repeated the same good-job-gang speech as that afternoon and probably tomorrow's matinee, Harry kept his eyes trained on her. "I wouldn't refuse any of those—unless, of course, you're trying to buy a grade in my class."

Duncan's snort drew the attention of several students around them. "I'm getting an A. I don't need to bribe the teacher."

"True." Harry patted his pockets to check for his keys and found them in the right front one of his pants. "Are you going to ace next week's test so I don't have to curve the grades?"

"Probably."

The director finally dismissed the cast and descended her perch, leaving the group to scatter in every direction.

Duncan joined the fray. "See you tomorrow!"

After returning the kid's wave, Harry headed for the parking lot, an involuntary grin tugging at his lips and his mood brighter than it had been in over a year. As much as he loved the cozy town of Wellington and teaching in a small high school, his social life had been dismal since his move four months ago. He'd met lots of people and been included in a number of gatherings with other faculty, but meeting a woman who interested him enough to date had met with abject failure. Truthfully, that had been the case long before his recent relocation.

Cold air blew through the defroster vents, triggering goose bumps to go with his shivers from the frigid night air. He blew on his hands and then rubbed them together before resorting to putting on the coat and gloves from the passenger seat a minute later. "Okay, car, can you warm up a little faster please?"

He trailed the line of taillights past a slew of empty spaces with almost no hope of getting warm prior to arrival at his rental house less than a mile away. Near the end of the row, a familiar head of wheat-colored hair appeared beside the lone vehicle without its lights glowing and the hatch open. She removed what looked like a jack.

Despite the cold, he turned into the space two slots down from Wallis Danforth and shut off his engine. An opportunity to prove his chivalry might not arise again soon.

With his collar turned up, he trotted the short distance to her car. "May I be of assistance, Lady Wallis? A carriage with a flat tire will not do at all."

She raised an eyebrow at him and chuckled. "Lord Harry to the rescue? Or is Tweedle Dee here to waylay me?"

"Harry the history teacher in attendance, offering to help remedy the situation." He bowed. "Or call the auto club, should you prefer a professional. I admit my experience is limited, but my dad was a mechanic and learning to change a tire was a requirement for getting my driver's license."

The jack clunked against the pavement when she set it near her feet. "I changed a flat a few years ago. In my driveway. In summer. During the day."

"Then between the two of us, we can probably get the job done before we freeze to death. Why don't I check the spare first? No point in wasting time on the jack if it's flat too." He reached into the dimly lit abyss. "Feels hard. Do you have a tire pressure gauge? Or should I get mine?"

Anabelle's voice came out of the near darkness toward the front of the car. "Is this it?"

Light reflected off the silver pen-sized tool that appeared a bit more than an arm's length away. A ghostly face with a blonde halo hovered beyond it.

He knelt on the lumpy ridge past the bumper and stretched toward the apparition, hoping he didn't fall into the hole. "Yes. Thank you, Miss Anabelle."

"You're welcome, Mr. Kreiger." A flash of headlights from an approaching car caught her Cheshire cat smile as she handed him the gauge. "I like you. You should date my mom."

I think I should too.

"I heard that, Anabelle Marie." The amused-sounding reprimand from behind made him jump, and his skull connected with what was most likely the plastic molding around the hatch. "Dance lessons and a new friend are fine, but I've had more than enough of dating nonsense in the past month to last me the next thirty years. Are you okay, Harry?"

He rubbed the barely noticeable twinge and stifled a disappointed sigh while he climbed back out of the vehicle. "I have a hard head, and I believe I might endeavor to change your mind about courting. I'm quite smitten, I'll have you know."

"Courting." The pleasure inflected in the word matched the expression on her face. "Smitten seems a bit rash, considering we only met this morning. How about if we try out the friends part and see if anything else develops?"

"'As you wish.'" He nodded once and pressed his lips together in an attempt to maintain a solemn expression.

Her smile widened. "A *Princess Bride* fan? It's one of my favorites."

His heart hiccupped. "Mine too."

"Maybe we can watch it—as friends—sometime." She aimed a mini flashlight at the spare. "If we survive changing the tire."

"That would be most enjoyable." A quick check of the pressure yielded a trustworthy replacement for her flat. "The spare seems to be in good shape. Tell me how I may assist you, lovely Wallis. Remove the spare? Jack up the car? Loosen the lug nuts? Your wish is my command."

She cocked her head to the side and studied him like he'd grown an extra nose. "You don't feel the need to be in charge?"

"In charge?" His eyebrows scrunched downward before he could stop them. "No. Should I? I'm sure you're quite capable, and it *is* your tire. You should be telling me what to do, not the other way around."

"And you're not just using your acting skills to fool me into thinking you're a nice guy?" Her lips quirked up on the left, hinting that she might be joking.

"He who attempts to fool a woman is a fool indeed." He set to work freeing the spare from the bracket holding it in place.

"I don't recognize that quote."

"It's an original by yours truly. I've watched many men make fools of themselves, the scoundrel this morning at the café among them." The tire now removable, he hefted it from the well and balanced it on the bumper. "Supervise me, my lady, while I repair your carriage."

She stepped away and directed him through the process of remedying her dilemma, providing the proper tools and plenty of encouragement along the way. Although his fingers ached from the cold, her cheerful voice and sweet disposition warmed him to his soul.

Smitten indeed.

Twenty minutes later, he closed the hatch and then wiped his dirty half-frozen hands on a fast-food napkin she'd pulled from her coat pocket. "The dealership should have no problem repairing the hole. The nail is fairly small."

"I really appreciate your help, Harry. The job would've taken so much longer by myself." She closed her gloved fingers around his and squeezed. "I hope you'll let me repay the favor sometime."

Pleased with the progress he'd made in their new friendship, he stifled the urge to ask her to dinner. "You already have. Remember, you agreed to be my partner for those dance lessons? I think we're even."

"I do remember." Her hand left his, bringing a moment of loss. "Thank you then."

"You're quite welcome." He withdrew his keys from his coat pocket and took a backward step toward his car. "Goodnight, Wallis. Drive safely and I'll see you on Monday at four thirty."

"You too. See you then. Goodnight, Harry." She hurried to the driver's door and ducked inside.

He waited for her to back out of the space and followed her to the road. His teeth chattered, even after she turned the opposite direction and her taillights disappeared from the rearview mirror. A hot shower to warm his body moved to top priority, overtaking a late supper. His heart, however, had transformed into a melty puddle of lovesick goo, much like he'd often witnessed in his teenage students.

The prospect of unrequited love at forty years old was more than a tad depressing.

CHAPTER 3

GOLDEN GLOW FROM THE FARMHOUSE WINDOWS COUNTERED THE bleakness of leafless trees and pitch darkness when Wally rounded the last turn in Tate's driveway. She chuckled at the triangular shadow in the living room's picture window. Big Jim had obviously convinced his wife the weekend before Thanksgiving wasn't too early to put up their first Christmas tree together. Colored lights flicked on as Wally shifted into Park.

Jim and Bobby would've gotten along famously.

I'm not jealous.

Well, maybe a little bit.

She'd gotten her happily-ever-after already, at least happily for fifteen years. Asking for another one would make her greedy.

The crunch of gravel greeted her when she opened her car door, and Petra pulled her pickup into the spot next to Wally. Her husband waved from the passenger seat. Auggie had evidently decided to ride with Jim down the road to Riley and Deke's house for guy's night.

Two more couples with well-deserved happily-ever-afters.

Yeah, so…I'm officially jealous.

Wally grabbed the grocery bag from the backseat and shoved the door closed with her hip.

Auggie jogged around the front end of the car with his arms extended. "Let me get that for you, Wally."

She shifted it higher and pushed the lock button on her key fob out of habit rather than necessity. "That's okay. It's not heavy."

Petra trailed after him at a leisurely saunter. "You better humor him. Today's the first day he's been allowed to lift anything heavier than a doughnut since the big V on Wednesday. He's been driving me crazy for four days."

A giggle snuck out before Wally could stop it. "Ah, the V that isn't for vendetta. Here you go, Auggie."

He hefted the bag and grinned like she'd given him his wife on a silver platter.

Staring toward her husband as he headed for the back of the house, Petra sighed. "It isn't for vagina, either. We have to wait at least three more days until we can have real sex again."

Wally didn't even try to hold in a hoot of laughter. "Sorry. Well, for him anyway. I'm pretty sure he isn't leaving you high and dry."

Petra snickered and bumped her shoulder against Wally's. "Wet as the ocean, but sometimes a woman needs her man, if you know what I mean."

"I'm not sure I remember. It's been so long. Not that menopause is being kind to my sex drive. Hell, I'd be happy with a conversation that included the guy saying he enjoyed my company."

"Still no luck with the dating app?"

Shaking her head, Wally walked beside her friend to the deck. "Wait 'til you hear about the loser I met for breakfast yesterday. I canceled my subscription when I got home."

"That bad, huh?"

Tate met them at the doorway. "What's bad?"

"Her date yesterday." Petra patted Tate's not-quite-there baby bump and grinned. "Hey, Tater, how's the little spud?"

Tate's withering sigh earned a snort from their butcher friend. "My brothers are already using that line. You'll have to come up with something else."

"How's the little fry?"

Snickers came from behind Wally, announcing Riley's arrival. "Good one, but my personal favorite nickname for Little Jim is sweet potato."

Tate rolled her eyes. "I yam so amused."

"I knew you would be." Riley gave her a hug and handed her a tote bag. "Free samples of some new herbs I'm trying out for the winter season. Still keeping breakfast down, bestie?"

"Breakfast, lunch, dinner, snacks. I'm pretty sure I'm going to gain two-hundred pounds by the end of June." Tate shooed them all inside and paused with the door almost closed. "Here comes Georgie. Petra, are you done being mad yet? You know she feels terrible about the whole Hugh Collier debacle, don't you? That's part of the reason she skipped Wednesday's book club meeting."

Petra glanced toward the deck. "I was done being mad the day after the food fight. She was right. Auggie and I could've—and should've—looked at the fake divorce papers right away. We also could've just talked to each other when she took my phone. Love puts your brain cells to sleep and makes you stubborn."

Aiming a smirk in Petra's direction, Riley removed her blazer. "Or, in our case, more stubborn."

"Very true."

The attorney in question appeared through the glass, her red trench coat looking much more festive than her closed-off expression.

Tate waved her inside. "Hi, Georgie! Glad you could make it tonight. Riley, coats can go in the hall closet. Wally, can you grab the veggies and dip from the fridge and check the bruschetta in the oven? Petra and Georgie, will you set the dining room table please? Dishes and silverware are already out."

After loading jackets and scarves in Riley's arms, everybody scattered for their assigned tasks, leaving Wally in the kitchen with their host. She transferred the perfectly arranged vegetable platter to the counter and removed the cover from the dip bowl in the center. "Your former-teacher skills are showing. Way to give our friends the opportunity to make up without an intervention."

"I know they'll be fine." Wielding a ladle, Tate stirred the contents of the soup pot on the stove. "Mostly, I'm concerned about Georgie. She always seems to hang back on the fringes, almost like she doesn't feel welcome unless she's handling a legal problem for one of us. Plus she still hasn't said whether she's coming to Thanksgiving dinner. I don't know if she has any other family besides Hugh and Joanie Collier, and I heard they left for Florida a few days ago. Snowbirds."

Wally slipped on a pair of oven mitts. "I've noticed that too. At least she doesn't have to worry about sperm donors, marriage contracts, and divorce proceedings in the book club anymore. I'm done trying to date after yesterday's public spectacle."

"That's too bad. You're an amazing woman with so much to offer." As she stepped away from the stove, Tate moved a pair of plates closer. "One's for the bruschetta and the other is for the snickerdoodles you brought. Hey, what about Harry? I saw him talking to you after dye-job Dan left."

"Harry who?" Riley peeked over Wally's shoulder and inhaled. "Yum. That smells so good."

Letting a wave of heat escape the oven, Wally reached for the potholders. "He's the new teacher at the high school."

Heavy boot steps announced the presence of Jim. He stopped behind Tate and wrapped his arms around her waist. "He wasn't at the pig roast, but he's in the café at least three or four times a week. Doesn't he teach history?"

Wally nodded. "Yes. He was also in the play at the performing arts center this weekend. And he changed my flat tire after last night's performance."

Tate's smile widened. "I knew he was a nice man."

Jim chuckled and then kissed his wife on the lips. "I see match-making in somebody's future. Auggie and I are heading over to hang out with Deke now. I love you, Mrs. Cochon."

"I love you too, Mr. Cochon. Drive carefully." The genuine affection in Tate's expression triggered another stab of envy.

Transferring the last of the bruschetta to the plate, Wally swallowed a sigh as Auggie and Petra shared a similar moment in the dining room doorway. Both couples deserved the happiness they'd found, but watching them made her revisit the loss of her own happy marriage and the companionship she had treasured with Bobby.

When the door closed behind the men as they left through the garage, Riley leaned against the counter and grinned. "What's this about you and somebody named Harry? Is he the guy you had breakfast with yesterday?"

"No, that would be dye-job Dan, asshole extraordinaire." Wally pulled the container of cookies from the bag and removed the lid. "I'll tell you all about that jerk once we sit down."

Riley directed traffic, making quick work of moving the goodies for their spread to the table. Then she took her place between Tate and Georgie. "Do I have to kick Danny boy into next week?"

"I'm pretty sure I won't have any more trouble with him." Everybody passed bowls and filled plates while Wally told the story their host had witnessed, earning groans from around the table. "I canceled my subscription when I got home, and I don't ever want to date again."

Georgie's deep frown eased enough that she no longer seemed on the verge of going renegade on the shithead. "And people wonder why I'm happy being a workaholic."

Tate shook her head. "Wally, I still think you should go out with Harry. I watched him when he was talking to you, and he definitely likes you."

Looking into her bowl of minestrone, Wally willed away the hot blush creeping up her cheeks. "When he was changing my tire, he told me he wants to court me. And that he's smitten."

"Courting and smitten!" Petra laughed and smacked her palm on the table, rattling silverware and dishes. "I haven't heard those words since I used to sneak my grandma's romance novels into bed with me when I'd spend the night at her and Gramp's house. Is he a proper English gentleman or a rake? A gentleman with rakish skills sounds like fun."

Riley tossed a carrot in Petra's direction, barely missing her soup. "No rakes. Teaching bedroom skills is easier than eradicating bad habits."

Who said anything about bedrooms?

Holding up her hands, Tate glanced back and forth between their two friends. "No more food fights unless we're outside and everybody is in agreement."

"Yes, Mom." Riley's smirk promised she planned to instigate a new battle as soon as the weather cooperated, whether anyone else agreed to it or not.

"I know that look." A half grin spoiled Tate's scolding. "It's exactly like Fiona's. Is your stepdaughter speaking to you this week?"

"She was pouty for one day at least two weeks ago. Amanda's mad at me now." Riley added a third cookie to her plate. "Deke told her she's too young to go to a movie with a boy, so she asked me—without telling me he'd already said no. I told her I'd say yes on one condition. She had to sit through my sex-ed spiel. When I got to the part about teenage boys expecting blow jobs instead of sexual intercourse nowadays, she turned about twelve shades of green and ran from the room."

Wally barely kept from choking on a bite of bruschetta. "I bet you told her they expect you to swallow."

Iced tea spurted from Petra's nose and Georgie cracked a smile behind her spoon.

"Of course I did. Good mothers have to prepare their daughters for the world of men." Riley tapped her glass against Tate's and then reached across the table toward Wally to do the same. "To motherhood. And blow jobs done right."

A chorus of hoots and giggles filled the dining room for several minutes before Riley passed around extra napkins for the tears running down everyone's faces.

Wally wiped her eyes and cheeks as the fit of laughter finally tapered off. "If you write the how-to book, I promise to stock it. I'm buying The Corner Bookshop tomorrow morning."

Tate added another balled-up napkin to her pile. "That's awesome about the bookstore, but please don't encourage her. And let me know if you need somebody to drive Anabelle to and from work."

"Congratulations." Georgie offered a truer smile than Wally had ever witnessed from the lawyer. "I'm so excited for you. It's a prime location and a really nice space. Are you going to host book signings?"

Wally nodded. "Book signings. Poetry readings. I was even thinking of adding a small stage for short performances like my play."

"I like that idea. Maybe this Harry person can help you with casting if he has acting experience."

Petra's nudge and wink warned Wally to expect more teasing. "You can find out if he's hairy like his name and has any other skills while you're rehearsing. He could end up being more dateable than the losers on the app."

Heat crept up Wally's neck again. "No dating. He mentioned needing to learn ballroom dancing for the spring play, so I agreed to be his partner for a few lessons, but only as friends. At least for now. And I was already considering asking him to be in my play. You know, the one with all the bad dating app guys? No kissing—or anything else—took place with any of them. He does have a bit of face scruff, so I guess you could say he's hairy."

"Ballroom dancing, huh? Nice." Riley waggled her eyebrows as she dunked her spoon in her soup. "Some of it's a lot like sex. You've seen *Dirty Dancing*, haven't you?"

"Yes, but..." Abandoning the real food in front of her, Wally grabbed a snickerdoodle and bent it in half until it broke. *Good, still soft.* "I don't know about the whole sex thing. Not that I think I'm... undesirable, I'm just not sure about letting a man see me naked anymore. Men seem to think women have to be perfect, even when their own bellies are squishy and their man-boobs droop to their belly buttons."

"Man-boobs?" Georgie pressed a napkin to her mouth, but it didn't hide the amusement in her eyes.

A bark of laughter came from Petra. "You lead such a sheltered life, woman. When was the last time you saw a naked man? The real thing. In person. One you wanted to see."

Color flooded Georgie's cheeks for the first time since Wally had met her four months ago. "I refuse to answer that question on the grounds that I'll incriminate myself on the charge of—"

"Being re-virginized?" Riley reached for the bruschetta platter. "I went over seven years between the big fortieth-birthday disappointment and Deacon."

Wally waved off her friend's claim to fame. "Not as long as me. Bobby was the last. It's been ten and a half years."

"Twenty years." Absolute silence descended on the table at Georgie's pronouncement. She shrugged and picked up her soupspoon. "My last year of law school. He broke up with me over Christmas break, and I decided to focus a hundred percent on my education and career for the rest of my life."

"Holy fuck." A slice of toasted baguette clattered onto Riley's bread plate. "*Twenty years?* I hope you own some really good toys. Women aren't meant to go orgasm-less that long."

Georgie tucked her chin to her chest and looked toward her bowl like the minestrone held the secrets of the universe, but it didn't hide the brighter flames on her cheeks. "I… I take care of…things."

"Not often enough if you're embarrassed about it. I can recommend several vibrators that get the job done better than a lot of men." Riley grinned. "And they don't snore."

A strangled cough punctuated another flood of pink on Georgie's face.

Pretty sure their lawyer friend would appreciate a little redirection from the very personal topic of masturbation, Wally heaved a sigh. "Anyway, I can't imagine any man understanding that Anabelle will never be completely independent, that she'll always come first in my life. Even before sex."

With a piece of bruschetta in one hand and a cookie in the other, Tate frowned. "I still think you should give Harry a chance. He's a really nice guy, especially to Anabelle, Darren, and the young woman I hired last week. And he's cute and smart and funny."

The rest of the book club members nodded, clearly willing to gang up on Wally for the sake of her social life.

She picked up another cookie. "Fine, I'll give him a chance—if he asks me out."

CHAPTER 4

HARRY FLIPPED THE MIRROR CLOSED, RAISED THE VISOR, AND scratched the rough stubble on his jaw. He would've preferred stopping at home for a second shave of the day, but skipping the after-school staff meeting in order to impress Wallis Danforth probably wouldn't have gone over well. "Hopefully, she likes the rugged look."

Computer bag slung on his shoulder, he pulled his keys from the ignition and climbed out of the driver's seat. A quick check that his car rested within the white lines assured him he would never belong to the bad-boy's club. Nerd was a much more accurate description.

"Hey, Mr. Kreiger!" The synchronous greeting cut through his self-assessment as he approached The Corner Bookshop. Four students from his second period class waved from across the street.

He lifted his hand and smiled. He had found the small-town familiarity he wanted when he'd accepted the new teaching position and moved to Wellington. The snowflakes hanging on the light posts along the sidewalk sparked a moment of wistfulness about the upcoming holidays, but it faded somewhat when he stood in front of the bookstore.

The new owner stood on the other side of the big glass window, removing books from a display and standing others in their place. Then she picked up a festively wrapped box and turned toward him. Her lopsided bun wobbled and her lips curved upward as she met his gaze.

His pulse kicked up a notch, proving the previous times hadn't been a fluke.

She motioned toward the entrance and her muffled voice carried through the window. "It's unlocked!"

He nodded once and bowed before heading to the door. Although her enthusiastic greeting tempted him to hurry, he channeled Dick Van Dyke in *Mary Poppins* and jigged his way the last ten feet.

Giggles welcomed him into the shop. A few seconds later, the woman who had occupied his thoughts almost constantly since Saturday morning popped out from behind a shelf of used books, the dirt smudge on her forehead not detracting from her beauty in the least. "Are you always in character, Harry?"

"My mom always said I didn't *play* characters. I *was* the character. My younger brother seemed to appreciate it." He gently grasped her extended hand, lingering a little longer than socially expected, but she didn't pull away. "It's a true pleasure to see you again, Wallis. I trust the closing went smoothly and you've had a busy but wonderful day."

The dimple formed in her right cheek, sending his insides somersaulting. "It did and I have, thank you. It's good to see you again too."

He offered his bent elbow. "May I escort you to the reading area to discuss the details of our dance partnership?"

"You may." After locking the door, she linked her arm with his and guided him toward the mishmash collection of oversized chairs and end tables near the children's section. "Would you like a cup of tea or coffee? I have cookies. Snickerdoodles. They're Anabelle's favorite. And mine."

"Mine too. Tea would be perfect. Can I help?"

"No need." She slipped her arm free and walked to the sideboard tucked out of the way in the corner. The Christmas-y scent of peppermint mingled with the pleasant smell of books when she set a tray on the closest table and poured. Steam rose in caressing wisps to her face. "Sugar or creamer?"

Breathtaking. He waited by the chair on the opposite side of the table for her to sit. "Um, no, thank you. You said you've wanted to learn to salsa for years, but do you waltz?"

"Not for close to twenty years. I'm more than a little rusty, I'm sure."

"It'll come back to you—like riding a bike, only you don't need a helmet."

"I hope so. You don't deserve a broken head any more than broken toes." She glanced toward him as she returned the teapot to the tray. "Where are my manners? Take your coat off and have a seat. And help yourself to as many cookies as you want. I have more at home."

A *thunk* came from somewhere in the rows of shelves as he tossed his jacket across the back of the chair. "Sounds like you have a really large bookworm living in your store."

Her laughter warmed him from the chilly walk outside and seemed to permeate every inch of the space around them. "My staff and a few temps are doing inventory so we can start with an accurate count when the store opens tomorrow morning. My accountant recommended it since the previous owner wasn't very committed to tracking orders and sales."

"Good plan." He leaned back into the squishy-marshmallow cushions. "Would your accountant be the one I've seen at The Homegrown Café with Mrs. Cochon and her husband? Deacon Jeffries, I think his name is."

"One and the same. He does Tate's and Jim's books for the restaurant and for Big Jim's Itty Bitty Pig Farm. Riley—Deke's wife— recommended him to Tate when she opened THC. Oh, and he does payroll for Riley's organic produce farm. He also handles the accounts of The Butcher and The Baker for Petra and Auggie Lochsley-Hofmeier or whatever last name they've settled on since they got married earlier this month. Riley likes to call Deke 'Everybody's Damn Accountant' when she's annoyed with him." Perched on the edge of her seat, Wallis grinned and picked up her teacup. "Before you ask, yes, there was a shop called The Candlestick Maker, but Mr. Collier retired and sold the building to Petra and Auggie so they could connect their businesses. He's quite the knave."

Mesmerized by her melodic voice, he almost lost track of what Wallis had said. "Clever. I've met Petra and Auggie—and Tate, of course. I didn't make it to Jim's hog roast because I had to go out of town, but you can hardly miss him. He's a big guy. Former football player?"

"High school and college." She shook her head and sighed. "Listen to me, monopolizing the conversation. How do you like Wellington?"

"You've been nothing less than polite and charming." He picked up a cookie from the tray to keep from grasping her hands and telling her he could listen to her recite the classifications from the Dewey Decimal System and never get bored. "I like Wellington and its small-town appeal. The people I've met have been friendly and welcoming. It seems like a good place to live."

"It is. I'm glad you're settling in. Did you find out anything about dance lessons? I have book club meetings on Thursday and Sunday evenings, but any other day should be fine."

"A book club? Hmm. I recall hearing something about it. Five friends who discuss books, eat delicious snacks, and enjoy each other's company. I believe Mrs. Crenshaw mentioned something about the marriage bug being catching in your club. Is it three surprise weddings in a matter of weeks?" *I wouldn't be opposed to making it four if things go well.*

"Yes, we were all single when we started meeting in September. Then Tate and Riley married Jim and Deacon in a double ceremony in October, and Petra and Auggie tied the knot at the county court-house earlier this month. I'm not sure I can picture Georgie getting hitched. Don't get me wrong. She's a very nice person, always ready to help her friends, but dealing with divorces and custody cases has disillusioned her, I think. For marriage and motherhood, not as a lawyer. She loves her job, even though she works long hours." A hint of color crept up Wallis's cheeks. "And here I am, talking too much again."

"Not at all. I like listening to you talk about your friends and the town. It's a slightly different perspective from Mrs. Crenshaw's gossip. She's a very sweet lady, but she seems to know everything that goes on in town. It's a bit disconcerting." He held his second cookie above his tea, ready to dunk and bite. "I wouldn't want to try to keep a secret."

"Definitely not. Mrs. Crenshaw and several of the other Garden Club ladies visit the beauty salon every Monday morning. Petra gets the lowdown at the butcher shop first thing when she opens. They're nothing if not creatures of habit. Hair, butcher, bakery, and home. The best time to make news is Monday afternoon or evening. It's usually forgotten by the following week." The sparkle in her eyes suggested she might've had personal experience using the strategy.

"Good to know. I'll try not to become the topic of gossip on a Sunday." After a drink of tea to wash down the last of his second snickerdoodle, he stood. "Since it'll be old news by the next gossip session, may I have this waltz while I fill you in on our dance lessons?"

She raised an eyebrow, even though she clasped his offered hand and arose. "What about music?"

"I would hum a song, but talking might be difficult, so we have two options. I can try to find something suitable on my phone or we can let our imaginations play the tune. The latter might attract less attention." Careful to maintain a respectable distance, he lifted their joined hands and placed his other hand at her shoulder blade. *A perfect fit.* "Perhaps 'Minute Waltz' by Chopin?"

Her tentative smile widening, she nodded. "Lovely choice."

"Just in case." He kicked off his loafers and nudged them under her chair. "Dancing, not toe squishing."

"Good idea." Resting her free hand on his shoulder, she toed off her running shoes. "Okay, I'm ready."

"Do you remember the count? For the waltz, not the *Sesame Street* character."

Her giggle became another and another. "You have a wonderful sense of humor."

"The proper term is goofball." The thrill of being able to make her laugh dragged him deeper into infatuation, but he guided her away from the furniture instead of scaring her off with a declaration of his feelings. Sharing a dance with her was reward enough.

"It's refreshing, whatever you want to call it." She straightened her spine and took a deep breath. "One-two-three, one-two-three?"

"Correct. You'll start by stepping back with your left foot. I'll do my best to try to lead. I'm a little out of practice, so we may need a few attempts before we get the rhythm and steps right. Here we go. And… one-two-three, one-two-three." Pleased when they managed the first basic box step without tangling their legs or tripping over each other's feet, he led her into a few more repetitions. "Excellent. Let's try a circuit around the reading area."

Her ability to follow his lead spoke of a woman who had been quite adept at the waltz years ago and whose rustiness needed only a brief polish to let her skill shine.

In the middle of a second circuit, he let the music in his head take over. "I've arranged for four private one-hour lessons starting next Monday night at six thirty. I just need to call and confirm, as long as that time works for you and your daughter."

She beamed up at him, her pretty brown eyes shining. "Anabelle meets with her occupational therapy group on Mondays from six to eight, so that's perfect. It's very thoughtful of you to consider her needs and my responsibilities. I appreciate it."

"Caring for a special-needs adult is a big commitment." He swallowed past the tightness in his throat and tried for a smile. "When our parents died in a car accident, I became the caregiver for my little brother with Down syndrome. He was sixteen and I'd just started my first teaching job."

"Wow, that's an amazing thing for you to have done. Does he still live with you? Anabelle and I would love to meet him."

Her enthusiasm made him wish that were possible. "He passed away a year ago, mainly from heart problems. He was born with a lot of health issues."

"I'm so sorry." Her words comforted him in a way no one else's condolences had. She'd probably had many of the same worries.

"Thank you. I tried to prepare myself because I knew from the time I was ten or twelve that he might not live past forty, but I still wonder if I did everything I could for him."

"You loved him, didn't you?" At his nod, she smiled. "And he was happy?"

"He said he was. He wanted me to celebrate his life rather than grieve his death. I had to promise him I'd concentrate on myself for a change once he was gone." Harry slowed as they completed another circle and guided her into an underarm turn as they neared her seat.

"Then you did everything you could for him." She brushed a few wayward curls from her forehead and sat. "Thanks for the waltz. I'd forgotten how much I enjoy dancing."

Already mourning the loss of holding her in his arms, he released a silent sigh and dropped into his chair. "It was my pleasure to partner with such a wonderful dancer. I'm really looking forward to our lessons together."

"Me too." She gestured toward the tray on the table. "More tea?"

"I wish I could, but I have essays to grade for one class and quizzes from two more tonight. A teacher's work is never done. It is, however, rewarding for the most part." He reached past her legs to retrieve his shoes and then slipped them on. A slight heaviness as he picked up his coat jogged his memory. "I almost forgot. I brought you a little some-thing. Well, not exactly little. Just something."

"Oh?" The brightening of her smile suggested she loved surprises.

He tucked away that information for later and handed her the extra-large treat he'd added to his grocery cart yesterday. "One of my students saw us talking after Saturday's show and told me Kit Kats are your favorite. I figure you'll need a snack to survive taking over the bookstore and getting through Black Friday this week."

"Thank you! That's so sweet." Her dimple made another appear-ance with a wide grin. "You know, I was wondering if you have plans for Thanksgiving, with you being new in town and I'm guessing no family. I thought you might like to join Anabelle and me for dinner at Tate and Jim's. And we'd enjoy your company."

"I would be honored to escort you." Should he have paused to pretend he had to consider the invitation instead of agreeing to it so quickly? Would she think he was too eager? *I like her, and pretending otherwise is foolish.* "It's a date."

CHAPTER 5

A DATE.

Wally gave up trying to slow her racing pulse and adjusted the neckline of her sweater for the umpteenth time. Fifty wasn't too old to show a little cleavage, was it?

A few new gray strands glittered in her hair, catching the light like Bobby's favorite twenty-pound fishing line.

I'm part unicorn.

Yeah, that's it. I'm definitely not old.

She added a swipe of peachy-pink lipstick and then yanked a tissue from the box on the counter to remove it. Why had she asked Harry to a major holiday event?

I panicked because I didn't think he was going to ask me out and I wanted him to.

Quit being an overdramatic teenager, Wally. It's just a date.

She stuck her tongue out at her reflection and tossed the unused tissue in the trash.

Anabelle popped into the bathroom doorway. "You're so pretty, Mom. Harry is going to be speechless."

The doorbell chimed, reigniting her nerves.

"I don't know about that, but I appreciate the compliment. You look pretty gorgeous yourself." Her heart hammering in her chest, Wally followed her daughter through the master bedroom to the living room and gave her a quick hug. "Why don't I answer the door while you call Darren and let him know we'll pick him up in about twenty minutes?"

Pulling her cell from her skirt pocket, Anabelle shot Wally a wide smirk. "Okay, but I want to see what Harry does when you open the door."

"Fine, but no laughing if he faints." Giggles erupted from behind Wally as she reached for the knob. The lighthearted sound chased away some of her nervousness. "Call your boyfriend and let me embarrass myself in peace."

"Yes, Mom."

The humor in her daughter's response distracted Wally for a moment, but the lack of footsteps on the wood floor warned her she had an audience as she turned the doorknob.

Harry stood on the front porch, a tissue-wrapped bouquet the size of *War and Peace* hiding the lower half of his face, but a smile shone in his eyes. A mini sunflower and several fall shades of chrysanthemums peeked out of the wrapping. "For you and Anabelle."

"Thank you, Harry." She cradled the flowers in her arm and stifled a swoony sigh. *Maybe I'll be the one to faint?* "They're beautiful. Um, come in."

"You're welcome. I'm glad you like them." He stepped into the living room, his mouth still curved upward. "They reminded me of you and your daughter when I saw them. Cheerful, vibrant, and pretty. You brightened my day with your invitation, and I hoped the flowers would do the same for you."

"They have."

As Wally waved him toward the kitchen, Anabelle squealed and clapped. "Hi, Harry! You brought flowers for my mom! That's so romantic. Darren sometimes brings me daisies because he knows how much I love them. He's ready for us to pick him up on the way to Tate's house."

"Hi, Anabelle. It's good to see you." Harry paused at the arched entrance to the kitchen. "Although I do love a good romantic gesture, the flowers are for both of you to enjoy. I wouldn't want to be too bold too soon and scare your mother off."

Maybe not, but you're doing a damn good job of sweeping me off my feet.

"Mom isn't scared of anything, except millipedes. She says nothing should have that many legs."

The mention of the creepy crawly buggers triggered a shudder up Wally's spine. "They shouldn't."

He pulled a pancake flipper from the utensil crock on the counter and raised it above his head. "I shall protect you from the thousand-legged dragons with my life, Lady Wallis."

And what if I'm scared of how easily it is to like you? "Alas, Sir Harry, the dragons have gone into hiding until spring. And I don't want to hit you in the head with the cupboard door while I look for a large enough vase. A knight with a concussion might need a rest instead of turkey and pumpkin pie."

"That would be a shame." He stood aside while she retrieved her largest vase and arranged the bouquet, his watchful gaze inciting a tickly sensation in her belly. When she set the flowers in the middle of the table, he followed her. "Beautiful. Not quite as enchanting as their recipients, but almost."

A blush warmed her cheeks and neck. Or had she suddenly developed the menopausal hot flashes Riley complained so much about?

Shaking off the disconcerting heat, she hurried to the fridge for the gallon-sized container of homemade cranberry sauce. "I hope this is enough. Tate said they're expecting about forty for dinner. I haven't cooked for that many people since Bobby and I used to host a picnic for his office years ago. Anabelle, will you get our coats please?"

"Okay, Mom." Her daughter flounced toward the closet by the front door.

"Bobby? Your late husband?" Harry's expression held no jealousy, only curiosity.

Wally nodded, caught between wanting to assure her date she was no longer in mourning and weirded out talking about her dead husband to a man who said he was smitten with her. Why did dating have to be so hard? "We should go since we still have to pick up Darren."

Thankfully, Anabelle picked up the conversational slack on the drive to Darren's house. Her chatter seemed to keep Harry's focus off the man Wally had been married to—while revealing he'd been engaged once but never married.

After casting a glance to the left, to the right, and again to the left, Harry made the turn into the neighborhood where Anabelle's boyfriend lived with his aunt and uncle. "My former fiancée told me I had to choose between my brother and her. It was an easier decision than I would've expected, and I've never regretted it. Charlie was the best brother. How long have you known Darren?"

"I can't remember." Anabelle rested her hand on Wally's shoulder over the back of the passenger seat. "When did he start coming to group, Mom?"

Wally opened the visor mirror to see her daughter's face. "About five years ago. Right before we moved into our house."

"Wow, that was a long time ago."

"It seems like it, doesn't it?" Laying her palm atop Anabelle's hand, Wally wallowed for a long moment in the bittersweet memory of selling the home she and Bobby had shared. "Harry, it's the fourth house on the right past the stop sign. Yellow with white trim and gray shutters."

He slowed as they neared the cross street. "I see it. My phone has gotten me lost on more than one occasion, so thanks for co-piloting. It looks like Darren's waiting for us."

Anabelle's face transformed in the mirror, expressing a kind of affection for her boyfriend Wally had never seen before. "He's very good at being on time."

"That's an excellent quality to have." Harry made the final turn into the driveway and shifted into Park. "Are we on time too?"

"Yes!" Anabelle popped out of the car and hurried along the side-walk toward the porch.

With a wide smile, Darren met her at the bottom of the steps. Then he dropped to one knee and held up a small red box. His words couldn't have been more obvious.

"Oh my." A rush of emotion brought tears to Wally's eyes. "I knew they liked each other, but... She has the most open heart, and now she gets to experience romantic love. I imagined... I just never expected..."

Harry extracted a paper napkin from the driver's door cubbyhole and dabbed at her cheek. "I had no idea our date would include a marriage proposal."

Laughter bubbled out of her, his sense of humor catching her off guard as much as her daughter's engagement. "Don't go getting any ideas."

His chuckle tickled her tummy. "I can assure you I only kiss on the first date."

Will he kiss me?

The thought didn't scare her. In fact, it intrigued her—his lips against hers and maybe a little tongue. Would she remember how to kiss?

She jerked her gaze from his mouth a second too late, based on his raised eyebrows and a pleased smirk. "Technically speaking, this could be considered our second date since we went dancing in the bookstore on Monday."

"Quite true." His mischievous tone set her insides tumbling and twisting. "I'll take that information under advisement when debating the appropriateness of kissing and asking for your hand in marriage today."

"As I said, don't go getting any ideas. I'm new to this dating thing. Maybe I need to title my play *Flirting at 50 and Other Failed Experiments*."

"Catchy, but I hope I don't fall into the failed category. I'd rather give you a happy ending." Bright pink circles bloomed on his cheeks, most likely matching the heat creeping up her neck. "I, um... Not that kind. At least not today. Maybe I should stop talking."

The click of the door behind her made her jump, and a gusty breeze chilled the warmth on her skin.

Anabelle ducked inside and slid across the backseat. "Mom, Darren and I want to get married. Will you walk with me in our wedding like Grandma walked with you?"

Switching gears from an embarrassing giggle fit to a joyous celebration produced a lump in Wally's throat, and choking sobs came out when she tried to speak.

Stupid menopause!

She swallowed past the ache and swiped at her leaky eyes, but neither had any effect on the elation for her daughter's happiness or the realization that her sweet baby girl had grown up. Three slow, deep breaths finally calmed her hormonal outburst enough to respond. "I'm so happy for you. I'll walk with you wherever you want to go."

Darren climbed in beside Anabelle, a frown firmly in place. "Why are you sad, Mrs. Danforth?"

"I'm not sad." Wiping away the last of her tears, Wally turned in her seat to smile at her future son-in-law. "Sometimes I cry when I'm happy. Did you tell your aunt and uncle you were asking Anabelle to marry you?"

Clutching her daughter's hand in his, he nodded. "Yes. They helped me practice what to say and Aunt Laura took me to buy the ring. She wanted to tell you, but then it wouldn't have been a surprise."

"It's a very nice surprise, Darren. I can't wait for you to be part of our family."

Harry reached past her to shake Darren's hand. "Congratulations to you both. Are you going to share the news at our Thanksgiving feast? I don't want to accidentally mention it if you're not ready to tell everyone."

Anabelle's gaze flicked toward the simple but elegant diamond solitaire on her finger and then toward Darren. "We have to tell them so they know to come to our wedding. It feels a little funny to wear a ring. I'll get used to it, though, because gifts from people you love are special."

"Yes, they are." Brushing his fingertips along the striped scarf around his neck, Harry seemed to lose some of his exuberance. "My brother gave me this scarf for Christmas two years ago. I wear it all the time, even though I hardly ever find anything to match it. Orange and purple were his favorite colors."

Wally bit the inside of her lip to keep from bawling her eyes out, but it didn't stop her heart from breaking for him. The desire to wrap him in a hug almost hurt.

He swiveled back to the steering wheel and shifted into Reverse. "Is everybody buckled? We need to get going. I wouldn't want to hold up Tate's dinner by being late."

After a pair of yeses from the newly engaged couple, he backed down the driveway and headed out of the neighborhood the same way they'd arrived. His subdued mood chipped away at her self-control on the twenty-five-minute ride to Big Jim's Itty Bitty Pig Farm. Inch by inch, she narrowed the space between her fingers and his right hand on the gearshift.

He glanced her direction at the first touch and the lines around his mouth softened. "Thank you."

"You're welcome." Was smitten-ness contagious? "In about a mile, you'll want to turn left just past the bright orange mailbox with THE BROWNS painted on the side. You can't miss it. Big Jim's has a sign at the road half a mile or so after the turn."

"Okay." He laced his fingers through hers, returning them to the same position after both turns.

Nearly a dozen cars already filled the gravel turnaround between Tate and Jim's house and the pole barn at their arrival, including the vehicles of the other four members of THC Book Club.

Georgie climbed out of her sporty roadster as Harry pulled in beside it. When Wally waved at her through the side window, her eyebrow shot upward in an uncharacteristic reaction. No sound carried through the glass, but the question on her friend's lips was unmistakable.

"Date?"

Determined to own her decision, Wally put on her bravest face and nodded once. Yes, she'd invited Harry. Her initial reasons, however, weren't as noble as she'd led herself to believe. Why had she thought she could fool anybody?

A hint of amusement shone in Georgie's eyes as she adjusted her hold on a cloth tote bag, clearly content to wait for the carload to disembark and walk with her to the gathering.

Anabelle, Darren, and Harry climbed out of the car, giving Wally no choice but to join them. Before she could pull on the handle, her date had rounded the front end and assumed the role of proper gentleman, opening the door and offering her a hand.

Smitten. Infatuated. Swoony. Ah hell, go with it.

She swung her legs around and rose with his assistance, reminding her of their dance in the bookstore. "Thanks."

"My pleasure." His mischievous grin suggested he'd witnessed and made a fairly accurate assessment of her interaction with her friend. Then he turned toward a smiling Georgie. "Georgina Swofford, it's good to see you. Harry Kreiger. You juggled all the hoops I had to jump through when I became the legal guardian of my brother Charlie."

Georgie's moderated glee instantly changed to lawyer mode. "Down syndrome minor. Parents deceased. Of course, Mr. Kreiger. I remember your case. It's good to see you again as well. How is Charlie?"

Harry let out a barely audible sigh, and Wally gave his hand a gentle squeeze. "He passed away last year. Please, call me Harry."

"I'm so sorry for your loss, Harry." Georgie shifted the bag to her other hand. "It's nice that you're here with Wally. She's a wonderfully kind and supportive person. Shall we go inside?"

Hefting the container of cranberry sauce, he glanced at Wally, setting off a new series of acrobatics in her tummy. "She is, and I thank you for the condolences. After you."

Georgie gave a curt nod and set off at a good clip toward the pole barn, its pumpkin and corn stalk décor announcing the location of the gathering. Anabelle and Darren followed, their voices carrying as they announced their engagement. Then the trio stopped at the entrance.

Georgie cocked her head to the side and raised a disconcerting eyebrow. "It seems a marital virus has infected Wellington. I wonder who's next."

CHAPTER 6

"Zero." Big Jim added another log to the fireplace in the center of the room and passed off the sleeping toddler in his arms to her father. A full belly and playing with her older cousins had likely contributed to the girl's condition.

Auggie glanced over his shoulder toward Petra and chuckled. "Only one. How about you, Deke?"

"Six? Seven? I don't know. I lost track a month ago." The accountant's smirk grew into a grin. "We like to keep things interesting. Besides, making up is worth it."

Oscar Banyan snorted. "Can you believe them, Harry? You'd think they're comparing something better than the number of arguments they've had with their wives since they got married. I never should've let them talk me into performing their ceremonies. Anabelle and Darren's wedding is my last—as long as it happens before my license expires at the end of December."

The man's grumpy tone didn't invite a response, but Harry couldn't help himself. "You're licensed to officiate weddings? Interesting. I'm curious, though. Why did you get licensed if you dislike doing it so much?"

After a noisy gulp of coffee, Oscar set his mug on the tray stand next to him and aimed a glare toward the group of women gathered around Anabelle, Darren, and Wallis on the other side of the room. A growl rumbled out of him. "I planned to use it and my notary license for something to do after my term as mayor ended. I hadn't decided whether or not to go back to corporate law."

Based on the chest-length beard and bushy ponytail, Harry was fairly certain The Grouch had chosen not to, but assumptions tended to get a guy in trouble. "Corporate lawyer? Mayor of Wellington?"

"Yes." The gruff response seemed to indicate Oscar had either detested both jobs or regretted them.

"Outstanding. You have quite the resume. I teach American Government, among other things, at the high school. Would you be willing to come speak to my class sometime before winter break? The students think public service is holding press conferences and going to fundraising parties."

Oscar's heavy sigh didn't bode well, but he unearthed a business card from his wallet. "Call me and we'll set up a date and time. But don't expect me to shave, get a haircut, or wear anything nicer than what I'm wearing now."

Deacon snickered and shook his head. "Don't mind Oscar. He's doing his best to convince everybody he's antisocial. He wouldn't be here if he really wanted to be a hermit."

"I'm here because Tate invited me when she brought an injured bird out to the sanctuary last week." Oscar frowned and crossed his arms, pulling his threadbare plaid-flannel shirt so tight on his elbow it split the fabric. "She didn't tell me we were having dinner in a barn with fifty people."

Jim's boisterous laughter echoed off the walls. "Says the guy who spends most of his time in a barn with wild animals. You came because Tate's the sweetest person on the planet, Auggie brought pies, and you wanted somebody to complain to. Oh, and we had forty-two people, not fifty."

"Close enough. I've complained and I had a piece of pie, so I'll be go—" Heaving another sigh, Oscar dug his phone from his jeans pocket. Then he grimaced and walked toward the exit as he lifted his cell to his ear. "Phone call. Thanks for dinner."

Auggie stuck out his hand palm up into the remaining lopsided circle of men. "Phone call, real or imaginary. You owe me five bucks, Deke."

Deacon's eye-roll suggested he had no intention of paying up. "He made it through dinner and dessert, and he didn't leave as soon as he saw Georgie was here, so *you* owe *me* five bucks."

"But he agreed to officiate Anabelle and Darren's wedding, and he actually showed up. Five bucks." The baker wiggled his fingers at the accountant. "Pay up."

Still figuring out the dynamics of the group, Harry scratched the beard stubble that had already gone from barely there that morning to almost time to shave again. "Georgina is Oscar's ex-wife? Ex-girlfriend?"

Auggie barked a laugh. "Uh, no. Definitely not. Greedy ex-wife's attorney. The divorce wasn't exactly amicable."

Leaning in, Jim lowered his voice. "Downright nasty is more like it. His ex made some false accusations that could've put him in jail and the poorhouse. It's why he keeps to himself most of the time. Technically, Georgie was only doing her job, but you could say he's a little bitter about the whole thing."

"Ah." Harry caught a glance of the man in question with his phone to his ear through the window. "I've heard him referred to as The Grouch a few times and wondered why. It seems he's earned the right to that nickname."

"Not that he likes it." Deacon passed a five-dollar bill to Auggie and grinned. "Remember to include it in gambling income."

Auggie raised an eyebrow. "Like you will if, by some long shot, you win the pool for guessing if Tate's having a girl or a boy and the day and time it's born?"

"Long shot? My guess is based on math and statistics, not a gut feeling." The accountant looked toward the approaching bride, groom, and wedding planners. "Besides, all I want is bragging rights. The money's going into an account for the baby if I win."

Staring in the direction of his wife, Jim looked as in love as Harry had ever seen a man. "That's still about seven months away, and we don't even have our first prenatal visit until next week. All that matters to me is a healthy baby and a happy Tate."

Riley slipped her arm around her husband's waist and beneath his sweater. Then she nipped at his ear. "Aren't Tate and Jim the most sickening sweet couple you've ever met? Even sweeter than Anabelle and Darren. Speaking of the newly engaged lovebirds, the wedding is planned, right down to the last detail."

Deacon stalled her roving hand with his and winked at her over his shoulder. "Since that's done, it's time to head to my parents' for second Thanksgiving. They asked if the girls can stay the night."

Familiar laughter came from behind them, rocketing Harry's pulse into overdrive. Then Wallis appeared next to the couple. "You two are such horndogs."

Riley's mischievous grin matched her husband's. "Yeah, so?"

"So try to make it home this time." Amusement glowed in Wallis's eyes, and dimples formed in her cheeks. "You almost gave Mrs. Crenshaw a heart attack last week."

"Fine. Point taken." Riley withdrew her hand from her husband's clothing and extended it toward Harry. "It was a pleasure to meet you, Harry, but you should know I'm not afraid of going to jail if you hurt Wally."

He tried to hide a wince at her unexpectedly strong grip. "The pleasure was mine, and I assure you that's not my intention. She's the most captivating woman I've ever encountered—even more than Holly Marshall from *Land of the Lost*, my first crush."

Auggie slipped his fingers through Petra's and chuckled. "I loved that show. You should come to our house on Sunday for guy's night in. We hang out twice a week and write a new chapter of the manual on understanding women. You haven't missed much, though. We've been meeting for about six or seven weeks and we're still on chapter one."

"Smart ass." His wife rolled her eyes, but she snuggled closer and seemed to whisper something in his ear.

"Hmm." A smirk slid across the baker's face. "We need to get going too. Thanks for hosting, Tate. Jim. We should do this again for Christmas."

A round of nods and yeses led to a fairly quick dispersal of the guests, and Harry walked his date, her daughter, and her future son-in-law to his car, with a pair of mini coolers containing leftovers in tow. Every step pulled him deeper into the fantasy that they were his wife and family, the only thing still missing from the promise he'd made to Charlie before his death. Talk of the wedding details only added to it as he drove Anabelle and her betrothed back to Darren's house for a feast with his family.

One proposal is probably enough for today.

Harry made the final turn into the driveway, parked, and pivoted to the passengers in the backseat. "Congratulations to both of you, and I enjoyed sharing Thanksgiving with you."

Leaning forward, Anabelle patted him on the cheek. "I'm glad you came with us, Harry. I like you. You should go on more dates with my mom."

I think so too. "I'll have to ask her. She might not want to."

"She does. Don't you, Mom?" The sparkle in the young woman's eyes suggested she'd fully intended to put her mother on the spot.

Wally's gaze skipped from him toward her daughter and back again. "Maybe. Probably. It depends on the invitation."

Anabelle giggled as she followed Darren out the rear driver's side door. "Mom likes music and dancing. And she loves books and food."

Relieved that his instincts had been right on target, Harry nodded. "Good to know. See you tomorrow at the café."

"A scone and a medium French roast coffee with one shot of skim milk." The door clunked shut and she waved as she hurried after Darren to the sidewalk.

"She remembers my order better than I do most days." He cast a glance at Wallis as he checked for cars on the street behind him. "Ah, to be young again, not that being middle-aged is all that bad. I probably wouldn't have been brave enough to talk to a woman as beautiful as you at twenty-something."

A lovely blush colored her cheeks and she ducked her head. "Sweet-talker."

"It's the truth." Would she notice if he took the long way to her house, allowing him to spend a few more minutes with her?

"Were you shy when you were younger? I have a hard time imagining that."

He made the turn onto the road headed south to Wellington. "Not shy, just nerdier than I am now and not very good at talking to women unless I was being a comedian. My former fiancée seemed to like it at the time, but looking back on it now, I think she just wanted to get married. The prospect of being partially responsible for my brother was clearly too serious a life for her."

Only road noise and the sound of the heater fan broke the silence for at least a minute.

Then Wallis sighed. "I've had the same concerns about dating and knowing Anabelle could potentially be a deterrent for most men. I don't ever want her to see that, whether she would understand it or not. I'd rather be alone than risk someone hurting her feelings."

"Charlie once asked me if he was the reason I didn't get married. I was honest with him about what happened, but I also told him I would've dumped her if I'd known how shallow she was." A smile tugged at his lips from the memory. "He said I deserved better—true love—and not to settle. We were both huge fans of happily-ever-after movies."

The light touch of her fingertips on his hand sent tingles through his whole body. "So that's where your romanticism comes from."

He shrugged. "And a certain woman may inspire it in me more than others."

Her throaty chuckle made his insides melt. "Charmer. Will you stay for a while and watch *The Princess Bride* with me? I'll make popcorn and hot chocolate."

Unable to pass up a golden opportunity, he inclined his head toward her. "'As you wish.'"

"We'll see." Her tentative smile remained each time he snuck a look at her on the rest of the drive, hinting she wasn't quite sure she believed his implication.

He stopped in front of the garage and shut off the engine, but his nerves revved higher. "I can carry your coolers into the house if you like. Don't want to be presumptuous."

Her tongue snuck out to wet her lips, giving his heart another workout as she unbuckled her seatbelt. "That would be wonderful, thank you. And before the movie, I want to show you something. Get your thoughts on it."

A vision of her standing in her bedroom doorway, clad in a modest Victorian ankle-length nightgown and crooking her finger at him, nearly forced a groan from his parched throat. *I am not a horndog. I am not a horndog.* "Oh? I'm, uh, happy to assist any way I can."

She turned and reached for the door handle.

Snapping his seatbelt free, he cleared the frog from his throat. "May I come around and open your door for you?"

With a slight nod, she leaned back in the seat. "You're the perfect gentleman, aren't you?"

"Not perfect, but I do try to be a gentleman." Her gaze seemed to follow him as he slipped and slid around the car, warming him against the icy drizzle falling from the gray sky. The pleased expression that greeted him when he offered his hand brought back memories of falling in love for the first time at six years old, but this was so much better. It wasn't puppy love, even though he sported enough hair on his face most days to pass for a werewolf ready for the full moon. "Shall I escort you to the front door before procuring your insulated chests of food-stuffs, Lady Wallis? I believe the pavement is becoming treacherous."

She stood and hooked her arm through his. "Your chivalry is greatly appreciated, Lord Harry."

"Always at your service." He accompanied her along the wet side-walk and up the two steps to the porch. The jangle of her keys served as his cue to return to his car. "Back in a minute."

Her pretty smile stayed with him while he retrieved the coolers from the trunk and retraced his steps toward the porch. Not even the icy pellets sneaking past his collar could chase away the hopefulness she inspired.

He shifted the grip on the handles to wheel his loads past his bumper. A millisecond too late, light reflected off what seemed to be a puddle in front of the garage. Before he could catch himself, he lay flat on his back with the echo of multiple thuds ringing in his ears.

"Oh my gosh! Harry, are you all right?" Wallis leaned over him, blocking out the gray sky and icy raindrops. Worry lines framed her eyes, but he'd never seen a more beautiful sight in his life. "Harry? Are you hurt?"

He blinked up at her. "I don't think so. Nothing feels damaged. Except my ego, of course."

"It's you I'm worried about, not your ego." She stared at him for about half a minute and then slid her hand beneath his shoulders. "Let me help you up. Tell me right away if you feel any pain."

With minimal effort, he managed to sit, although the dampness seeping through his khakis wasn't exactly comfortable. "I think I'd better try to stand by myself. No reason to risk making you fall too."

"Okay, but I'll get the food." She righted the still-latched coolers and, dodging the slick spot on the driveway, wheeled them to the sidewalk. "And you need to take off those wet pants."

CHAPTER 7

THANKFUL FOR A FEW MINUTES TO RECALIBRATE HER BRAIN-TO-MOUTH filter, Wally stirred the pan of hot chocolate and then pressed the Start button on the microwave for the popcorn. *Nothing like inviting a man to undress on the first date. Okay, second date. Sort of.*

"Can I help?" Harry strolled into the kitchen like he hadn't taken a tumble on her icy driveway. The sweatpants she'd loaned him covered only two-thirds of his calves and his pants dangled over his arm. "I can keep an eye on things here or put these in the dryer if you point me in the right direction."

She tried to take the damp clothes from him, but he held tight to his khakis. "You should be resting on the couch, just in case you strained a muscle or something. I slipped on the ice last winter and I was sore for a week."

"I'm fine. I promise. Besides, I'm used to taking care of myself. Laundry room over there?" He pointed toward the open doorway opposite the stove.

"Yes, but—"

"I promise to go sit down as soon as these are in the dryer." After a cross-my-heart gesture, he skated across the tile floor in his stocking feet.

She almost smothered a laugh at his antics but let it escape. So what if it encouraged him to act goofy? Laughter was a huge improvement over the annoyance and frustration dye-job Dan and the other dating app jerks had instigated.

The popping from the microwave tapered off as he came out of the laundry room. Although he hesitated partway to the living room like he might offer to help again, he shuffled past her. "I'm going. I'm going."

His dejected expression challenged her not to give in and let him empty the bag of popcorn into a bowl. "I'll be out in a minute."

A second after he disappeared around the corner, her phone buzzed on the counter. Several more vibrations followed in quick succession. A quick check of the messages triggered equal amounts of trepidation and anticipation.

Darren's aunt clearly had the situation under control. *"Freezing rain started shortly after you dropped off the kids and the roads are covered in ice. Is it okay if Anabelle spends the night? She's worried about us driving her home later."*

Anabelle's text confirmed it. *"Are you home? Can I stay here?"*

Unsurprised by the concern, Wally responded to her daughter first. *"I'm home. Yes, you can stay. Love you." "Sounds good, Laura. Thanks! Call me in the morning and we'll figure out the logistics."*

Her daughter responded within seconds. *"I love you too mom."*

Movement in the doorway announced Harry's reappearance. "I heard your phone buzzing. Is everything okay?"

She raised a just-a-second finger and answered a group message from Georgie. *"Made it home. Going to watch a movie and veg out the rest of the day."* "The roads are getting bad, so Anabelle's staying at Darren's tonight, and Georgie was checking to make sure everybody got where they were going safely."

His lips pursed above the thick stubble on his chin. "Maybe I should—"

"No, you're not driving or walking anywhere. Except to the couch." She set aside her phone and picked up the ladle and a mug. "You can sleep there or in the spare bedroom if we decide the weather's too bad for you to leave."

Wide eyes stared back at her. "But my car's in your driveway. What will your neighbors think? I could never do anything that would tarnish your reputation."

"Keep arguing, and I'll give the neighbors something really good to gossip about. You know Mrs. Crenshaw lives across the street, don't you? And she always waves if she sees someone through the living room window." Tossing an exasperated glance at him, she filled the second mug. "Since you're so insistent on not doing as I asked, grab the popcorn from the microwave and pour it in the bowl next to the sink. Don't burn yourself on the steam when you open the bag."

"I promise to be careful." He pushed off the wall and saluted. "Perhaps we should close the draperies to avoid being spied upon."

Double-checking that she'd shut off the burner, she picked up the mugs. "You prefer to invite speculation?"

"Ah, a double-edged sword. If I dare to earn a kiss from you in plain view, we'll be the talk of the beauty parlor Monday morning. If we hide behind closed curtains, a kiss might be the least of the chin-wagging, especially if I spend the night." The popcorn now in the bowl, he held up the empty bag. "Trashcan?"

"Under the sink." She put an extra wiggle in her walk as she headed out of the kitchen in front of him. "I don't think I've been chin-wagged about nearly enough. Sounds entertaining. I guess the question is whether to let them witness or speculate about our debauchery."

A squeak came from behind her. "Debauchery? Are you propositioning me, Lady Wallis?"

"I don't know. I haven't decided yet." A pair of coasters already positioned about a foot apart on the coffee table provided the perfect excuse to share the couch. She delivered their warm drinks and gestured for him to sit. "Go ahead and get comfortable. I'll be back in a second."

The weight of his eyes followed her down the hall to her bedroom, creating the kind of feeling in her lower belly she hadn't experienced in a long time. Maybe she'd known him for less than a week and maybe she'd given up on finding an occasional male companion, but she genuinely liked him and the opportunity to share a night with a man without having to explain his presence to Anabelle probably wouldn't happen again for ages.

Do I even remember how to kiss or make love?

She clipped together the stack of papers in the printer tray on her desk and took a slow, calming breath.

One step at a time.

When she returned to the living room with the final draft of her play, her guest sat on the sofa with his plaid-socked feet propped on the coffee table, his audible exhale carrying across the room. "Whew! I wasn't sure what to expect. To be honest, the thought of you possibly slipping into something more comfortable scared me a little, not that I… Let's just leave it at I'm way out of practice with dating."

A giggle snuck out before she could stop it. "Sorry. Comfortable to me is yoga pants and a sweatshirt. And the practice I've had dating hasn't exactly been…productive, shall we say? Speaking of bad dates, here's what I wanted to show you. The play I wrote. I'm planning to host poetry readings and book signings at the bookshop and am considering adding short performances like my play too. I thought you might be interested in being part of the cast for this one. Or all the male parts if you think it's doable. I can only afford to pay you in cookies and tea for right now, though."

"Your company is payment enough." He flipped the script over and chuckled. "Ah, so this is the record of your recent experiences with cads like dye-job Dan. *Dating Disappointments and Disasters.* Is it okay if I read some of it?"

"Yes, of course. I'll get the movie ready." She hurried to the shelf of movies and ran her finger along the alphabetized cases, even though she could find the right one in the dark with her eyes closed. Then she readied the DVD to keep from watching him read.

What if he hates it?

The crinkle of paper was followed by a low growl. "Don't get me wrong. I know this is supposed to be funny—and it is—but these scoundrels should be strung up by their suspenders. I hope you informed the app's customer service department of their transgressions and canceled your subscription."

His indignation on her behalf warmed her heart. "I did. They were quite unapologetic, so I left a very detailed review about the kind of men they allow on the site. Would you believe I got an invitation for another free month a few hours later? I blocked their email."

"Persistent, aren't they?" Papers shuffled again. "Hmm. Portraying jerks will be challenging, but I do enjoy transforming into many different characters. The script is well written and easy to follow. We could have our first reading after the movie if you like. Get a feel for the lines. Inflection and timing are important, and I want to get it right."

Finally brave enough to face him, she stood and turned toward him. "You're not just saying that so I don't feel bad? You really like it?"

"It's very good. I promise." He set aside the script and patted the cushion beside him. "Come sit so we can watch the movie and feed each other popcorn. Then we can stand in front of the window to read through our lines, look like we're having a lover's quarrel, and obviously making up when my car is parked in your driveway overnight. I want to be sure Mrs. Crenshaw has fresh gossip for Monday."

"I'm fairly certain having you stay the night will incite plenty of gossip." After a moment's hesitation, she crossed to the drapery pull near the front door. Shadowy movement in Mrs. Crenshaw's picture window all but confirmed her suspicion and dared her to do something worthy of a beauty-shop rumor. "Let's make most of it speculative. We can decide how much of it's actually true as we go."

He leaned back into the corner of the couch, the popcorn at the ready in his lap. A hint of mischievous gleam lured her closer to throwing caution to the wind and relocating their snack to make room for herself. "You're enjoying this, aren't you?"

"Yes. As a matter of fact, I am." *I like him and he says he likes me. Why shouldn't I enjoy more than just conversation with him?* Hoping her courage didn't desert her, she walked around the coffee table, snagged the remote and then the bowl, and dropped in the vee between his thighs. "Can you reach to turn off the lamp?"

"Um, maybe? I think so." A strangled groan accompanied a wiggle, and the light clicked off as the outline of what seemed to be a semierect penis made an imprint on her lower back. The sweatpants she'd lent him did nothing to disguise or confine the body part pressing against her.

She nearly choked in an effort to hold in a whimper. Heat spread over her neck, face, and chest, but menopause wasn't to blame this time. Had sexual attraction ever set fire to her before? Had she ever reacted this way to Bobby?

No, no, no. Stop. Didn't I promise myself I wouldn't compare any of the men I date to him?

Focusing on the remote, she pushed the Power button and counted backward from ten to cool her overheated hormones. She hadn't spent the last ten years sowing any wild oats, other than the occasional self-induced kind, and she wasn't about to start now. Of course, that could be the reason her body had reacted like a hormone-driven teenager.

Or my sex drive had a long winter's nap and is recharged.

Skipping the previews and assorted advertisements, she navigated to the movie, pressed Play, and set aside the remote. "Popcorn?"

"Good idea. Thank you." His arm brushed the side of her breast as he reached into the bowl. He jerked away, sending popcorn flying into her low-cut sweater. "Sorry, I didn't mean to... This position... I'm not being much of a gentleman."

After finding the Pause button, she plucked the fluffy salt-dusted kernels free of her cleavage and plopped them in the bowl. Setting aside their snack, she swiveled toward him on a courage-mustering breath. "I like you, Harry, and I'm thinking we should get the first kiss out of the way so we can relax and enjoy the movie. And to be clear, I'm not saying we should sleep together tonight or anything. Well, unless we both agree it's the right thing to do. It's just that—"

His lips cut off her rambling as his fingers slid into the hair at the back of her head. The gentle pressure released the tension from her body and carried her away on a cloud. A rush of anticipation raced along her skin, leaving goose bumps in their wake.

When his tongue traced the seam of her mouth, she clutched at his shoulder to keep from melting into a puddle on his lap. *What do I do? God, I haven't kissed a man in ten years!*

A millisecond later, his lips were gone. "Forgive me for being too forward. I—"

She tugged him back and slipped her tongue into his open mouth before she could second-guess her actions. Making out might not have been part of her plan for the day, but damned if it didn't hit the spot.

A tentative glide turned into a sensuous slow dance, each stroke and counterstroke as seductive as the tango. Soft hums vibrated through her jaw, but heaven only knew if she or Harry had generated the sounds.

"Mmm." *That was definitely me.*

She leaned closer, savoring the skitter in her pulse when his erection pressed into her hip and generated a uterine contraction. Maybe kissing fell into the same category as riding a bike. Muscle memory suggested sexual dexterity wasn't something easily forgotten, either.

He eased away, panting against her chin and moving his hand to cup her cheek. Then he rested his forehead on hers. "Wow. I believe smitten might be an understatement."

"It might, huh?" The world seemed to stand still while hope coursed through her veins. Giving in to it didn't seem wise so soon. "We'll see how you feel in a week."

"After spending time with you today, tonight, Monday evening, and perhaps more, I think I can safely say I'll either have fallen madly in love with you and asked for your hand in marriage or you'll have decided to kick me to the curb. I'm not one for procrastinating." He touched his lips to hers in a breath-stealing barely there caress. "Shall we watch the movie now that we've dispensed with the first of what I hope will be many wonderful and amazing kisses? Some cuddling to ensure my ego is suffering no ill effects from my mishap would be most welcome as well."

"Your candidness scares me a little, even it is refreshing, and some snuggles sound wonderful." She patted the seat behind her until she made contact with the remote and then settled against his chest. The weight of his arm curved around her back brought a comforting sense of affection and familiarity that resembled the love she'd felt for her husband—so much more than the simple companionship she'd all but given up hope of finding. "This is nice."

He let out a breath as the opening credits started, pulling them both deeper into the throw pillows decorating the couch. "Yes, very nice."

Despite the persistent lump against her hip, he kept his hands and mouth rated G throughout the movie, only kissing her fingertips when she fed him popcorn and resting his palm near her waist on the outside of her sweater. His uninhibited laughter rumbled through her during every deserving scene to confirm he truly enjoyed Westley's and Buttercup's story.

When the last of the closing credits scrolled by, he wrapped her in an almost intimate hug and kissed her temple. "Today has been the best date I've—"

A crack and a crash thundered outside, making them both jump. The TV screen darkened and the light above the kitchen sink flicked off, leaving them in utter silence amplified by near darkness.

She buried her face in his shoulder and bit her lip until the urge to laugh subsided. The world had evidently conspired to push her toward much more than friendship with Harry Kreiger. "I should report the outage and check to see where the tree branch fell. It didn't sound like it landed on the house, but you never know. Oh, and I'll need to start a fire in the fireplace if the power's going to be out for a while."

"What can I do to help?"

Pretend to be less perfect, so I won't ravage you?

CHAPTER 8

WALLY STRETCHED HER ARMS OVER HER HEAD AND GROANED. "I DON'T think I've ever burned that many calories at one time in my entire life."

Snickers came from at least two of the quartet sprawled across the remaining chairs they'd shoved into a circle at the back of the store for Sunday night's book club gathering.

Petra nudged Wally's leg with her wool-socked foot. "Are you sure about that? I heard you had an overnight guest on Thursday to go with the power outage. If you're doing it right, sex definitely uses more calories than restocking after a Black Friday weekend."

Riley's grin widened. "You slept with Harry? Good for you! Is he hairy all over?"

Heat spread like wildfire from Wally's neck and chest to her ears and her cheeks. "He was a perfect gentleman. All we did was sleep."

Georgie's left eyebrow rose, the only sign of amusement on her face.

Wally sighed and crossed her arms under her breasts. "Okay, so maybe we kissed a little bit, but we were both fully clothed the whole time."

Petra's hoot of laughter echoed through the bookstore. "With tongue? Or don't you kiss and tell?"

"God, I should've known teasing you about Auggie would come back to bite me on the ass." Grabbing the last piece of brick cheese and a cracker from the tray on the center table, Wally willed away her embarrassment. "Yes, with tongue. And I'm not afraid to admit I thoroughly enjoyed it. He's a very good kisser."

Georgie scooted to the edge of her chair and folded her coat over her forearm. "I'm glad you finally found a nice man to spend time with, whether it's talking, kissing, sleeping, or having sex. He seemed very polite and attentive at Tate and Jim's. You deserve someone who treats you well." Nods and affirming hums accompanied her smile. "I need to go since I have an early meeting tomorrow morning, but I'll see everyone on Thursday."

Wally rose with her friend and stacked their empty plates together. "I'll walk you to the door."

"No need." Georgie's trench coat billowed like a bullfighter's cape as she slipped her arms in the sleeves. "Thanks for hosting tonight. The bookshop makes a wonderful place to meet, especially with the changes you've made already."

"Thanks. I'm just glad the new furniture was delivered on time." The burst of pride almost distracted Wally from the recent improvement in her friend's disposition. "Drive safely."

"I will." Amid a chorus of goodbyes, Georgie disappeared into the rows of shelves.

As soon as the attorney's steady heel clicks faded and the bell on the front door chimed, Riley leaned forward. "Has anybody else noticed how different Georgie's been acting the last few times we've met? It's almost like she's getting laid or something."

Gathering the rest of the paper plates and napkins, Wally aimed an eye-roll at Riley. "Why do you and Petra always think everything's about sex?"

"I know you're not getting any if you have to ask that question." Her butcher friend stuffed one of the two remaining snickerdoodles in her mouth and handed the other to Tate.

After a moment's hesitation, Tate wrapped the cookie in a napkin and set it with her purse. "I can't eat another bite. Did anybody else notice the weird vibes going on between Georgie and Oscar at Thanks-giving? I get why he'd hold a grudge against her after what happened with his divorce, but this seemed…different. I caught him staring at her several times, like he wanted to go talk to her or something. And then she left almost right after he did. Do you suppose they're dating and they don't want anybody to know?"

Petra swung her feet to the floor and stood. "Oscar and Georgie? I don't think so. They'd probably go all praying mantis on each other before they got to the best part."

The mischievous gleam in Riley's eyes warned Wally to swallow the gulp of lukewarm tea in her mouth. "You say that like eating during sex is a bad thing."

Tate snorted. "It is when it's your head." A second later, a flood of color rushed across her normally pale cheeks. "The hairy one. I mean the one that… Ah, crap, I give up. You two can turn anything sexual."

"It's a gift." Looking up from zipping her boots, Riley giggled. "Deke appreciates it."

Wally cleared the decimated serving trays and carried them to the sideboard. "Says the woman who needed a jumbo tube of vaginal itch cream from fooling around in a patch of poison ivy."

"We didn't know it was there. I was kind of distracted by my horny husband at the time." As Riley pushed up from her seat, she hooked her fingers and thumbs through the handles of the four mugs on the table. "Speaking of horny, how many dates are you going to have with Harry before you sleep with him? It seems silly to punish yourself by waiting if you're attracted to him. You *are* attracted to him, aren't you?"

"Yes, but… I don't know. We have our first salsa lesson tomorrow evening." With the questions that had been rattling around in her brain given a voice, Wally plopped into the closest chair and sighed. "I have stretch marks on my stomach and breasts, and stray hairs suddenly appearing on my chin out of nowhere. And don't even get me started on the gray invading my scalp. I'm okay with being less than perfect, but letting a man see me naked? I'm not sure I'm ready for that."

Tate perched on the overstuffed arm and grasped Wally's hand.

"Not that I think Harry would ever say or do anything mean, you can ask him to leave any time you want to, even if you just change your mind at the last minute. Take charge. Make sure you're happy, first and foremost."

Leaning over the back of the loveseat she'd moved back into place, Petra winked. "And an orgasm or two is a step in the right direction."

The squirming butterflies in Wally's stomach took flight, and a measured breath failed to calm them. Did that mean her sex drive hadn't deserted her after all? "Okay, I'll think about it."

"A LITTLE FASTER. THAT'S IT. ADD MORE HIP MOTION. YES. GOOD. Very nice." The female instructor—Kim—turned up the volume on the music and then joined Larry, her co-instructor, on the dance floor.

Fifty-five minutes into the lesson, the count in Harry's head continued without conscious thought, letting him enjoy the rock and sway of Wallis's body moving in time with his. While holding her and not being able to kiss her tortured his libido, he wouldn't trade a second of it for all the money in the world.

"One, two, three, pause. And one last under-the-arm turn. Pause." Kim called out the motions as he spun the love of his life in a single rotation and guided her back to their starting position. "Terrific! If I didn't know better, I'd think you two have been dancing together for years. Fantastic chemistry and style."

The music stopped as he bowed to his partner.

Brushing a loose strand of hair toward her ponytail, Wallis curtsied. "You're amazing teachers, and Harry leads so well. Decisive but subtle. I can't remember when I've had this much fun."

"Super!" Kim glanced toward Larry as she gestured in the direction of the exit. "I'm sorry to rush you out the door, but we have a beginning waltz class starting in a few minutes."

"No need to apologize." Harry plucked their coats from the hook on their way to the hall. "Thank you again for the private lesson."

With the tote holding her purse and boots hooked over her shoulder, Wallis clicked along beside him in her dancing shoes. "Yes, thank you, Kim. Larry. See you next Monday."

A synchronized good night followed them into the small gathering of people outside the room, and Harry slipped his hand around hers to walk with her to the reception area. Her fingers tightened around his, spreading heated shivers along his forearm. Nothing in his twenty-odd years of interacting with women had prepared him for the mix of emotion and desire she inspired.

Hopefully, he wouldn't have to wait five years to propose the way Darren had with her daughter. Nine days had already seemed like an eternity.

"Ready." Wallis popped up from the bench across from the desk, her boots now on her feet and her coat buttoned up to her chin. Reaching out with her gloved hand, she renewed their physical connection.

Snow flurries greeted him at the sidewalk, but being with her warmed every inch of him, inside and out. "I thoroughly enjoyed tonight. Dancing with you is such a pleasure."

"You too." She huddled closer and smiled up at him. "Do you want to have some tea and practice our lines when we get back to my house? Anabelle won't be home until at least eight thirty, and I'm hoping we can put on our first performance before Christmas."

"With such a short play and just the two of us, we should have our lines polished in three or four more rehearsals at most." He thumbed the key fob to unlock his car as they crossed the tiny strip mall's parking lot. "How's the work on the stage coming along? Was the construction crew able to start today?"

She climbed into the passenger seat while he held the door. Her golden hair practically glowed under the security light, turning her into an angel. "They're almost finished building the platform. Once it's installed, they'll add the stairs on each side and stain the whole thing."

"That's excellent news." Still mesmerized, he rounded the hood of the car and climbed in beside her. "I have several colors of wigs, mustaches, beards, eyebrows, even a few bald caps. We can look at character profiles after tonight's practice and decide what to use for costumes."

"I think you're as excited about this project as I am."

"I am. It's a fun play." He started the engine and adjusted the settings for the heater, not that he needed any more warmth than what his feelings generated.

At the exit onto the main road, she leaned across the center console and pressed her cool lips to his cheek. "I'm glad you stopped at my table."

"Me too." Navigating through the steady traffic saved him from pulling her onto his lap like a barbarian and kissing her until they were both short of breath. What would stop him when they were alone in her house?

Willpower, I'm counting on you for a lot of assistance.

Her frequent glances in his direction on the drive gave his heart a more strenuous workout than their salsa lesson, especially when the streetlights revealed her impish half smile and sparkling eyes.

I'm in so much trouble. Good trouble, but trouble all the same.

He flipped on his signal for the last turn into her driveway and focused on his grip on the steering wheel. "I'll come around to open your door. No ice, so I should make it without falling."

Her lips curved upward a little more. "I salted, just in case. Can't have you getting injured every time we have a date."

The cold night air only somewhat helped him regain his equilibrium from her sultry voice and he swallowed to keep from choking or drooling. Teaching high school students for almost twenty years had evidently made him susceptible to all those crazy pubescent hormones.

She grasped his hand and stood. "Are you okay, Harry? You seem distracted."

Unable to force out a response, he nodded and walked her to the front porch.

As she slid her key in the lock, she cast a grin at him. "Good thing I closed the drapes before we left. Mrs. Crenshaw's watching us from her rocking chair."

"Were...a-hem." Cursing his suddenly dry throat, he followed her into the lamp-lit living room. "Were we the topic of gossip this morning at the beauty parlor? I haven't heard."

"According to Petra, the whole town is now aware that you spent the night on Thanksgiving, but most of the talk was about Anabelle and Darren's engagement. Tate was kind enough to share that bit of news with everybody who came to the café all weekend." She stopped at the hall closet and set her tote at her feet. "Let me take your co— Hold on a sec. I just got a text. I have to check it right away in case Anabelle needs something."

"Of course." The reminder that he no longer shouldered that kind of responsibility sparked a brief pang in his chest, but he held the collar of her coat so she could slip her arms free. "I'll handle this while you make sure your daughter is safe."

Her smile as she pulled her cell from her purse assured him he'd said exactly the right thing. After numerous taps on the screen, she grabbed his hand and led him toward the kitchen. "She said some of the people in her group want to perform at the bookstore, so they're staying over a few minutes to talk about ideas."

"Will you need to pick her up? I'm happy to drive if you like."

"Darren's uncle is on carpool duty tonight, and he texted to confirm he's driving her home." She switched on the burner beneath the teakettle and then moved to the cabinet with mugs. "Did you have a good support system when your brother lived with you?"

Touched by her interest in his caregiver experience, he wanted to wrap his arms around her waist from behind and hold her close. "Somewhat, but being a sole guardian was still difficult. Rewarding, yes, but most definitely hard. Will you dance with me again?"

After a long moment of hesitation, she placed her hand on his shoulder and hummed the theme song from *Gilligan's Island*.

He led her into a waltz, guiding her around the kitchen while the kettle heated. On the final step, he twirled her once and braced for a dip.

Her hand hooked him by the neck, urging him downward until their foreheads almost touched. "Will you kiss me again?"

"Anytime you wish." His knees buckled with the soft brush of her lips, and he barely managed to keep from collapsing in a heap. "Perhaps we should adjourn to the couch?"

She nodded as she turned off the burner. Then she tugged him into the living room. "Tea can wait, I think."

"Yes, I'm quite warm already."

"Me too." Her boots clunked on the floor beside the coffee table. "You can take off your sweater if you're too hot."

The invitation created a battle between his determination to be a gentleman and his wide-awake libido. He waffled for several seconds before pulling the half-zip sweater over his head, toeing off his shoes, and joining her on the couch.

She leaned into the corner and her hair cascaded over her shoulders. "I dreamed about kissing you the last three nights."

"I dreamed about you too." A hot flood of desire engulfed him. Sharing that those dreams had included X-rated activities was probably a bad idea, especially when he'd done his best to be the antithesis of the rude man in the café.

Tilting her head to the side, she grinned. "Want to make out? Or maybe it's called canoodling now. I'm a bit out of the loop."

He swallowed to distract himself from his instant erection. It didn't help, not with thoughts of making love to her inundating his brain. "Like kissing and…petting?"

She walked her fingers from his belly button to the opening at the top of his button-down oxford, lighting a bonfire along the way. "Unless you don't want to."

"I want." The words tumbled out before he could censor them.

"Good." Her slight tug on his shirt brought him down on top of her, a pair of supple breasts obvious through her clothing and her hair enveloping his face in a cocoon when he nuzzled her neck. "Me too."

He slipped his hands behind her, tunneling beneath her sweater to her silky skin by happy accident. "I didn't mean to—"

"More. Hooks are in the back." She sucked his earlobe between her teeth, stealing his ability to think. Her fingertips grazed his chest as she deftly unfastened two buttons and started on the third. "Mm."

A groan rumbled from his throat to accompany the steady flow of desire surging through his body. He nibbled his way to her mouth, needing to connect with her and taste her, while he followed her spine to a wide band of elastic and lace. The hooks released with two careful twists of the strap at the same time she freed another button and eased her tongue past his lips.

Every stroke and glide imitated their dance—sensuous, synchronized, scintillating—and she had to feel his pounding heart under the palm that now rested over it. Shallow breaths allowed him enough oxygen to stay connected to the woman he wanted to kiss for the rest of his life. The barrage of sensations implied virginity, or at least some very early level of novice, even though he could've sworn he'd lost that status in his early twenties.

She swept his sleeves to his elbows, baring his chest, shoulders, and upper back as she arched into him. "I swear I'm not a sex fiend, but I want to touch you and be touched by you. Dancing with you tonight was…so damn hot. I just need a little relief."

Her admission boosted his bravery enough to strip off his shirt and shove her sweater and bra up to her underarms. The long skirt covering her legs presented a problem with one immediate solution that didn't involve destroying her clothes.

He climbed off her and offered her a hand up. "I'll do my best to remedy that if we can swap places."

She stood, yanking her top and bra over her head while he adjusted the erection behind his zipper and sat in the spot she'd warmed with her body heat. Her nipples jutted toward him, making his mouth water and his body harder than it had ever been.

"You are utterly exquisite. Shall we try lifting your skirt up to your hips and you sitting on my lap facing me?" His plan for them to dry-hump each other like a couple of teenagers posed only one hitch. More than likely, neither of them would be dry when they were done.

She gathered the fabric, exposing her shapely calves and thighs, and straddled him, putting her wonderful breasts in direct contact with his chest. Then she wiggled until her lace-covered pubic bone rested against the telltale lump at the front of his pants. Her mouth covered his before he could groan at the delicious pressure. Rocking her hips forward and back, she created enough friction along his length to make him wish they were naked from the waist down as well.

Every stroke of her tongue along his matched those of her body, and he smoothed his hands up her spine to her loose hair. The soft strands tickled his forearms as he traced the curve of her shoulders. He trailed his fingers over the ribs leading him to her breasts. Still finding his way with his eyes closed and mouth engaged, he cupped the full mounds and caressed the peaks with his thumbs.

She moaned and pressed her lower body harder against his aching erection. A tremor vibrated through her as he rose to meet her. An utterly feminine cry broke their kiss, and he opened his eyes in time to watch the euphoria on her face when a contraction pulsed through her torso. Wet heat accompanied a rush of pleasure and lightheadedness, forcing another groan from his throat.

Her lips found his again for a slow and sexy kiss as she melted sideways onto the couch with him. Then she grabbed the throw blanket behind him and spread it over their bare skin. "Your best was very, very good—for both of us, I think."

"Indeed."

A *thunk* from the direction of the kitchen interrupted a post-coital cuddle.

"Mom, I'm home."

CHAPTER 9

Wally pocketed her car keys and gave a cursory glance left and then right before jogging across the street to The Homegrown Café. Light filtered past the edges of the blinds and through the glass door, promising a cozy welcome from the snowy evening.

She hurried inside, stomped her boots on the rug, and whipped the scarf from around her neck. "Sorry I'm late. The shop was busy right up until the last minute, and the crew finished the stage this afternoon, so Harry and I had our first real rehearsal after the store cleared out. What do we have for snacks tonight? I'm starving."

Four sets of eyebrows rose and four giggles erupted as she removed her coat.

Tate held up a plate, her wide grin suggesting an inside joke. "Peach cobbler cupcakes, sauerkraut balls, mashed potato bites, artichoke dip with pumpernickel bread, a relish tray, and the usual fruit and veggies."

The various scents carried to her nose as Wally walked to the spread. "Cravings?"

"Mm-hm." Tate joined her at the buffet table, still grinning like a possum.

Riley's bark of laughter echoed in the small dining room. "Sort of like yours? That's some hickey you have on your neck there, Wally. Is Harry part vampire?"

Heat flared worse than a hot flash, and Wally yanked her sweater toward her chin. "A *hickey*? Oh God."

"I hope it was oh-God good." Riley dunked a piece of dark-brown bread into the mini mountain of dip on her plate and scooped up a healthy serving. "Anabelle told Tate she caught you and your boyfriend making out on the couch the other night. She thinks Harry's going to propose to you. Honestly, I have to agree with her. Maybe not right away, but the way he looks at you... Why is it the men around here throw themselves off that cliff without any reservations whatsoever? I know simple lust when I see it, and that man wants your heart at least as much as he wants your body."

Wally swallowed the bite of cheesy-potato goodness and added a cupcake to her plate. Denial would get her nowhere, even if her heart and her conscience had decided to ride a seesaw since Monday night's visit to the playground. "You might know lust, but you were completely oblivious to love for the past year. Poor Deacon suffered in silence until you were desperate for a husband. Besides, Harry and I have only known each other for twelve days. That's hardly enough time to fall in love and decide you want to marry somebody."

Refilling her teacup from the pot in the middle of the table, Petra snorted. "That you know exactly how many days since you met him tells me it's plenty of time. I can't imagine you snogging—and who knows what else—with just anybody. So, was there any *what else*?"

A volcanic flash of heat scorched Wally's cheeks. "I can't believe you asked something like that!"

"Holy shit, you did fun stuff!" Petra leaned back in her chair and rubbed her hands together. "Details, woman, details."

"We had most of our clothes on. At least the ones that mattered. And a blanket. We were covered when Anabelle got home." With her face buried in her hands, Wally sighed. She'd earned an interrogation fair and square after demanding the same kind of information from her newly wedded friends during their testing-the-waters days. She lowered her hands and raised her chin. A little foreplay wasn't something to be embarrassed about, was it? "Fine, we...humped each other."

Georgie's jaw dropped and her eyes widened. "You mean like underwear on, no penetration, and rubbing body parts until you...you know?"

Stuffing a sauerkraut ball in her mouth, Wally nodded, praying for an end to the questions but not holding out much hope. Not that long ago, she'd been the one to tell Tate the best-laid plans usually included getting laid.

Riley positioned a baby carrot in the inner curve of a piece of celery and slid them back and forth. "The word you're looking for is orgasmed. The big O. *La petit mort*. Dry humping has been the safe-sex choice for millions of horny people for millennia—since humans figured out sperm's sole purpose in life is making babies. You've led a very sheltered life, Georgie. And good for you, Wally. It was good for you, wasn't it?"

With another curt nod, Wally grabbed a second cupcake and plunked two more scoops of artichoke dip on her plate before she sat. Maybe an admission would appease her friends, if not the part of her brain that liked to remind her Bobby had been her true love. "I like him, okay? But that doesn't mean I'm in a hurry to get serious—or married. And, no, he hasn't asked." *Thank God.*

Tate dropped into the seat beside her and wrapped a dip-slathered hunk of bread around a sauerkraut ball and a black olive. "*You* could always ask *him*, although he seems like the more traditional type."

"Ew!" Petra pointed toward their host's snack and scrunched up her nose. "And everybody thought Guinness and a Boston cream doughnut was gross. That's just nasty."

"Don't knock it 'til you try it." Grinning around her mouthful, Tate made another appetizer combo with a mashed potato bite and a sweet gherkin.

The butcher raised her hand to her face and curved it around the outer corner of her eye, probably blocking their pregnant friend from view. "Anyway, most guys aren't into humping. They want the real thing. Harry may be traditional, but he clearly has an adventurous side.

I think he's just biding his time and waiting for the right opportunity to proclaim his feelings and sweep you off your feet. In the meantime, a few hints about his sexual knowledge and generosity can only be good. A man who doesn't give a damn about his partner's satisfaction should stick to blow-up dolls."

Seizing the slim chance to redirect the conversation, Wally straightened her spine and cleared her throat. "Speaking of sexual knowledge, Tate, I was hoping you can point me to a book Anabelle and I can read together to prepare her for marriage. I mean, we've talked about the usual stuff—periods, where babies come from, sexual intercourse, and contraception. I'm just not quite sure how to approach the possibility that she and Darren might want to have sex. I don't want to scare her with horror stories about the first time, but she needs to know it might hurt. Did you come across any resources like that when you were teaching special education? I was thinking that maybe after I talk to her, Darren and his aunt and uncle should join the conversation. They're both so innocent, and I don't want them to give up on intimacy if it doesn't work perfectly from the beginning."

Tate leaned forward and launched into a discussion about her experience with young adults with learning disabilities and sex education, effectively ending the inquisition.

Over an hour later, the rest of Wally's friends seemed to have forgotten her escapade and said their goodnights. Unfortunately, the reprieve didn't apply to her brain. Every second of the ten-minute drive home was filled with thoughts of Harry, sex, and marriage. Not once in the ten years since Bobby's untimely death had she considered remarrying. Even dating hadn't been on her radar until very recently. Everything was moving so fast. *Too fast?*

No closer to any conclusions, she pulled into the garage and closed the door behind her. With her purse flung over her shoulder, she trudged into the kitchen. *God, I'm exhausted.*

Anabelle popped around the corner from her mother-in-law-suite apartment. "Hi, Mom. How was book club?"

Shrugging out of her coat, Wally closed the space between them and kissed her daughter on the cheek. "Good. What did you eat for supper?"

"Soup and a sandwich." Anabelle's crooked frown and a furrow between her eyebrows sparked a flicker of concern. "Were you and Harry having sex when I got home from group on Monday?"

❧

"No. No. No. Good God, no." Wallis let out a heavy sigh and frowned at the laptop on the table situated near the front of the stage. "Hmm. Benjamin. Forty-nine. Data analyst. Geeky but interesting. Enjoys reading, backpacking, socializing, and winetasting. Looking for a good conversationalist, someone who likes good food and parties. Okay, Benjamin, let's see if you're a nice guy."

His bald cap and bushy gray-blond eyebrows and mustache in place, Harry popped up behind the large cardboard cutout made to look like a computer screen. "Good evening, Wallis. It's a pleasure to meet you! Your profile says you're a former librarian and you enjoy cooking, eating, and discussing books with your friends."

She aimed an eye-roll at the row of folding chairs that represented the audience, breaking the fourth wall for her soliloquy. "Yes. I know what it says. I wrote it."

The pretentious blond buffoon puffed out his chest. "Do you have experience hosting parties? I'm looking for somebody to serve as a hostess. Plan menus, make appetizers, greet guests. Stay after the party's over, if you know what I mean."

"So you want a Step...a Stepford...mistress?" A giggle slipped out before she could stop it. "Sorry. You sound just like him—half used-car salesman, half politician, all misogynistic weasel. And is that a fake chin?"

"It is." He leaned through his prop and patted the silicone appendage. "I thought it was a nice touch. Wait until you see what I've chosen for Daniel of the infamous dye job."

She tried to regain her composure, but more giggling echoed through the mostly empty space. "Good thing we're having a dress rehearsal. I wouldn't have made it through the first five minutes of the performance without laughing my head off."

His sweet smile made her heart pitter-patter and her insides flutter. "I'm pleased that I can entertain you. You're beautiful when you laugh. Shall we try again?"

She nodded once, unsure how she could rein in the tumbling emotions that seemed headed straight for love. Was she ready—and willing—to delve into a serious relationship again, one that could potentially lead to something more?

Focus. One marriage in the family is enough to think about right now.

Prepared for a bit of creativity in the costuming department, she started from the opening scene again. His transition from buffoon to slimeball to bozo to pervert challenged her to stay in character, but she managed until dye-job Daniel swept through the fake café entrance for the final scene.

His white dress shirt pulled and puckered at the buttons, straining against the stuffing that transformed Harry into the turkey who'd insulted her daughter. Dark dribbles stained his neck and a pair of platform shoes added at least two inches to his height. The crowning glory rested on the tip of his nose—a lumpy green wart the size of Rhode Island with a wiry black hair growing out of it.

Her bark of laughter quickly morphed into breathless chortles and teary eyes. "Oh my God, that's brilliant!"

He grinned and bowed, sending one of his buttons skittering across the stage. "I'm glad you approve. The scoundrel deserves no better than to be ridiculed and run out of town."

Dabbing at the trails of wetness on her cheeks, she leaned back in the chair to catch her breath. "Between me and the traffic stop as he was leaving Wellington, I'm pretty sure he won't be showing his face here again anytime soon. Let's run through our final scene and pick up something to eat on the way to my house. Anabelle's having dinner with Darren and his family tonight."

"As you wish, milady." He retrieved the runaway button and hurried past the curtain. "Ready."

The temptation to overanalyze his use of the well-known line accompanied her swooning heart, but she concentrated on a meditative breath to prepare for the closing spectacle of the play. He'd probably meant it as a distraction, not a declaration.

His spot-on rendition of Daniel promised rave reviews from the book club and anyone else who had witnessed the actual incident. As his character scurried out of the makeshift café, Harry raised his right arm and extended his index finger. "Stay where you are! I have an idea for an ending I'd like to try out."

Curiosity encouraged her to ask questions, but she sat glued to her chair without speaking when he vanished behind the curtain.

A minute passed, and then two.

At three minutes, he reappeared through the café door in his Tweedle Dee costume, with the whirligig cap on his head and a to-go coffee cup in his hand. He crossed the stage to her table and smiled. "Excuse me. Do you mind if I set my coffee on your table while I look for my keys? I hope I didn't lock them in my car again."

Touched that he remembered how they'd met, she smothered another giggle at his high-water red pants hiked up to his chest paired with the white-collared yellow shirt and droopy blue bowtie beneath his corduroy blazer. "Take your time."

"Thanks." He patted the front and back pockets of his trousers and moved on to the large one on his shirt. After checking beneath his whirligig cap, he stuffed his hands into his jacket pockets. "I feel like I should apologize for all the decent guys of— Aha! Found them. Anyway, your date was a cad. You're beautiful, no matter your age, and way too good for the likes of him. And Anabelle—your daughter, right? She's better than most at waiting tables and taking orders. Always polite and helpful. She's quite fortunate to have you for a mother."

Giddiness warmed her heart. "Thank you. You're very kind to say so."

"Just calling it like I see it." He scratched at his reddish-brown beard stubble with his keys and then picked up his to-go cup. "I'd better get going to play rehearsal or I'll be late. It was a pleasure to meet you, Anabelle's mother. I hope to see you again."

"Me too." She stood, albeit a little weak-kneed, and leaned across the tiny table to kiss him. "It's perfect. Thank you."

His fingers feathered through her hair, sending a wonderful shiver along her spine. "You inspire me, dear Wallis, from the moment I saw you. We'll need to write another brief monologue for my costume change, but we can work on it over supper."

"How about pizza on this wonderful Friday evening?"

He pressed his lips to hers again before he eased away. His look of utter contentment matched the feeling in her soul. "Pizza, it is. My treat this time. Order what you like while I turn back into a teacher."

"Okay." She sank into the chair, half afraid she might be falling in love. Her heart fluttered as he retreated behind the curtain. Had she felt this way when she'd met Bobby?

Bobby. How did I forget about him?

"PIZZA'S GETTING COLD." WALLY SNUGGLED AGAINST HARRY'S FURRY chest, pondering whether or not she'd fallen head over heels for this wonderful man but not quite ready to give it too much thought. She had, however, given in to her desires and had real sex with him. *Amazing sex. And sex doesn't have to mean love.*

"I like cold pizza." He tightened his hold and nuzzled the top of her head. "I love you."

The steady thump of his heart beneath her ear barely calmed the immediate mix of panic and elation, and her throat seized, preventing a response of any kind—which was probably good. What if she didn't love him? Was she lonely and missing her husband because of the holidays?

His fingertips caressed her hip, reigniting the fading tingles throughout her traitorous body. "I just want you to know. I don't expect you to say the words unless…until you feel it too."

Grateful he hadn't pressured her to proclaim feelings she wasn't even ready to analyze or acknowledge, she hid her face against his neck. "Thank you. Everything's moving so fast, and I'm still figuring out... I don't know. Things. I wasn't expecting to meet someone like you."

"It's okay." Although he sounded like he meant what he said, she couldn't help questioning his truthfulness. "You don't have to explain. I'm not going anywhere—unless you want me to."

"I don't, at least for now." She wrapped her arm around his waist and hugged him. "I like you very much."

"I hope it makes you as happy as it makes me." The smile in his voice assured her he wasn't exaggerating. "Although I'd prefer to stay right here forever, Anabelle will be home soon. I should dispose of the condom and get dressed."

The coarse mat of chest hair tickled her cheek when she nodded, almost distracting her from her confusing thoughts. "Remind me to tell you about our conversation after book club on Wednesday. She asked if we were having sex on the couch when she got home from group."

He stalled halfway to sitting and propped himself up on his elbows. "What did you tell her, if I may be so bold as to ask?"

"The truth—that we like each other and decided we're ready for a physical relationship. It actually gave me a great lead-in for expanding on the birds and the bees talks we've had." As he pushed upward and sat on the edge of the bed, she cuddled with the pillow he'd been using. "I want her to have a marriage with sexual intimacy if that's what she wants. She deserves to enjoy sex with the man she loves."

He rose, giving her a wonderful view of his sexy butt. "As I said before, she's very lucky to have you for a mother. I'll be back in a few minutes."

"And you're incredibly kind." She breathed in his musky scent and followed his progress to the master bath. When the door clicked closed, she flopped on her back.

I think I'm falling in love with you, Harry Kreiger. I just don't know if I'm ready for it.

Her phone buzzed on the nightstand, dragging her from the wonderful yet disconcerting notion. She rolled toward the sound and reached for her phone. Anabelle's future aunt-in-law's name flashed on the screen as she picked it up.

"Invitations are ready to send. The happy couple decided to watch a movie. I'll let you know when we're heading your way. :)"

Wally tapped on the reply bar and scooched to the edge of the mattress. *"Thanks, Laura! You're a lifesaver. See you later!"*

At Laura's thumbs-up, she switched on the bedside lamp and returned her phone to the nightstand. Harry's wallet lay open beside it, along with a foil wrapper. The sweet smile on his driver's license drew her gaze and lured her into the emotion she never expected to feel again.

So...maybe I am in love with him.

Unable to look away, she sighed.

I wasn't expecting this. How can I love someone as much as Bobby?

His birthday stood out beside the picture, revealing he'd turned another year older last month. Then the year came into focus.

That can't be right.

She stood and grabbed the reading glasses beside the lamp for confirmation.

Forty years old? Oh my God, I'm robbing the damn cradle. Ten years. Six, seven, eight months. And three days younger than I am.

The floor swayed under her bare feet and a cold sweat swept across her cheeks and neck. She staggered three steps before she managed to find the bed again. Even lying flat on her back with her arm flung over her closed eyes didn't stop the wooziness.

Petra's comments two months ago at book club about the age difference between Tate and Jim played in Wally's head. *"Who cares if he's younger? If he doesn't care how old you are, why should you care how young he is?"*

Nearly eleven years wasn't the same as seven. Experience had taught her nine years was too many.

And I still love Bobby. How can I feel this way about someone else?

She yanked the comforter over her body and curled in a ball. Her heart sank when light footsteps carried to her ears. How could life be so cruel?

"Wallis, are you okay?" The mattress shifted and a hand closed over her ankle. "Do you regret making love?"

Her eyes stung and her heart ached, but she pushed upward until she sat face-to-face with him. He deserved honesty and a clean break. "Yes. No. I should. Why didn't you tell me how old you are? You've known my age since Daniel announced it to the whole café."

He frowned, adding to her pain. "Does it matter? We're both adults, capable of making adult decisions, and age has nothing to do with how we feel about each other."

She swallowed, hoping to chase away the lump in her throat, but it lodged tighter. "I'm more than a decade older than you, Harry."

"It isn't important. I love you, and I know you care about me. That's all that matters."

He reached for her, but she scooted away. If he touched her, she wouldn't have the strength to follow through with the right choice. "Bobby was nine years older than me. Yes, we had a good marriage, but... When I'm eighty and in need of hearing aids and a walker, you'll still be dancing everywhere you go."

I can't put you through losing someone who's been your whole life for too short a time.

His rough sigh warned her to expect another rebuttal. He opened his mouth, closed it, and then picked up the pile of his clothing from the floor. Without a word, he dressed and tucked his wallet in his back pocket. He paused at the bedroom doorway, his shoulders sagging and his tight jaw revealing his frustration. "I had hoped for... I'll be at the bookstore thirty minutes before tomorrow's performance. It's probably best if we end the play with Daniel's departure."

CHAPTER 10

WALLY STUFFED THE DAMP TISSUE IN HER ROBE POCKET AND SHUFFLED to the front door. Only one of her book club friends had responded to her group text half an hour ago, but at least Georgie's practicality meant she would more than likely support Wally's decision.

Frigid evening air swirled around her ankles when she let her friend inside. "Tea, hot chocolate, or something stronger? I have pizza too."

"Tea is fine, thanks." Georgie walked with her to the kitchen, still as put together at six forty-five at night as she'd probably been at the same time this morning. "What's wrong? You seem upset. Did Harry say or do something to hurt you?"

Biting the inside of her lip to keep from blubbering all over the place, Wally shook her head and turned on the burner beneath the teakettle. Then she joined her friend at the kitchen table. "We had sex earlier—real sex—and he told me he loves me."

"And you're regretting your decision to sleep with him?" Georgie's bland expression changed to attack-lawyer sternness in an instant. "Of course you are. Otherwise, he would be here instead of me, and you wouldn't look like you've been crying. Did he pressure you?"

Dropping her face to her hands, Wally shook her head again and sniffled. "No, not at all. After—"

Her phone buzzed in her pocket at the same moment Georgie extracted hers from the leather jacket she'd hung on the back of her chair. "It's Riley. She just saw your text and she wants to know if you're okay. She's at her in-laws' house for dinner, but she can leave if necessary. I'll tell everybody I'm here and will let them know if they should stop by later if they can. For now, let's talk about what happened."

Wally swiped at her watery eyes and cursed her stuffy, runny nose. "Afterward, he went to the bathroom and I saw his birthdate on his driver's license. He's barely forty years old."

Georgie set aside her phone, her disapproving grimace in tune with the hissing kettle. "You looked in his wallet without his permission?"

"It was laying there open on the nightstand from when he got out the condom." Needing to do something to distract herself from her aching heart, she pushed her chair away from the table to go prepare cups for their tea.

"Sit." The stare Georgie aimed at her as she stood probably scared the daylights out of opposing counsel. "I'll make the tea. He used protection. That's good. Can I presume he lied to you about how old he is?"

The gentle *clunk* of closing cabinet doors and mugs being set on the counter gave Wally an excuse not to immediately answer.

Spoons clinked and then came a long stretch of silence. "Did he lie to you about his age?"

"Well, no, but everybody in the café heard dye-job Dan announce my age and Harry never told me how old he is." Annoyed with her defensive tone, Wally focused on her disappointment instead of stamping her foot and demanding Georgie take her side. "He knew how much younger he is, but he didn't tell me. He says it doesn't matter."

"Does it matter to you?"

"Yes." *At least that was an easy question to answer.*

Her lawyer friend tossed out another minute of uncomfortable quiet. "*Why* does it matter to you?"

The whistle of the teakettle almost drowned out the sound of the mudroom door closing, but the new question echoed through Wally's head.

"Hi, Mom." Anabelle removed her coat as she entered the kitchen. "Hi, Georgina. It isn't Thursday or Sunday. Are you having book club tonight?"

Georgie greeted Wally's daughter with a nod. "Hi, Anabelle. No book club tonight. I'm here for a visit. Would you like a cup of tea?"

"No, thank you. I have to practice my reading and go to bed. I'm working early tomorrow at the café." Anabelle wrapped an arm around Wally's shoulders and kissed her cheek. "Goodnight, Mom. I love you."

Relieved that Anabelle seemed too intent on her tasks to notice the newly dried tears, Wally tried for a smile. "I love you too. Sleep well."

As soon as the door to the apartment closed, Georgie set the pair of steaming mugs on the table and made a second trip for the pizza box and paper plates. "Why does the age difference matter to you? Tell me every reason. They're all valid. I promise I'm just here to listen. Absolutely no judgment from me and no advice unless you want it. I learned a hard lesson about interfering in my friends' romantic relationships."

"They know you meant well." Wally let out a shaky sigh. "Bobby was nine years older than me. I never considered that he might die before me when we started dating. He was this incredibly kind man who was so much more mature than the guys my own age. Neither of us was interested in hookups or one-night stands. We wanted the same things from life and our relationship. I learned what it means to really love someone."

Georgie slid the box closer and lifted the lid. "Have you eaten today?"

The scent of yeast, Italian herbs, and tomato sauce wafted upward, tempting Wally to devour the whole deep-dish pie by herself. "Oatmeal for breakfast and soup for lunch. Have you?"

"Peanut butter toast, half a veggie wrap, and part of a fruit cup. I was in meetings most of the day. Let's eat while we talk." Not bothering with utensils, Georgie plunked two thick slices on a plate and slid it in front of Wally. Then she added an equal serving to the other plate. "Do you regret marrying Bobby?"

With the pizza halfway to her mouth, Wally frowned. "Of course not. Why would you ask me a thing like that?"

Georgie dabbed at her lips as she chewed. "Just curious. He was a bit older than you—not old, by any means, when he passed away—and I wonder whether you'd change your choices if you could do it over again. I always ask my divorce clients the what-if question. It can be very enlightening."

"I wouldn't change any of it—marrying Bobby, having Anabelle. They've made me a better person for having known them." Wally bit off a huge mouthful and closed her eyes to savor every calorie. Brownies, under a mountain of ice cream, would make the perfect dessert to top it off. Too bad she didn't have a batch ready for demolition.

"How long were you married?"

Grief no longer lived in her heart, but a tiny pang reminded Wally of the loss. "Fifteen years. Anabelle was thirteen when he died. I can't imagine how hard losing him would've been without her."

"I'm glad you had each other." In an uncharacteristic show of compassion, Georgie squeezed Wally's hand. "It sounds like you and Bobby built a strong family together, but the connection between your marriage and Harry's age confuses me. I've seen lots of couples with much larger age differences—some successful and some not. The ones who love each other almost always succeed and the ones who marry for superficial motives usually fail. If you don't love Harry, you made the right decision to stop seeing him. If you love him or think you might love him, you have a reason other than age for pushing him away, whether you realize it or not."

"You should've been a marriage counselor." In need of more comfort food, Wally popped the last bite of crust into her mouth and headed to the fridge.

"In a way, I am. I do what I can when I think a relationship is worth saving. I get paid in either case, so I have no incentive to encourage divorce."

Wally set a can of whipped cream on the counter and pulled a box of graham crackers from the cupboard. "Sprinkles?"

"Of course." Georgie refilled their mugs and returned to her seat. "You're going to have to analyze what you're feeling sooner or later."

Adding the dessert supplies to the table, Wally stuck her tongue out at her friend. "You already did, so just cut to the chase and tell me what you think this other reason is."

"Reasons. Are you sure you want to hear them from me? I won't sugarcoat my observations."

The cream sloshed in the can as Wally shook it. "Yep. I'm tired and cranky and feeling like a jerk for hurting Harry."

Georgie held out a piece of graham cracker. After a squirt of whipped cream, she topped it with a healthy dose of sprinkles. "This is an educated guess, based on the fact that you slept with him today and then found out he's somewhat younger than you are. It's my objective opinion that, although you care for Harry, you feel like you're being unfaithful to Bobby. Not necessarily with your body, but definitely with your heart. That's in addition to being concerned the age gap means you'll die and put him through the pain you experienced when you lost your previous partner. I think you're also afraid Harry will die and you'll be left to survive without that love again. They're completely normal reactions, but you're hurting yourself as much as him. Self-sabotage. Don't you think Bobby would want you to be happy, even if it means you fall in love with someone new? And you're just as likely to have a long and satisfying relationship with Harry as not. Isn't that a risk worth taking?"

Stuffing a loaded graham cracker into her mouth, Wally shrugged. A specter of her husband wearing his fishing hat popped into her head. How many times had he said his favorite hobby would always come in second to making her happy? Even when he lay dying, he'd used the last of his strength to tell her how grateful he was for every minute they'd had together.

She swallowed past the tightness in her throat, surprised at her somewhat-repressed friend's insight. "Damn it, you're right."

Georgie loaded another mound of whipped cream with sprinkles. "Then what are you going to do about it?"

APPLAUSE AND SHRILL WHISTLES CARRIED PAST THE CURTAIN AS HARRY made a final adjustment to the bushy eyebrows that transformed him into Benjamin the pretentious butthead. Butterflies dive-bombed his stomach and he gulped a swallow of water in an attempt to drown them, not that he expected it to do any good. Seeing the woman he loved and knowing this was likely the last time she would ever speak to him promised to be every bit as painful as he'd imagined through a sleepless night and month-long day.

"Welcome to The Corner Bookshop's first Readings and Writings performance." Wallis paused through a second round of applause, hoots, and hollers before continuing. "While no arithmetic was harmed in the making of tonight's presentation, I can guarantee one plus one doesn't always equal a couple. Settle in for a short play titled *Flirting at 50 and Other Failed Experiments*, written and performed by Wallis Danforth—me—with special guest Harry Kreiger."

Despite a preparatory deep breath to steel his unusual case of nerves when he stepped through the curtain, he had to stare into the audience of forty or so patrons to calm the hyperactive butterflies and his pulse. Only a lifetime of playacting saved him from stumbling over his feet and his lines. "Good evening, Wallis. It's a pleasure to meet you! Your profile says you're a former librarian and you enjoy cooking, eating, and discussing books with your friends."

Every cad, from Benjamin to Daniel, called on him to pretend the woman opposite him wasn't the love of his life. When he finally ducked through the curtain with dribbles of hair dye on his neck, he jerked off the sable wig and tossed it in the suitcase with his other costumes. Applause and laughter marked the end of the play and time spent with her. The quicker he departed, the better.

"Harry, will you come out and take a bow?"

His heart thumped out of control at the voice directly behind him. He nodded once and grabbed the wig to suit up again.

"Leave it." Wallis grasped his hand, igniting a fiery sensation up his arm, and tugged him onto the stage. A few steps from the edge, she gestured toward him. "Everyone, this is Harry Kreiger—talented actor, master of disguises, high school teacher, and all around wonderful guy. He deserves a standing ovation for his performance tonight and for helping me make this play a reality."

The small crowd rose, clapped, and hooted as he bowed, but the recognition didn't bring the same joy and energy it usually did. Pasting on a smile, he waved at the audience, more than ready to take his leave. "Thank you."

At least most of them don't know I'm one of the failed experiments.

The noise finally dwindled to low chatter and scraping chairs, signaling an opportunity for his exit. Unfortunately, Wallis still gripped his hand.

She glanced at him and back toward the audience. "Thank you so much for attending tonight's performance. Refreshments are being served in the reading area, and please feel free to browse. We're open until eight o'clock this evening."

Moving like a flock of birds, the potential customers shifted to the right and headed for the double doors leading into the main area of the bookstore. At the tail end, a group of women led by the owner of The Homegrown Café broke off and approached the stage, with Anabelle close behind.

Tate grinned up at them and held out a colorful bouquet. "Fantastic show, you two. I haven't laughed that hard in ages."

Without letting go of his hand, Wallis took the flowers. "I'm so glad you liked it. Thanks for these—they're gorgeous—and for being here. Harry, you remember Tate, Riley, and Petra, don't you? And Georgie of course. She's really good at helping people see what's right in front of their faces."

A fraction of a smile appeared on Georgina's otherwise unreadable face. "Good to see you again, Harry. I'm also good at reminding people to follow through when an important task needs to be done. Wally, do you still want me to drive Anabelle home like we talked about earlier?"

"If you're sure you don't mind."

Georgina tucked a few strands of white-blonde hair behind her ear and cast a glance toward Wally's daughter. "Of course not. We have wedding plans to discuss. We'll see you later."

After a few more goodnights, the friends trailed after Anabelle and her chauffeur, leaving him alone with Wallis.

"Your show was a success. Thank you for inviting me to be part of it." He took a step toward the curtain, but her grip on his hand kept him from leaving. "I should go. I have papers to grade and you have a store to run."

Still not letting go, she looked him in the eye. "I owe you an apology."

"It's fine. I'm fine." He wasn't, but he refused to tarnish his last interaction with her with a disagreement. "I should've told you and given you the choice, even if I didn't think my age mattered. It was important to you. I'll be finished packing up my costumes in a few minutes and will see myself out."

"Harry, listen to me please." Her frown tried to break his will. "I panicked. Everything between us happened so fast, and you're the first man whose company I've truly enjoyed since my husband died. I didn't expect to fall in love, so I wasn't prepared for all the feelings I had about—"

"You...love me?" He couldn't possibly have heard her correctly, could he?

"Yes." She closed the few feet between them and licked her lips, tempting him to kiss her. "I love that you talk to me like a Victorian gentleman. I love how you dance a jig to make people smile as you're walking down the sidewalk. I love that you're not afraid to love me. You're not too young for me, it isn't too soon to love you, and I'm allowed to be happy about how I feel. Life is too short not to let love happen."

His resident butterflies finally settled into a light flutter. "Would you, perhaps, consider a marriage proposal after a short wooing period then?"

She looped the hand with the flowers around his neck and pressed her soft lips to his. "I'd like to sleep on it, but I've always preferred happy endings."

AND BABY MAKES 2½

CHAPTER 1

"IF I HAVE TO BE IN A COMMITTED RELATIONSHIP TO GET CUSTODY, YOU have to pretend to be engaged to me." Oscar Banyan resisted the urge to slip the elastic band from his wrist and gather his shaggy hair into a ponytail. The unkempt image suited him better these days.

"I won't lie to social services or the court. I could lose my license to practice law." Georgina Swofford's controlled outrage chewed on his last nerve.

The gall of the woman. "Bullshit. You lied so my ex-wife would get a big settlement. If I hadn't kept meticulous records, you would've stolen my house, my car, and my money, not to mention my reputation and my freedom. You're lucky I agreed to pay your legal fees to get rid of her. You owe me."

"I acted in good faith. She lied to me when I asked why she wanted to end her marriage to you." Head up, spine straight, and no hint of unnatural color on her neck or cheeks had made her the ultimate adversary during his divorce, more so than his greedy ex.

Nothing had changed in the counselor's demeanor, but her secret soft spot for a happy ending wasn't so secret. Soon enough, she would discover he'd done his homework—beyond the facts that she'd graduated *magna cum laude* from a prestigious law school, was forty-four years old, and had never been married.

He gulped a mouthful of lukewarm coffee and spit a long arc of it across the porch railing in hopes of triggering a reaction—any reaction —from her. "A likely story. Look, I want to give my nephew a good home and you agreed to represent my interests. Since you don't seem to have any confidence in your ability to win my case, I'm asking you to be my fiancée for a few weeks so that can happen."

She glanced toward the lane, but her expression remained stone-cold. "Be? Or pretend?"

The tension in his jaw multiplied exponentially, adding to the headache she'd already gifted him since her arrival nearly half an hour early for their appointment. *God, I hate being around argumentative people.* "Semantics. I'll buy you a full-carat diamond ring if that's what it takes. You can keep it after I dump you."

"You think I can be bought?" Swofford looked down her not-quite-perfect nose at him, her act of superiority laughable. "And spitting? Really? No wonder Kayla left you."

"She left because I refused to put up with her lies and you know it, so spare me the judgmental load of crap."

Her chin rose an almost undetectable notch. "And what if I want to dump you?"

Because a woman like you would never be on the receiving end of a broken engagement. "If you help me gain permanent custody of my nephew, you can tell the whole damn world I'm a terrible lover and wouldn't know how to please a woman if I had a manual for all I care. Like I said, you owe me. I expect payment in full for the nightmare you put me through five years ago."

"Or what?"

Jesus, did the woman bait rival attorneys and clients alike? No wonder he'd gone through three spineless divorce lawyers before representing himself out of necessity.

He aimed his rock-hard corporate-counsel stare at her, even though he was more than half a decade out of practice. "Or you don't have a soul. I'm that kid's next of kin after my sister. How she's managed to be pregnant for eight months and not hurt him is beyond me, especially when she doesn't even know she's expecting. She isn't capable of caring for herself, let alone a baby."

"And you are?"

The cross examination is done. Not bothering to hide an exaggerated eye-roll, he pushed to his feet and descended the porch steps in a single bound. "Yes, I am."

"Prove it." The rocker creaked and then rhythmic clicks on the floorboards announced her intent to shadow him while he finished his morning med checks and feedings.

"If it'll shut you up, fine. Follow me." He set off for the closest outbuilding, his pace on the uneven stone walkway sure to leave her in his dust, especially in those ankle-breaker heels she wore. At the exterior door, he stopped, prepared to wait while she navigated the path, but she stood a pace and a half behind him in her blood-red designer shoes and matching trench coat. *God, I spent too much time in the big-business world of custom suits and expensive footwear.* "You can come into the observation room. No farther."

Her curt nod reinforced the impression that she preferred giving directions to taking them as much as he did and made her own damn rules when she felt like it. "How will watching you play nursemaid to wild animals prove your fitness to raise your sister's child?"

Ignoring her question, he gestured for her to go in first. Then he closed the door and withdrew the makeshift necklace from his shirt. The suede lacing dug into the back of his neck as he slid the key into the knob, forcing him to lean forward. "Stand still. Don't move at all while the door's open. Stupid red coat. Are you trying out for bull-fighter of the year?"

She muttered something incoherent under her breath, but he stepped into the next room without asking her to repeat what was surely nothing he wanted to hear anyway.

Careful to close the door quickly and quietly, he twisted the lock to prevent her from entering. Most people couldn't be trusted, and she seemed like the type to purposely disregard his explicit instructions out of spite.

He crossed to the sink, first washing his hands and then mixing a fresh batch of formula for the four possums he'd rescued a week and a half ago. One by one, he lifted the babies from the pouch he'd fashioned out of their mother's road-kill hide and fed them their breakfast. They still hadn't grown big enough to move them into the rehabilitation barn, but that they'd survived at all was a miracle. A few drops of water on his finger served to clean their faces when they were done eating.

Next, he changed the dressing on the young raccoon some idiot had decided to keep as a pet—until it had become smarter than the fool who thought it could be trained like a dog. The poor thing hadn't lasted a day without injury after being dumped on the side of the road a mile from town. When her leg healed, she would probably end up in a nature center or a zoo, condemned to a life of entertaining humans.

She sniffed at the fresh bandage and then nuzzled his hand as he placed her back in the cage.

"Good girl, Alice." He dumped a handful of sunflower seeds and cracked corn into the far corner of her cage, refilled her water bowl, and cleaned her litter box. "I'll bring you an egg and some vegetable scraps for lunch."

Tempted as he was to head outside and shake Georgina Swofford's hand without washing off the raccoon feces and possum drool, he made a last stop at the sink. It also gave him another minute's respite from her self-serving excuses for not simply agreeing to his plan.

She barely waited until he closed the inner door to yap at him. "What are you? Radagast? Grizzly Adams?"

I bet you've never even read Tolkien. "Wow, that sounds like a compliment. I didn't think you had it in you."

"Your gift with animals *might* mean you potentially have good parenting skills, but it's questionable for convincing a judge you can take care of a newborn child." Her pompous response continued, even though a cell phone buzzed somewhere in her purse or coat pocket. "Like you, both characters could've benefited from a shower and a shave, although Beorn is probably a more accurate match of your personality since people refer to you as The Grouch."

Here we go again with the nickname crap. Don't people have better things to do with their time than make up insulting names or speculate about how somebody got theirs? "I'm not a skin changer, a wizard, or a fugitive. *Ghostbusters II* came out after I was born. And I'm not named after the trashcan Muppet from *Sesame Street*, either. My disposition comes from having to interact with people, especially the kind who make judgments without knowing or even wanting all the facts. You know, like taking care of the animals usually precedes taking a shower, especially when your seven-thirty appointment shows up at five after seven." He ushered her out of the building and toward the house instead of citing her condemnation of him during the divorce proceedings as an example of why he'd been dubbed The Grouch. His patience for humans had reached its limit for the day. Thankfully, they'd also reached her ridiculous status-symbol black roadster. "You have until five o'clock today to accept my terms."

"Are you attempting to coerce me?" Rage almost engulfed her face, but stoicism took over at the last second.

Gotcha. "No, I'm appealing to your conscience and your sense of justice, if you have either one. I heard about the bulldozing job you pulled on Tate Cochon. Convincing her to try to make Jim sign a sperm-donor contract—after the fact—so she'd see that she cared more about him than having a baby. You and the book club women conspired to con her into marrying him. I believe the term is manipulative matchmaking. And don't even get me started on Deacon and Riley. How those two haven't killed each other is anybody's guess. Auggie and Petra. That was just low on anybody's scale of duplicity. At least you kept your nose out of Harry and Wallis's relationship. Anybody I forgot?"

Her red lips stretched into a thin line.

"Now about my nephew. He belongs with me. It's the right thing and you know it. Otherwise, you wouldn't have agreed to represent my case." He pivoted on the gravel, giving her his back. "Five o'clock."

"Some free advice, Mr. Banyan. Get a haircut and a shave. The backwoods look doesn't typically inspire a judge's confidence in the suitability of a single man to raise a child any more than nursing abandoned and injured animals back to health." A car door clunked shut and a purring engine drove the birds from the trees surrounding his house.

Like hell it's free advice. I already wrote a retainer check for the cost of that damn ring I promised you.

The woods called to him, offering an escape from "civilized" life, but he climbed the porch steps and grabbed his mug on the way to his kitchen. She was right about one thing, and one thing only. He needed a shower.

Even though the hot water eased the tight muscles in his neck, he hurried through scrubbing his hair, his beard, and his body. With a call to his sister's obstetrician and three notary appointments this morning, his schedule didn't allow for much downtime, but a long look in the mirror while he slicked a comb through his more-than-shoulder-length waves and then his chest-length whiskers reminded him of Georgina Swofford's recommendation.

"I don't give a damn if she's the best family law attorney in the whole state or my fake fiancée. I'm not getting a haircut or shaving off my beard." He shoved the electric trimmer to the back of the drawer and slammed it shut.

His cell phone buzzed on the nightstand while he pulled on clean underwear and grabbed a t-shirt from the dresser drawer. If not for the caller's name, he would've let his voicemail pick up and save him the trouble. Instead, he stabbed the Answer button and switched to speaker. "Unless you're ready to agree to my terms, I have nothing to say to you."

"The polite greeting is 'hello.'" Swofford's admonishing tone warned him she had no intention of playing the role required to guarantee he gained custody.

"Say yes to my proposal or I'm hanging up." He yanked the shirt over his head, wincing when his fingers caught in his beard.

"I've drawn up a contract."

"I told you I already have one, with no loopholes you could walk a crooked lawyer through. Yes or no?" Fairly certain the jeans balled up on the end of his bed were clean, he tossed a pair of socks and a flannel shirt onto the pile.

"I've added some terms." Her voice dared him to challenge her for the third time in roughly sixty seconds.

"Of course you did. I'm not—" His phone buzzed, announcing another call. The name below the number triggered a knot in his gut. "Hold on. My sister's obstetrician is calling." He switched to the incoming call as he lifted the phone to his ear. "Oscar Banyan."

"Mr. Banyan, this is Dr. Falling's office. The hospital just notified us that Constance has gone into labor. She—"

"I'll be there in about half an hour. Thanks for letting me know." A tap on the screen reconnected him to his nemesis, and he had to work harder than expected to cover his panic. "My sister has gone into labor. It's now or never. Are you going to meet me at the hospital or make me represent myself in court again?"

CHAPTER 2

"Hi, Wally. This is Georgie." Flipping on her turn signal, Georgina moved to the center lane in front of the hospital. "It's five after eight on Tuesday. An emergency situation has come up and I'm not going to make our eight-fifteen appointment this morning. The next few days may be a little busy, so let's talk after book club Thursday evening. I'll probably be unreachable for the next several hours, but I plan to check my messages when I can. See you Thursday."

A break in traffic allowed her to turn as she pressed the End Call button on the steering wheel. Her stomach complained about missing breakfast, but she couldn't be in two places at once, and the irritating twinge of guilt wouldn't go away until she made restitution for almost taking down the former mayor of Wellington. Kayla Perkins-Banyan had snowed them all.

Georgie parked in the first empty space she came to, opting for a significant walk to focus on the remorse from that particular case instead of the bigger regret a visit to the hospital always triggered. The Banyan divorce had come damn close to destroying her career and, truth be told, Oscar had every right to hold a grudge against her, his ex-wife, and the people who'd almost succeeded in removing him from office and tossing him in jail over her false accusations. Of course, she wouldn't necessarily admit it to him, not until they stood on equal footing again.

The scent of disinfectant hit her the moment she stepped into the lobby, jerking her thoughts from courtrooms to operating rooms. Her expectations and goals had changed overnight, even if her actual accomplishments hadn't fallen short. She'd adjusted and adapted, channeling her energy in a different direction. Neither was better or worse.

At the maternity floor, she took a deep breath and walked out of the elevator. The surge of wistfulness caught her off guard, but she quickly located the nurses' station. Dodging people in scrubs and a very pregnant woman, she walked to what looked like an information desk. "Can you please tell me the room number for Constance Ban—"

"You're here." The familiar gruff tone practically shouted he hadn't thought she would keep her word.

"Never mind. Her brother found me." Turning away from the harried-looking woman on the opposite side of the counter, Georgie gathered her patience. She lowered her voice and set off toward the waiting area, aware of and away from prying ears. "Yes, just as I said I would be. Since we're supposed to be engaged, you might try pretending you like me."

He matched her step for step. "You agree to be my fiancée until I gain custody of my nephew? And you'll sign the contract I drew up?" His suddenly professional bearing seemed at odds with the dark-brown ponytail and scraggly beard, unlike the crass hermit she'd talked to less than an hour ago and the one who'd greeted her less than a minute ago.

"Yes and yes, with the addition of two terms." Prepared for his backlash, she chose the pair of chairs farthest from the corridor and withdrew her iPad from the messenger bag she tended to use as a purse. The document she'd drafted while waiting at the railroad crossing lit up the screen when she logged in. "Here's the preliminary language for the addendum. After you've reviewed it, we can talk about possible edits. Did you bring your contract? I'll need to read it before I sign. How is your sister's labor progressing?"

His resting prick face turned to stone. "The doctor said it'll be at least four to five hours. You talk too much."

Transforming her instant annoyance to pragmatism, she handed him the tablet. "If I were a man, you'd say I have good communication skills. Unless you have the contract with you, I'm not sure why you asked me to meet you."

With a withering sigh, he pulled an envelope from his coat pocket. "Good communication uses fewer words and gets straight to the point instead square dancing around it for three paragraphs, no matter the orator's gender. You're here because you're my attorney and you owe me. Read the damn thing before I change my mind. I've updated it since our discussion earlier."

"You've certainly earned your nickname, haven't you? And I evidently proposed to you since your temperament doesn't exactly support you asking me to marry you. At least no one will be surprised when I break off the fake engagement." She donned her reading glasses and snatched the envelope, prepared to dissect every word.

"I'd rather be a grouch than a bitter old maid." His insult sliced open the twenty-year-old wound that had never quite healed.

Yanking off her glasses and grabbing her iPad from him, she stood, letting the envelope fall to the floor. The ache in her throat added to her anger. "I'll return your retainer as soon as I get to the office."

Not waiting for an acknowledgment, she marched out of the waiting lounge, stuffing her belongings into her bag as she passed nurses, doctors, and other visitors. The elevator opened as she approached it, saving her from the nearly nonexistent chance Oscar Banyan had followed to apologize. He wasn't the type to say he was sorry, let alone admit he'd done anything wrong. They were even now as far as she was concerned, and she no longer gave a damn what he thought of her tactics.

The doors closed, but the lid on her box of bruised feelings refused to do the same. She'd accepted her choice not to marry long ago. The bitterness, however, had resurfaced and festered as each of her four "old-maid" friends had found love over the last few months. The first twinge of envy had morphed into an ever-growing green-eyed monster she despised as much as she wished her book club buddies all the happiness they deserved.

Life wasn't fair, but she didn't have to roll over and play dead. Nor did she have to let her emotions control her.

Snow flurries greeted her at the exit, intensifying her irritability. She folded up the collar of her trench coat and dug her matching leather gloves from the front pockets as she stepped outside.

A man in a Santa suit waggled his glued-on bushy white eyebrows at her from the bus-stop bench a few feet ahead. "Hell-ooo, Mrs. Claus. Want to sit on my lap and tell me what you want for Christmas?"

Donning her practiced platinum-blonde persona, she batted her eyelashes at him and pasted on a Marilyn Monroe smile. "I know exactly what I want for Christmas, Santa. For men to stop behaving like jackasses, you creep. I'm a lawyer in a bad mood, so unless you want me to file harassment charges against you that *will* stick, I highly recommend you learn some manners."

"Geesh, somebody's PMS-ing." The idiot laughed at his lame joke.

She reached into the messenger bag angled across her torso, retrieved the emergency supply of feminine hygiene products she kept on hand for her clients, and heaved the handful of pads and tampons at him. "You need these more than I do. Your brain and your mouth are hemorrhaging."

While he sputtered a few choice expletives and juggled the items like a bunch of hot potatoes, she stalked past him without a backward glance. The gusting wind cut through her wool trousers and the multi-plying snowflakes blew into her turned-up collar as she passed row after row of parked cars. When she arrived at the second-to-last line of vehicles, the promise of heat pushed her to hurry around the massive SUV a space down from her convertible.

Finally. Eyeing the mini bakery box on the passenger seat, she slipped her gloved hand into her coat pocket. *To hell with being responsible. I'm eating that cupcake while I get warm.*

"Looking for these?" Keys jangled behind her, but the relief the sound brought was tempered by the gruff voice that accompanied it. "And you have a flat tire."

"I don't suppose you're joking?" She dared a peek at the back tire as she took the keys dangling from Oscar Banyan's fingers. The damn thing could've passed for a pancake. "This day keeps getting better and better. Thank you for returning my keys."

"You're welcome. I also owe you an apology for the old-maid crack. It was rude, even for me, and I'm sorry." He crossed his arms in front of his chest and frowned, as if being polite had pained him. "I followed you. You're hard to miss in the red coat and shoes. I could've just as easily been the jerk in the Santa suit. You should be more careful."

She raised her left eyebrow at him. "Worried about me?"

"Concerned for your safety, just like I would be with anybody else." With his eyes locked on hers, he stuffed his hands in his coat pockets. "We can discuss the contract while we wait for the auto club."

"What makes you think I can't change my own tire?" If not for the weather, she would. "Or that I have any interest in discussing your case?"

"I'm sure you can. Will you reconsider?" A twitch of his shaggy beard said asking her to revisit her decision about representing his custody pursuit had cost him more than the apology.

A sigh escaped before she could stifle it. "All right. We'll discuss your contract—and my addendum. Go around to the passenger side. And don't sit on my cupcake."

He rounded the back end of her car while she slipped into the driver's seat and started the engine.

Moving the bakery box to the center console, he climbed in beside her. "Special occasion?"

When did you become so chatty? She scrolled through the contacts on her phone for roadside service and then tapped on the number. "It's my birthday, if you must know."

A grunt seemed to indicate his acknowledgment, but the standard wish for a happy birthday didn't come. Instead, he once again produced the envelope and unfolded its contents while the line rang.

She focused on retrieving her iPad and logging in rather than the mix of annoyance and gratitude that Oscar hadn't exercised the usual protocol for birthdays through the brief call for assistance. "It's going to be over an hour, possibly two, before someone will be here since it's a non-emergency. Evidently, the roads are slick and people have forgotten how to drive. Here, you read my addendum while I read your contract. Once we've finalized and signed the paperwork, we can go inside to wait. The dispatcher said the driver will call when he's on his way."

He gave a curt nod and took the tablet from her. Although he didn't utter a word during her thorough eight-minute review of his document, the tension rolling off him inhabited every inch of the small space.

"Are you done yet?" The low growl in his words conveyed his impatience loud and clear.

"Yes." The typewritten agreement underscored his contract-law background, and the precise language left no wiggle room for either of them as individuals, should one or the other want to end their obligations. "You do realize you're bound by these iron-clad terms as much as I am, don't you? Mutual dissolution is the only way to terminate the contract prior to its pre-defined conclusion."

"Yes, I'm aware. I wrote it." He set the tablet on his lap and exhaled long and deep enough to fog up the side window.

"And I don't want or need a ten-thousand-dollar engagement ring. I can suggest several worthy charities if you feel the need to throw your money away." Her rumbly tummy and the cupcake less than an arm's length away tempted her to forgo politeness and eat it without offering her guest a bite.

"I made a reasonable assumption that a woman who drives a Mercedes Roadster and wears designer clothing and footwear would require an equally expensive ring. What you do with it after the contract expires is up to you." He shook his head and grabbed the box. "Here, eat this. You didn't skip breakfast because you think you're fat, did you? You're not."

The glare she leveled at him should've incinerated him, based on her current disposition and his penchant for baiting her. "For your information, I was supposed to meet a client for breakfast at eight fifteen. However, I had to reschedule—and not eat—to be here. Therefore, my missed meal is your fault. My body image and the cost of my attire are none of your business. Furthermore, the car was a gift from a wealthy client who appreciated not losing custody of his children to an irresponsible former spouse, not that that's any of your business, either."

"Hangry much?" He unfastened the lid and peered inside at the treat she'd bought herself on the way to his house this morning. "Sprinkles? What are you? Twelve? Eat. We'll stop in the cafeteria when we go back inside. Any other questions or concerns about the contract?"

She traded the contract for the box. "I like sprinkles. Again, not your business. I also question the wisdom of my moving into your house. If we're engaged and living together, why aren't we married?"

"I have trust issues. Wouldn't you if your first marriage ended with you being falsely accused of spousal abuse because the person you were married to got caught cheating?" Bitterness permeated his words, reminding her how close she'd come to destroying his life.

"*Touché*. Fine, I agree to your terms. Do you agree to mine?" Her stomach growled again, demanding she eat her birthday cake. She peeled a small section of paper liner from the side and bit into the sugary goodness she'd planned to savor after lunch.

"No. I'm not shaving off my beard or cutting my hair." His unwavering stare bored a hole into her, but the chill from it dropped the temperature in the car by at least twenty degrees. "I also take offense to the implication that I'm going to take advantage of our engagement by touching you without your explicit permission. What kind of monster do you think I am?"

The mouthful she tried to swallow stuck in her throat, the accusatory tone of that particular term suddenly clear from his perspective. When had she lost the ability to see both sides of an issue?

When the person I'm protecting is me.

She forced the sweet ball of cake and frosting past the tightness. "I'm sorry. I didn't mean to imply that you're untrustworthy. You're not the only one with trust issues, especially after more than fifteen years of watching the horrible things couples do to each other and their children during divorce and custody negotiations. That said, maintaining an appropriate attorney-client relationship is important to me, despite the outward appearance to the contrary. I think it's best if we're both clear on the expectations of spending time and physical space together. As to the second term, a haircut and shave won't kill you. The ponytail and beard will grow back after custody is finalized."

"That's not the point." His animosity couldn't have been any more obvious if he'd shouted. "The point is my ability to take care of a baby shouldn't be judged by the amount of hair I have. What if I was bald?"

"I understand your argument, but judges are people and they have biases like everyone else. I'm trying to improve your chances of gaining permanent custody." Fighting the impulse to berate him for being stubborn, she concentrated on the snowflakes landing and melting on the window behind him. "You *do* want permanent custody of your nephew, don't you?"

"I've already told—" He shoved his hand in his coat pocket and withdrew his phone. After a tap on the screen, he lifted the cell to his ear. "Oscar Banyan. Okay. I'm in the parking lot. I'll be there as quick as I can."

She closed the rest of the cupcake in the box as he returned the phone to his pocket. "What's wrong?"

"They're performing an emergency C-section. The baby's in distress." Fear had replaced the predictable crossness etched onto his features. "We need to go. Now."

CHAPTER 3

OSCAR COUNTED EIGHT STEPS AS HE PACED AWAY FROM THE VISITORS'
lounge and eight more on the return trip to keep from checking the
clock on his phone for the fifth time in less than twenty minutes.
Georgina sat in the chair closest to the doorway, still talking on her
phone through wireless earbuds and typing a thousand words per
minute on the tablet balanced on her lap. The woman was clearly as
much of a workaholic as he'd been during his corporate law days.

My fake fiancée.

She hadn't given him much choice but to agree to her ridiculous
terms and hope she didn't hold him to the first. It irked him to no end
that she expected him to get a damn haircut and shave off more than
two years' beard growth to impress a judge. She did, however, make a
valid point about managing the expectations of their cohabitation, not
that he would ever touch her in a sexual way. Physical attractiveness
aside, she wasn't his type. Her intensity and argumentative nature fell
far outside the scope of his life now, and his nephew deserved his full
attention.

"Oscar. Oscar?"

He halted mid step as he began another lap. "What?"

The warning glare she aimed at him came solely from her eyes over a pair of glasses resting halfway down her nose. The rest of her face remained impassive, giving no one witnessing their exchange a reason to suspect the engagement was a sham. "Come sit with me for a few minutes."

Fairly certain her cajoling tone was for the benefit of any nosy bystanders, he dropped into the seat beside her and clasped his hands in his lap to keep from drumming a hole in his leg. "I prefer pacing."

"I prefer not being engaged. Hold my hand and pretend you like me." She forced her fingers between his palms and kissed his cheek. "I just spoke to a judge I work with from time to time and explained that you only recently found out about your sister's pregnancy and that her mental and physical health would be detrimental to her child's welfare. As next of kin, you want to assume guardianship. Although you haven't gone through the home study and inspection process the court requires, the status of our relationship—engaged and living together—would likely mean approval since I've already completed the requirements and have experience as a foster parent. I told her we'll provide expert evaluations from your sister's doctors no later than tomorrow morning and submit a request for emergency placement of your nephew with us by the end of the day today. We may have to jump through a few minor hoops, but she doesn't foresee any issues. Do you have any questions?"

Questions. The lingering imprint of her lips had caught him off guard, dulling his usual razor-sharp focus. "You're a foster parent?"

A ghost of a sigh hinted his question wasn't at all in line with what she had in mind. "Yes. It's come in handy during a few of my cases."

Think, damn it. "Hoops. What kind of hoops?"

"A home inspection, a background check for you, and an interview with both of us—all expedited so we can take the baby home when he's released. Barring any medical issues, that's typically one or two days." She held the tablet over their joined hands. "Maybe you should read the notes I made while I was talking to her. It's a lot for someone who isn't familiar with family law to take in."

Bullet points and sub-points filled the screen, a testament to her thoroughness. His brain refused to process the information despite the urgency of the situation. "You used your connections to help me."

She smiled at him, but it didn't look quite genuine. "I said I would do whatever was necessary and legal."

That clearly included telling the judge she had accepted a marriage proposal from him, unconventional though it was.

"Thank you." He brushed his lips against her forehead to support their ruse. Contrary to her hardline personality, her skin was soft. "Is that pretend enough for you?"

"Yes. Any more affectionate, and those who know you would suspect you've developed dissociative identity disorder."

"Very funny."

"I'm not trying to be funny. We have to be able to convince everyone this is real." She withdrew her hand from his, set the tablet on his lap, and swapped her glasses for a wallet from her bag in quick succession. "Why don't you review my notes while I go down to the coffee shop? We can discuss anything you need clarification on when I get back. Regular or decaf?"

"Decaf. Large. Two creams."

"I'll be back as quick as I can, Oscar." After a brief one-armed hug that seemed far more sincere than her smile, she rose, adjusting her bullfighter's coat when it slipped from where she'd draped it over the arm of the chair. "Try not to worry about Constance and the baby."

Her heels clicked on the tile floor as she hurried down the hallway, reminding him of the fast-paced world and sixty- to eighty-hour work-weeks he didn't miss. He might have managed to hoard most of his income, but it hadn't brought him happiness, only the ability to live as a recluse much of the time.

He tried again to focus on the detailed notations Georgina had made. The chatter and beeps outside the waiting area distracted him, letting his mind wander to the warmth of her hand in his and the strange sensation her lips on his cheek had caused. Human interaction ranked low on his priority list. It had from the moment his mayoral term had expired mere days after the divorce was final. Then he'd dropped off everyone's radar for months, only coming out to restock his food supplies. The solitude had done him good, loneliness never having been an issue, but raising his nephew would ensure he didn't become a hermit.

The iPad darkened a moment before he touched his finger to the screen. Taking it as a sign, he set aside the device and cradled his head in his hands. The woman he had no intention of marrying could explain everything to him later.

"Mr. Banyan?"

He jerked upright and turned toward the gentle voice. "Yes?"

The nurse who'd informed him the obstetrician wanted to speak to him before the C-section wore a wide smile. "The doctor is just finishing up, but I wanted to let you know the surgery went well, and Constance and the baby are doing fine. You should be able to see them in about ten or fifteen minutes."

Relief eased the tension in his muscles and he relaxed into the chair. "Thank you. Will my fiancée be allowed to go in with me?"

The word rolled off his tongue a little rougher than he would've liked, but the nurse didn't seem to notice. "It shouldn't be a problem as long as Constance isn't upset by it."

"Okay. We'll wait right here." At her nod, he fished his phone from his pocket and tapped in a text to Georgina. *"Surgery's done. We can see Connie and the baby in ten minutes. Hurry up."*

Several seconds later, his cell buzzed against his palm.

"I'm going as fast as I can. Walk, elevator, walk, line, order, wait, walk, elevator, walk. I'm in line. No, ordering. And I've had one bite of cupcake since a late lunch yesterday."

He shook his head and swallowed a pointless sigh. *"Why didn't you say so when we came back from your car?"*

"You said, and I quote—We need to go. Now." More dots appeared in the next text bubble. *"Waiting. I had phone calls to make so you can take your nephew home when he's released from the hospital. Would you prefer I prioritized eating over handling important details for your case? Because I'm quite certain my stomach would appreciate it."*

The woman clearly had no issues speaking her mind, something that could make living with her for the next several weeks unbearable. Quiet had become his way of life, and only a helpless baby deserved the right to make noise and demands of him.

He bounced his heel up and down on the floor, but the motion didn't relieve his annoyance like pacing did. *"Just hurry up."*

Thankfully, his phone remained still and silent since he refused to respond to any more of her longwinded explanations and excuses. Fake fiancée or not, she talked too damn much.

Five more minutes passed before the steady *click, click, click* of high heels penetrated the hum of voices in the corridor. The rhythm didn't slow, stop, or falter until Georgina entered the waiting area with a drink carrier in one hand and a paper bag in the other.

She placed both items on the end table as she sat and then a harsh squeak broke the relative silence when she twisted the closest cup free of the holder. "Your coffee. I bought a breakfast sandwich for you too."

He took the offered drink and then a paper-wrapped lump she pulled from the bag. "Out of the goodness of your heart, or am I am getting billed for it?"

"Eat, you ungrateful— Never mind." Her hissed order probably looked like a whispered endearment to any observers, given the realistic smile curving her blood-red lips. She removed the lid from her cup and blew across the rising steam, sending a pungent scent his direction.

Ungrateful what? "What's that god-awful smell?"

She glanced sideways at him before removing what appeared to be a single-serve carton of ice cream and a spoon from the bag. "Do you mean your decaf coffee with two creams or the bacon, egg, and cheese croissant? Because my half-sweet chai latté with soy milk and oatmeal with dried cranberries and almonds smell fine."

Again, her expression gave away none of the facetiousness in her voice. If he'd had any doubts about her ability to fake affection for him, they were gone now.

He grunted and peeled back part of the wrapper on his sandwich, not about to verbally admit he was hungry. Having a conversation with her made his ears tired. Thankfully, she ate instead of grating on his last nerve.

As he washed down the last bite with a gulp of coffee, the nurse reappeared at the entrance to the waiting area. "Mr. Banyan, you and your fiancée can come back now if you'd like."

"Thanks."

Before he could crumple the wrapper, Georgina grabbed it from his lap and stuffed it into the paper sack with her empty oatmeal container. Then she draped her coat over her forearm and shouldered her messenger bag as she rose. "I'll take care of the trash. Do you mind carrying my chai until we find a trashcan?"

Her sugary tone seemed to fool the nurse, but a hint of tension in her jaw revealed her irritation with him. She'd come damn close to snapping with his supposition that she expected him to pay her back for the trip downstairs. What would make her lose control—besides calling her an old maid?

He put on his jacket as he stood. "Of course not. Why don't I meet the service truck when it gets here so you don't have to go traipsing all the way back to your car? The parking lot's getting slippery, and I don't want you to fall, Georgie."

She relaxed her shoulders like she appreciated his offer, but annoyance glowed in her eyes when she looked up at him. "That's so sweet of you, Oscar darling, but you need to spend time with your sister and nephew. I'll ask the mechanic to pick me up at the lobby, and I promise to change into my boots at the car."

Darling? A shudder skittered up his spine. Nobody in their right mind would believe he'd allow his fiancée to use an endearment like that, especially in public. God, but the woman seemed to get a thrill out of pushing people's buttons. "Did you get everything, sweetheart?"

Her eyelid twitched, assuring him his jab had hits its mark. "Yes, let's go."

Halfway down the hall, she dropped the paper sack into a trashcan, providing the perfect opportunity to pass her spicy-scented drink to her and hurry her past the invisible malodorous cloud with a hand at her lower back. If she insisted on drinking the stuff at his house, he would assign her living quarters in the basement.

Their guide finally slowed, yanking his thoughts to Constance and the baby.

"She was just waking up when I came to get you, so she might still be a little groggy from the anesthesia." The nurse led them into the recovery room and to his sister's bedside. "Connie, Oscar's here."

His sister blinked up at him, clearly trying to get her bearings—not that she had much concept of reality anymore. "Oscar. You came to see me."

Careful to avoid the scars on her wrist, he grasped her fingers and gave them a gentle squeeze. "For a short visit. How are you feeling?"

She scrunched up her nose. "Tired. Did I hurt myself again?"

His heart hurt at her automatic assumption, but seeing her almost fully lucid for the first time in two weeks tempered the pain. "No, you haven't done that in a long time."

"Good. When can I go home?"

"In a few days. When you're feeling better." He kissed her forehead and forced a smile. The transition to a different mental health facility, one that paid attention to the wellbeing of their patients, would mean a new home for her. At least he'd had the money and connections to make that happen quickly. "Time to rest now. I'll see you soon."

"Okay. See you soon." Her eyes drifted shut, easing some of his concern that she might ask questions he didn't want to answer.

Releasing her hand, he turned toward the nurse and hoped for an easy escape.

Without speaking, she walked to the exit and then led them back the way they'd come. "The nursery is this way."

The click of Georgina's heels announced her presence beside him, but the tension rolling off her could've been every bit as effective. At some point, she would demand to know why he hadn't told her the details of Connie's illness. Even the thought of sharing them rekindled the guilt for not having caught the problems that had brought his sister to this point.

Georgina slipped her fingers through his, a gesture that prompted a surprising amount of comfort, despite her edginess. For several long moments, her solace seemed real enough to make him wish he hadn't become so cynical and weary of humanity.

It's all for show.

Hardening his emotions, he counted the steps that carried him to his nephew—the child he would raise as his own.

CHAPTER 4

He's not telling me everything.

Georgie increased her pace ever so slightly to break their synchronized steps and channeled her irritation at the involuntary action into creating a mental list of all she and Oscar had to accomplish today. If he didn't level with her between the tasks, she would make damn sure he didn't go to sleep tonight until he did.

The nurse finally paused at the entrance to the nursery. "Wait here while I see if your nephew's ready for a visit yet."

Oscar nodded and then stood stock-still, facing the door she'd entered, but he didn't release Georgie's hand. "I'll talk to Connie's doctors as soon as we're done making sure the baby's okay. I just need to know where they should send their diagnoses and recommendations. After your tire's fixed, we need to go buy a ring and move your clothes into my house. Am I correct in assuming you have the necessary paperwork to file for emergency placement?"

His rundown included nearly every item on her list, reassuring her they might actually be able to get along until the case was finalized and she could go back to being un-engaged. "I talked to my assistant while I was waiting in line for breakfast. She'll have it ready when we stop by the office on the way to my condo. Once I file the request, Family

Services will run your background check. Then we need to prepare for the home visit and interview. Do you have the appropriate furniture and supplies for a baby? Crib, changing table, diapers, formula and bottles, newborn clothing? If not, we'll need to go shopping since I don't have any of those items on hand. I've only fostered older children. You have to be ready to take care of a baby."

"Everything was delivered last week."

"Okay. That's one less thing we have to squeeze into today's busy schedule. Do—" Her train of thought derailed with the appearance of the nurse in the open doorway with a swaddled infant in her arms. Shoving the instant regret back in its box and shutting the lid, Georgie forced a slow breath.

"Mr. Banyan, you and your fiancée can come back to the cuddling room." The nurse smiled and gestured toward the corridor behind her with her elbow. "Then I'll help you put on your matching ID band."

Oscar hesitated only a split second before moving in the direction she'd indicated. Most people wouldn't have noticed his moment of uncertainty, but it had coincided with Georgie's and years of negotiations had trained her to spot every possible weakness. Hopefully, he'd been too distracted by his own anxiety to catch her millisecond of tenseness.

She walked beside him, taking carefully measured breaths as they followed their guide into a homey space that resembled the kind of baby's room she used to picture for her own child. The subtle scents of baby wash, fresh-from-the-package diapers, and clean laundry permeated the air as she set her bag and coat on the floor beside the nearest rocker.

A tiny grunt came from the bundle as the nurse placed it in Oscar's cradled arm. Then a genuine smile spread across her fake fiancé's face and he tempted his nephew with the bottle she handed him. "My thoughts exactly. What do you think of the name Oliver? Oliver Reed Banyan."

The baby sucked the nipple into his mouth and blinked up toward his would-be father with wide blue-gray eyes.

"I'll take that as a yes. I'm your uncle Oscar, but you can call me

Dad. My sister—your mom—is too sick to take care of you, so I'm going to raise you."

An unexpected surge of respect and something resembling emotion caught Georgie off guard. Oscar was right. His nephew did belong with him, and anyone with half a heart could see their immediate connection. The man might prefer the company of himself and animals, but he clearly had no problems getting along with those he chose to.

Not me.

The nurse smiled as she finished fastening the ID band on Oscar's wrist. "You're a natural. I'll give you some privacy to get acquainted. The changing station is stocked, but let me know if you need anything. I'll be right across the hall."

When the door clicked closed, Georgie walked to the supply of diapers and wipes, occupying herself with preparing for the inevitable diaper change. It didn't relieve the unexpectedly sharp pang of jealousy watching her client bond with his newborn nephew sparked or the empty ache of knowing she would never experience it.

She moved from the changing table to the framed picture above the bassinet. Reciting Ohio guardianship code didn't distract her from the realization that weeks from now she would've developed an attachment to this child, only to have to say goodbye.

"Do you want to hold him?" Oscar's voice seemed gentler, much like it had while he'd cared for his animal charges.

Although she would've preferred staying detached, their pretend relationship dictated she show at least some interest in getting acquainted with the baby who was supposed to be her adopted son in the near future. She crossed the room to her make-believe husband-to-be. "Of course."

He frowned at her as she sat in the rocking chair next to his. "Oliver's going to know you're uncomfortable holding him."

"Who said I'm uncomfortable?" She willed her muscles to relax and her tone to stay even. "I told you I wanted to."

"People say things they don't mean all the time." Setting aside the now-empty bottle, he stood, looking entirely at ease with a newborn cradled in his arm. "Have you ever held a baby?"

"Yes." Holding her much younger cousin at eleven years old counted, didn't it? Besides, numerous clients brought babies and young children to their consultations.

He raised an eyebrow. "In the past five years?"

"What does that have to do with anything?" She bent her elbow, ready to support Oliver's head the way Oscar had. Her heart hammered in her chest, despite her ability to face down any insolent spouse, merciless opposing counsel, and uncooperative judges. *I can do this.*

"Why do you have to act like you're an expert at everything?" Positioning himself in front of her, he placed his nephew in the crook of her arm and guided her hand to a point near the bottom of the blanket. "He likes when you talk to him."

"I didn't say I was an expert. I said I've held a baby before." She'd been careful not to raise her voice, but Oliver scrunched up his face and let out a surprisingly strong cry for someone so small.

"I told you. He knows you're uncomfortable." Judgment filled every word from Oscar's mouth.

"I'm—"

A miniature fountain of undigested formula spewed forth between cries, creating a horror-movie-worthy splatter across the front of her suit jacket, her blouse, and her neck. Warm liquid seeped along the edges of her bra, but the sting of failure came with unwelcome tears. Uninhibited laughter added anger to embarrassment and heartache.

She elbowed The Grouch out of the way as she stood and then hurried to the changing table. A few quick wipes with a tissue removed the few dribbles on Oliver's cheeks before she laid him in the bassinet and gave in to the desire to brush her palm over his downy head. Not even his blanket had been soiled and his crying stopped as soon as she turned toward her belongings.

A restroom behind the rockers beckoned her, offering a place to clean up and stuff her emotions back inside where they belonged. She grabbed her messenger bag on the way, ignoring the jackass still laughing at her expense.

Forget ring shopping and the details of his sister's medical issues.

The sooner permanent custody is decided, the better—even if it means working nonstop for the next two weeks.

She flipped on the light switch and locked the bathroom door behind her. Fan noise exorcised the ring of laughter in her ears as she stripped off her vomit-sodden clothes and dabbed the worst of the mess from her blouse and jacket. At least the mild smell didn't make her gag, and several layers of paper towels created an effective wrapping until she could drop off her clothing at the dry cleaners.

Thankful she'd thought to pack a camisole and cardigan in case of a spill at breakfast with Wally, she unzipped the larger pocket of her bag. Vibrations from the smaller outside compartment interrupted her.

Hoping for a bigger temporary reprieve from the contract she'd signed, she answered her phone. "Hello. Georgina Swofford."

"Miss Swofford, this is Tom from Mercedes Roadside Assistance. I'm on my way and should be arriving in about fifteen minutes. Can you please confirm your location?"

She recited the name of the hospital. "If you'll pick me up at the main lobby entrance, I can show you where I'm parked."

"Not a problem, ma'am. And you have a flat tire, correct?"

"Yes. Rear driver's side."

"Okay. I'll see you shortly."

"Thank you." She swapped her mussed clothes for the zip-top bag of clean ones as she ended the call. Three minutes later, she exited the restroom and made a beeline for her coat and chai without sparing a glance at Oscar. "The auto service called. I have to meet the truck downstairs in less than fifteen minutes."

Not waiting for a response, she hurried out of the silent nursery and cursed her forty-fifth birthday—the absolute worst of her entire life.

T*IRE FIXED.* C*UPCAKE EATEN.* D*RY CLEANING DROPPED OFF.*

Georgie scrolled through her missed calls and tapped on Wallis Danforth's number before setting aside her phone and shifting into reverse.

"Hi, Georgie. Is everything okay? You're not sick or hurt, are you? I can bring a pot of soup over during my lunch hour." Wally's instant caregiver mode triggered an involuntary smile. Too bad the most maternal woman in her close-knit group of friends from the book club couldn't share some of that immense natural ability with her.

"I'm fine. It's work-related. One of my cases needs some extra attention. That's all." Triple-checking both directions, Georgie made the left turn toward her condo community.

"Are you sure? You seem upset about something."

How did Wally always see through Georgie's attempts to hide her emotions?

"It's just been a frustrating day. A client screwed up my schedule." *And my life for the next who knows how long.* "Then I thought I lost my keys, I got a flat tire, a baby puked on me, and…it's my birthday. I hate birthdays." *Let's not forget a fake engagement.*

"Happy birthday, girlie. You know, it could be worse. You could be six feet under."

"You're right, of course." At the security gate blocking the entrance to her private street, Georgie tapped in the six-digit number on the keypad and waited for the barrier to roll aside. "Damn it. Now the code to get into my neighborhood isn't working."

"Remember what I told you about trying to suppress your feelings? The littlest things get blown out of proportion and it makes everything seem much worse than it really is. Ready for a deep breath? Close your eyes and slowly breathe in for five. Hold it for five. And out for five. Five times."

The count of five lasted about two seconds each time and a flash of light caught Georgie's attention through her eyelashes as she inhaled the fifth time. "It's not working, and it's making my fingers tingly."

"Shhh. Again. No peeking this time, Georgie, and stop making yourself hyperventilate. If somebody's behind you, they can wait. It isn't the end of the world. Now breathe and count."

"Fine." Some of the tension left her shoulders after the third breath, but she continued until the final exhale.

"Okay, now try again. Take your time and focus on each number."

Four. One. Five. Two. Three. Nine.

The iron gate shuddered and glided to the left.

Georgie put the car in gear and bumped over the guide rail. "I'm in. Thank you."

Wally chuckled. "You're welcome anytime. Whose baby needs an exorcism? The jerky client's? You could add the cleaning expense to your bill."

"I don't want to talk about it." *I can't if the plan is going to work.* She pressed the garage opener button and turned into her driveway. "I called to confirm that Thursday after book club is good for you and Harry."

"Actually, Thursday is Christmas Eve so we won't be having book club. That's why I called. If you're not available tomorrow or Wednesday, we can meet next week instead."

Christmas. "Of course. I'm not sure where my brain is today. Let's plan for next Tuesday at eight fifteen again."

"Sounds good. Sorry, I have to go help the new cashier. Happy birthday again! Check your email. I just sent you a card. Talk to you later."

"Thanks, Wally. Talk to you soon." Georgie pressed the button on her steering wheel to end the call, shut off the engine, and closed the garage door, slightly cheered by the chat with her friend. As she grabbed the handle to climb out, her cell buzzed in the cup holder. The number matched the two before Wally's missed call and the three after it. She had little choice but to answer. "Hello. Georgina Swofford."

"Where the hell have you been?" Oscar's hissed question held as much rage as an ear-splitting bellow. "I've been calling every ten minutes for the last hour. When you didn't come back, I went looking for you and your car was gone."

She leaned against the headrest, wishing she had the option to hang up on him. "If my jacket and blouse had any chance of being salvaged, I had to take them to the cleaners right away. Or would you prefer I add replacements to your expenses instead of a dry cleaning bill?"

"I would've preferred not thinking a creepy Santa impersonator carjacked you and dumped you in a ditch somewhere." The hint of fear in his voice surprised her, revealing another crack in his grumpy exterior. A sigh suggested he hadn't planned to tell her he'd been concerned about her safety. "And I shouldn't have laughed when Oliver threw up all over you."

"No, you shouldn't have." She sank deeper into the driver's seat and closed her eyes. His concession deserved one in return. She would not, however, tell him how much his nephew's unintentional rejection hurt. It was no one's issue but her own. "I should've called to let you know I decided to run a couple errands before I came back to the hospital. I'm not accustomed to anyone other than my assistant needing to know where I am or how to reach me."

"Fair enough. I know what it's like to live alone and not have to report to anybody. I also understand why you're mad at me for laughing. Mutual apologies?"

His peace offering was probably the best offer she would get. "Mutual apologies."

"Where are you now?" Something, possibly a car door, slammed in the background.

"I'm at home. I'm going to text you the name and fax number for your sister's medical reports. Then I need to pack and go to my office to finish preparing the placement request." She switched to speaker and scrolled through her contacts.

"As soon as I call Connie's doctor, I'm coming to your house. We were supposed to handle those things together, along with buying a ring. That was part of the deal."

Breathe in for five, hold for five, and out for five. "I don't want a ring. We can tell people we haven't had time to go shopping, which is entirely believable given the circumstances."

His low growl rumbled through her phone. "We have a contract—that you signed—and it states that I'll provide an engagement ring for you to keep when our agreement concludes. I'll even provide a proposal free of charge, if that's what it takes. Georgina Swofford, will you marry me?"

CHAPTER 5

I PROPOSED TO GEORGINA. GEORGIE.

His ex-wife had begged and pleaded for a commitment until Oscar had caved to her demand, killing two birds with one stone—satisfying his boss's request for a settled image and proving he wasn't using her for sex. However, coercion didn't equal a proposal, and he hadn't realized Kayla had only wanted him for his money and prestige until too late.

Six years later, he'd willingly, albeit for purely self-serving reasons, asked a woman to marry him, using some of the right words—but not the most important ones.

Still mulling over that bizarre development, Oscar loaded the last of his fiancée's luggage into his SUV and closed the rear hatch. At least he didn't have to go through with the legal entanglements this time.

Georgie's silhouette moved out of the shadowy garage into the light. Red jeans and black knee-high boots emphasized her long legs and the take-no-shit attitude he normally employed rather than admired. Snowflakes dotted her hooded suede jacket, adding an unexpected touch of femininity to the hard-nosed attorney's image, but the driving gloves she pulled on awakened his five-years-dormant libido.

Really? That's happening now? With her?

Evidently, her instincts about adding the second term to their contract had been right on the money. He tried to summon the anger he'd had no trouble mustering early this morning, but her purposeful walk distracted his brain.

She stopped near the hood of his vehicle. "The doors are locked and the alarm is set. Let's go. We should drive separately so we don't have to make another trip back here after we stop at my office and the jewelry store."

While she didn't sound any more enthusiastic about ring shopping than he was, she'd agreed to his proposal and they had no choice if they expected the plan to succeed.

"Okay. I'll follow you." At her curt nod, he climbed behind the wheel and backed into the empty street.

Although the main roads had been salted and she stayed well within the speed limit, he tensed every time her brake lights lit up on the twenty-minute drive to her office. If she'd won full custody in a nasty divorce for him, he would've given her a car designed for driving year round. Flashy wouldn't get her in and out of his driveway when the six to eight inches of forecasted snow dropped on them tomorrow night.

Something else for her to get mad about.

She finally turned right into a parking lot and chose a spot with another empty space next to it. When he pulled in beside her, his phone buzzed in his cup holder.

"This is a test. If we can convince my assistant we're engaged, we can convince anyone. Handholding is good. A kiss on the cheek is good. Anything more and she'll never believe it. I don't do PDA."

What will you do in private? Frowning at the crazy thought, he tapped in a thumbs-up emoji and stuffed his cell in his coat pocket. His nephew required his full attention, and a forty-five-year-old woman who had never been married or had children had clearly chosen to live her life without those commitments.

He pocketed his keys as he rounded the front end of her car to meet her at the driver's door, never taking his eyes off her. "I told the nurse we'd be back after lunch. Do you want to feed Oliver next time instead of holding him after he eats? I need to practice changing diapers and being barfed on."

Her lips twitched and a hint of a smile transformed her emotionless expression into something almost welcoming and friendly.

Stunning.

She slipped her fingers through his and gave his hand a squeeze. "Maybe he'll give you a shower while you're changing him. *That* would make us even."

The strange tickle in his stomach had to be caused by the breakfast sandwich she'd made him eat. It certainly couldn't be from holding her hand. "A sense of humor? I didn't think you had it in you."

Her left eyebrow arched toward the white-blonde bangs sweeping across her forehead. "You're one to talk. Speaking of which, please let me do the talking unless my assistant addresses you directly."

Did she really believe he didn't possess the ability to keep his thoughts and feelings to himself? Self-control was his middle name, both personally and professionally.

"Yes, ma'am. Anything else, ma'am?" He dropped to half a step behind her, even though he'd already made his point.

"I said please." She stopped at the entrance to the building, her bland look once again unreadable. "We have to be able to convince everyone our engagement is real, and this is the first test. A failure here means we have to come up with an alternative plan."

If she wanted realistic, he would give her realistic.

Willing the muscles in his face to relax, he leaned in and touched his lips to her cheek. The combination of smooth and cool skin seemed like the perfect analogy for his fake fiancée. Was she soft all over to make up for her chilly personality? "We can do this, Georgie. Oliver is counting on us."

Her breathy sigh warmed his chin. "You're right, but I'm still... concerned."

"Are you sure you don't mean nervous?" He tucked her hair behind her ear, an action that seemed all too natural, and then he threaded his fingers through the silky mass at the back of her neck. "It's okay to admit you're not made of stone."

She stared up at him, some unidentifiable emotion appearing and disappearing in the blink of an eye. "I have to be to do my job."

"You have to be able to turn it off to make people believe we're in love. Well, maybe not off, but you need to show a little vulnerability. You have to trust me." Although the concession violated every instinct he'd put in place during his divorce, he had no choice but to meet her halfway for the ruse to work. "I trust you."

Silence hung between them for nearly a full minute before she gave a curt nod. "Okay. Just follow my lead. Margaret proofread the motion I wrote, so she surely figured out we're engaged."

He returned her nod and reached around her to open the door. "Ladies first."

"Thank you." Without releasing his hand, she led him down the hall and past several doors. She stopped at the etched plate on the wall proclaiming the office as hers. "Ready?"

"Ready." He exhaled and willed his jaw to relax. It wasn't as easy as it had been during his corporate days, but he would do what needed done to gain custody of his nephew.

The Christmas-y reception area contrasted considerably from the cold, impersonal waiting room he'd entered numerous times during his divorce negotiations. Georgie had been a partner in a fairly large firm at the time, not a family law specialist with her own practice. Had she been pushed out because of Kayla's lies or had she made the decision to leave?

"Georgina, good morning." The silver-haired woman behind the desk pinned him with an unwavering stare as she held out a handful of pink message slips to her boss. "Your messages. None need your immediate attention and I informed the callers that you're out of the office the rest of this week. I made a pot of tea right before you walked in and there's fresh coffee in the carafe. The document you asked me to look over is on your desk. I've spoken to Judge Lansing's secretary, and she's expecting your request."

"Excellent. Thank you." Georgie's fingers flexed between his and she cast a genuine-looking smile at him. "Margaret, meet Oscar Banyan. Oscar, this is Margaret, my assistant."

The tickle in his stomach returned, but he met the older woman's steady gaze. "Nice to meet you, Margaret."

"And you, Mr. Banyan." Margaret's attention flicked toward Georgie. "Let me know if you need anything."

"Of course." His fiancée gave his hand a firm tug and led him across the reception area.

The heavy feel of eyes boring into his back followed him into a spacious office, confirming the necessity of passing this first test. Some people had a sixth sense and Margaret, without a doubt, possessed it. When the door clicked closed, he silently released the breath he'd been holding.

"Have a seat." Georgie gestured to a conference table next to a basket of toys and a small library of children's books as she slipped her fingers free from his.

While she crossed to her desk, he flexed his hand and took in the details of her professional space to distract himself from the unwanted sense of loss. Only a single framed photo of a serious young girl and a slightly older version of Georgie stood among the law tomes lining the shelves on the far wall. That personal glimpse into her life sparked far more questions than it answered. "You have a lot of clients who bring their children with them?"

"Yes. A number of them can't afford the extra childcare expense, so I do what I can to accommodate them. I can also get a feel for the children's home situation." A folder in hand, she joined him at the table. Her knee brushed his when she set the papers and a pen in front of him, setting off a jump in his pulse. "You'll need to read through the motion carefully and note any additions or corrections to the information. Then I'll have Margaret prepare the final copy for signing. Would you like a cup of coffee or herbal tea?"

How about something to shut down this crazy attraction? "Tea would be good. No milk. No sugar." He shuffled through the pages, hoping her thoroughness meant the request would be approved. "Please."

"I'll be right back."

Too aware of her movement toward the reception area, he forced his mind to the paperwork that could grant him temporary guardianship. The justification for the request spoke of a person who missed nothing and used every word to her advantage, someone with the knowledge and attention to detail he needed. For the first time since making the decision to pursue custody, he truly believed it would happen. If Georgina Swofford couldn't succeed, no one could.

Without a word, she set a tray with a flowered tea set on the table and then poured candy-cane-scented liquid into the delicate cups. Wisps of fragrant steam curled into the air, reminding him of childhood Christmases with his sister and their parents.

Good memories. Oliver deserves those kinds of memories. With family.

Oscar tapped his thumb against the paper to refocus his thoughts on the matter at hand. The sooner he reviewed the information, the faster Georgie would submit the request.

The document included several fragments about her personal life and supporting evidence of her experience fostering, but he continued reading instead of letting curiosity get the better of him. He wasn't in the market for a real fiancée, wife, or girlfriend. Their relationship was a means to an end.

Laying the final page face down on top of the others, he silently admitted to having new respect for her intelligence and professionalism. "I didn't find any errors, not even a comma out of place. Your reputation is well-earned."

"I appreciate the compliment. Do you have any questions or need clarification on any of the content?"

"No, it was more straightforward than I expected." The lack of herein, aforementioned, and whereto littering every paragraph had been a nice change from contract law.

"Good." She set her cup on the saucer with the faintest of clinks as she stood. "I'll have Margaret prepare the final copy. Once we've signed, she'll email a copy to Judge Lansing and send the original to her with the messenger service. We should receive a ruling within twenty-four hours."

"You don't do anything half-assed, do you?"

"No. I do it the best I can or I don't do it. What's the point, otherwise?" Her quick exit evidently meant she didn't require or expect an answer.

The flash of red tempted him to watch her leave, but he forced his gaze to the teacup and took a drink. Her intelligence was sexy enough. He didn't need to drive himself crazy by cultivating the physical attraction too.

Maybe I am *lonely, but I don't have time for a distraction.*

A gulp of tea failed to dispel the earlier image of her walking out of her garage from his mind. It did, however, remind him that they would be spending Christmas and New Year's together and had to make their relationship look believable. What was a man supposed to buy his fake fiancée for Christmas, especially when he'd bought her an engagement ring only days before?

What if she doesn't celebrate Christmas?

What if she's Jewish? Or Buddhist? Or Muslim? Atheist?

Although he couldn't care less if or how she practiced religion, not knowing could blow their entire plan sky-high.

"Margaret is printing the final copy now." Georgie reached toward a glass tumbler of pens on the other side of her desk, giving him a bird's eye view of snug red denim hugging her curvy backside.

He tried and failed to pull his attention away from her butt. *Holy moly, this is going to be a rough few weeks.*

Subtle throat clearing from the doorway warned him he'd been caught checking out his not-quite future wife. "Georgina, here's the final draft. Would you prefer I wait here or out at my desk while you sign?"

Looking over her shoulder, Georgie straightened. "Here is fine. It'll only take a minute."

His eyebrow almost rose of its own accord, but he lifted the teacup to his mouth to cover the twitch. If she wanted to risk exposure, she could come up with a new plan when they had to scrap this one.

Margaret set the official motion in front of him and took up a watchful position on the opposite side of the table. Once again, her steady gaze drilled into him.

Georgie's finger brushed his as she handed him a pen, igniting a strange tingle up his forearm. "Other than being printed on letterhead, the document is identical to the one you reviewed. Your signature line is on the third page below the first affidavit paragraph."

"Okay." He skimmed the text of the first two and a half pages, because old habits died hard. At the statement indicating all the information contained in the motion was accurate to the best of his knowledge, he scrawled his name on the line and dated it. The action should've brought some relief, but concern about the ruling lingered.

Georgie covered his hand with hers and gently squeezed, triggering a hiccup in his pulse.

Stop that, damn it.

Then she slid the papers across the corner of the table and signed below the next paragraph. "Try not to worry, Oscar. We'll know soon, most likely by late this afternoon since Judge Lansing is expecting the request. Based on the circumstances, this should be just a formality."

A nod was all he could manage between anticipation, nerves, and uncertainty—of Oliver's future and sharing his personal space with her.

"I'll send the motion over right away." Margaret gathered the pages and tapped them against the polished surface, cutting through a long moment of silence. "Not that I mean to stick my nose in where it doesn't belong, but it seems congratulations are also in order. You're clearly quite taken with each other and I'd like to offer my best wishes. Have you set a wedding date?"

Georgie's gaze met his, barely communicating a cautious but victorious gleam, before flicking toward her assistant. "Thank you, Margaret. We haven't discussed a date yet, and the early arrival of Oscar's nephew has put that on hold for now. He's our top priority, especially with the court's slowdown over the holidays."

"Of course." The older woman patted Georgina's arm and smiled on her way toward the reception area. "Why don't you two go enjoy each other's company for a little while? Having a baby in the house won't leave much time for quiet moments alone together."

Pushing to his feet, he grasped his fiancée's hand. "That sounds like a good reason to go ring shopping and have lunch before we head back to the hospital."

"I like you, young man." Margaret shot him a grin from the door-way. "You'll do very well."

CHAPTER 6

WAITING FOR THE GARAGE DOOR TO RISE, GEORGIE GRIPPED HER steering wheel to keep from toying with the exquisite diamond-and-ruby ring Oscar had asked to see within seconds of entering the jewelry store. He'd slipped it onto her finger and it had stayed there. Ten minutes later, he'd led her out of the shop like he dropped nearly ten grand on an engagement ring every day. The owner had invited him to come again soon.

She fought a snicker and lost at the memory of his muttered rant about suck-ups on the way to the parking lot. The Grouch certainly fit his disposition at times, but he'd easily convinced Margaret of his sincerity and earned her blessing.

A growing sliver of light finally peeked out from under the door on the left, and she pulled into the empty space when Oscar waved her forward.

He unloaded the last of her luggage from the back of his SUV as she gathered the few things she'd stowed in her trunk. "Do you know how to use a stove? I need to run down to the nursery barn to check on Alice and the babies."

Tossing a frown at him, she slung the strap of her weekender bag on her shoulder. "Of course I do."

"Then you can heat the soup and make sandwiches while I feed the possums." He hefted all four suitcases and headed for the door that probably allowed entrance into the house. "I'll put your luggage in my room for now. I doubt we'll fool anybody if your clothes are in the spare room."

She followed him through a mostly clean mudroom and into a functional yet homey kitchen. The wall of windows in the adjoining living room offered a gorgeous view of the leafless trees and falling snow, but the stone fireplace with its carved mantle took her breath away. While Oscar seemed to prefer a somewhat minimalistic exis-tence, his home was by no means cold or unwelcoming.

"This way." He crossed to a dim hallway and finally set down her bags inside the last door on the left. "Most of the closet is empty. If you need more space, you can use the built-in drawers under the bed on this side."

"And the bathroom?"

His huffy sigh implied he didn't like sharing his private domain with her anymore than she wanted to be there. "Through the door closest to the slider that goes out to the deck. Most of the shelves in the linen closet are empty. That's probably the best place for your stuff until the home inspection and interviews are done."

"Yes, the house needs to look like we live together as a couple. They'll notice if we have separate sleeping quarters."

Gruffness hovered around him like a storm cloud as he brushed past her and the bag on her shoulder to go back the way he'd come. "The soup and the turkey and cheese for sandwiches are in the fridge. I'll be back from the nursery in about fifteen minutes."

Rather than letting her attention linger on his moodiness and the massive bed they could—but wouldn't—easily share without ever finding each other in the dead of night, she moved her suitcases to the first door to her left and opened it. Other than two white dress shirts, one black suit, and one blue suit hanging at eye-level and a pair of leather wingtips on the shelf above immediately inside, the walk-through closet was an empty cavern. The three weeks' worth of clothing and shoes she'd brought with her barely filled a third of it. She added a few washable items to the laundry basket, tossed her night-gown on the end of the bed, and placed a pair of her reading glasses on the nightstand before deciding the master bedroom passed the lovers-slept-there test.

Ignoring the temptation to find the baby's room, she hurried to the kitchen. Woman, lawyer, fake fiancé—she claimed all those identities, but mother would never be among them. She would leave Oliver in his uncle's capable hands as soon as she met the most important term of their contract. Securing custody would end her part in their lives.

A search of the refrigerator and kitchen cabinets yielded everything she needed to prepare their meal, forcing her mind from the single disappointment she couldn't seem to overcome. As she added glasses to the place settings on the breakfast bar several minutes later, the sound of boots pulled her attention to the mudroom.

Oscar frowned at her, but his grumpiness seemed different this time. "Is lunch ready?"

"I just have to ladle soup into the bowls. Is something wrong?" Her thoughts jumped to the worst-case scenarios. "Your sister? Oliver? Did the hospital call?"

He shook his head and crossed to the bar. "One of the possums died while I was gone this morning. It's not uncommon for the weakest of the litter to die, but they had all been doing better than I expected."

The tiny pang in her heart urged her to comfort him, but she filled his bowl instead of closing the space between them. "I'm sorry. You obviously care about the animals you nurse back to health. It must be hard to lose one."

"It is, even when I know none of the litter would've survived without somebody to feed them and keep them safe from predators."

She set the bowl at his place and reached for his glass. "What would you like—"

"I'll pour the drinks while you finish getting the soup." He slid the glasses away from her. "I'm having milk, but there's also water and juice."

"Milk is fine." *I would've guessed you were an all-day coffee person most of the time.*

"It's skim, not soy or almond or any of those other not really milk things." A hint of a smile suggested he meant to tease her.

A joke?

She swallowed the defensive retort on the tip of her tongue as she transferred the second bowl of soup to the bar. "I order soy milk in restaurants because it has a much longer refrigerated and unrefrigerated shelf life. One taste of spoiled cow's milk was enough to last a lifetime. You have to take a drink first."

"I had some in my coffee this morning and it was fine."

"Then you won't mind tasting it before I do." Climbing onto the stool, she aimed one of her courtroom stares at him.

He narrowed his eyes at her as he set the full glasses by their plates and joined her. "Are you always this stubborn?"

"About this, yes. At home, it has to pass the sniff-and-sip test *after* I check the sell-by date."

"Okay, you made your point." Instead of picking up his spoon or his sandwich, he lifted the glass to his lips and took a long swallow. "Tastes like milk."

She spread her napkin on her lap and smoothed it flat. "Smartass."

His sideways glance included a raised eyebrow. "A one-word response? How did you manage that?"

"And you proved me right again." Content to let him dig his hole deeper, she picked up half the sandwich and bit into it.

"Now who's being a smartass?"

Still you. She followed a second bite of sandwich with a sip of milk. Satisfied that he hadn't tried to trick her, she took a real drink.

His spoon clinked against the bowl. "Good to know you don't trust me. And, just so you know, I like the silent treatment."

I like it better, so stop talking and eat.

Twenty minutes of relative silence later, she carried her dishes to the sink with Oscar right behind her.

He pivoted the faucet away from her. "I'll load the dishwasher while you do whatever you need to do before we go. We're leaving in fifteen minutes."

Not bothering to acknowledge his clear insinuation that she couldn't be ready on time, she headed to the master bath to brush her teeth and freshen her lipstick—a three-minute task at most. When she emerged from the closet with her coat, he stood at the end of the bed with his fingertips skimming along the lace overlay of her nightgown's bodice.

A shiver raced over her skin and her lower belly tensed, a sensation she hadn't experienced in ages. Shouldn't revulsion have been her body's response? Since when did a grouchy former courtroom adversary touching her pajamas invoke a sexual response? "I'm ready to go."

He jerked his hand away and stalked past her to the bathroom. "Good. I'll meet you in the kitchen in a few minutes."

Before she could respond, he shut the door.

Are you mad because I caught you feeling up my nightie? Or because you're attracted to me?

No, I don't want to know.

A physical relationship to go with their fake romantic one would create too many complications to untangle when the contract ended, not that her reaction to the pajama-groping man meant she wanted to have sex with him. He wasn't her type by any stretch of the imagination.

So what if he's intelligent and he'll be a good father? The long hair. That god-awful beard. And he's even more obstinate than I am.

She draped her coat over her forearm and marched to the kitchen to check her email.

Three minutes.

Five.

After answering, deleting, or moving every message in her inbox, she emptied her junk mail and returned to the home screen.

Twelve minutes. And he had the nerve to imply that I couldn't be ready to go in fifteen minutes.

She hung her coat on the closest barstool and took a step into the living room.

Oscar appeared at the hallway, stepping into the light from the wall of windows. His brows and his frown curved downward more than usual, but the bird's nest missing from his chin and the visibility of his neck and ears stopped her in her tracks. "Don't say a word."

Although his jaw still sported a bit more than the popular scruff males had taken to wearing in recent years, with the close-cropped sides of his haircut, he closely resembled the man she'd nearly helped Kayla Perkins-Banyan destroy. The top had been clipped longer, in a style similar to those of her younger colleagues. Handsome seemed too trite a description when his dark eyes locked on hers.

Wow.

Breathe.

Maybe he is my type after all.

She swallowed to wet her suddenly dry throat. "I know you didn't want to. Thank you."

Heaving a sigh, he grabbed her coat from the chair and held it like a civilized gentleman. "I should've known you couldn't keep from commenting."

"You said not to say a word. I said…eight words." She slipped her arms into the sleeves, nearly gasping when his fingers brushed her shoulder.

He's a client. Off-limits.

Remember the contract?

Yes. Anything beyond public handholding and a kiss on the cheek requires mutual agreement.

"Georgie." His gruff tone cut through her thoughts, suggesting she'd missed something. "Are you ready to go?"

"Yes." Slinging her purse across her body, she followed him into the garage.

Her eyes strayed to his profile numerous times as he drove, drawn by the stark difference in his presence. This version of him struck her as much more dangerous than the man she'd met five years ago and again this morning. Everything about him seemed sharper, angular.

More determined. More controlled. And completely focused.

"Why?" The question slipped out before she could stop it.

His grunt sounded the same. "I want the custody issue resolved as soon as possible."

A moment of confusion preceded a pinch of disappointment. "Of course. These things take—" Insistent buzzing came from her purse, urging her to find her phone. Her assistant's name lit up the screen. "Hello, Margaret. Any news about the motion?"

"Hi, Georgina. Judge Lansing has granted your request for temporary guardianship on Mr. Banyan's behalf, contingent upon the background check, Family Services' evaluation, and verification of Constance Banyan's health issues. The background check is in progress and Family Services will be contacting you to schedule the home inspection and interviews."

Relief eased the tightness in Georgie's neck, but tension rolled off the man beside her. She nodded and gave him a thumbs-up in hopes of easing his worry. When had she become so personally invested in this case, this family? "I'll let Oscar know. We're on our way back to the hospital now, but I should be reachable if anything urgent comes up."

"Very good. Would you prefer a call or a text message if I have any updates?"

"A text is fine. Now go take a lunch break. Out of the office. I'll talk to you later this afternoon." Georgie disconnected before Margaret could argue that eating at her desk fit the definition of lunch break.

"Well?" Oscar's brusque question came as she returned her phone to her purse and he turned into the hospital parking lot.

"As long as there are no problems with Family Services and the background check, Oliver can come home with us from the hospital. You have temporary guardianship."

He turned into the nearest empty space and shut off the engine. His noisy exhale filled the silence. Then he turned toward her, looking at her with the same heartfelt gratitude she'd seen in the eyes of numerous former clients. "Thank you. I mean it. I know this is just the first step, but… Thank you, Georgie."

His voice cracked over her name, revealing how deeply the small success touched him.

This is why I love my job.

She covered his hand with hers atop the gearshift and basked in the physical and emotional warmth of the moment. "You're welcome, Oscar."

CHAPTER 7

A SOFT WHIMPER CHANGED TO GASPING CRIES SEPARATED ONLY BY shallow breaths, but Oscar kept his back to the set of rockers as he rearranged a diaper, the package of baby wipes, and a tube of rash ointment on the changing table for the fourth time. Although Georgie seemed slightly more comfortable holding Oliver than she had earlier, his nephew clearly sensed her maternal instincts needed a lot of practice to become maternal and instinctual.

I better not say that out loud—unless I want to be called a sexist pig.

He added a clean drawstring-bottom nightshirt to his pile of supplies when the tiny cries grew louder.

No wonder she disappeared this morning. Motherhood clearly isn't as natural as society thinks it should be. God, I'm glad I'm not female.

Running water carried to his ears in between the sobs he wanted to do something—anything—to stop.

"I'm sorry, Oliver. I didn't know the nipple would squirt like that. Hold still while I wipe your eye. There. That's much better, isn't it? Now let's go try again. A lot of people get cranky when they're hungry. Low blood sugar has that effect. Maybe you need to eat more often." The chair creaked behind him, barely audible through his nephew's wailing, and then near silence blanketed the nursery. Faint sucking noises announced his fiancée's success as much as her slow exhale.

Success? Tenacity is more like it.

She left because of me this morning, not because Oliver threw up on her or her lack of experience with babies. Not because roadside assistance called, either. I may not be a sexist pig, but I acted like a jerk. And I probably need to eat more often too.

He dared a glance over his shoulder and caught Georgie with her cheek against the crown of Oliver's downy head and her eyes closed. A more maternal image didn't exist. Did she regret her choice not to marry and have children? Or had she never met a man she wanted to spend her life with?

A twinge near his heart caught him off guard.

Life? Right.

Cynicism had replaced his plan for a wife and children after one short year of marriage, but the failure hadn't stung as much as the loss of hope. Had she given up on the ideal like he had?

At least he would have Oliver when their farce ended.

She brushed her lips against his nephew's forehead as she straightened. Her gaze met his for only a second before she looked away and frowned. Sadness hovered around her in a gray cloud instead of the usual annoyance and impatience.

Regret.

The twinge became an achy tightness in his throat.

There's more to her than she lets anybody see.

Her initial reaction to his proposal made perfect sense now. Going back to her sterile existence wouldn't be easy after living who knew how long in his house and spending time with Oliver, not when she already seemed emotionally attached to the baby in her arms. How had she fostered kids, knowing the arrangement was temporary?

"Oscar, can you get my phone out of my purse please? I think it's vibrating, and Family Services is supposed to call to set up the appointment."

He hurried to her chair and retrieved her cell from the outside pocket. "It says Laura's calling."

"That's Family Services." Glancing from him to her lap and back again, she pursed her lips. "Can you hold it to my ear?"

With a nod, he answered the call and slipped the phone behind the fall of white-blonde hair hiding that side of her face.

"Hello, this is Georgina Swofford." Her neck and shoulders barely tensed as she seemed to don her professional persona, and Oliver's nose scrunched up like he'd noticed and might protest. She visibly relaxed and tipped the bottle a little higher. "Hi, Laura. Yes. Thank you. No, we haven't set a date yet. The baby arrived a couple weeks earlier than we expected. Yes, the doctor assured us he's healthy. Okay. Three o'clock is perfect. Yes."

Her hair caressed his wrist below the ID band when she looked up at him, but he couldn't read her expression with the urge to kiss her sidetracking him.

She licked her lips, adding to the pull. "I hadn't considered that, but you're right, of course. Okay. Thank you for arranging everything so quickly. We'll see you at three."

At her nod, he slowly lowered the phone, letting the silky strands glide across his skin. Did he really want to complicate their already complex fake relationship? "What hadn't you considered?"

Her sigh didn't bode well. "Laura suggested we get the marriage license to show our intent to wed. I couldn't very well tell her no without arousing suspicion."

Of all the words she could've chosen... "Applying for a license doesn't mean we have to have a wedding. Even if we had a ceremony, we wouldn't be legally married until the officiant files the signed license at the county office."

"I'm well aware of that." She spared him a frustrated grimace. "If you recall, we had this discussion when Riley and Deacon almost ended up not married because you didn't file theirs right away. I still can't believe you told Deke you'd destroy it without talking to Riley."

"But I didn't after hearing the whole story, did I? I also recall that you tried to trick Auggie and Petra into thinking the other had filed for divorce." He raised an eyebrow at her, daring her to refute it.

"I was trying to do some damage control after I discovered Hugh

Collier's ridiculous contract terms in the purchase agreement. If they'd opened the envelopes, they would've seen I put blank papers inside."

He shook his head. "I don't understand why some people think they should interfere in the personal lives of their friends."

"I didn't do it to hurt them. I save as many marriages as I end." She eased the half-empty bottle from Oliver's mouth and wiped away a dribble of formula with a cloth diaper the nurse had given her. "Just because a couple, or even one of them, wants a divorce doesn't mean it's the right solution for their situation. I'd rather have to apologize for my methods than have them give up on a relationship worth saving."

"So you *do* have a heart."

Her eyes shuttered in an instant, cutting off any hint of her reaction, but her voice stayed low and calm. "Yes, I do."

The lack of emotion in her response told him more about her past than an angry outburst would have. Somebody had hurt her badly enough to turn her into the hardened lawyer she let the world see.

She was, however, much more human than she allowed anyone to know.

He stepped back, waiting for her to make the next move rather than simply picking up his nephew. "We'll stop at the probate office and get the license on our way home for the interview and inspection. I'm paying for it out of pocket so there's no record of it in your expense report."

A curt nod without eye contact assured him she'd retreated behind whatever walls she'd built to keep everybody out. "We can leave sooner if you visit your sister while I finish Oliver's feeding and change his diaper."

Her dismissal grated on his exhausted nerves, but butting heads with her again wouldn't accomplish anything. "Do you want me to have the nurse come in, in case you need help?"

"No." She lifted the baby to her shoulder and rubbed her hand up and down his back as she rocked. Although her movements were smooth and steady, tension rolled off of her in waves. At least Oliver didn't seem to care this time.

And I thought I was good at shutting people out.

He set her phone on the table next to the bottle before heading for the door. "I'll be back in about fifteen or twenty minutes."

"Okay." Her one-word answer was no less clipped than her response to his previous question.

The nurse rounded the corner near the nursery exit as the door behind him gently thumped closed. "Can I help you with something, Mr. Banyan?"

A debate over whether or not to ask someone to check on his fiancé and nephew raged in his head for several seconds. "Everything's fine. I'm going to visit my sister for a few minutes while Georgie and Oliver have some bonding time."

Her bright smile oozed approval. "I was just coming to see if you needed anything, but I'll give them a few minutes alone before I pop in. Have a good visit."

Problem solved. "Thank you."

He walked out of the maternity wing and to the private room Connie had resided in during the last three weeks of her pregnancy. The five-minute trek allowed him to recite his practiced explanation if she asked why she was in the hospital. Telling her the whole truth wasn't an option, not with her mind so far gone already.

A slow breath at her doorway did little to soothe the tightness in his chest and the ache in his soul. Life wasn't fair, but he couldn't do a damn thing to change it.

Her eyes remained closed as he approached the bed, giving him a few moments to pretend the older sister he'd grown up with still lived within the prone body with its familiar face. Her chest rose and fell in an easy rhythm, and peace surrounded her.

He sat in the bedside chair, hesitating for several seconds before slipping his hand through the side rail to carefully grasp her fingers. The faint sound of her breathing brought relief if not hope. He'd lost hope fifteen months ago, when her intermittent connections to reality had mostly disappeared.

Footsteps announced the presence of someone else in the room, but he kept his attention focused on Connie's serene expression.

"Good afternoon, Mr. Banyan." The nurse stopped at the IV bag hanging above the opposite side of the bed and checked the tubing. Then she lifted the blanket at his sister's waist, more than likely examining the incision site. "She was uncomfortable at lunchtime, so the doctor increased her pain medication. She'll probably sleep for another hour or two. Otherwise, she's had no issues related to the surgery. Everything looks good. Do you have any questions?"

He shook his head. "Thanks for the update. I have to leave soon for an appointment, but I'll be back again this evening."

"I'll let her know when she wakes up." After noting Connie's vital signs, the nurse headed toward the exit. "I'm working a double shift, so I'll see you later."

A nod was all he could manage. Even if his sister knew she had a brother, the chances she would remember he planned to return later were practically nonexistent.

He rose and leaned forward to kiss her forehead. "I promise to take care of everything."

She sighed as if she'd heard him and understood she had nothing to worry about.

"I love you, sis." Despite the appeal to stay a while longer, he returned the way he'd come, carrying her peacefulness with him back to the nursery.

Georgie stood at the changing table when he opened the door, her thumb caught in Oliver's tiny fist as she stretched a sleeve toward his hand. "This isn't a very efficient method of dressing. Little sleeves. Little arms. I don't want to injure you. Babies' pajamas should have detachable sleeves that snap to the shirt part after you slide them on like socks."

His nephew tugged her thumb toward his mouth but missed when the door thunked closed. Clear blue eyes seemed to lock on Oscar's when the baby turned his head toward the sound.

Without glancing to see who had entered the room, she crooked a finger over her shoulder. "We need another set of hands."

Glad her mood had obviously improved, Oscar joined her instead of risking another round of glaring and snarling. Although the tiny diaper was crooked across Oliver's belly, it rested below the short stump of umbilical cord and covered the necessary parts. "I'll loosen his fist while you pull your thumb free. Then you hold the sleeve straight up so I can guide his arm into it."

"It won't hurt him?" Her red lips formed a crooked frown and the faint aroma of peaches mingled with the mild scents of baby wipes and diapers.

He cursed the involuntary reaction behind his zipper and dragged his gaze from her mouth. "No, he's pretty flexible. You just have to be gentle."

"He's so small and helpless." Her hand brushed his as he freed her thumb, triggering another surge of unwanted attraction.

Why her? Why now?

In less than a minute, she managed to complete the job she'd started—without biting his head off or fussing at him for not doing everything exactly the way she wanted. Anyone watching them would've thought they worked well as a team and maybe even were the couple they pretended to be.

With one hand resting on Oliver's chest, she took half a step back, but she still stood close enough for the hint of fresh peach to carry to Oscar's nose. "Do you want to hold him again before we go? I need to wash my hands."

"Just for a minute or two." He reached for his nephew, careful to avoid contact with her soft skin. "He's already falling asleep and we have a lot to do this afternoon."

She nodded once and then hurried toward the restroom, her swaying hips drawing and holding his attention until she closed the door.

"Not happening." Cradling the baby, he crossed to the closest rocking chair and sat. "And not just because she'll say no. I don't want the complications."

Oliver blinked up at him and his tiny mouth stretched into a yawn.

"Yeah, well, I like boring." The door clicked open behind him, making him glad he'd kept his voice low.

"We'll have to stop by the County Clerk's office for a copy of your divorce decree before we go to the probate office to apply for the marriage license." Georgie picked up her purse from the floor as she sat. "Unless you happen to have your copy with you, which I would guess is very unlikely. Without it, the license won't be processed."

See? The feeling clearly isn't mutual. "I used it to line the bottom of the cage for my first litter of skunks."

"I can't say that I blame you." The apologetic look in her eyes made his stomach twist in knots. "It's the one case in my career I truly regret. I'm usually a better judge of character. I'll pay for the new copy and keep it in my files…in case you need it at some time in the future."

"I won't." A twinge in his heart pushed him to his feet, and he carried his soon-to-be son to the exit where the nurse peeked in the window. "Be ready to go when I get back."

CHAPTER 8

BREATHE IN FOR FIVE.

Hold it for five.

Breathe out for five.

Georgie forced her shoulders lower as she exhaled, not holding out much hope the tightness in her neck would ease without a dose of ibuprofen. An unplanned fake engagement—complete with the requisite marriage license and ring—and mothering a newborn baby who would never be hers had only added to the stress of representing a man she was quite certain despised her.

Stretching out flat on the living room rug, she tried again to relieve the tension knotting her upper spine. *One, two, three, four—*

Heavy footsteps approached from the hallway, vibrating the floor beneath her. "Georgina?"

Goose bumps skittered along her bare arms in direct opposition to the sudden warmth in her lower belly at Oscar's sleep-husky voice.

Five. She bit back a scathing reply to being interrupted and her body's foolish response as she rose to sit cross-legged. The glow from her laptop cast enough light to make out his shadowy outline several feet away.

"Something wrong with the bed in the spare room?" Then he

stepped closer, revealing a slightly hairy chest paired with low-slung sweatpants.

Holy stud on a stick. "No. I don't sleep much." Her nightgown tangled around her calves when she tried to rise, tugging the top lower on her breasts. His gaze dropped for a long moment and returned to hers, but she suppressed a whimper triggered by the visual caress that made her nipples tighten as she stood. "Did I wake you?"

He shook his head. "I don't sleep much. And I saw the light from your computer. Working?"

"For the most part. I have a lot to catch up on after all that happened today. Yesterday." A glance at the dimming screen confirmed midnight had come and gone more than an hour ago.

"And you decided to take a catnap on the floor in between cases?"

She picked up her robe and shrugged into it. "I was getting a tension headache, so I did some breathing and relaxation exercises."

His low chuckle feathered along her skin, causing a shiver. "Good luck with that. As a former workaholic, I can recognize it in other people from a hundred paces and can assure you the only real cure is retirement."

"It isn't from work." He waved her toward the kitchen and she followed, tightening the tie around her waist as she walked. "At least not directly."

"Me then." He flipped on the light above the stove and picked up the teakettle as if to weigh it. After setting it back on the cooktop, he switched on the burner. "Tea?"

"Yes, thank you."

When he glanced over his shoulder at her, his left eyebrow quirked upward without his expression revealing his mood. "Me and tea or just tea?"

Caught by the propositional nature of his question, she accidentally allowed her attention to fall to his naked back. Strong, lean muscles traversing each side of his spine suggested he spent time at the gym or did a lot of physical labor, probably the latter. She frowned at the spark of heat that spread through her body in an instant. *He isn't offering himself.*

"I'm paying you more than enough to cover a few visits to a psychologist." A pair of mugs clinked as he removed them from the cabinet. Then he pulled a box of teabags from a different cupboard. "Besides, if I can handle being in a fake engagement, I'm sure you can. At least this one won't end with a divorce."

"Or a marriage." She shoved the bitterness back behind the walls she'd erected twenty years ago. How did he find every possible way to provoke her? "You're not the only person to survive a bad breakup, and I don't need a therapist to know what's causing my stress or how to deal with it."

The hiss of the heating water almost drowned out his sigh. "Can we call a truce? I didn't get out of bed to argue with you about which of us has more relationship and career baggage."

"Excuse me?" The muscles at her nape snapped taut again. "I don't have baggage. I own my strengths and weaknesses, and I've learned from them."

"Who said you didn't? I sure as hell learned from mine and the baggage is still there, whether I like it or not." His relaxed movements as he added a teabag to each mug scraped against her last nerve. "You put on a pretty good act at the courthouse and for your Family Services friend. Now that it's just you and me, you're being defensive and combative. Again. I get that you're as set in your ways as I am in mine, but I don't want Oliver seeing or hearing us snipe at each other day and night."

"I didn't say you were the cause of my headache. You made that assumption." Fighting the need to massage her neck, she turned her back to him and walked into the living room. "I'm going in the bedroom to work."

"Georgie, w—"

The teakettle's whistle drowned out his words, giving her time to gather her laptop and notepad.

"Will you stop?" Footfalls warned her he'd followed her. "I don't know why we can't seem to go more than fifteen minutes at a time without butting heads, but this seems different. You're running away, and I know from experience you don't back down from a challenge. What are you afraid of?"

She straightened and focused on their indistinct reflection in the floor-to-ceiling window instead of facing him. She'd fooled Laura during the home inspection and interviews. She'd fooled everyone at the hospital. Oliver, however, had seen through her concerns and drawn her into the fantasy of motherhood.

"Are you afraid of me?" Oscar's near-whispered question brought a twinge of guilt.

"No." Her voice seemed loud in the dim light, especially when she spent every night in the dark with her own company.

"Then who? Or what?" He stepped closer, his presence palpable without invading her space.

Her leg muscles twitched, but she stood her ground. Moving backward into his arms wasn't any better option than hightailing it to the spare bedroom. "I'm not a—"

"Baloney. You're as skittish as the doe I rehabilitated last spring." His deep exhale ruffled her hair, igniting fresh shivers along her back and shoulders. "If you don't want to tell me, that's fine, but at least admit you have an issue. We have to live together for God knows how long, and I'd rather not lose my mind during that time. I don't tiptoe around people's feelings."

"I have…concerns…about a personal issue." She clutched her belongings to her chest and fought a wave of melancholy, the same one that struck every year around Christmas. "It's my problem and I'll deal with it."

"This is about Oliver, isn't it?"

"I don't know what you mean." She spoke the truth, even if her response was a deflection. Fighting for her clients had taught her well.

Another warm breath feathered along her ear. "You're realizing you have regrets about not having kids, and avoidance is how you deal with personal issues. And work, of course. The workaholic's solution for everything."

How did he read her so easily, not that he'd guessed her reasons with a hundred-percent accuracy? Her closest friends didn't often see more than she wanted them to. "I wouldn't say regrets. Sometimes plans don't happen the way we originally wanted. It doesn't necessarily mean there's anything wrong with how everything turns out."

"And you still didn't answer the question." He turned toward the kitchen. "We're not that different, you know. Tea's ready."

"Redirection to make me lower my guard. It's the oldest trick in the lawyer book. You can't fool me." Despite his attempt to lead her into revealing her secrets, she set her armful on the end table and followed him. "As I said, it's my problem."

He stopped near the stove and disposed of the tea bags. "God, you're stubborn. Sugar? Milk? You're out of luck if you want fake sweetener."

"I'm stubborn? You're the one who said we're not so different. Do you have any local honey?"

His curt nod accompanied a frown. "From my hive. How are we supposed to convince the people we associate with that our relationship isn't a scam if you won't tell me anything about you?"

She picked up the bottle he plunked on the counter, careful to avoid making contact with his hand. *Two can play at the redirection game.* "I'm curious why you didn't tell me the details of your sister's illness if you're worried about fooling our friends. It seems to me they probably know more than I do about it."

"They don't know anything. I haven't told anyone but you about Connie and the baby. I doubt they even know I have a sister." He braced his hands on the edge of the sink, adding tense layers of muscle to his bare shoulders and neck. "She was diagnosed with early onset Alzheimer's a few months after my divorce and attempted suicide about a year later. Last fall, the companion nurse I hired reported her missing and the police found her wandering around in a park a couple miles away, so I moved her to a long-term memory-care facility. Despite its excellent reputation, an employee sexually assaulted her and was able to hide her pregnancy for months. Then the facility covered for him. I video-chatted with her every day, but she lives in another world a lot of the time. She had no idea she was pregnant, and

I didn't find out until I made an unplanned trip to visit her right before Thanksgiving."

Georgie released her tight grip on the honey bottle, but her stomach continued its churning and roiling. "I'm sorry she was treated so heinously. Have you filed any charges? The employee—"

"It's done. He signed away his parental rights and entered a guilty plea. I also filed a formal complaint against the facility with the licensing agency. Once Oliver's home, I'll decide whether or not to pursue further charges." Oscar straightened, giving her a clear view of his stern reflection in the window above the sink. "As soon as my sister recovers from childbirth, she's moving to a new facility, one where I can keep a closer eye on her care."

The urge to comfort him almost won. "It's not your fault. You did what you thought was best for her at the time."

"I know. A hundred percent of the blame belongs to the sick bastard who deserves to have his dick cut off and a very long prison sentence." His eyes met hers in the glass again. "I spilled my guts. Now it's your turn for a concession. Or confession. Whatever you want to call it."

A last drip of honey stretched into Georgie's tea and she stirred to avoid focusing on the dull ache in her chest. What did she have to lose by telling him? "I can't have children."

He pivoted toward her, his momentary silence suggesting he planned to choose his words carefully. "Pretending we're engaged and becoming Oliver's legal guardians puts you in a position of potentially becoming attached to him and then having to leave him behind when the paperwork is finalized. That's the chink in your armor."

Spine stiff and heart hardened, she reached around him to set the spoon in the sink. The loud clink punctuated the door to her private life slamming shut with no conscious effort. "Bravo. Do you feel powerful now that you have a weapon to use against me and know where to aim?"

His frown deepened. "You really think highly of me, don't you? I'm a grouch, not a monster. What happened?"

She picked up her mug and walked to the living room windows to watch the snow falling through the trees. Giving him any more personal information he could use to manipulate her wouldn't be wise.

Quiet footsteps trailed her, but he stopped at the couch and sat. "You do what you can to protect kids through the legal system to make up for what you consider a fatal flaw."

"It isn't a flaw—certainly not a fatal one. I'm playing the hand life has dealt me, and I have plenty to be grateful for." Wisps of steam blurred her reflection, but she focused on the view beyond.

"Your defensive reply tells me somebody thought it was a flaw, even if you're bound and determined not to acknowledge that rejection. What happened?"

"You don't have the patience or disposition to be a psychotherapist." She turned away from the window, ready to face Oscar and his scrutiny head-on. "Ruptured ovarian cyst. I had both ovaries removed when I was twenty-five and the man I'd been dating for two years decided using his sperm to propagate was more important than the woman he asked to marry him. I chose to make the best of the situation by focusing on my studies and career. By anyone's standards, including my own, I've been very successful. I don't need you or anyone else to feel sorry for me. A tiny window closed, but a large door opened."

Even in the dim light, the storm in his eyes flashed bright enough to see. "And a jackass taught you to turn off your feelings and lock everybody out, just like my lesson about trust from my ex. It all makes sense now. Oliver picked up on your discomfort with having to crack that window open, knowing it'll close again when all this is settled."

She shrugged and brought her mug to her lips. "Life never promised to be fair."

"Maybe not, but I might not have insisted you play this part if I'd known."

"Oh, please." Without taking a drink, she set her tea on the end table and fought the need to cross her arms in front of her. "You wanted payback for my part in your divorce and you would've used what you assumed to be a weakness against me. I know human nature."

He mirrored her action at the opposite end of the couch. "Even when you hate being human because it means having feelings? You can only try to channel your anger and disappointment into other people's problems for so long. Did you ever cry or scream—or both—about not being able to have a baby? And, for the record, I would've asked you instead of insisting."

Her chin rose before she could stop the involuntary response. "Neither would've changed anything. Besides, allowing my former fiancé to see my pain would've been more humiliating than his Dear Jane breakup announcement in the hospital. We won't ever know exactly how you would've chosen to proceed, so I prefer not to speculate."

His frown deepened as he closed the space between them. "Damn it. There you go, getting defensive again. You have to stop doing that, or nobody's going to believe we're a couple, let alone in love and engaged."

She planted her feet, determined not to retreat from his space-invading bluster. "I told you from the beginning we'd never be able to fool anyone."

"Then it's time to make sure we can." He cupped her jaw, his calloused fingers gentle despite their roughness. His eyes locked on hers as he slowly lowered his head, setting off tiny tremors in her belly.

The instantaneous desire to kiss him caught her by surprise, and the battle between standing her ground and escape lasted less than a second.

His lips touched hers, tentative at first and then bolder when she braved a lick along the seam. He slipped his hand into her hair as he opened his mouth. A low growl accompanied the slow glide of her tongue past his lips to find his, and she braced herself with a palm to his bare chest. The heat of his skin set fire to her body, razing any intention to surrender to no more than a brief taste.

I'm toast.

CHAPTER 9

OSCAR GRIPPED THE STEERING WHEEL HARDER THAN NECESSARY, multiplying the tension in his neck and shoulders, but it beat giving in to the urge to do more than lock lips with the woman in his passenger seat. The coffee in his travel mug disguised the delectable scent of her hair, thank God, or he would have much bigger problems. If she hadn't run off to the spare room partway through their kiss last night, he might've complicated their fake relationship beyond the silent treatment.

This isn't how the plan was supposed to go.

He turned into the hospital parking lot and aimed for the empty space at the end of the closest row. A quick check in the rearview mirror as he pulled into the spot gave him a glimpse of the infant seat he'd strapped into the backseat at two in the morning. With luck, the doctors would release Oliver today and add a buffer to the strained equation the contract with Georgie had created.

She jumped and then slid her phone from her purse. Tapping a staccato beat on the screen, she pursed her kissable red lips.

What now?

For the first time during their silent ride, she looked directly at him.

"Tate and Jim are having an impromptu get-together on Christmas Eve and she wants to know if I'm free. While it would provide an excellent opportunity to announce our engagement, I'm not sure we should take Oliver out in the cold more than necessary when he's only two days old, besides the fact that tomorrow might be his first day home from the hospital. In any case, I shouldn't go by myself if we're going to convince everyone this is real, especially since I'll have to explain the ring."

"We aren't taking Oliver anywhere other than checkups at the doctor's office for at least a few weeks." He slid the key from the ignition and sifted through the possible invitees and solutions instead of analyzing her overlong rapid-fire explanation. Most likely, her nerves were as shot to hell as his from last night's kiss, even if she would never admit it. With the exception of Georgie, all of the couple's closest friends had married in the last three months, setting up the ideal scenario. "Tate and Jim can do all the planning and cooking they want, but we're hosting the party since we have some announcements to make. And it has to be small. It's cold and flu season. Anyone who wants to see Oliver can go into his room for a minute or two and we can limit exposure. We'll pick up a tree and decorations this afternoon."

Her narrow-eyed stare could've drilled another hole in his head. "*You* want to host a party? With people? And socializing? And Christmas decorations? Who are you and what did you do with The Grouch?"

A bark of laughter freed itself before he could even consider trying to stop it. She wasn't wrong about him behaving out of character, but he hadn't expected to discover such a strong bond with his nephew or to enjoy sparring with the woman who had once tried to destroy him. Her support and companionship over the last twenty-four hours had made dealing with life easier. Feeling human again wasn't so bad. God, he'd laughed more in the past day than he had for years. No wonder the urge to kiss her had won over common sense.

He jangled his keys and ignored the cell buzzing against his upper thigh for the moment. "We have limited options. I chose the one that makes the most sense. Tell her you'll be there and I'll take care of the change of venue."

"Oh-kay." Her fingers zipped over the tiny keyboard once more.

Fairly certain Jim had sent the same text to him, Oscar wiggled his phone free from his pocket. He typed in his response at a far more sedate pace than his fiancée. *"Important stuff going on right now. Might tell you about it if you have the party at my house. You and Tate can still plan and cook."*

"At your house?" The three dots indicating more conversation in progress bobbed in the text bar. *"Are you sure??? Probably about 15 people. For at least 2, maybe 3 or 4 hours. When the food's gone and everybody's done visiting."*

The effort to stay true to character proved more challenging than usual. *"Make less food. You're not feeding an army."*

Faint buzzing came from Georgie's phone, but she didn't immediately respond, although her sexy red lips twitched like she was trying not to smile. "She wants to know if I'm okay with attending if the party's moved to your house. Unforeseen circumstances are her reason. She also says your house is a shorter drive."

"Keep your answer short and simple for a change." Her instant frown sparked a pang of regret. "I'm teasing."

"Since when do you tease?" Three quick taps preceded a slower fourth one. "I said yes. Nothing more. Nothing less. Are you happy now?"

He reached over the center console for her left hand. The ring he'd bought to add legitimacy to their relationship glinted brighter than the sun reflecting off the new-fallen snow. "I'd be happier if you weren't pissed off at me all the time. About last night... I don't regret it. It was...insightful."

"Last night? Insightful?" She stiffened, but she didn't pull away. "I don't know what you mean. In fact, you make it sound like we did much more than practice kissing. Once. In case we need to do it in public at some point. And I'm certainly not angry with you all the time."

"Then you don't regret sticking your tongue in my mouth, and you're ready to practice again? You know, now that we're in public." Poking the bear probably wasn't his wisest move. It was, however, the kind of challenge she wouldn't back down from. He lifted her hand to his mouth. "We *are* supposed to be lovers after all."

She licked her lower lip and raised her chin. "I have very few regrets in my life, and mediocrity isn't worthy of that label."

"Ah, so that's why you ran away." He pressed a light kiss to each of her knuckles, breathing in the subtle fragrance of scented soap or lotion on her skin. "Are you sure you don't want to try again to see if we can do better?"

A faint flush colored her cheeks, the first hit of embarrassment she'd ever displayed in his presence. She tugged her hand free and grasped the door handle. "I didn't run away. I had work to do and you'd distracted me long enough."

"What am I distracting you from now? Or are you running away this time?"

Her glare as she released the handle warned him she had probably hit her breaking point. "Why are you provoking me? Is this more payback for five years ago? I admitted I made a mistake. What more do you want?"

The faint tremble in her voice sparked an unexpected jolt of remorse. She came across as tough and unyielding ninety-nine percent of the time, hiding the woman who'd given up on having a family of her own—the woman who recognized how difficult walking away would be at the end of their charade. Had he subconsciously chosen to taunt her with that weakness for what his ex-wife had put him through?

"Yes, I was angry about it, but it's done and I've moved on. What Kayla did wasn't your fault." He leaned back in the driver's seat and let another more likely possible explanation for his taunting stew in his brain, one he wasn't ready to share with her. "We're both under a lot of pressure in this situation. Besides knowing what you're giving up when this is done, I'm concerned about what'll happen to Oliver if we fail. Unfortunately, that's made you a convenient target for my frustrations. I'll try to do better. We do, however, need to get comfortable with behaving like a real couple."

Her solemn stare and curt nod twisted his insides in a knot. She might not show her emotions, but he didn't have to work hard to guess what she was feeling. The penance for her part in his divorce far outweighed the unintentional transgression. "You're right. It's almost time for Oliver's feeding. We should go."

Despite her less prickly tone, her instant regression to avoidance mode gave him no choice but to unbuckle and open the driver's door. "Wait there. I'll come around for you."

A barely audible sigh announced her annoyance. Amazingly, she didn't argue for once.

Patting his pockets to be sure he'd remembered his keys and his phone, he stalked past the rear bumper to the passenger side. He'd mastered avoiding people and conversation shortly after his mayoral term had ended, and stubborn was practically his middle name. Georgie, however, could give him a run for his money.

He opened her door and offered her a hand. Instead of warm skin, cool leather connected with his palm and fingers, triggering an irritating twinge of disappointment. "Careful. There's a slick spot right below the running board."

She didn't acknowledge his gruff recommendation as she gingerly touched one boot on the pavement and then the other. Her silence while they walked hand-in-hand to the hospital entrance tempted him to pick another fight to fill the tense space between them. Since when did he prefer conversation to quiet?

The automatic doors slid open in front of them and she slipped her hand free. He refused to analyze the sense of loss while she removed her gloves. Stress from his sister's illness, the birth of his nephew, and the complications related to both had clearly weakened his usual resolve. Despite an unexpected physical attraction to her, he couldn't possibly like her—not romantically anyway.

He stopped at the elevator and pressed the call button. "Will you come with me to visit Connie after we're done in the nursery?"

Georgie's expression and body language gave nothing away. "Only if you're sure my presence won't confuse or upset her."

"She still knows and trusts me, so it should be fine." The doors swished open and he gestured for her to enter. "Having visitors usually makes her happy."

"Okay." Georgie stared straight ahead as she entered the elevator, her outward appearance giving no indication of the turmoil he suspected stirred inside her at the prospect of spending more time with his nephew.

A flash of compassion stung, but he didn't dare mention his thoughts—unless he wanted to start another argument. "Do you mind if I feed Oliver this time?"

"Of course not. You're going to be his father." The trace of relief hidden in her confident statement probably would've gone unnoticed by most people, but knowing her weakness made it easy to hear. "I need to check in with Margaret this morning, so I can do that while the two of you get to know each other better."

"Okay." When the elevator stopped its ascent, he slipped his fingers through hers. "Given a choice, I know you wouldn't be here, but I appreciate all you're doing to make this happen."

"You issued an ultimatum, but I had a choice. And you're welcome, in spite of my initial misgivings." She stepped toward the door as it opened, clearly ready to grab another day by the balls and wrestle it into submission.

He fell into step beside her in the corridor, far more comfortable than he would've dreamed a day ago. This is what he'd wanted from his marriage—a partnership that included support and loyalty, not only sexual attraction and affection. He hadn't put much stock in romantic love then, but the twinge in his chest, the slight tingle where they touched, and the edginess in his gut warned him their fake relationship might not turn out to be the simple pretense he'd planned.

After a check of his wristband, one of last night's nurses led the way to the cuddling room and repeated the process when she returned with his nephew. The near weightlessness as she placed the precious bundle in his arms and the trust in the blue-eyed stare warmed his soul.

Georgie touched her finger to Oliver's tiny fist and kissed his forehead, sparking a jolt of something in Oscar's heart.

Empathy?

Wishful thinking?

She wasn't as callous and unfeeling as she tried to convince the world. Then again, he'd gotten pretty good at hiding his feelings too.

He took the bottle and settled in the closest rocking chair, reluctant to analyze his reaction and what it would mean a few weeks from now. His gaze strayed across the room, where she stood near the changing table with her phone to her ear. Her hair tumbled past her shoulder when she dropped her chin, obscuring her profile and making him itch to tuck the silky strands behind her ear.

A full minute passed before she looked toward him and gave a curt nod. "Thank you for the update, Margaret. Yes. Today, if at all possible. Okay. I'll message you as soon as it's done."

Her slow exhale as she lowered the phone spoke volumes about the seriousness of whatever she had to handle right away. She licked her lips and took another measured breath.

Goose bumps prickled his skin, a sign he couldn't ignore. "What's wrong? Has Family Services changed its mind about Oliver's placement?"

"No." She walked toward him, her pace much slower and more tentative than normal. Then she sat in the other chair, her posture rigid and her jaw tight. "I requested a hearing date when Margaret submitted the motion since you've been granted only emergency guardianship. The hearing's been scheduled for Monday."

"That's good, right?"

"Under most circumstances, yes." She rubbed her palms on her jeans-clad thighs. "We drew a judge who... She always has the children's best interests at heart and I respect her decisions, but she's very traditional in her thinking."

Her hesitation sent a cold shiver up his spine. "I'm not sure I understand what you mean. We have the single-male issue covered."

"That's not the problem." Georgie stood and paced to the door. "Unless a cohabitating couple has significant medical, legal, or financial reasons that prevent them from doing so, she expects them to be married. As we're living together and have a marriage license, she's going to ask why we haven't taken the final step. I truly thought engagement was the best strategy for helping you gain permanent guardianship. ”

Panic tried to set in, but he focused on the serene baby in his arms and the problem. What options did they have?

Option. There's only one. “We're getting married today, aren't we?”

CHAPTER 10

GEORGIE NODDED, TOO DUMBFOUNDED BY HER LACK OF FORESIGHT AND the consequences of it to speak. Once again, she'd allowed Oscar Banyan's intensity to influence her ability to do her job. Last time, it had nearly cost both their reputations and his money. This time, it would cost him so much more if she failed to make the necessary sacrifice.

The chair creaked behind her, and his presence announced his close proximity to her as much as his footsteps. "It wasn't part of the plan, but I'm willing to do whatever it takes to get permanent custody of Oliver. If getting married is our only option, then we do it—unless you object."

She shook her head. "I'm sorry. I should've foreseen—"

"There's more than enough guilt and blame to go around." His reflection appeared in the glass next to hers, revealing a softer expression than she deserved. "I'm the one who insisted you owed me for what happened with the divorce, and we wouldn't be here if I'd kept closer tabs on Connie's care. Let's do what we need to do and deal with the rest later. Besides, I can think of worse women to marry."

His hint of a smile surprised her, and relief joined resignation. "Really? Who would that be?"

"My ex-wife, for one." He swayed back and forth like so many of the new mothers and fathers she'd represented, as if the motion was instinctual. "I'm pretty sure we can agree on that. So what's the plan? I have contacts at the courthouse if Margaret hasn't already made an appointment with a justice of the peace."

"She offered, but I told her I'd take care of it, in case you decided against doing something so rash." Turning toward him, Georgie braved looking him in the eye. "Are you absolutely certain this is what you want to do?"

"Yes." His lack of hesitation came as no surprise, but the tiny spark of hope in her belly did.

Before the ember could ignite an uncontrollable fire, she extinguished the flame with reality. He had one motive for wanting to marry her, and it had nothing to do with her. "You understand this means a second divorce?"

He aimed a disconcerting stare at her for several long seconds. "Who says it has to?"

The man represented himself during his divorce proceedings. He couldn't possibly have forgotten the requirements for an annulment.

Strange prickling crept along the back of her neck, but she held his unwavering gaze. "Do you understand that we're living together and we've demonstrated to the court that our relationship goes beyond platonic acquaintances who share a residence? Dissolution won't be an option."

"I'm aware of that." He finally blinked, drawing her attention to his long dark eyelashes.

"Then you know the only way to end our fabricated relationship is divorce."

"Once I—we—have permanent guardianship, you're free to split your time between my house and your condo, if that's what you want. We stay married, raise Oliver together, and you become his sole parent if anything happens to me." His Adam's apple moved up and down as he swallowed, but his expression remained unchanged. "It's the most logical solution, not only for the custody issue, but to make sure he isn't subjected to your departure once everything's finalized. I would've thought you'd be happy not to go through getting attached and having to leave."

Although his comment suggested she'd been an afterthought, the fact that he'd considered her feelings at all made her eyes sting. "What happens if you meet someone you want to date or marry? Do you expect me to surrender my parental rights?"

His frown formed before she finished speaking. "I didn't date for the last five years and I don't plan on dating at any time in the future, especially if I have a wife. A commitment is a commitment, no matter the circumstances. Agreed?"

Annoyed by a tiny surge of relief, she nodded once instead of scrutinizing the possible reasons. "Agreed. Infidelity would undermine the image we're trying to project, not that I have any interest in dating, either."

The tension in his jaw eased somewhat. "We're good to go ahead with a civil ceremony then?"

"Yes." She could only hope this part of their deal didn't become the biggest mistake of her life.

"I'll make a few calls when Oliver's done eating." He adjusted his hold on the nearly empty bottle and walked to the chair he'd vacated before their discussion.

"Thank you. I'll be back in a minute or two." Rather than join him, she retreated to the restroom to calm her churning insides.

Several slow breaths did little to put the situation into perspective. Oscar Banyan had turned her entire world upside down in a matter of days, much like he had the first time they'd met.

Marriage. A baby.

The two aspirations she'd sacrificed half a lifetime ago stood within reach again. Despite the absence of love, this unconventional arrangement offered her so much in exchange. She'd given up on happily-ever-after long ago, at least for herself, and hiding the unwanted attraction to her convenient husband wouldn't be an issue for someone with her ability to bury feelings when necessary. Shouldn't she be celebrating her second chance to have it all—or most of it?

Marriage without love wasn't the end of the world. At least he didn't hate her anymore.

She straightened the hem of her sweater before opening the door and pouring every ounce of confidence she could muster into her exit.

With his back to her, Oscar murmured something too soft for her to hear as he laid Oliver on the changing table. Then her soon-to-be husband hurried through a diaper change as if he'd done it a thousand times. "Full belly. Dry diaper. Do you want to visit Georgie while I ask Judge Simmons for a favor? I guess we should start calling her Mommy since there's going to be a wedding soon. It feels kind of strange, but we'll get used to it."

She halted four steps into the room and grabbed the high-backed rocker for support, his matter-of-fact statement triggering more fear than hope. Indecisiveness had never been one of her weaknesses, but doubts threatened to chase her out of the door, down the hall, and away from the hospital. More than anything, she wanted to bury herself in work. It had been her safe place for twenty years, and a retreat into that habit was the only way to ensure she didn't allow anyone to see her flaws.

"Georgie, are you okay?" Oscar stood an arm's length away with the baby cradled against his chest. "If you don't want to do this, you need to speak up now."

She swallowed the hard knot in her throat and met his soul-penetrating stare. "You say that like I can choose not to."

He shoved his hand through his mussed hair, frowning when his fingers slipped free sooner than he was clearly used to. "You can, just like I could have. I'll find another way if that's my only choice."

"But—"

"No buts." His determination hovered around him in an invisible but tangible force. "You said it yourself. This isn't a temporary fix. The upside is I think we can make it work. Will you marry me?"

§•

Oscar cursed the critters running laps in his stomach. He didn't get nervous. He hadn't for the bar exam or the interview that had landed him a high-paying job at a prestigious firm shortly thereafter. Hell, even the overblown event commemorating his worst mistake had left him bored and detached.

Georgina Swofford, on the other hand, challenged, interested, and worried him. Nothing else could explain why he'd proposed to her.

Twice.

He trusted his gut, in spite of its current condition, and he planned to listen to it this time.

The young man behind the desk spoke into his headset and then rose. "Mr. Banyan, Judge Simmons will see you now."

"Thank you." Giving his fiancée's icy hand a gentle squeeze, Oscar rose from the waiting area chair.

Her bland expression as she stood said she didn't have a care in the world, but her eyes darted toward the door beyond the receptionist's station. She was no deer in headlights. If she wanted to run, she would've done it by now.

Marriage license. He'd put it in his wallet yesterday, returned it to the money slot this morning after another look at it, and shown it to Georgie before they left the hospital. *Check.*

Rings. He shoved his hand in his pants pocket, and his fingers collided with the velvet jewelry box containing the other half of her engagement set and the complementing men's wedding band they'd picked up before lunch. *Check.*

Bride. He took a step and she moved with him, confirming his belief that once she made a decision, only indisputable facts could change her mind. *Check.*

Simmons met them at the entrance to his office and waved them inside. His former law-school classmate still sported the same crooked nose he'd supposedly gotten in a fistfight when he was thirteen. "Oscar, it's good to see you again. What happened to the ponytail? And the *beard*? It was almost long enough for you to become an honorary member of ZZ Top."

Georgie extended her free hand. "Georgina Swofford. I asked him to trim his beard, and he decided he prefers the scruffy look."

Asked? Right.

"Bradley Simmons." Brad chuckled as he shook her hand. "He must love you a lot to do something that drastic. Georgina Swofford. I know that name. Family law, right? High-profile adoption and custody cases. Divorce attorney."

"Yes." Clearly not in the mood for small talk, she continued into the mostly tidy office.

Brad's eyebrow jerked upward and his eyes widened, announcing he'd connected the dots. "I guess you two buried the hatchet. Interesting. I wouldn't have thought that was possible after—"

Oscar aimed a warning glare at his friend—acquaintance, former classmate, instigator. Was the clown really foolhardy enough to bring up that debacle? *I dare you to mess with Georgie.* "We have another appointment at four. Can we move it along?"

"Yeah, sure." The hint had evidently hit its mark, because Brad gestured toward the alcove by the window. "Are you still licensed to perform weddings? Ministry of Everlasting Ordained Weddings or something like that, isn't it? MEOW?"

Resisting the urge to roll his eyes and shake his head, Oscar escorted Georgie to the makeshift chapel. "Ministry of Ordained Officiants. The ceremony I presided over a couple weeks ago was the last one. My license expires at the end of the month."

"That's right. MOO. I knew it was an animal sound." Simmons stepped behind the podium and flipped several pages of the spiral notebook setting on it. "Did you write your own vows or are we going traditional?"

"Traditional." His bride's chin rose an inch or two. "No obeying. And no mention of death."

"Yes, ma'am." Finally settling on a page, Brad looked up from the book and grinned. "I assume you brought the license?"

Oscar shot another glare at him and pulled the paper from his wallet. "Of course I brought the license. Here."

The jackass made a show of inspecting the document. "Everything looks like it's in order. Do you have rings?"

The jeweler's box already in his palm, Oscar huffed out a sigh. "Yes, we have rings. Can we get to the ceremony now?"

Brad set aside the paper and smirked in Georgie's direction. "Is he always in this much of a hurry?"

Her silent stone-faced stare nearly forced a laugh from Oscar, having been on the receiving end of that take-no-bullshit expression numerous times.

With a shrug, the joker positioned a pair of reading glasses on his crooked nose. "Wow, you two are definitely made for each other. Oscar Banyan, do you take Georgina Swofford to be your lawfully wedded wife? To honor and cherish for better or worse, for richer or poorer, in sickness and in health as long as you both shall live?"

"I do." The words didn't stick in his throat and choke him like they would've last year, last month, or even last week. Hopefully, that meant his gut hadn't steered him wrong.

"Georgina Swofford, do you take Oscar Banyan to be your lawfully wedded husband? To honor and cherish for better or worse, for richer or poorer, in sickness and in health as long as you both shall live?"

The grip on Oscar's fingers tightened a fraction, but Georgie gave no other indication of her uncertainty. "I do."

"You've chosen to exchange rings as a symbol of your love and commitment. Oscar, please place the ring on Georgina's finger and repeat after me." Brad recited a long sentence without looking down.

Almost there.

Oscar flipped up the lid of the velvet box with his thumb and let go of her hand to remove both rings. Then he slipped the smaller one past her knuckle and against the worthwhile investment he'd given her yesterday. "I, Oscar, give you, Georgina, this ring as a symbol of our future together and do willingly pledge to share my life with you."

"And, Georgina—"

She sighed and cast a long-suffering glower at their justice of the peace as she took the second wedding band. "I can handle it from here.

I, Georgina, give you, Oscar, this ring as a symbol of our future together and do willingly pledge to share my life with you."

Simmons shook his head and chuckled. "Oscar and Georgina, with the exchanging of vows and rings, you have committed yourselves to each other in marriage and I'm happy to announce that, by the power vested in me by the State of Ohio and the Lorain County Court, you are now husband and wife. Congratulations! You may kiss…your husband, Georgina."

CHAPTER 11

GEORGIE TRIPLE-CHECKED THE BELTS AT OLIVER'S CHEST AND WILLED her husband to the driver's seat.

Instead, he hovered behind her at the rear passenger door. "It's latched. Let's go so we make it home before his next feeding."

"I'm being careful. Car crashes are the leading cause of death in children and the majority of babies' injuries in car accidents are caused by the improper use of car seats." She straightened and climbed in beside the child she would raise as her own. Maybe a little distance from Oscar would stop the conflicting emotions that had started again with their first kiss as husband and wife, close-mouthed and short as it was. Tomorrow night's gathering would undoubtedly require more displays in front of their friends. Expectations and complications were normally at the top of her list of things to avoid. "I'll ride back here."

He placed his hand on the door, preventing her from closing it, but he didn't frown or engage her in a staring contest. "Georgie, he'll be fine."

"Yes, he will." She pulled the shoulder belt across her body and fastened it at her hip.

"This is about us, isn't it?" Despite the overcast sky, his wedding band glinted when he shoved his fingers through his hair, but at least his mood didn't seem to match the gray clouds. "We did what we had to do and it's going to take some getting used to. Avoidance won't change anything."

"I'm not avoiding you." She held up her hand when he furrowed his brow and opened his tempting mouth, more than likely to contradict her. "I need some space right now to sort out my thoughts, and you should be happy I didn't ask you to drop me off at my condo when we were done at the courthouse."

He sighed and stepped away from the door. "Okay."

Nothing in his bearing suggested impatience or anger, but she tugged on the handle and shut him out before he could argue. Life decisions deserved more consideration than she'd given the situation, even if she would've come to the same conclusion in this instance. Why had her feelings chosen to assert themselves now?

Oliver slept and Oscar remained silent on the drive to Wellington, giving her time to stew over the unexpected events that had led to her gaining a husband and son. Two days ago, her biggest concern had been convincing her newest client he needed to present a suitable living environment at a custody hearing in two to three weeks. After an engagement, a birth, and a wedding, she had bigger worries—not the least of which was how to navigate a marriage when she'd planned to stay single and insulated from that kind of relationship the rest of her life. Developing friendships with her book club cohorts had been enough of a challenge.

A turn and the slow entrance into the stand of trees announced their arrival at Oscar's snowy refuge in the woods. He followed the plowed drive to the home they would share for the foreseeable future and parked next to her car in the garage.

Home? Her heart stuttered and her stomach tangled in confusing knots. *It was the most logical decision. I've finally made amends for my mistakes five years ago.*

As the door hummed closed behind them, he climbed out of the driver's seat and made quick work of releasing the top of the car seat from the base. "Can you carry in the hospital bag and feed Oliver while I bring in the tree and decorations? Please."

Politeness? How was she supposed to fend off an irrational attraction when he'd morphed from The Grouch into father-of-the-year and nice-guy-next-door material?

She bit back a cheeky retort. Now wasn't the time to channel her friend Riley's snark. "Yes."

"Thanks." He lifted the seat by its handle and headed toward the entrance to the kitchen.

A tiny peep urged her to hurry as she followed him past the stack of firewood and into the house. By the time she reached the nursery, the waking noises had changed to fussing. At least solving that problem didn't require addressing the question of how she would survive night after night sleeping across the hall from Oscar. Sexual awareness took the occasional need for sexual release to a whole new level.

She finally settled on the couch, leaning back in the plush cushions with Oliver. Sucking noises had replaced his demanding cries, and the scent of baby almost lulled her into surrendering to the dream of family she'd set aside long ago.

Oscar sliced through the packing tape on the enormous box a few feet away and then returned the pocketknife to his pocket. "I noticed your condo wasn't decorated for Christmas. When was the last time you put up a tree?"

Only years of practice kept a defensive reply from escaping. "I have one at the office."

"Did you decorate it?" He looked up at her when he hefted a large bundle of imitation pine tree from the box. "Or did Margaret?"

"What difference does it make?" She fought a frown and barely won. "Why are you baiting me?"

"I was making conversation. We're going to be parenting and living together. Don't you think we should get to know each other beyond our attorney-client association?" The second section of the tree rustled against the first as he set it on the floor. "I haven't decorated for Christmas since I was in college. My mom always insisted we do it as a family, but she passed away before I finished law school, so that tradition ended. My dad didn't like celebrating holidays after she was gone. I didn't have—or make—the time when I started working and then my ex-wife preferred doing it all herself. I never saw the point after that since I lived alone. Things are different with you and Oliver here."

Fairly certain he'd spoken more words in that single snippet of conversation than he had during most of their previous discussions combined, she wasn't sure how to respond. Could she tell him about her experiences without being judged?

Not likely. Deflection was easier than talking about her childhood and being shuffled back and forth between two equally inattentive parents. "Different how?"

He pulled a smaller piece from the box, along with a paper. "I want him to grow up happy, knowing he's loved. That means I have to let go of the anger and regret I've been holding on to, the feeling that I failed because I made one lousy choice. He deserves better than a father everybody calls The Grouch. It's also time to bring back the traditions I enjoyed as a kid. I want him to have good memories of his childhood."

Watching him face his personal demons head-on and admit his weakness prompted newfound respect and something more than the physical attraction she'd been battling. "You're a good person and I know you'll be a good parent."

After a brief study of what seemed to be the assembly instructions, he set aside the paper and reached into the box again. The metal apparatus he picked up reminded her of the stand Margaret had used when she'd set up the pre-lit fir tree in the office several weeks ago.

He loosened the screws and then locked his gaze on her. "The same is true of you. You don't have any ulterior motives for being here. I don't have to watch my back, because you say what's on your mind and you don't hide who you really are. This may not have been what either of us expected to happen when I asked you for help, but you've proven that I can trust you to do what's best for Oliver. I appreciate the sacrifice you made to be sure he's here with me, and I'm glad you're getting something in return, besides money. Something that matters to you."

She bit the inside of her cheek to keep her emotions in check, but her throat ached and her eyes stung. He could have used what she'd told him against her, but he hadn't. How was she supposed to resist the man she'd been at odds with more often than not after he'd thanked her so sincerely and sweetly—after the second chance he'd given her?

Unable to look him in the eye without blinking back tears, she turned her attention to the wide-awake child in her arms. Oscar's olive branch hadn't been a detached thank-you, catching her by surprise, and no words were sufficient to express her gratitude for his gift. "I'm grateful that you trust me, especially after—"

"It's done, and I know you're sorry for it. It's time we put the past behind us and focus on the present and the future. We're on the same side now." He slipped the bottom of the tree into the stand and then tightened the screws. The limbs flopped downward when he untied the string holding the bundle together. "What do you want for supper? Soup and sandwiches again or breakfast?"

Too confused by his chattiness to immediately respond, she eased the half-empty bottle from Oliver's mouth and lifted the baby to her shoulder. She stood to give the less-than-instinctual bouncing-and-swaying motion a try. "Whichever you prefer is fine. I can make it if you need to check on your animals."

He glanced toward her as he slid the last piece into place. "I didn't know what our schedule would look like, so I made arrangements for one of the vet's assistants to take care of them today and tomorrow. Let's have breakfast. I'll do the prep if you do the cooking."

"Okay." His lack of gruffness put her on edge, but she could only guess that the stress of not knowing his nephew's fate had been a major influence on his mood. *Bounce and sway. But not so much he vomits all over me again.*

"Tree's up. Do you want me to change Oliver's diaper before you finish feeding him?" He stood little more than an arm's length away, inciting a tickly feeling in her belly.

Her phone buzzed on the end table, saving her from trying to speak while her insides reacted inappropriately. Margaret's name vanished before Georgie could read the message. "Sure. Thank you."

He lifted the baby from her arms, his fingers grazing her nipple through her sweater and making her jump. "Problem?"

She tried to put a step between them, but the couch stopped her. "I, um... You shocked me. The air must be dry. Maybe we need a humidifier."

One corner of his mouth quirked upward, as did an eyebrow. "I have a whole-house humidifier hooked up to the heating system. Any more humidity and the walls will start growing fungus. Besides, the only thing I felt was a pleasant surprise, not a shock."

OSCAR SHUT OFF THE SHOWER AND CURSED HIS INCLINATION TO FACE the truth head-on for the hundredth time since accidentally copping a feel of his wife.

My wife. Married. Again.

Somehow, that fact didn't bother him at all—not when they'd exchanged vows and not in the dead of night twelve hours later.

He wiped the water droplets from his skin, but being dry didn't relieve the goose bumps. Unfortunately, his dick still hadn't gotten the message. How many ice-cold showers would he have to take before Georgie acknowledged she might be willing to explore extending their marriage to the bedroom?

Despite the chaste kiss that had concluded their wedding, she wasn't the unfeeling woman she pretended to be. She'd proven it last night during their first kiss, one he would never forget. Passion lay beneath her cool exterior.

While he hadn't been thrilled about his sexual attraction to her, fighting it fell under the heading of futile. His body had made up its mind, and his heart seemed to be well on its way to following suit. Not in a million years would he have believed he'd fall victim to the happily-ever-after dream his friends had succumbed to. Hell, he'd even developed casual friendships with several men over the last two years. When had he made the decision to give up his hermit's life? Did it matter?

He tossed the towel over the shower door and padded out of the bathroom to find a pair of pajama pants. Oliver would wake soon for another feeding, if he hadn't already, giving Oscar the perfect excuse to haunt his house at three in the morning.

A gasp came from behind him as he grabbed the first bit of flannel he found in the dresser drawer. He turned toward the noise and got a generous peek at his wife's bare shoulders and back.

She glanced toward him and then jerked away as the nightgown barely covering her breasts slipped from her grasp. Skimpy red underwear hugged her butt, and gorgeous pale skin drew his gaze down her sexy legs.

He almost moved the folded handful in front of his naked groin, but fate had offered him an opportunity to discover whether or not she wanted him as much as he wanted her.

"What's the matter, Georgie? Never seen a naked man before?" A millisecond too late, he wished the teasing comment back. "I'm sorry. I shouldn't have said that."

"It's not your fault. I should've moved some of my clothes to the spare room. Oliver and I had a mishap again, but he's fed and changed." She hooked her bare toes under the puddle of silk, but it slid free when she lifted her foot. "Damn it. Will you please turn around?"

"We're living in the same house. At some point, we were bound to see each other naked." Determined to forge ahead, he took a step toward her. "We can even have sex if we want to, which would definitely make being attracted to you more manageable."

A whimper seemed to suggest the feeling was mutual but she didn't necessarily agree with her body's assessment.

He closed half the remaining distance between them. "Do you want me sexually? If not, that's fine. I'll just need to decide if taking cold showers or jacking off is the right solution. And, no, I'm not going to sleep with anybody else. I want *you*, unexpected though it is."

Her hair feathered across her upper back when she slowly inhaled and exhaled. Then she pivoted toward him, her lower lip caught by her teeth. The look of uncertainty—of sudden shyness—shattered the last remnants of the walls he'd thought would stay in place for the rest of his life. One lover had taught her not to trust and she'd given up on everyone, like his ex had done to him.

Despite the overwhelming need to touch her, he stood his ground. He would suffer through his hard-on for as long as she took to make up her mind—and then some if she said no.

She lowered her arms to her sides, baring herself to him, and finally looked him in the eye. Caution lingered there. "Yes, I'm attracted to you, but you need to know something upfront. If, after I told you about what happened in my last relationship, you decide that you need to produce your own biological child to be a man, I can promise I'll become your worst enemy. What I did five years ago won't begin to compare—"

"I'm not going to do that to you, Georgie. I promised to honor you, and I don't break promises." He shook out the bunched flannel and discovered an armhole with his foot—a bad sign. His dick would hate him for what he was about to do, but his conscience gave him no choice. "Maybe we aren't ready for this yet. Let's try to get some sleep before Oliver wakes up again. I'll take the next feeding."

The weight of her stare tempted him to skip his pajamas and climb into bed naked, not that she would join him. He should've kept his mouth shut and let his brain dictate his actions.

"Are you withdrawing your proposition? Offer. Suggestion. You know what? Never mind. You've already decided for me, which tells me you didn't want to hear my answer unless it was an immediate yes." She sighed and pick up her nightgown. Halfway to the door, she glanced back at him with a frown. "It's been twenty years since I've had an intimate relationship. Waiting five minutes for me to make my own decision wouldn't have killed you."

Twenty years? The sleeve refused to let go of his foot and it ripped in his hurry to stop her. "I wasn't trying to decide for you. I meant for us to sleep in the same bed and take things slowly."

Her abrupt about-face challenged him to stop before he plowed over her. "Then why didn't you say that?"

"Because you confound me." He scooped her into his arms and carried her to the bed. Her silky skin nearly defeated his intention to plop her on the near side of the mattress.

Then she grabbed him by the back of the head and kissed him. Soft lips and an insistent tongue turned his knees to rubber and his control to dust, and the urgency of her mouth lured him down on top of her.

Her breasts pressed into his chest and her legs tangled with his as she rolled him toward the middle of the bed. His back landed on the cool bedspread with her body trapping his erection between them, but he didn't give a damn if she took charge. Her pent-up passion had escaped, and only kissing her and finding a way to connect with all of her mattered.

He slid his fingers into her hair, hoping she didn't pull away. Every aggressive thrust of her tongue urged him to run his palms down her back and along her hips to the scant bit of silk and lace that prevented him from being skin to skin with her. He waited for a sign instead.

Her lips were suddenly gone and warm breath heated his neck. "I don't want to sleep or take things slowly."

"Are you sure?" His balls might turn blue if she said no, but he would live.

She wiggled against him, adding to his pleasurable discomfort. "Yes."

The impatient quality of her response brought relief, as did the slow glide of his palms down her spine to the graceful curve of her backside. He nudged his fingertips beneath the elastic of her underwear and cupped her butt. "I don't have any condoms, but I got tested after…"

Another breath caressed his ear. "I was tested too—a long time ago —but I haven't been with anyone. I willingly give my consent for unprotected sex."

"Same." Grateful for her directness, he pushed the thin layer of fabric past her hips and partway down her thighs. When she repositioned her legs, he managed to work the inconvenient article of clothing past her ankles with his foot. "What do you like? Fast? Slow? Top? Bottom?"

She tensed beneath his palms for a fraction of a second. "I, um… I don't know."

"Let's find out." He guided her mouth back to his for a lingering kiss while he explored the contours of her upper body and committed them to memory.

Her lips softened with each slow stroke of his tongue, fueling a heady combination of want and need sparked by the faith she'd placed in him with her confession. The tentative pressure of her hands on his shoulders became more confident as he kissed a path along her jaw to her neck and shifted her underneath him again. When he reached her breast, she arched upward. The breathy moan that accompanied a gentle suck of her taut nipple tempted him to move on to the main event, but a quickie wasn't the way he wanted to start their marriage.

He switched to her other breast and let the gentle curve of her waist lead his hand to the shallow dip along her lower belly. Her muscles quivered against his palm, urging him to hurry.

"You're going too slow." Her husky reprimand held none of its usual annoyance, but the implied challenge was every bit Georgina Swofford. She pushed his hand over the pale curls to the heat between her thighs. "I'm ready. Are you?"

More than you know. He traced a slippery path from her vagina to her clit to confirm her statement, and she rewarded him with a sexy moan. After another quick taste of her nipple, he rolled toward the middle of the bed, putting her on top again. An adjustment of the pillows behind him brought him sitting almost face to face with her. "Ready. You're in charge."

Her firm grasp on his erection as she straddled him threatened his self-control. Then she sank onto him, stealing his breath with each slow inch. "I… Ooh… Wow."

He grunted and clutched at the covers to keep from grabbing her hips and thrusting upward. "Understatement."

Her lips parted and her head fell back when a tremor rippled around him. "Top. I like top."

"Me too." If his instincts didn't fail him, top would have to share the status with bottom and every other position they tried. "I won't last long."

She rocked forward, deepening their physical connection and

making him hope for so much more. "Quality over quantity. I don't remember sex feeling this good."

"I don't, either." The lack of a condom probably had a lot to do with it, but actually liking his wife definitely made a difference. He leaned forward to nuzzle her neck and wrap his arms around her. "Fast?"

"Mm-hm." She swayed back and forth in a steady rhythm, keeping time with her shallow breaths and the pounding pulse where his lips met her jaw.

Her muscles flexed beneath his hands, but she didn't slow her pace. Only when her hips stuttered and she let out a frustrated whimper did he guide her up and down his length. Then her cries begged him to give in to release. He surrendered control and growled into her shoulder. Pleasure tore through him in a mix of desire and never-let-go adoration.

She melted against him, all the tension and restraint gone. She'd trusted him and he'd trusted her. Somehow, she—a woman as self-reliant and reserved as he was—had kindled the intimacy that had eluded him in his previous marriage.

Reluctantly, he broke their physical connection and laid her on the bed beside him. After covering her with the blankets, he switched off the lamp and pulled her into the curve of his body with an arm at her waist. Contentedness dragged him closer to sleep, despite his wish to savor the minutes, hours, and days with her.

So this is what real love feels like.

CHAPTER 12

GEORGIE ADJUSTED OLIVER'S BLANKET A LAST TIME BEFORE EXITING his bedroom. The guests had arrived, along with the time to make her entrance and the announcement that she and Oscar were married.

A real marriage.

Riley's familiar laugh met her as she walked into the living room, and her husband—her lover—awaited her by the fireplace. His steady gaze reignited the disconcerting warmth in the vicinity of her heart. Falling in love with him hadn't been part of the plan or their agreement, and hiding it was imperative. Sex didn't equal love, especially in the context of their fake-turned-real relationship.

He greeted her with a brief kiss on the lips that made the heat spread lower. His intense stare was every bit as hot. "Is Oliver sleeping?"

Not trusting her voice, she nodded.

"We're as ready as we'll ever be then." He cleared his throat, even though most eyes in the room were already aimed in his direction. "I know you're all wondering why I wanted to have the party at my house. Don't bother to deny it."

Chuckles and snickers filled the room.

"I have some announcements." With his arm around her shoulders, he glanced down at her and back toward their guests. "Georgie's helping me gain permanent guardianship of my nephew, who was born on Tuesday. My sister isn't able to take care of him, so I'm going to raise him. Since Oliver's too little to be around a bunch of people breathing on him, I told Jim and Tate I wanted to have the get-together here. He's asleep right now, but you can see him for a few minutes when he wakes up. Next, for those who don't know, Wallis and Harry asked me to perform their wedding ceremony this evening. We'll do that after we eat."

"They already told us, and that doesn't explain why you were kissing your lawyer." The observation came from a clearly amused Riley.

"I was getting there before you interrupted." Oscar's hand skimmed along Georgie's lower back and he linked his fingers with hers. "We got married yesterday. I think Tate and Jim have the food ready, so head over to the breakfast bar and grab a plate."

Petra sidestepped Riley and perched her fists on her hips. "You can't tell us you and Georgie got married and then say it's time to eat. We didn't even know you were engaged. Or dating. Or speaking to each other. How long have you been"—she waved her finger back and forth—"doing whatever you've been doing? Oh, and congratulations."

His noisy sigh sounded real enough to deceive the book club, but he didn't fool Georgie. The Grouch enjoyed his tendency to be blunt. "None of your business."

Riley peeked around Petra's shoulder. "You've been dating or whatever for at least a month if what we noticed at Thanksgiving was right. Is congratulations the proper acknowledgment?"

Georgie barely stopped a frown. What had they noticed?

"Speaking of announcements…" Jim walked his wife to the center of the group and placed his hand on her barely there baby bump. "Tate and I found out we're having twins."

Riley's stepdaughters squealed and high-fived, their excitement only slightly more exuberant than Wally's, Petra's, and Riley's. The women gathered around the expectant parents and hugged Tate. Their husbands and soon-to-be-husband joined them, taking turns shaking Jim's hand.

Oscar gave Georgie's fingers a gentle squeeze. "We couldn't have asked for better timing. Twins are evidently more interesting than the whatevers of our relationship at the moment."

"We can only hope." The physical connection with her husband soothed and aggravated the battling feelings inside her. "They seem really happy about it. We should go congratulate them and let everyone get the interrogation out of their system. It shouldn't take long if we remind them the food is ready."

He raised an eyebrow. "I doubt it'll be that easy."

Under the pretense of not wanting to be overheard, she leaned closer and inhaled his freshly showered scent. "I have insider information. Tate's hungry all the time."

Breaking from the crowd, Wally grinned and walked straight at Georgie. "Congratulations, you two! I should organize a live rendition of *The Newlywed Game* at the bookstore. We'll certainly have enough couples after tonight."

Oscar cringed and shook his head. "We're not disclosing details about our personal life. That's why it's called personal."

"The Readings and Writings Theatre is a family venue. I'll have my part-timers make up questions about favorite foods, shoe sizes, and dream vacations. None of the sexy stuff." Wally crooked her finger at Georgie. "Short book club meeting in the kitchen. Your attendance is required, Mrs. Swofford-Banyan."

Steeling herself for an inquisition, Georgie took a step toward her retreating friend, but Oscar's hold on her hand stopped her.

He closed the arm's length between them and kissed her again, inciting all the nerve endings throughout her body. "It'll be fine. Only one thing matters in my mind, and it's the truth. Oliver brought us together."

She held his gaze, trying to read him, to see some hint of emotion in his eyes, but he was at least as skilled as she was at stoicism. The fact that he hadn't come back to bed after the baby's five-o'clock feeding and had disappeared somewhere outside half the morning and for several hours in the afternoon seemed to make his feelings perfectly clear. He liked her well enough for sex and a marriage that guaranteed guardianship of his nephew.

With a curt nod, she hurried after Wally to the kitchen. Happily-ever-after had fallen off her list of expectations long ago, and nothing had changed.

Eight eyes drilled into her when she rounded the breakfast bar and approached the quartet gathered by the garage door. Riley, Tate, and Wally wore matching grins.

Petra blinked at her and opened and closed her mouth twice before she finally broke her silence with a squeaky whisper. "Oh my God, you and Oscar? We saw him watching you at Thanksgiving, but I figured he was pissed off because he had to breathe the same air as you, not because you guys didn't want anybody to know you were swapping body fluids."

Tate scrunched up her nose and grimaced. "That sounds disgusting."

In complete agreement with their pregnant friend, Georgie frowned at Petra. "He was concerned about his sister and the baby. I was still reviewing the case to see if and how I wanted to proceed. And then our professional relationship developed into something more. Neither of us expected it, but look what happened to all of you. You found love when you weren't looking."

All four women smiled, obviously accepting the truthful but slightly misleading explanation. They looked past Georgie toward the living room and the men who loved them, sparking a twinge of envy in her heart.

Instead of wallowing in her disappointment, she gave Tate a brief hug. "You and Jim are going to be wonderful parents, and I know this is what you wanted. Congratulations. I'm sure the twins are hungry, so why don't you start the food line?"

"I think I will, thank you. Congratulations to you and Oscar, and I can't wait to meet Oliver." Tate grinned as she turned toward the platters and trays lining the counter. "After growing up with four younger brothers, I have to ask if you got a shower during a diaper change yet."

Georgie gestured for Riley, Petra, and Wally to follow. "No, but I had to make a trip to the dry cleaner after the first time I held him. I'm not sure how he was able to vomit more than he drank from the bottle."

Riley made gagging sounds. "Ew. Keep your babies and I'll keep my slightly melodramatic and hormonal stepdaughters."

Hooking her arm through Riley's, Petra snickered. "I'll keep my have-sex-whenever-and-wherever-I-want life, thank you very much."

Wally hung back as their friends lined up at the stack of plates, her thoughtful expression far too all-seeing and all-knowing for Georgie. "Ah, the baby that puked on you, along with the flat tire, lost keys, and the client who screwed up your schedule."

Did I just ruin everything? Unwilling to incriminate herself any further, Georgie nodded.

After moving deeper into the corner, Wally lowered her voice. "You could've told me what was going on. Are you going to enjoy being married and raising a child? It isn't everyone's cup of tea, and you've always said you didn't need those things to be happy."

Wally's unconditional shoulder to lean on tempted Georgie to confide everything in the mother of their group, but she couldn't—not the whole truth.

"I thought I didn't. Then... I love them, Wally." The admission brought a measure of relief tempered by the knowledge that Oscar might be grateful and physically attracted to her, but he couldn't possibly feel the same, despite the fact that he'd forgiven her.

Her friend's sweet smile only magnified the ache. "It changes everything, doesn't it?"

"It does." Grasping Wally's hand, Georgie shoved her problems behind self-control door number one and locked it. Maybe later she would reexamine them and devise some solutions or a more effective coping mechanism. "Let's eat so we can have your wedding."

§

Oscar cast a lingering glance at Georgie and savored the soothing warmth of affection that spread from his heart to the rest of his body and his soul. The multicolored lights from the Christmas tree left hints of blue, green, pink, and purple in her hair, giving her a soft glow. Falling in love wasn't as bad as he'd imagined it would be.

Pocketing the license he would sign and file at the county courthouse on Monday, he fought a smile as he faced the final couple he'd agreed to marry. His distrust in happily-ever-after had waned in the past twenty-four hours and the possibility of renewing his license had begun percolating in his head.

He let the smile win. "We're gathered here in the presence of friends and family to join Harry Kreiger and Wallis Danforth in matrimony. They've chosen to commit themselves to each other in marriage as they've done in their hearts. Harry, do you take Wallis to be your lawfully wedded wife? And do you promise to love, honor, and cherish her for as long as you both shall live?"

Harry grasped her fingers and kissed the back of her hand. "I do."

Not bothering to look down at the notes on his phone, Oscar turned toward Wally. "And, Wallis, do you take Harry to be your lawfully wedded husband? Do you promise to love, honor, and cherish him for as long as you both shall live?"

The bride cupped her groom's stubble-laden jaw with her free hand. "I do."

Holding out the rings the couple had given him minutes ago, Oscar recited the same words about the symbolism of an endless circle he often included, but their meaning finally hit home. He wanted that forever with Georgie. "Harry and Wallis have written their own vows and will share them as they exchange rings."

Harry slipped the smaller band into place on Wally's finger. "Wallis, you brought joy into my life and my heart the moment I met you, and I love you more than I could ever put into words. This ring is a token of my commitment to you and the feelings I hope will always make you smile. My heart is yours for always."

She sniffled as she took the remaining band from Oscar's palm.

"My dear sweet Harry, I adore you and the way you swept me off my feet with kindness and your generous soul. I look forward to dancing through the rest of my life with you at my side. Wear this ring to remind you that my love for you never ends."

Oscar's attention drifted to Georgie again for a moment before he caught himself. "Harry and Wallis, you have promised yourselves to each other and exchanged rings as a token of that promise. By the authority vested in me by the State of Ohio and the Ministry of Ordained Officiants, I pronounce you husband and wife. Share a kiss and make it official."

Applause and a few raucous cheers came from the spectators, and then his wife disappeared into the hallway, her red dress tempting him to follow her. Would their guests call him rude if he kicked them out so he could carry his own new bride off to bed?

He chuckled, fairly certain they already thought he was as bad-mannered as he'd been bad-tempered the last five years.

Jim clapped him on the back. "You okay, dude? I don't think I've seen you laugh in years."

"Never been better." Hoisting his nearly empty glass of Tate's homemade eggnog, Oscar tapped it against his friend's recently refilled glass. "To happiness and having the right people in your life."

"You got that right." Jim downed half his eggnog. "How about if Tate and I encourage everybody to clear out after cake? You and Georgie probably aren't getting much alone time with a baby in the house."

Another flash of red snagged Oscar's attention again. "You might have a hard time convincing everybody to leave now. Oliver's awake, and Tate looks like she may never leave, at least not until the twins are born."

Half a giant step away, the former college linebacker grinned over his shoulder. "She won't be alone. Come on, Dad. Introduce me to the little guy."

Oscar trailed after Jim to the half circle the rest of the partygoers had formed around Georgie and Oliver.

She met his gaze for a second and then looked down toward the baby in her arms. Despite her smile, she seemed tense—and Oliver's fussiness confirmed it, especially since his next feeding was still an hour away.

The younger of Deacon's daughters frowned at Oscar as he excused his way through the gathering. "Why's it crying?"

"He." Oscar touched his finger to a tiny fist and smiled when Oliver grasped it. The fussing stopped, but the tension in Georgie's jaw remained. "Sometimes, he's grumpy like me."

"You mean *grouchy*, don't you?" The girl cast a side-eyed glance toward Riley, who shook her head and coughed past a laugh.

Behind them, Deacon smirked. "Fiona's not wrong."

Oscar shrugged and aimed what he hoped was a meaningful look at his wife. "I have good reasons not to be grouchy anymore. Plus, Auggie brought a wedding cake."

Fiona grabbed her father's hand and pulled. "Cake! Hurry up, everybody. You can see the baby while we eat."

A SOFT GRUNT BROKE THE SILENCE, BUT IT DIDN'T WAKE GEORGIE. She'd awakened over an hour ago, still torn between pretending her husband loved her and facing the fact that sex was his motivation for inviting her into his bed again. She turned down the volume on the baby monitor as she eased out from under his arm and then slipped free of the blankets. The air chilled her bare skin, but she quickly found her robe in the near darkness.

By the time she reached Oliver's room, the grunting had changed to the insistent cries of a hungry baby. He quieted when she picked him up and renewed his efforts while she hurried through a diaper change.

The cries continued while she prepared his bottle in the kitchen, prompting a need to join him. She hadn't wept in twenty years, but tears escaped as she finally settled on the couch. Her heart hurt after watching her friends celebrate with their true loves, despite the attempt to bury her jealousy.

Content now that she'd provided his two-o'clock feeding, Oliver suckled and stared up at her. His face in the glow from the Christmas tree lights blurred as more teardrops formed and fell.

How did I let this happen?

Light footsteps approached, and she ducked her head to hide the dampness on her cheeks. The last thing she needed was for Oscar to discover her feelings for him.

He stopped in front of her and brushed his fingertips over Oliver's dark hair. "You should've gotten me up. I told you I'd take the next shift."

With her nose running, she had no choice but to sniffle. "I was already awake."

Had she sounded like she'd been crying?

He sat beside her and hooked a finger under chin, gently lifting it until she had to look him in the eye. "What's wrong? You're upset about something."

She shrugged, not willing to lie to him and having no alternative. "It's nothing I can't handle."

"That's not the point." He rubbed his thumb through the trail of wetness, reminding her of the tender way he'd touched her in bed. "We're supposed to work together and, above all, I want us to be honest with each other."

A deep breath and a forced swallow didn't help her courage as much as she wanted. "I think I should go back to sleeping in the guest room."

He frowned. "Did I hurt you? Did I do something you didn't want me to do?"

She shook her head. "I just think it's best if we—"

"I think it's best if we talk about what's bothering you." The stubborn set of his jaw suggested he would wait all night for an explanation, but it conveyed frustration, not anger. "Maybe I should go first, because I've had something on my mind since last night."

The worst possible scenario—that he planned to make clear he wanted only the physical aspect of their marriage—hijacked her thoughts, giving her one option. "I'll go first. I... I have...romantic feelings for you, but I don't expect you to feel the same and I won't mention it again. It's my problem and I'll deal with it."

A smile slid across his face and a laugh followed.

Embarrassment and fury heated her neck and cheeks. "How gentlemanly of you, you—"

"I'm sorry I laughed, but if you would've let me go first, you'd know I have *romantic* feelings for you too." He kissed her on the lips before she could respond and then leaned his forehead against hers. "I love you, Georgie. I don't know exactly how or why it happened, but I do. For better or worse."

Disbelief overshadowed every other emotion. "But… You can't possibly—"

"I feel what I feel. I think you should open the Christmas gift I put under the tree for you." He popped up from the couch and marched across the room.

"You bought me a gift after spending a small fortune on this ring?" She held out her hand, even though he now knelt next to the lowest branches.

"I made something for you. For us. Two things, actually." When he emerged from the tree, he held one large and one small package. After he set them at her feet, he scooped Oliver from her arms. "I'll finish feeding Oliver while you open them."

Plain brown paper served as giftwrap, but both presents affirmed his perfectionist tendencies. She picked up the smaller of the pair and carefully removed the tape holding the seams closed, much like she'd done with the treasured gifts she'd gotten from her aunt and uncle as a child. A wooden sphere fell into her hand when she tipped over the box.

He switched on the lamp beside her. "I carved it yesterday for our first Christmas together."

Their names and the year stood out in the intricate design circling the sphere as she turned it under the light. "It's exquisite."

He stepped around the larger package and sat next to her. "The other one is a collage picture frame I made a few months ago. I thought we could have a family portrait taken next week. Then Tate texted me some pictures she'd taken at the party, so I printed the best ones and added them to the frame. Because I love you and we're a family. The kind I always wanted."

Hope bloomed in her chest, replacing the ache, and love filled the empty spaces she'd ignored nearly half her life. She rested her head on his shoulder and kissed his scruffy jaw. "I love you too."

EPILOGUE

"Sixteen." Tate lifted the whiteboard with her answer from her lap, careful not to knock the tiny green John Deere cap from Ethan's head.

The umbrella above them no longer blocked all of the late-afternoon sun from the sleeping baby and her arm, but Jim shifted his chair to the right, putting his body between the sun and their fair skin. Then he raised his own board as he leaned in to kiss her. "Nine and a half."

Ellie's yellow cap tumbled to the deck, revealing a fully awake twin smiling up at her daddy. The sight reminded Tate how lucky she was to have this kind, loving, and thoughtful man in her life. She'd never expected to find happily-ever-after a year ago.

"Correct." Mrs. Crenshaw nodded at Fiona, who readied an eraser in one hand and a dry-erase marker in the other. "That's another ten points for Tate and Jim, putting them in first place with one hundred."

Hoots, hollers, and clapping came from the hog-roast audience seated at the picnic tables beyond the deck railing, Tate's parents and her brothers and their families among them.

The retired schoolteacher raised her hand, bringing immediate silence to the adults and school-age children in the crowd. "Mr. and

Mrs. Fenniman-Jeffries, you're next. Riley, what is Deacon's shoe size?"

Tate's bestie looked down toward her husband's feet from her perch on his lap. Then she wiggled her bottom against him as she raised her answer board. "Hmm. Based on his...recent need for new hiking boots, I can unequivocally say that he wears a size eleven."

Deacon grunted and tightened his hold on his wife as she lifted a second whiteboard. "Because of the number of shoes in my wife's closet, I know she wears a very sexy size six."

Several chuckles came from the audience and from the next newlywed couple in their game.

Pursing her lips, Mrs. Crenshaw cleared her throat. "Correct, but keep it rated G please, Deacon, or I'll have to deduct another five points. You've moved up to second to last place with eighty points. Try not to lose any more of them. Fee dear, add ten points to your mother and father's score. Petra and Augustus, you're next with a chance to stay ahead of Riley and Deacon."

"He wears a ten." Petra aimed a grin toward Auggie. "I discovered that little tidbit when I strung up his shoes with his underwear last fall."

One of the younger Garden Club women cackled from her seat in the front row. "Does he ever wear the bananas?"

Petra's grin widened. "Nope. Not the bananas, the hearts, or the devils, if you know what I mean."

Auggie leaned closer to his wife and kissed her on the nose. "Are you trying to get us disqualified, Pet? Sorry about that, Mrs. C."

The old woman shook her head, but not a strand of her teased-and-styled snow-white hair moved an inch. "Petra always was a handful. Your answer?"

"The size that fits on her feet." He snickered, along with most of the audience. "Seven, I think? All I know for sure is I love her exactly the way she is."

"Suck-up!" The heckler stood among a group of high school boys loitering near the dessert table.

Petra flipped him the bird behind Auggie's back as Mrs. Crenshaw turned toward the scorekeeper.

"I saw that, young lady." Without a backward glance, their game-show hostess frowned. "You earned ten points for having the right answers, but I'm taking away five for the inappropriate hand gesture. The Lochsley-Hofmeiers are now tied for last place with eighty points. Kriegers, you can tie for the lead if you answer the question correctly. Wallis, you're first."

Wally lifted the whiteboard from where it rested against the leg of her chair and shared a smile with the man who cradled their clasped hands. "Harry wears a twelve, unless he's playing a character with much larger feet of course."

Returning her smile, Harry raised her hand to his lips. "And Wallis wears a seven and a half, although her new dancing shoes are sevens."

Mrs. Crenshaw consulted the top index card and then moved it to the back of the stack she held. "Well done. Ten points to Harry and Wallis. We'll have a three-way tie for first place if Georgina and Oscar respond correctly."

The baby on Georgie's lap grabbed a corner of the top whiteboard resting on her husband's thigh and pulled it toward his mouth. She waved a cookie in front of him, clearly hoping to distract her son. "Num-num. A cookie for you and the toy for Mommy."

Oscar withdrew his arm from around her shoulders and scooped up the baby and then the cookie, freeing the inadvertent teething target. "*Food* is for eating, Ollie."

Oliver's semi-toothless smile vanished and his lower lip popped out. "Ma-ma-ma-ma-ma-ma."

The utter joy in Georgie's eyes spoke volumes about how much motherhood agreed with her, even if it had started out a little bumpy. She held out her arms and caught her son when he dove toward her. "Cuddle time. Oscar, would you show Mrs. Crenshaw our answers while I warm a bottle?"

"I'll get it." Oscar propped the boards on his seat facing the audience as he stood and then headed into the kitchen. "Georgie wrote eleven and I wrote six and a half. I'll be back in a minute."

With a nod from her supervisor, Fiona changed their score.

Mrs. Crenshaw shuffled the cards in her hand again. "We have a three-way tie for first place going into the final round. This question is worth fifty points, which means all five of our newlywed couples have a chance to win or tie. The latter will result in a tiebreaker. As soon as Oscar returns, I'll ask the question. The husbands will have one minute to write down their answers."

Footsteps on the stairs brought Tate's attention to her approaching niece. Corey's curls bounced every which way and her over-sized Big Jim's Itty Bitty Pig Farm t-shirt flapped against her thighs, giving an occasional peek at the pink shorts beneath as she skipped across the deck.

She stopped in front of Jim and perched her fists on her hips. "Unca Jimbo, are you done yet? I wanna go see the piggies. You promised. Dint he, Aunt Tater?"

Jim laughed and Ellie cooed. The sounds sparked more joy in Tate's heart and soul than she would've thought possible when she'd moved back home to Wellington.

He leaned forward, putting him at eye level with their niece. "One more question in the game, Curlicue. Then we'll go to the feeding pens. How do you like your new shirt?"

"It's my *fave-rit!*" After a quick twirl, Corey brushed her fingers over Ellie's shock of red hair. "I can't wait 'til the babies are big enough to play. All they do is sleep 'n eat 'n make poopy diapers."

"You used to do the same things not that long ago, squirt." Jim gestured toward the sliding door with his elbow. "Here comes Uncle Oscar. Head on back to your mom and dad until we're finished."

"O-kay!" She trotted to the steps and jumped down each one, the thudding from her work boots drowning out Mrs. Crenshaw's attempt to quell the chatter from the audience.

"Quiet please." The old woman tapped the stack of notecards on her podium as Oscar handed the bottle to Georgie and sat. "Ladies, put your blindfolds in place. No peeking and no speaking until I say so."

Tate donned the sleep mask hanging from the arm of the chair, blocking out all but a few slivers of early evening sunlight.

"Gentlemen, here is your final question. If your wife went on vacation without you—and the children, for those of you who are parents—what would she take with her? And keep it suitable for our audience."

Dry-erase markers squeaked for twelve of Tate's count to sixty, suggesting all five men had immediately thought of an acceptable answer.

"Time's up, husbands. Put your markers down. Wives, you may remove your masks."

At Mrs. Crenshaw's go-ahead, Tate slipped hers to her forehead in time to see Riley slide her blindfold onto Deke's head.

The gleam in her friend's eyes warned Tate to expect a possibly disqualifying remark. "We get to keep the masks, right? You know, for hide and seek."

Petra snorted, but she kept whatever she was thinking to herself—with a little help from a pair of Auggie's fingers across her lips.

Mrs. C. cleared her throat and raised an eyebrow. "We'll start with the Lochsley-Hofmeiers. For a chance to take over first place with one hundred thirty points, let's see your response, Augustus."

With his free hand, Auggie raised his board. "The book club."

Laughter spread through the crowd, but Jim and the other men on the deck laughed the loudest and the longest. Then, as one, they showed their answers.

Mrs. Crenshaw smiled and swapped her stack of note cards on the podium for one from her skirt pocket. "Well, it looks like everyone agrees that the ladies will take along their book club friends. All five couples have earned fifty points in the final round, bringing their totals to one hundred fifty for Tate and Jim, Wallis and Harry, and Georgina and Oscar. Riley and Deacon finish with one hundred thirty, and Petra and Augustus have one hundred thirty as well. The tiebreaker—"

Corey thundered up the steps, drowning out the rest of the retired teacher's words. "Come on, Unca Jimbo! It's time!"

A cry came from Ethan and then another from his sister, setting off the telltale tightness of feeding time in Tate's breasts. She shifted the waking baby to her shoulder, but his fussiness only grew louder. Ellie added to the stereo effect. "The twins are hungry, so we'll need to take a short break."

Wally popped up from her seat next to Harry. "Since the kids are getting restless, I think we're content to share the bragging rights, Mrs. Crenshaw. Thanks so much for emceeing our game show today. How about a round of applause for Mrs. C., everyone? And help yourselves to more food and drinks. Big Jim, hand me Ellie so you can take Corey and the rest of the kids down to see the pigs."

Amid the chaos, Tate's husband passed the baby to Wally and swung Corey up to his shoulders. He kissed Tate as she stood, inciting the same flutter in her belly that had struck when he'd been towering outside the service door of The Homegrown Café a year ago. "Love you, Mrs. Cochon. Back in a little while."

She tugged on the front of his shirt and kissed him again. "I love you too, Mr. Cochon."

His smile promised her words still made him as happy as the first time she'd said them. Then he headed toward the steps and their guests gathered in the yard.

Riley hooked her arm through Tate's free one and walked toward the doorway into the kitchen. "Deacon's setting up a horseshoe tournament with the guys. Book club meeting in the living room while the babies eat."

Ellie's cries quieted behind Tate, and the muffled conversation announced the rest of her friends trailing her into the house she shared with her husband and children, the family she'd always wanted.

Riley and Petra sprawled out on the couch and Georgie cradled Oliver on her lap at the near end of the loveseat, each one obviously at home.

Settled in the recliner, Tate wedged a pillow beside her on the right and positioned Ethan to nurse. The Jim-sized chair allowed plenty of room for the second pillow on the other side. "Ready."

Wally laid Ellie in place and then joined Georgie on the couch. "The babies are getting so big already. I can't believe they're already two months old, and Ollie's first birthday is only three months away. He'll be walking before we know it."

Tate made a silent vow to treasure every moment—sleepless or otherwise—while their kids were little. "Speaking of birthdays, happy anniversary, everybody. Can you believe it's been a year since our first meeting of The Homegrown Café book club?"

"I'm so glad Riley talked me into joining." Georgie eased the bottle from Oliver's mouth and raised the sleeping baby to her shoulder. "You're the best friends I've ever had, and you've taught me a lot about how to trust people. I probably wouldn't have given my relationship with Oscar a chance if I hadn't seen how happy falling in love made all of you—once you got past thinking you didn't want to anyway."

Kicking off her wedge slides, Riley tucked her feet under her legs. "You better not apologize for your interference again. We all needed a kick in the a— Ahem. Behind."

Petra's laughter was a little quieter than usual. "Sperm donor contracts, unfiled marriage licenses, fake divorce papers. Even Wally needed a good talking to. How did you manage to have an uneventful engagement and wedding, Georgie? We should've been allowed to give you advice."

Georgie cast a glance toward each of them in turn. "I wouldn't say it was uneventful. Oscar and I... I suppose I can tell you the truth now that the case is closed. We pretended to be in love and engaged to convince the judge to grant him guardianship and permanent custody. And then we got married to help the cause."

Wally's mouth dropped open and she stared in their friend's direction for several long and silent seconds. "You mean to tell me you two have been faking it all this time? No way."

"Only at the beginning." Georgie pushed to her feet and paced to the fireplace, lightly bouncing Oliver as she walked. "Despite our past animosity, we were attracted to each other, and circumstances dictated we spend time together. Things happened. And changed. Pretty quickly. We discovered we were much more compatible than either of us expected."

Petra chuckled again. "Oh, so the sex was mind-blowing. That always helps, speaking from experience of course."

A blush crept across Georgie's face, but she didn't deny the allegation. "We're more alike than I thought we would be. He's very sweet and considerate. And, honestly, his grouchiness was justified."

Sliding the index finger of her right hand back and forth through a circle formed by the thumb and fingers of her left hand, Petra smirked. "Plus, hot nookie."

"Okay. Yes." The color in Georgie's cheeks deepened. "Hot nookie. But we also love each other."

"Of course. The two aren't mutually exclusive."

Wally rolled her eyes and waved a hand toward Petra. "Ignore her teasing, Georgie. We're thrilled that it worked out well for both of you and you felt like you could confide in us about how your relationship started. We're here to support each other."

Unsurprised by Wally's ability to redirect the conversation, Tate raised an imaginary glass. "To friends and happily-ever-after."

In synchronized motion, her friends mimicked her gesture and spoke in unison. "To friends and happily-ever-after."

THANKS FOR READING! IF YOU ENJOYED THIS STORY, PLEASE CONSIDER leaving a review on the retailer's website, BookBub, and/or Goodreads to help other readers find their next book! Join my Facebook reader group for fun discussions and subscribe to my newsletter to receive the latest news about releases, sales, book signings, and more. You'll receive 3 free short stories just for subscribing!

Ready for more? Check out all Mellanie's books on her website at https://www.mellanieszereto.com!

ABOUT THE AUTHOR

Mellanie Szereto is the *USA Today* Bestselling Author of over sixty romances, most with characters who have plenty of life experience like herself. Mid-life isn't so bad! She enjoys gardening, cooking, and baking—as well as hiking to work off the fruits of her labor—and incorporates food into all of her stories. Mellanie lives in rural Indiana with her husband of thirty-nine years.

Visit her website at https://www.mellanieszereto.com